THE BOOK OF
MORDRED

THE BOOK OF
MORDRED

by Vivian Vande Velde

An imprint of Houghton Mifflin Company
Boston

*This book is dedicated to all writers
who have ever been tempted to give up.*

Text copyright © 2005 by Vivian Vande Velde
Illustrations copyright © 2005 Justin Gerard

www.houghtonmifflinbooks.com

The text of this book is set in Centaur.

Library of Congress Cataloging-in-Publication Data
Vande Velde, Vivian.
The book of Mordred / by Vivian Vande Velde.
p. cm.
Summary: As the peaceful King Arthur reigned, the five-year-old daughter of Lady Alayna,
newly widowed of the village wizard Toland,
is abducted by knights who leave their barn burning and their only servant dead.

ISBN 0-618-50754-X (hardcover)
ISBN 0-618-80916-3 (paperback)

1. Arthur, King—Juvenile fiction. [1. Arthur, King—Fiction. 2. Mothers and daughters—Fiction.
3. Mordred (Legendary character)—Fiction. 4. Knights and knighthood—Fiction. 5. Wizards—Fiction. 6.
Great Britain—History—To 1066—Fiction.] I. Title.
PZ7.V2773Bo 2005
[Fic]—dc22
2004028223

ISBN-13: 978-0618-50754-2 (hardcover)
ISBN-13: 978-0-618-80916-5 (paperback)

Manufactured in the United States of America
HAD 10 9 8 7 6 5 4 3 2

So I said to Sir Malory, "Thomas, you've written of the adventures of Sir Galahad and La Cote Male Taile. You've devoted one whole book each to Sirs Launcelot, Tristan, and Gareth. What of Sir Mordred?"

"Mordred?" he said. "Mordred set knight against knight and brought about the destruction of King Arthur's Round Table."

"True," said I. "But before all that, he rescued his fair amount of damsels and had several 'good' adventures, if you will. Even if we didn't have the documentation for it, we'd know that he must have had a reputation as a fair and honest knight, or the others would never have chosen him above Arthur."

Then Sir Malory's eyes grew hard. In the years we had spent compiling the stories of Camelot, he had grown to love Arthur, as of course had I, so that now he said, *Le Morte D'Arthur* is my book, written in my way."

"But surely," I said, "you don't expect that by ignoring Sir Mordred's more noble endeavors you can make people forget they ever occurred?"

Sir Thomas raised his eyebrows at me. "Oh, no?" he said.

—*from a letter by Brother Lucien, a scribe and a friar of the Holy Order of St. Benedict, to his sister, Claire. Spring, 1471*

PART I

Alayna

CHAPTER 1

After looking everywhere in the house, Alayna found Kiera in the barn, talking to the horses.

Alayna knew that—given the chance—most children of five years would talk to horses. But Kiera was crying, sobbing, her voice coming out in gasps and hiccups, barely able to get the words out, and what she was saying to the horses was "No, I'm sorry. I couldn't tell. But something terrible."

She was still in her night dress, and she had her arms flung around the neck of the mare, Alayna's own horse, who was nuzzling her as though to offer comfort. The other horse, Toland's old nag, looked up as Alayna entered and gave a soft nickering sound.

"No," Kiera said as if in answer. "Why should I? She never believes me anyway."

"Kiera." Alayna's voice came more sharply than she'd intended, for it was one thing to talk to horses; it was something else entirely to think they talked back.

Her daughter turned and stood there, still crying, but not speaking.

"What is it?" Alayna asked. "What has happened?" Then, because Kiera was her only child and Alayna did have a tendency to worry: "Are you hurt or ill?"

Kiera hesitated and the mare used her head to gently bump Kiera's back, forcing her to take a step forward. Looking and sounding torn between reluctance and hope, Kiera said, "I had a dream. A very bad dream. Something bad was about to happen, but I don't know what."

Alayna crouched down among the straw bedding, unmindful of the hem of her gown, and held her arms out, and Kiera ran to accept the hug. Alayna stroked her hair, soft and shiny but still tangled from the night's sleep. "Everybody has bad dreams," Alayna assured her in a gentle murmur.

Kiera pushed herself away. "This was *not* that kind of bad dream."

Not again, Alayna thought. "Come back to the house," she said, and she swept Kiera up in her arms as she stood, which was getting more difficult lately, with Kiera looking to grow all tall and gangling like her father. Cheerfully Alayna announced, "I'm to bake bread today." Sometimes Kiera could be distracted from these moods. "You may add the raisins and the seeds."

"Something bad is coming," Kiera insisted. "We have to warn Ned, too."

"Do you remember how two years ago you dreamed that the well collapsed? And do you remember how you refused to go anywhere near there all that summer long? And every time your father"—she was able to get the word out without a catch—"or Ned or I went near, you cried? And nothing bad ever happened anywhere near the well."

"Two years ago I was just a baby," Kiera said. "Now I can tell the difference." Alayna kept walking and Kiera twisted to call back to the horses. "Be careful. Oh, please be careful." So seriously, so anguished—it nearly broke Alayna's heart.

Alayna glanced to the peach tree on the little hill, where Toland was buried, and managed not to feel resentful.

Ned was just coming out of the house. "Found the little one, eh?" he said with a wink for Kiera. Of course Alayna would have awakened him in his little room at the back of the house with all her slamming of doors and calling for Kiera. He was carrying a bucket of slops for the pigs and didn't pause, for the bucket was heavy. "Everything all right, then?"

"Fine," Alayna assured him.

Kiera said, "Ned, be extra careful today!"

"Of what?" he called back over his shoulder.

"I don't know. But something is wrong."

"All right, young miss," he told her, disappearing around the corner of the barn.

Kiera gave a loud sigh of exasperation, which Alayna knew Toland would have said was a mannerism their daughter had definitely inherited from her mother's side.

In the kitchen Alayna put her down and told her, "Go get dressed. And this time don't forget to brush your hair."

Baking day always made her impatient. She had never mastered the art of making bread, but until a year ago she hadn't realized it. Growing up on the wealthiest of her father's several estates, she had never *needed* to learn. And with her father's young second wife eager to avoid the reputation of demanding stepmother, Alayna had been allowed to spend her time as she wanted—and what she'd wanted was to accompany her older brother, Galen, through sword and riding lessons rather than learn how to run a household.

Then, married at the age of fifteen, it never occurred to her that the effortlessly wonderful bread she baked could have anything to do with the fact that her husband was a wizard. It wasn't until Toland died that she realized just how much help he had secretly given around the house.

So now, twenty years old and on her own for the first time, she pounded and kneaded a slab of dough, and knew for a fact that some of the loaves would end up mostly big holes, and some would be too hard to bite through.

Her hands sticky with dough, Alayna blew at a stray lock of hair that had come loose and kept falling into her eyes. What she wouldn't give for a few household servants now. But there was only old Ned, and good as he was at tending horses and fixing thatch and working the garden, it was too much to expect that he should be able to bake, also. She thought again of how her parents had advised against her marrying Toland, how they'd warned that life with a village-wizard would be nothing like the life she'd led so far. But she'd loved Toland enough to give up everything for him, even enough to put up with the queasy feeling she got at the thought of twisting nature through magic.

She'd defied her father, who in all likelihood *would* welcome her back home despite what he'd said almost six years ago; but she was determined to keep the home she and Toland had built together—bad bread or no bad bread. And, unless Galen had told them, her parents didn't even know Toland had died.

Emotions mixed together, like the flour and water of the bread she was kneading: Missing him blended with annoyance, for he had always sworn that he wasn't meddling.

She was so intent on not crying, not again, and on getting the bread right that she didn't hear anything from outside.

No warning, until someone kicked in the door.

She didn't have time to turn. Someone grabbed her from behind, slapping a sweaty hand over her mouth to keep her from crying out. Alayna bit as hard as she could, and the hand jerked away.

"Miserable wench!"

Alayna managed to twist around. The one who held her was a short, dark-haired man wearing a stained woolen shirt and breeches. The other two crowding through her doorway were in full plate-metal armor despite the heat of the day. Their helmets covered much of their faces and they wore no identifying insignia.

Knights? Knights were attacking her? The absurdity of it was enough to stop her, so that she lost her advantage, and the first man—the commoner—tightened his grip again.

"Forget her," one of the knights told him. "Just find the whelp."

Whelp? *Kiera?* Why in the world would knights be interested in Kiera? There was no time to work it out: Nothing was as it should be. "Kiera!" she screamed, hoping to get Kiera out of the house and at the same time warn Ned—Please, *please*, let him be close enough to hear—that something was wrong. "Kiera, run!" She had barely gotten those words out before the second knight struck the side of her head with his armored fist.

Alayna's head was throbbing and there was a roaring in her ears. She didn't have the energy to open her eyes, much less to lift her head.

Useless, she thought. *Foolish and useless.* She'd provoked them for nothing: Even if Kiera had heard and obeyed without question or argument—which in the best of circumstances was unlikely—how could a five-year-old child possibly hide from determined knights?

And what could knights possibly want with her anyway?

With her thoughts come full circle, Alayna became aware that the noise in her ears was not the result of the blow to her head, and that the heat in the room was much more than sunlight through the casement and the fire in the hearth.

She sat up. Instantly thick smoke coated her throat, stung her eyes. She dropped to her hands and knees and fought the instinct to self-preservation that told her to crawl directly to the door.

"Kiera!" She tried to scream, but her voice, thick and slow, wouldn't cooperate.

She started to crawl, but almost immediately banged into a wall. So. The stool she had dimly glimpsed through the smoke wasn't where it was supposed to be. One of the men must have pushed or kicked it aside, and now her directions were all confused.

She followed the wall, but the smoke and heat seemed more intense in that direction. Her eyes streaming from both smoke and frustration, Alayna turned back the way she had come. But when she reached a doorway, it was the one leading to the rest of the house, not outside. And smoke was billowing from there also—a fire in each room.

"Kiera!" she tried again, and broke off, choking. She fought against the idea that Kiera could be in there. Surely, whoever those knights had been, whatever they had wanted, surely they wouldn't . . . they couldn't . . .

The front door would be just about opposite. Coughing almost to the point of retching, Alayna decided the risk of cutting across the unseen room was less than that of taking the time to feel her way around.

She crawled.

And crawled.

The cottage, so small after her father's manor, suddenly seemed vast; and she was chiding herself for another wrong decision when she felt the door jamb and fresh air on her hot face.

Shakily she got to her feet. "Kiera!" Her hoarse scream came out little more than a whisper, but she repeated it in all four directions.

Nothing.

She called, "Ned! Where are you?" and stumbled toward the barn, also aflame. The horses must be gone—her mare which her father had presented to her on her fourteenth birthday, and the old nag Toland had used to make his rounds—surely they must be dead already or the men had taken them, for they weren't in the enclosure and if they'd been trapped inside, they'd be frantically trying to get away from the fire. Yet she could hear nothing of them.

She found Ned's body behind the barn, and she did not need to turn him over to see that he was dead.

The body of a stranger, perhaps squire or attendant to one of the knights, lay nearby. Ned, who had taught Alayna and Galen all about riding and weaponry and survival in the forest, had been past sixty, yet she saw that it had taken a sword blow from behind to kill him.

More tears ran down her face, this time nothing to do with the smoke.

"Kiera!" she called again, her voice finally gaining strength. She gulped a deep breath though it felt like nails scraping the inside of her throat. "Kiera!" she screamed.

There was no answer.

She turned at a loud cracking sound from behind and saw the house cave in. The air quivered in the heat as she watched the end of all that had remained of her life with Toland.

Alayna dug her fingers into her hair, sank to her knees. She covered her face with her hands and rocked back and forth. "Kiera," she moaned one more time.

But, of course, there was no answer to that either.

CHAPTER 2

Alayna forced herself to steadiness, for she'd be no use to herself or Kiera in this state. Toland would have been better suited to handle such a situation.

But then she thought, *Or perhaps not.* His magic had been unable to stave off the sickness that had started in chills and fever, and had ended in his death. The person she needed was Galen, who was a knight as well as being her brother. But whether he was at home with their parents or at court at Camelot, or someplace else entirely, there was no waiting for him.

She returned to the still-blazing barn, to Ned. With detached coolness that she knew could not last forever, she noted the wind and the amount of dry grass in the area and saw that the fire would consume Ned's body and that of the attackers' squire before dying out itself. Fire was the old way, frowned upon by the Church as a heathen rite, but she hoped Ned would forgive.

In any case she had no choice.

"*Pax,*" she said, holding her sleeve to her face, against the stench of burning. Remembering how Ned had agreed to leave her father's service to go with her and Toland, knowing he deserved better—she sprinkled a handful of dirt over his body. "Pray God for the dead," she said out loud, then murmured, "Dear, dear teacher."

The other corpse, the man who had come with her attackers, had nothing she could use: neither insignia, ring, or clasp from which to learn his identity, nor blade or water flask for her to take with her now. She didn't give him another thought.

Now it was time to turn her attention back to the living.

The tracks of five horses led across the field in the direction of the east-west road first cleared by the advancing Romans. Two knights she had seen, and two attendants—including the dead one. That would have required only four horses. Either there had been one more attacker she had never seen, or they had taken Alayna's own gentle mare with them. If they had taken Kiera—*They must have taken Kiera*, Alayna assured herself, unwilling, unable, to think of the alternative—if they had taken Kiera, they may well have wanted the mare for her to ride. In any case, apparently Toland's sturdy old nag had not been considered worth the taking and had been left to burn.

She knew it was useless to go running after them on foot. But still she had to fight the inclination to do so, and to head—instead—for help.

The nearest holding was old Croswell's, to the north, nearly half the morning away, for Toland had believed a wizard should live somewhat remotely, separate from the casual bickerings and rivalries of near neighbors constantly wanting to bespell each other. Alayna started down the path, but it had become overgrown since Toland's death. Hardy, clinging weeds overlapped the edges and snagged the skirt of her dress. She had to lean over to pull herself free, and she noted for the first time that her hands were still speckled with bits of dried dough. *Well*, she told herself grimly, *at least I won't starve to death.*

She kept her head down to watch the path. Her feet, in light shoes never meant for outside use, quickly became bruised and sore. She tried to recapture the energy she'd had as a child, training with Galen, when physical exertion had been an enjoyable challenge. But every time she looked up to note how far she'd come since the last glance, it was always a disappointment.

Instead, her mind filled with thoughts of last spring.

She remembered Toland sitting at the table, a blanket wrapped around his shoulders, unable to get warm though she and Kiera had already put aside their winter woolens. Looking back, she knew it for the first sign of his sickness, though at the time she hadn't seen that.

At the time they had been arguing.

"Oh, Toland!" she cried, coming in from airing out the bedding and finding her husband and their child with heads close together, mixing bitter-smelling herbs into a pasty green substance she couldn't begin to guess at. "I've asked you not to do that in front of Kiera."

Toland had looked up from his work, his expression guilty and defiant at the same time. "What? This smells foul, but it's only to help chickens lay. It isn't dangerous."

"That's not the point." Alayna had glanced at Kiera, who sat still on the edge of the table and said nothing. The child's face, always too pale and serious for her age, remained impassive.

Toland had sighed. "Oh, Alayna. I'm not corrupting our daughter. She has the power. Train her in magic, and she'll be able to control it. Ignore it, and she'll just be less adept."

"Kiera," Alayna had said, "tables are not for sitting on. Go get water for washing our hands before supper."

Alayna remembered how Kiera had turned to her father, as if waiting for his permission. Toland had kept his face expressionless, and Kiera had gone, sulkily, still never saying a word.

"Alayna . . ." Toland had started.

Alayna had put her back to him, poking at the fire, and eventually he, too, stormed out of the house without a word.

For love of him, she had left her ancestral home, left despite her father's warning to be sure this was what she wanted, for—if once she left—she would not be welcomed back. She had learned to do without servants or rich clothes.

But it was one thing to be married to a wizard; she would *not* raise one. Too often she had heard of folk suddenly blaming all their problems on magical interference. Too often suspicion would boil over into violence, sometimes directed against people who had no more magic than Alayna herself, often against old women who had lost their wits and young excitable girls. Toland was capable of taking care of himself. Twice they had packed up what little they owned and fled to avoid mounting hostility. Alayna would *not* let Kiera be subject to that.

Magic was the only thing about which she and Toland had ever argued. And, in the end, it was Alayna who had the last word. For when Toland died, she had gathered his potions and herb pots and talismans, and had burned them all.

Just as the knights today had burned all the possessions *she* treasured.

Alayna forced her mind into blankness and kept on walking.

When she finally did see Croswell's cottage, the old farmer was hitching his horse to a wagon, apparently about to leave for town. "Wait!" she called, waving to get his attention. "Please wait!" But she used all her breath running. When she finally reached him, she could do no better than to pant, "Need your help. Your horse please. No time to lose."

Croswell squinted at her. "Eh?" he said.

"Please. My daughter's life is at risk."

Croswell looked apprehensive. "What?" he asked, trying to pry her fingers loose from his arm.

Alayna forced herself to slow down and suddenly found herself trembling and crying.

Croswell peered into her face. "Eh, now," he said. "Ain't you the lady from the cottage down yonder? The wizard's woman?"

Alayna nodded.

Croswell finally gave her a steadying arm. "Why, what's happened? Why'd you come the back way, on foot?"

"Have some men been by here?" Alayna was finally able to get out.

"Who? What sort of men?"

"Two knights. Five horses."

"Five horses for two knights?"

This time Alayna pulled loose and grabbed the little man by the shirt. "They've taken my daughter!" she cried, shaking him.

"Who?"

"The two knights!" she screamed. "Did they come by here?"

"That's the road that leads to Camelot," Croswell said, nodding just beyond his front door. "Men pass all the time."

Alayna, suddenly realizing what she was doing, released his shirt. "Please, I need to use your horse."

"My horse?" He scratched his head. A dry old man who smelled of dusty earth, he had lost his entire family to a virulent winter flux the year Galen had gone off to squire. Now he seemed to be out of the habit of talking and to be having trouble concentrating. "But why didn't he help?" he asked.

"Who?" Alayna tried to keep her voice even.

Croswell gave her a look that indicated she was a simpleton. "Your husband. What's the good of having a wizard in the family—"

"He's dead," Alayna told him, though Croswell had attended the funeral mass last year.

But perhaps he had attended too many funeral masses to keep them straight. "I'm so sorry. They killed him *and* took the girl?"

Alayna refrained from shaking him again. Instead she pronounced each word slowly and distinctly. "May I take the horse?"

Croswell shook his head. "What's the world coming to?" His lusterless eyes appraised her. "Take the horse, why don't you?" he suggested.

Alayna's hands trembled as she unfastened the traces. The horse was old, incredibly old, and bony, and she hoped it wouldn't die of age before she reached the road. She swung onto its back. Her skirt was wide enough that she could ride straddled, which she hadn't done since she was twelve and her father and stepmother declared it was time for her to start behaving like a lady. But there was no way to ride sidesaddle without a saddle, and she wasn't concerned about looking like a lady. "Thank you," she told Croswell as she dug her heels into the horse's sides.

She could hear Croswell yell, "Easy, she's older than you are, you know." Then softer, once again, "What's the world coming to?" And then she was too far out of range to hear any more.

CHAPTER 3

The men had probably gone east. Camelot was a half-day's journey to the west—even less with a decent horse—and it was well known that King Arthur would not tolerate murder and abduction. Alayna felt she could assume the lords of those baronies that were closest geographically would be least likely to be involved in actions sure to offend the King.

Still, she had to fight the inclination to head east after the men.

Even if she had a sword, she told herself—and she hadn't picked one up since her parents had finally put a stop to her training when she'd reached twelve—even if she *had* a weapon, and even if she was in as good form as she'd ever been—which she knew she was not—and even if she could ever hope to overtake them—which with Croswell's horse she could not—even *then:* What could she do against two knights and their man?

She hesitated on the road, looking down the way she was certain they'd gone. *And Kiera,* she prayed. Surely that was why they had taken the mare. Surely . . .

She turned west, toward the help she could seek from Camelot.

But soon it appeared that all the agony of making

her choice had been meaningless, for Croswell's horse suddenly slowed and, after a few moments of consideration punctuated by Alayna's cursing, it slowly sank down and lay on the road.

Alayna jumped at the last moment to keep from getting her feet caught underneath. Now she started tugging and pushing.

"You *worthless* animal!" she cried. "Horses aren't supposed to lie down in the middle of the road. Come on. Up! Get up!"

She stooped down in front of the horse's face. The animal looked at her with dull, unresponsive eyes.

"Nice horse," she tried, scratching gently between the eyes. "Good horse. Are you hungry?" She plucked a handful of flowering wild grass from the roadside and waved it in front of her tired mount's face. "How would you like some nice sweet grass?"

The horse snorted and looked away.

"By the blood of St. Francis, get up off the road!"

The horse gave a knowing snort, indicating her sincerity had been at question all along.

Alayna threw the grass to the ground and started walking. As soon as she was too far away to do anything about it, she heard the horse get to its feet and start off toward home at a steady clip.

I don't need you, Alayna thought.

Let everyone and everything conspire against her, she would *still* get Kiera back.

Eventually, from behind, Alayna heard a horse trotting in her direction, moving faster than Croswell's decrepit animal had managed in years. She turned. A knight was approaching. She felt a moment of dread. Twenty years of assuming she knew how the world worked had shattered. Knights, she had to remind herself, were honorable men, were men to be trusted. This was a single rider, which pointed at the probability that he wasn't one of the pair who had attacked her home. And, therefore, she told herself a second time, he was to be trusted. She stood in the center of the road and raised her arm, signaling the rider to stop.

But the man ignored her and changed neither speed nor direction. At the last moment Alayna took a step to the left and felt the horse's warm breath on her cheek, and the knight's metal-clad foot brushed against her arm.

"Thank you, gentle sir!" she called after him.

The man tossed a small coin over his shoulder.

Alayna looked down at her dress, soiled and tattered from the fire and her walk through the fields, looking like a high-born lady's cast-off rag. She could only imagine the state of her hair and face. She sighed. Knights pledged to help ladies. Nobody expected them to waste their time running errands or settling quarrels for peasant women.

She resumed walking.

The next time she heard someone approaching, much later and again from behind, she resolved not to take any chances on being mistaken for a beggar. She stopped and sat on a rock by the edge of the road. She would have wished for the element of surprise, but for just that reason all large trees and boulders were kept clear from the road.

The horse was a destrier, a fine light gray warhorse, though the rider, unarmored and without a helmet, looked quite young. Somebody important, then, she thought. Or the son of somebody important. So be it. He was going slowly enough for Alayna to hope she could stop him without getting herself killed.

She waited until he was abreast of her, knowing that the horse was aware of her presence even if the youth wasn't. At the last possible moment she jumped up and grabbed the reins for one instant, and then leaped back off the road.

Immediately the horse, trained for battle, reared up on its hind legs and flailed with its front hooves at the space where Alayna had been an instant before. She had counted on the young lord to keep his mount from trampling her despite his surprise, but he slid out of his saddle and hit the road, rear end first.

The horse, fortunately, was satisfied, and galloped away.

"Sorry," Alayna said, running up to the felled rider. Most of all she regretted yet more delay, but she hadn't meant for him to fall, and she hoped he wasn't hurt. "Sorry."

He was swearing in some foreign dialect—possibly Gaelic—and trying, with only moderate success, to get to his feet.

Alayna let him pull himself up on her arm.

"What were you thinking, woman?" he demanded, which she took as a strong indication that he would recover.

"I said I was sorry."

"Oh. Well. That fixes all, then."

Cornish, she settled on. Just the faintest hint—more in inflection than pronunciation. "Fine horsemanship," she observed icily.

His dark gray eyes widened, then narrowed, and he took a deep breath. But he bit back whatever he was going to say and turned his back on her. Without a word, he started walking.

Young, Alayna reflected. He was even younger than she had first thought, probably not even her own age. And thin-skinned, apparently. Not the kind of person she'd have chosen. But she didn't have the luxury of choice. And, after all, it would have been worse if he'd been the kind to take out his annoyance on her. She hurried to catch up. "I *am* sorry," she repeated.

He kept on walking, without bothering to look at her. When he finally spoke, it was to the air before them: "You could have been killed."

Which was not what she'd expected him to be brooding about.

"I had to take the risk, sir. It did not occur to me that my action endangered you, also." Alayna took care to speak slowly and evenly in the accents of a lady so that she wouldn't be mistaken again for a peasant. She didn't mention that had he been a better rider, he wouldn't have fallen. "I am truly sorry, but please, I need your help."

"You might have tried asking, you know."

"Yes. Certainly. And you would have stopped."

The young man—the knight, he had to be, with that horse, for all that he wore no armor and he was shorter and of a more slender build than average—finally did stop, finally did look at her. "Yes, I would have," he said.

Hard to judge.

And of little consequence now.

Alayna resumed walking. "Well, then, I thank you. But one of your fine compatriots passed me by already." She wasn't even going to *start* explaining that it was knights she needed help against.

He stopped again and pulled her around to look directly at her. His dark eyes were quizzical. "Who are you?"

"Lady Alayna De La Croix. My father is Sir Guy of the Towered Gate." Maybe she *would* tell. "This morning—"

"You're Galen's sister?"

Alayna felt a surge of relief. "You know Galen?"

By the knight's smile, it was a happy acquaintance. "We squired together. I'm Mordred of Orkney."

Her breath momentarily caught. "The King's nephew?" she gasped, though she knew both her father and her brother believed the rumors that he was actually Arthur's son, by the King's own sister, the witch Morgause.

Mordred's smile tightened, and he neither acknowledged nor clarified his exact relationship to the King. He tried to kiss her hand, but—nephew or son—he was the heir apparent to the throne, and she was already dropping into a curtsy. "M'Lord," she murmured.

He looked embarrassed and quickly got her back to her feet. "Tell me what happened."

"Two knights broke into my home—I don't know who they were. They stole my daughter, killed my retainer, and left me for dead in a burning house."

"Stole your daughter?" Mordred repeated. From his renewed scrutiny of her face, he must be trying to guess how old she was, as though to gauge whether she could have a daughter who might be of an age to warrant abduction.

She resented the hesitation—she wasn't *that* much older than he. "She's five," she said.

"What did they want with her?" he asked.

"I'm not sure." But she'd been thinking about it while she walked. She added, "My husband—he died last year—he was a wizard." When the young knight didn't comment, she continued, hesitantly, "And . . . Kiera may well have . . . inherited . . . some of his powers . . ."

He raised his eyebrows at this.

"She can . . ."—she bit her lip, finding this hard to put into words, for she had tried so long to ignore it away—"talk to animals . . . and make herself understood, and understand them. And, once in a while, she might mention something that hasn't happened yet and then it . . . well . . . happens." Alayna swallowed hard. "Sometimes." She swallowed again. "Will you help me?"

He sighed, which in a moment of panic she took as reluctance. But then he said, "Of course I will," and he looked down the long road that stretched empty before them. "As soon as we find that damn horse."

They began walking.

And walking.

And walking.

Alayna had begun to limp and was leaning heavily against Mordred, when he pointed off to the left. "The road curves around the old Roman quarry, but there's the castle. You can see the north tower through the trees."

Despite its proximity, she had only been there once: for Galen's investiture as a knight. "Camelot," she whispered in awe.

"Mmmm," Mordred said. She couldn't decipher his tone, but it definitely wasn't awe. "Camelot."

They didn't try to cut across the quarry, which would have been treacherous going in any case, and kept instead to the main road in the hope that someone would be sent when Mordred's horse showed up at the castle riderless.

And, in fact, it wasn't too long after that when they heard the sound of horses. One of the house guards came around the corner, the gray charger in tow. "Sir Mordred," the man said with a grin. "You seem to have lost a horse and gained a . . ." He raised his eyebrows. "Could it perhaps be . . . a Lady?"

"Yes," Mordred said, quietly and evenly.

The man smirked, obviously doubting this, obviously giving his own interpretation of why Mordred was in her company.

No need to take time pondering what *that* was. Alayna felt herself blush, though this man's opinion of her was of no consequence. Still, that anyone could think that of her . . . She hovered between shame and anger, even as she felt herself diminished as a mother for letting these concerns distract her at this moment.

Mordred looked from the man, to her, back to the man. He smiled, showing a lot of even white teeth but absolutely no warmth. He said, "And, of course, since you didn't bring a mount for her, you will have to give her yours."

"M'Lord?" The grin wavered as the guard tried to determine how serious Mordred was.

"Off."

The man gave Alayna a disgruntled look, but slipped off the horse.

Mordred helped her up, a politeness probably for the guard's benefit since she was already halfway there, and if the guard had doubted before that she was a lady, her straddling the horse couldn't have helped.

Mordred swung onto his own horse. "I will send someone back for you," he leaned down to tell the guard. Then he gave his cold smile again. "If I remember."

Alayna flicked her horse's reins and took off at a headlong gallop. It was a small gelding, no match for Mordred's mount which would catch up in a moment, but it felt like riding the wind after her own small mare and Croswell's plow horse.

And at last, now, she felt as if she were doing something. *I'm coming,* she thought to Kiera.

CHAPTER 4

Camelot was aswirl with color. Alayna remembered that had been her first impression four years ago also, when she—and Toland, and Kiera, who hadn't been quite one-year-old at the time—had come to see Galen named a knight. In the intervening years, she had remembered the impression of color, but had forgotten the colors themselves.

There were banners, and awnings, and shirts and dresses: all in different shades and textures, not looking as though they were all dyed together—the way the shirt Toland had been buried in matched exactly the blue of the family's best tablecloth, which was the same as the blanket Kiera used on chilly nights. Or had—until this morning.

Even on her father's manor, her stepmother and the servants would dye all the season's wool in just one or two batches, since the work was so time consuming and messy. As a result, each piece of cloth was linked to a particular year and its events: blue from woad (the year her father remarried), and a lighter blue from a different batch of woad six years later (when Galen was sent to Camelot to be a squire), scarlet the year all four of them had gone to the Canterbury fair where her stepmother bought madder, and a rich russet the year Alayna left to marry Toland.

But here in Camelot, with so many people, colors were bright and endlessly varied, with no two exactly alike—a noisy, cheerful, festival atmosphere.

Alayna tried not to let it irritate her. The people of Camelot weren't the ones behind Kiera's abduction; *they* had no way of knowing how anxious she was about her daughter's safety, or how their bright colors and friendly laughter seemed to mock her distress.

People called greetings to Mordred as he and Alayna rode through the streets, but he gave only cursory acknowledgment, never slowing except to take care that the horses would not trod on anyone.

In the courtyard, servants came to take their horses. Dismounting, Alayna almost collapsed when her pained and bloodied feet met the ground. She clutched at the shoulders of the wide-eyed groom who tightened his grip on her. "My Lady," he said, distressed, but she managed to gasp, "I'm well enough." Her hips and thighs ached too, from the ride. But Mordred hadn't seen her undignified stagger, for he'd been dismounting at the same time. Now, as he turned, she forced herself as straight as she could manage, for she would not allow the indignity of letting herself be carried in. "I'm well enough," she repeated, releasing the groom, and Mordred led her into the castle itself, which seemed only slightly less crowded than the public streets.

She followed him at a cramped and stooped half-run as he went up the stairs and down a long hall. Here, finally, they left the clamor and press of people behind. There were only three or four women in this region of the castle, quiet and elegant, slipping in and out of rooms along the hall. But though they were wearing gowns as fine as any Alayna had ever had in her father's house, she guessed they were servants, because some were bearing freshly laundered linens or cut flowers, and because they bowed as Mordred passed.

Mordred brought her into a large sunlit room where a half dozen women were gathered: One was strumming a gentle tune on a rebec, two were working at a loom and an embroidering frame, one was brushing another's hair, and the last looked up from a book from which she had been reading out loud. The women inclined their heads as Mordred entered, all but the one who was embroidering the tapestry. That one paused, her needle in midair. She was an older woman—at least thirty-five, or maybe even forty years old—but she had a gentle look to her, as her gaze went from Mordred to Alayna.

Mordred had not shared with Alayna the specifics of his plans. He'd said he would inform King Arthur immediately about what had happened, but now she suddenly realized that—of course—she wouldn't just be let into the council room for an audience with the King. Obviously he was first taking her to the apartments of one of the noblewomen, to be cleaned and tended, bandaged and made presentable.

Just as she was wondering who this noblewoman was, Alayna noticed that Mordred had inclined his head with deference and waited for a sign to approach, and Alayna knew—just as Mordred said, "Guinevere."

"Mordred," the Queen greeted him. Without turning around, she said, "Juliana, we have a guest who is in obvious need of succor."

The young woman who had been getting her hair brushed hastily rose to her feet and rushed to Alayna's side, but still managed to look graceful. "I beg your pardon, mistress," she told Alayna, curtsying. "Would you care to sit?" She took Alayna by the arm and was leading her to a cushioned seat before Alayna could nod. "May I bring you something to drink?"

Alayna hesitated to sit, she was so filthy. "I don't want to ruin . . ." she started, but her legs were suddenly wobbly after all the anxiety, and the walking she'd done, and the unaccustomed riding, and the headlong rush up the stairs. She was too tired, too unsteady, to match the servant woman's courtly manner of refined speech. "Isn't there somewhere—" But as she glanced around the room, she saw *everything* was too fine for someone in her condition.

After a quick glance at Queen Guinevere, Juliana assured Alayna, "Sit here. Please."

Alayna sat, because to delay was to risk collapse. Even so, she lost several moments of time, and somehow another of the women was suddenly standing beside them with a bowl Alayna had neither seen her fetch nor approach with. By the smell of it, the bowl contained rose water, and by the cool wetness of her face, the serving woman, Juliana—who was dipping a cloth into the water and wringing it—had already wiped her face at least once.

"Thank you," Alayna said breathlessly.

"Poor soul," Guinevere murmured. She had put her embroidering needle aside and was standing nearby, something else Alayna had not seen happen.

Someone brought a stool. Alayna sat there staring at it dumbly, assuming she was meant to summon the energy to remove her filthy self from the fine chair and onto the almost-as-fine stool—until one of the women knelt and took her bruised and bleeding feet and put them up. Juliana knelt also, and she took Alayna's right foot while the other took her left, and each woman tenderly worked to remove the stones and tattered bits of Alayna's thin slippers that had worked their way into her flesh as she walked so long over rough ground. They washed her feet, seemingly unmindful of the blood and dirt that seeped into the cushion of the stool.

Time was being wasted, but Alayna had to fight to keep her eyes open.

"Rest. Rest, Alayna," a gentle voice murmured, and that was something else she had missed, Mordred telling them her name. When she forced her eyes open, she saw him standing next to the Queen and she was aware of his quiet voice, though she couldn't make out the words. She closed her eyes again for a moment, just to gather her strength, yet when she looked again there was no sign of him, and the gentle voice—it was the Queen, Alayna realized—said, "All will be well. But now it is time to regain your vigor."

Alayna saw the sense of it and knew she was not a bad mother just because she couldn't sustain the level of panic she'd experienced when first walking to Croswell's holding. She let herself doze, refusing to give in entirely to sleep; instead, she drifted in a state where she remained somewhat aware of her surroundings, of the quietly efficient voices around her, of someone brushing the twigs and tangles from her hair. But most of all she was aware of the fact that she was just catching her breath—waiting for Mordred to come back for her, to bring her before the King, who would help her regain her daughter.

She was aware enough to recognize a male voice among those hushed feminine voices about her, and she forced herself to come fully awake then, and opened her eyes though they were reluctant to cooperate.

Mordred was leaning over her. "Lady Alayna," he said. "Are you able to come with me? The King has convened an emergency session of the council. I have told them what you told me, but it would be better—"

"Yes," she assured him. It was what she had hoped for, what she had anticipated. She sat up, with help from one of the Queen's ladies-in-waiting. Her muscles had set, once she'd stopped moving, and she ached all over.

Kiera would be sore, too, for she was not used to riding. Alayna focused on that thought, and wouldn't allow her mind to skitter off to any other. To *any* other.

Mordred took hold of her arms and gently lifted her to her feet, which hurt more now that they were salved and bandaged than they had before. "Are you well enough?" he asked at her pained intake of breath.

"Yes," she said, her voice a sibilant whisper.

Guinevere said, "Juliana will attend to you."

"Thank you." Alayna looked around the room to include all of the ladies, though their kindness was from the Queen. "Thank you all for your tender charity."

Guinevere made a hushing sound, with her finger to her lips as an adult to a child, too secure in herself and her position to be concerned about maintaining her dignity. "Our prayers go with you, that you speedily find your daughter safe and well."

The other women murmured their good wishes, too, and all the words of kindness seemed to fly directly to the inside of Alayna's chest, where they sat, a lump waiting to take its shape depending on what happened to Kiera.

"Are you certain you are well enough?" Mordred asked several times more as they walked, very slowly now, back down the stairs and through several halls. He had hold of her left arm, supporting her, while Juliana hovered at her right side, ready to be of assistance if needed.

"Yes," Alayna said each time.

And finally they stood before huge oaken doors decorated with a golden ring at least as big as the circumference of a barrel.

Mordred knocked, and the doors swung open.

They were in a big room, not as immense as the Great Hall where the King held public audience and where Galen and his friends and relatives had gathered for his investiture, but big enough to hold a circular table that had twelve chairs around it.

And Galen was there, too.

She hadn't realized how much she had been hoping—until, for one awful moment, she thought he wasn't. But it was just that he wasn't seated. He was standing by the door, not one of the twelve and he came forward and hugged her. He had grown a droopy mustache since the last time she had seen him, which made him look more like their father. She threw her arms around him, burying her face in his chest and he rocked her back and forth, which was also like their father—a very long time ago—and he said, "There, there. All will be made right. I'm sure she's safe. She *is*, Alayna. There would be no sense in taking her away to do her harm."

Alayna fought back the voice that wanted to say, *But I don't know for sure they DID take her away. She might be dead beneath the cinders of the house.* A part of her wanted to say it, to hear Galen's reassurances. But another part of her warned that his reassurances could only be guesses; and to give voice to her fears—only to be reassured by guesses—was to give the fears too much strength.

Once she was sure she wouldn't cry, wouldn't embarrass her brother in front of his comrades, she stepped back from him, glad to have had the support of his arms. She nodded to show that she was in control and remembered that among the men watching and kept waiting was the King.

Arthur was, in fact, the only man of those who sat there that she recognized, for it was only four years ago since she had seen Galen swear fealty to him.

She curtsied, aware that Juliana also curtsied, except deeper, because she was a servant—and Mordred bowed. Then Mordred indicated for her to go closer. There were chairs along the far wall also, and one of these had been pulled forward. She couldn't be expected to sit, not in the presence of the King. It had been bad enough when she had practically collapsed in the Queen's chambers.

But Mordred brought her directly to the chair, and the King smiled, a grave but friendly smile, and the King said, "Sit, child. You have been through too much to stand on ceremony."

Alayna hastily looked away, partly to make sure she didn't miss when she attempted to sit, but mostly so that King Arthur wouldn't see the tears in her eyes. She blinked several times, and the tears went away without overflowing her eyes.

Galen stood beside Alayna while Juliana stood behind the chair. Mordred took his place at the one remaining chair around the table. Arthur's councils were selected as they were needed: Arthur and eleven men of his choosing, so that there would never be a lack if someone was away from court.

"Lady Alayna De La Croix," Arthur said, "please know that you are most welcome here, and we sincerely hope that you will avail yourself of anything we might possess to make your time at Camelot more comfortable, though we understand the reason for your coming is one none of us would have desired."

Alayna hesitated, having no idea how to answer this. But if she was left speechless by the King's greeting, that didn't bode well for explaining her mission. She finally settled on, "Thank you, my Lord."

Arthur indicated the man on his right. "This is Sir Gawain."

Alayna inclined her head in greeting, which Gawain returned, and Arthur continued with the next man. "Sir William Fitzwilliam . . ."

Belatedly she realized he hadn't singled out Gawain as someone she needed to know; the King was simply going around the table. Alayna tried to concentrate, mentally repeated each name as Arthur spoke it, and lost in turn each name as Arthur moved to the next. The only names that stayed with her were Gawain, since he'd been the first, and Percival, since he was last—and also he stood out because he was the only one of the twelve, besides Mordred, who wasn't her father's age or older.

Once done, Arthur said, "Please tell us, as you will, what happened."

Alayna nodded and took a deep breath. "Two knights—"

"Did you know them?" interrupted a man several places to Arthur's left. He had darting eyes and fidgeting fingers.

"No," Alayna said. "If I—"

"Then how do you know they were knights?"

"They were dressed as knights," Alayna started. "I—"

"How?" the man interrupted again. "Exactly."

"Plate armor—"

"Painted? Any devices? Insignia?"

Alayna started to shake her head, and the man didn't wait for her to vocalize her answer. He asked, "Did they carry shields whose pattern you might recognize?"

"No, I—"

"What makes you think they were knights then, and not just thieves?"

Alayna glanced at Galen to see what he made of this man who wouldn't let her get out more than two or three words at a time. But Galen, she saw, was in company among whom he did not dare speak out as an equal. And Mordred was busy watching the King. She spoke in a rush to get her question all out: "Thieves who stole armor from knights?"

"Why not?" the fidgety man snapped. "Or from an armorer? Might they not have been?" His tone suggested he was sure she planned to argue.

"I don't know," Alayna said "They might—"

"What of the horses?"

"Sir Lambert," Mordred finally intervened, "will you give Lady Alayna a chance to answer any one of your questions, or must she wait until you have asked them all first, then answer the sum of them at the end?"

There were some quick smiles, and the first man, Sir Lambert, explained, "Please pardon my zeal for the truth, only I find it difficult to believe knights would accost a woman and her child in their own home."

"Oh, verily," said Mordred, in such an ingenuous tone there could be no doubt his words meant the opposite of what he said, "such a thing has *never* been done before."

"Not in recent memory," Lambert protested. "Not in King Arthur's lands. Perhaps in the backcountry of Cornwall, where—"

Mordred sighed and looked away. Apparently this was an old argument. The burly Gawain must have been Cornish also, for he brought his arms down heavily onto the table.

"Enough," Arthur said in the long-suffering tone of a father experienced with bickering children. "Let Lady Alayna tell her story." As though to get her started again, he prompted, "Two knights broke into your home—"

"Two men dressed as knights," Lambert corrected.

Praise God Arthur was king, and not Lambert.

"It happened so suddenly," Alayna resumed, "I didn't get a good look at them. I am not certain I would be able to recognize them again, but I might." She thought of their man who had grabbed her, how she had spun around and found herself no more than the breadth of a hand away from him. "I think I would be able to recognize the man they had with them."

"What did he look like?" Lambert asked.

"Ugly," Alayna said, and knew Lambert was going to ask it before she had even closed her lips on the word.

"Ugly, how?"

Ugliness was a subjective quality. "Big nose, pocked skin." She added, "And he had dark hair." She indicated just below her ear before Lambert could ask and added, "Neither curly, nor exactly straight."

"Any scars, distinguishing features?"

"No," Alayna said.

Lambert made a dismissive gesture. "Could be anyone."

"No," Alayna insisted. "I would recognize him."

"You think," Lambert reminded her.

The younger knight with the fair hair—Percival—said, "Tell us about the child."

Beside her, Galen rested his hand on her shoulder.

"My husband," Alayna said, "was a wizard. Kiera may have some of his"—even after all this she hesitated—". . . ability."

"What sort of ability?" asked a man at the table who had not previously spoken, a stout man with very little hair. "Precisely."

"Precisely, it's hard to say," Alayna said. "You know how little children are." But there was a good chance they did not. Guinevere, despite being a queen, despite being childless, would probably understand. Men, even fathers, rarely knew as much about young children or noticed things as women did. "She might or might not be able to talk to animals. *Sometimes*," she admitted, "she truly seems to be able to; sometimes, she seems to be simply playing a game."

She expected the men would be losing patience with her, but—with the exception of Lambert, who was sitting on the edge of his seat but had his head tipped back so that he was staring at the ceiling—they gave no outward signs of wanting to hurry her.

"Sometimes," she continued, "she tells me something will happen, and it does." She found it difficult to break her old habit of trying to find natural explanations for Kiera's unnatural abilities, and couldn't help but add, "Though sometimes it does not. This morning . . ." She licked her lips: *Why* hadn't she paid closer attention? Why hadn't she believed? Could all this have been prevented if she had done something based on Kiera's warning? But it had been so vague: *Something bad is coming.* How could one prepare for that? But still, Kiera safe at home, Ned alive and well: It was an alluring picture. She swallowed hard and said, "This morning she was afraid of something. She said she saw something bad happening, something dangerous. I thought she'd had a bad dream."

The knight closest to her, the stout, balding man, reached over to give her hand a squeeze.

Lambert sighed. Loudly.

Percival asked, "How many people know of the child?"

"Know of her?" Alayna repeated.

Lambert sighed yet again and said, "I think what Sir Percival is trying to ask is this: How many are aware of her so-called abilities? From the way you have presented the matter, you yourself are not certain whether they truly exist or not. Does this mean you ignored these abilities, or have you worked to conceal them?"

"I . . ." One made her sound a fool, the other—someone who would use people and try to manipulate them. Was that what she was?

Quietly, evenly, Mordred said, "Anyone who knew the father was a wizard might suspect the child. Whether the child truly has power is unimportant; the fact that she *might* may well be the reason she was taken."

Percival, with a glance at Lambert—who hadn't had a chance to say anything— said, "I think what Sir Lambert is trying to say is he agrees."

"Much more reasonable," Lambert argued with a sour look for the younger man's mockery, "that some ruffians, wearing stolen or discarded armor chose a well-born lady living alone at a remote residence, and—intent on extorting a ransom—"

"They burned her house down around her," Mordred pointed out. "Hard to collect a ransom, if you destroy all the property; harder yet if you kill the person most likely to pay the ransom."

"Please do not interrupt," Lambert said. "That would still leave Sir Galen, who might—"

This time it was Arthur who interrupted. "Mordred and Percival may well have a point," he said. "There seems little reason to suppose that abductors would choose the roundabout way of seeking ransom from an uncle rather than a parent. *Or*," he added quickly since Lambert was opening his mouth, apparently ready with a rebuttal, "if the mother did not have as much money as the abductors hoped to gain, why not hold her as hostage, too, and call on the ties of brother, as well as uncle?"

"A child is easier to control than a grown woman," Lambert objected.

Arthur nodded but said, "Nonetheless . . ." and—incredibly—Lambert finally bowed his head to acquiesce. "So," Arthur continued, "we have a child taken, apparently by knights, apparently because of her abilities—real or imagined—in the art of magic. Therefore, we will start our search by questioning the wizards of the realm."

Mordred said, "I will call upon Halbert of Burrstone."

Lambert said, "You always suspect Halbert of everything, ever since you lost that joust with his nephew Bayard. Lances *do* break, you know, without magical intervention."

Mordred gave a tight smile and said, "Halbert is also closest, which makes him most likely to have heard of this child."

The other young knight, Sir Percival, gave the name of another wizard, and said he would ride to that one's home. Several of the other knights called out the names of wizards they would seek out.

They were discussing her daughter, and nobody looked ready to explain the direction the discussion had taken, so—feeling like a child unable to understand the discourse of adults—Alayna raised her hand and timidly asked, "Why wizards?"

Arthur answered, "Ever since Merlin left Camelot to be with Nimue,"—Alayna saw a few smiles, a few smirks around the table, but Arthur never blinked—"there has been no clear leader, no master magician. Some have started actively vying for power."

Alayna cleared her throat and asked the King in a whisper, "How do you mean 'vying'? Magical contests?"

"Well, yes, contests," Arthur said. "Sometimes." Then he admitted, "Sometimes assassinations."

Alayna couldn't help herself, even though this was the King of whom she was demanding answers. "What are you saying?" She was aware that several of the men around the table leaned forward to hear her better, but she couldn't get her voice above a whisper. Beside her, Galen squeezed her shoulder, which might have been a warning that she shouldn't interrupt the King. But she continued. "Do you think that Kiera was eliminated as a potential rival?"

Arthur didn't answer. Mordred was looking steadfastly at his own hands. Galen, she saw, was chewing the inside of his cheeks—a habit she remembered from their childhood whenever their father unexpectedly summoned them before him. Kiera had picked the trait up from him.

Alayna felt an ache in her chest—a need to be reassured that her daughter was warm and well treated whether in a wizard's captivity or elsewhere. "Kiera is still alive," she said steadily. "I am her mother; and I can feel it."

Arthur and Mordred exchanged a glance, but had the good grace not to offer their opinions.

CHAPTER 5

Although Galen had not participated in the council, now he spoke. "I would like to take part in the search for my niece. I do not know any of these wizards of whom you speak, but if someone tells me the name of one who might be involved, and where he is likely to be found . . ."

Arthur said, "The five who have just been spoken for *are* the most likely. There are, of course, always village-wizards and country witch women, but if we begin to question all of them . . ." He shook his head. "That would be a task for more knights than there are in all of Camelot, if we were to seek them out in a timely manner. And I think it unlikely that the wizards of other lands would concern themselves with a five-year-old girl whose abilities may or may not surpass her father's."

He was reminding them, Alayna thought, in as gentle a way as he could in front of Toland's widow, that Toland himself had been nothing but a village-wizard, not powerful enough to attract attention, so his daughter's fame was not likely to spread far.

The stout, bald-headed man seated beside Alayna said, "But the earlier the power manifests itself, the stronger it is likely to be."

"So it is said," Arthur agreed. Turning back to Galen, he said, "Still, Sir Galen, if there is a wizard behind this, it is likely to be one of the five just spoken of. Leave that quest to the older knights."

"Such as Sir Mordred?" Galen asked, for Galen was probably closer in age to Percival, with Mordred being the youngest.

But the King did not take this boldness amiss. He smiled indulgently—again Alayna was reminded of a forbearing father. "I agree it would be an excellent arrangement for you to accompany Sir Mordred," he said, which wasn't, exactly, what Galen had asked. "And at the same time, we will see if a ransom is demanded. And the child will be remembered in our prayers." He stood to indicate the council was over. "I believe supper must be almost ready, if not already set out."

The others stood also and began to move toward the door.

Prayers. Was that all that was left to her now? Was praying the most she could do to help Kiera?

Mordred said to Galen, "I would be honored to have you accompany me," in too smooth a tone for Alayna to decipher if he meant what he said or its opposite. But if, in truth, he wasn't disposed to have Galen's company thrust on him, she thought, he certainly would not be pleased to hear that she, too, wanted to face Kiera's abductor.

Mordred was continuing, "Castle Burrstone is three days' journey to the northeast, assuming a fairly fast ride. I recommend simple breastplates—giving up some measure of protection for the extra speed that lightness will bring. How much time will you require to prepare?"

Alayna answered before Galen could. "I lost everything in the fire, so I must depend on the charity of someone here, please." Trying to make light, as though that would prove she would not be dead weight to slow them down, she added, "Of course, I never did have a breastplate."

It took several moments for either Mordred or Galen to grasp her meaning. In fact, she thought it was Sir Percival who understood first. She saw him stop, his expression exhilarated, unwilling to leave before this new, interesting diversion was settled.

In the doorway, Arthur turned back to say something to Percival, saw the younger man was no longer beside him, and paused also—which left the entire council to either push ahead of their king or remain and listen to Alayna argue with her brother.

"You can't come with us," Galen said, aghast.

"Firstly," Alayna said, "that would be Sir Mordred's choice, not yours, because— after all—*you* are accompanying *him*." And then, because—judging by Mordred's face—he was no more inclined than Galen to have her, she added, "Secondly, do not forget, I *saw* the men. I would recognize them."

Lambert, annoyingly precise, said, "You think."

"I would come closer to it than anyone else." Alayna could hear the displeased murmur of the knights about her.

"Don't be absurd," Galen started, sputtering a bit—more and more like their father—at the same moment Mordred said, quietly, reasonably, "Lady Alayna, sure-ly the child's best interests—"

"I would not slow you down," Alayna said—she honestly didn't think she would. She was certainly lighter than the men, and yet capable of riding a good horse. "Without me, you go to this wizard you suspect, you question him, you look around: What else will he say but *no*, he had nothing to do with stealing away Kiera? But there is a good chance I will know. *I* can say *yae* or *nay*. *I* can say: *This is the man, no matter what he tells you*, or *We are wasting our time; he wasn't there*."

Mordred said, "The wizard was not likely one of the two knights himself."

Alayna brushed this argument away with an impatient hand. "His men, then. If he has nothing to hide, he will have no objection to presenting his knights to me."

The burly Gawain—who had not spoken up at the council—now said, "This is not women's work."

Galen said, "Alayna, use some sense. I know you are distraught—"

Someone interrupted, "If it comes to a fight, you are likely to get everybody killed, the girl included."

Alayna couldn't let herself believe that. She said, "I was trained to fight."

Her statement was met with looks and snorts of derision.

"Until I was twelve."

This was meant to show that the training was beyond a young child's playing, but obviously they were not impressed.

"I know I am not as strong as a man," Alayna said over their upraised voices. "But neither am I a helpless maiden who can do no more than clutch her hands together and faint at the first sign of trouble."

Unexpected ally, Mordred said, "Of which we have ample proof, by the fact of your being here."

Alayna weighed this as likely mockery or not, decided not, and gave a terse nod of appreciation for even this much support.

There was a murmur of comments, as the knights found themselves unable to argue Mordred's point, but unconvinced by it.

Gawain said, "The idea is ludicrous and irrational."

"Unworkable," Mordred modified, though it still came down to his being against her.

Everybody was agreeing.

Except Arthur, who seemed to be just watching, waiting to see what would happen.

And except for Percival. He said, "As the child's mother, she has the right."

The voices continued for a few more moments until his words sank in.

There were a few jeers, to which Percival didn't respond. He stood, tall and commanding with his arms folded across his chest, and once the room was totally silent, he repeated, "It *is* her right."

Even the balding man who had squeezed her hand in comfort was shaking his head. He said, gesturing to Percival, "Arthur, tell this young pup that he has been out too long in the sun."

Arthur looked at Percival. "Perhaps he has," he said. "But even so he is correct: It is her right. Far be it from me to stand between a mother and her child."

Neither Mordred nor Galen appeared pleased, but neither would they argue with the King.

"So then," Alayna said, unsure whether Percival's support extended so far as to be an invitation, "I will accompany you?"

"That," Percival said with a smile, "would be unseemly: a woman and a man with no bond of kinship. You should go in the party that includes your brother."

Galen scowled.

"We are wasting time," Alayna said frantically.

Not even addressing her, Lambert protested, "But even if she *did* know how to use a sword, she does not have one, nor is there armor that would—"

"One thing of which Camelot is not lacking," Percival said, unbuckling his sword belt, "is swords." He handed belt and sheath and sword to Alayna. She didn't trust her voice to work and only mouthed the words *Thank you*. Percival continued, "And surely a leather jerkin can be found to fit her, to offer some amount of protection."

The fact that he was pointing out to all that her bosom was not especially ample did not in this circumstance bother Alayna.

"This is preposterous," Galen complained.

With a glance toward Arthur, Mordred said, in that annoyingly indecipherable tone, "It has been decided." He held his arm out, indicating for her to precede him out of the council room. He told Galen, "Gather what you will need as quickly as you can. We will leave at dawn tomorrow."

Alayna bit back a plea to get started immediately, but she knew there was no time. It would do Kiera no good to have them rush out ill-prepared and stumbling in the dark. Better to start fresh in the morning.

Though she had not eaten all day, she would forgo the meal that the servants were in all probability setting out—in favor of bed. She didn't know how much longer she could stay on her feet. She hoped that—despite the sure knowledge that the knights would be grumbling about her—they could not dissuade Percival, who had spoken up for her, and Mordred, who had, however reluctantly, eventually backed her also. In fact, Mordred said to her now, "I disagree with what you have decided. But I admire it."

She waited to see if this would come around again to a condemnation, but it didn't. He only added, seeing her expectant look, "It is not every mother who would fight so strongly to protect her child."

Gawain said, brusquely, "Don't go on about our mother," and brushed past her and out the door, even ahead of the King.

And, with that as an example, knowing she hadn't heard the last of the arguments, Alayna too walked past everyone, her brother included, and out the door. She walked down the hall with her head high, for she had gotten what she wanted, and she knew it would be best for Kiera.

But she also knew that once she got to the end of the hall, she would have to wait for Mordred, for she had no idea where she was going.

The next day, Alayna fidgeted in the morning sunlight, which streamed in through the open window.

The lady-in-waiting who was arranging her hair giggled.

"Celeste."

In the mirror—a real glass one, not just polished metal—Alayna could see Queen Guinevere's disapproving look.

Celeste giggled again.

Guinevere approached and took the hairbrush, then dismissed the servant with a motion of the head.

Alayna caught Celeste's reflection in the glass, turning back in the doorway for a final look, no doubt relishing the amusement of a lady dressed in boys' clothing, a lady who proclaimed herself ready to take on a man's task.

Guinevere moved behind Alayna and blocked her view of the door. "Silly girl," she said, but Alayna couldn't tell, not for certain, which of them the Queen meant. She rearranged Alayna's long brown braids into a much less elaborate knot, one which would stay up without needing a good deal of attention. Guinevere's hands were very thin and very white and had a tendency to tremble with nervous energy when they weren't occupied. But now they worked quickly and deftly. "I do wish you would reconsider," she said softly. "The men are trained for just this sort of thing, you know."

"I can ride as well as any man," Alayna told her. "I am not going to hold them back. Kiera must be so frightened. She needs me. She needs to see me as soon as possible." Her own hands were rough, and she nervously picked at a piece of skin by her thumbnail until—just as she thought, *I must stop before I cause it to bleed*—it began to bleed. She held on tight to stop the blood but also to hide it.

"Still . . ."

When the Queen didn't finish her thought, Alayna looked up from her hands to Guinevere's reflection in the mirror. The Queen was looking beyond her, over the mirror, and out the window. Alayna followed her gaze to the courtyard below, striped by early-morning light and shadows. Mordred was approaching, and Galen was with him.

The two young men wore simple breastplates, which was what Mordred had suggested the previous day—that they should give up some measure of protection for the extra speed that lightness would bring.

"Galen!" she called, and her brother found the right window and smiled up at her, which was a relief.

Alayna clutched Guinevere's hand, unmindful for the moment that she was probably getting blood from her thumb on the Queen. "Thank you," she said with all her heart, but she was already thinking ahead to seeing Kiera, to holding a rescued Kiera in her arms. "Thank you for all you have done."

Guinevere rested her hand on Alayna's head. "Be assured our hopes go with you," she told Alayna. Then, with a smile that said she knew there was no use saying any more, "Go."

Alayna ran down the stairs just as the men came in, and she threw her arms around her brother's neck. "Oh, Galen, I'm so glad to see you. I half suspected you might leave without me."

"If I had thought of it . . ." Galen said. But he didn't mean it, she could tell by his eyes. Still, "Alayna," he started in a tone that warned he was intent on trying to talk her out of this.

"Galen," she said, matching his tone, as they had done when arguing as children.

Galen sighed, relenting. He took her by the shoulders, a demand for her attention, for seriousness. He said, "You know you can always depend on me."

It was true. He had always taken care of her, even though he was the elder by less than a year. He had always taken her side when she had come into conflict with their father or their stepmother. And last year, when Toland had died so suddenly, Galen had arrived, without being summoned, following a premonition that something was wrong.

Now he smiled at her, even as he shook his head at her page's leggings and leather jerkin.

She felt her face go hot and red. To hide her embarrassment, she turned to wave to Guinevere at the top of the stairs, but the Queen had already gone.

They passed through another door and into the main courtyard of the keep. Into a crowd. Squires were brushing and exercising their knights' horses. Even this early, washerwomen carried great baskets of laundry. Pages ran messages. Servants trying to get platters of breakfast food from the kitchen to the main hall had to dodge people, barking dogs, and a flock of sheep, which had somehow worked its way up from the lower bailey. A cluster of children were trying to tag each other and bumped into everybody.

King Arthur was there, also, looking as permanently tired as his wife. He took Alayna's hand in his own. "Godspeed," he wished, and to Galen, "Our prayers go with you—a safe trip and a happy conclusion to this unfortunate matter." He gave each of their hands a squeeze. Then—and there was obviously some matter between them—"Mordred."

Mordred gave just the slightest inclination of his head.

The squire who had attached Alayna's things to her saddle stepped back, and there was nothing more to delay them.

Alayna paused before mounting and rested her hand on the sword Sir Percival had presented to her. She hoped she was not being just stubbornly prideful, that her presence wouldn't endanger Kiera. She offered up a brief prayer. Then she swung onto her horse and followed Galen and Mordred through the press of people and animals.

Knights touched sword pommels as they passed—a wish for luck—and several ladies waved and blew kisses. No wonder. Galen, his hair golden in the sunlight, looked magnificent. Mordred, darker and slighter, was a handsome youth. Together they looked like heroes from a ballad. Alayna still hoped that her pride wasn't endangering Kiera, but she spared a brief hope that, also, she wouldn't make a fool of herself.

They made their way through the lower bailey and a throng of peasants who looked at the knights with mild interest and gaped at her. By the time they got through the portcullis and over the drawbridge, Alayna was finding the crowds suffocating.

Perhaps Mordred felt the same, for he immediately set off at a gallop that they all knew couldn't be maintained for long.

CHAPTER 6

It had been long years since Alayna had spent all day in a saddle. Her horse had no trouble keeping up with Mordred's and Galen's, but by the end of the day she had to concentrate to stay on her mount. Despite her anxiety to get to Kiera she was grateful when the sun finally set, giving her the chance to rest her aching body. She was not eager for their first real chance to talk, for she feared she knew what the men would have to say.

And, in fact, once they finished setting up camp and eating, Mordred asked, with a nod toward the sword she had set down beside her, "How good are you?"

She stretched out on her side, unable to sit any longer than the time necessary for the actual eating of their evening meal. She knew Mordred must have asked Galen already. He was testing her assurance. Or the level of her pride. Two different matters, requiring two different answers.

"Competent," she answered. She didn't know what to do with her hands, and plucked at the grass before her. Mordred was buffing the breastplate he had been wearing all day. Galen was poking at the fire with a stick. Alayna said, "When we were children, I could keep up with Galen."

Mordred concentrated on rubbing a section of the metal.

But something about his manner made Alayna add, "And Galen is quite good."

"Oh, yes," Mordred agreed. "He has done well in tournaments."

Alayna considered this for a moment. "Yes?"

Galen grinned. "Despite the fact that I have beaten Mordred nearly every time we've been up against each other, he insists he's the better fighter."

"That," Mordred said, "is not exactly true. What I've told him is that battle is not a joust: no points racked up for snapped lances, no one to break things up if they get too heated. Your brother is in love with the ideals of chivalry. Tournaments, of course, are a sports event—nobody is supposed to fight all out. Galen thinks tournament rules apply even in real life."

With a grin Galen said, "Mordred has been advocating slash and maim."

Mordred looked about to protest, but in the end did not.

Alayna's thoughts went—as they did in any free moment—to Kiera. Before the men could switch from baiting each other to badgering her, she said, "So, tell me about this wizard Halbert of Burrstone, that you seem so sure has Kiera."

Mordred glanced up, but said nothing.

The campfire threw dancing shadows over all their faces.

Galen stopped poking at the fire and took a drink of ale from his wineskin. "Well, for one thing, he is perhaps the strongest wizard since Merlin is gone."

"Strongest in wizardry," Alayna asked, "or strongest in men and money and holdings?"

"Good question," Galen acknowledged, and she felt a flash of irritation at the condescension, as though she were in the habit of asking foolish questions, which she didn't believe she was. The fire had grown too hot on her arms, but she didn't move back.

"Both," Mordred finally said, when it became apparent Galen wasn't going to say anything.

Their eyes danced from one to the other—Alayna's brown, Galen's blue, Mordred's gray—each eager to read the others' reactions but reluctant to be read.

"That's one thing . . ." Alayna prodded, reminding Galen that he had hinted at more than one point.

Mordred reached to readjust a branch in their fire. *He always chooses his words carefully*, Alayna thought, and though there was nothing wrong with that, it was uncommon in one so young, and she did wonder at it.

"Merlin," Mordred said, "never concerned himself with acquiring wealth or personal glory. He did not use magic"—Alayna noticed how he practically spat out the word "magic" and wondered at that, too—"for petty personal gains or to settle grudges. Perhaps I am just used to his manner. He kept aloof, and did not use magic to inflict spiteful miseries or to affect the odds on wagers."

Galen said, "Mordred admires aloofness, as you may have already guessed."

Mordred gave a smile that was the picture of aloofness.

"And as for grudges," Galen added, "*he* does hold them."

"Certainly," Mordred admitted, "but I don't use magic to settle them."

"You have a grudge against Sir Halbert?" Alayna asked.

"Yes," Mordred said.

"Because he uses magic in a way of which you don't approve?"

"Because he used magic against me."

"Once," Galen told Alayna, "and perhaps."

"It is a place to start," Mordred said with yet another aloof smile. "Rather than this, we would do better to discuss our approach to Castle Burrstone."

Before Alayna could complain that she had thought he knew how to get there, Galen sighed. Loudly. "Stealth," he said as though it were an old argument, "is for thieves, and foxes in the chicken coop. Not for the righteous."

"Someone who steals a child *is* a thief," Mordred countered. "Does one meet a thief's stealth with chivalry?"

"We don't know for a certainty that Halbert is the culprit."

Mordred gave a grin that had nothing of aloofness in it. "Nor will we," he said, "if we approach openly, declare and challenge. That will give him more than enough time to hide away anything he does not want us to see."

At least, Alayna thought, watching her brother settle in to convince Mordred of something Mordred was all too obviously set against being convinced of, it would take their minds off her, and the question of whether she should be there.

At worst, it freed her mind once more to agonize about Kiera.

They reached Castle Burrstone two days later. Sand-colored walls were reflected in the clear water of the wide moat, and bright banners snapped in the breeze. It was . . . *prettier* was the best word Alayna could come up with . . . it was prettier than she had anticipated. Was this the home of someone who stole away children? Yet she was relieved, too—in case it *was* the home of someone who stole away children.

Galen must have seen the surprise on her face. Grinning, he asked, "Did you expect swamps and dragons?"

Without raising his voice, without sounding alarmed, Mordred said, "Archer in the north bartizan."

Crossbow, Alayna noted. Her father would have disapproved, saying that Christian men should fight each other as Christian men were meant to: face-to-face, relying on their God-given strength and skill. Bows were for hunters, and the newer crossbows were to be used on boar, deer, and heathen Saracens.

Two knights dressed in full field armor stepped out onto the lowered drawbridge just before them. They stood with feet apart and both hands on the hilts of their sheathed swords, which were pointed—at least for the moment—downward.

"Declare and challenge," Mordred muttered, having been in the end worn down by Galen's scruples, and obviously wanting to remind them—should they get killed—who was at fault for it.

"Straightforward is the best," Galen assured them both. But she noticed that he quietly placed himself between her and the archers.

She had wavered last night, knowing that Mordred's way was safer, Galen's more decent, but they hadn't sought her opinion, and she had been glad to let them work it out, being reluctant to commit herself to either. But in the face of those guards, Mordred's arguments gained, too late, considerably more strength.

The three of them passed between the two guards, whose eyes remained perfectly forward.

In the courtyard another knight stood waiting, dressed in a simple hauberk instead of cap-à-pie armor, and his attitude was less openly aggressive.

"More archers," Alayna muttered, catching a movement at one of the archer loops above. There was no way to tell if the others heard, but they no doubt expected it in any case.

But the knight certainly didn't look as though he meant to intimidate them, and as they pulled up he even smiled at them, still mounted, in greeting. "Welcome, my Lady," he said smoothly, as if he often greeted ladies in leather jerkins and hose. "My Lords. I am Sir Denis, seneschal at Castle Burrstone. May I be of assistance to you?"

"Our business is with the wizard," Mordred said brusquely.

But Sir Denis refused to take offense. "And may I have your names to tell Sir Halbert?"

"Mordred of Orkney," Mordred said. "Sir Galen and his sister Lady Alayna De La Croix."

Denis bowed and motioned for a boy to come take their horses. Still, Alayna wasn't fooled by his meek manners. Denis might be in charge of the castle's stores, but he looked no more like the overfed, lazy steward of her father's estates than Galen did. And, for a moment, comparing his voice to one burned into her heart, Alayna thought he *might* have been one of the knights she sought: the one who had snarled, "Find the whelp." Then they swung off their horses, and Sir Denis turned out to be barely as tall as she—a good head shorter than any of the intruders.

They followed him indoors to the Great Hall. "I will summon Sir Halbert," Denis said, with a slight bow. He backed out of the room, still bowing, which might have been courtly manners—or suspicion, a reluctance to expose his back to them.

Alayna inclined her head in acknowledgment and forced a smile, reminding herself that these people might be innocent, no matter Mordred's conviction.

The room was large, with two entrances on the far wall, besides the one through which they had come. Heavy tapestries covered the walls. They were much richer than those at any of her father's estates, and not as well chosen or tasteful as what she'd seen at Camelot.

She moved past a picture of a dragon, quite striking in reds and golds, then paused in front of an intricately worked hanging obviously based on Greek themes. She'd studied it for long moments before realizing that in the background, behind the dancing women in white kirtles and the men playing flutes and drums, among the trees there was a human sacrifice taking place: a youth bound on an altar, with tiny stitches of red thread signifying his blood. She put her back to the weaving in time to see Galen rub his upper arms and glance nervously to each of the three entrances.

Mordred had been checking behind the tapestries—Alayna could only presume to learn whether anyone was lurking behind—but he finally seemed satisfied that they were truly alone in the room, and at last stood still.

Alayna sniffed. Somebody was burning incense. She sighed impatiently and hoped that whatever was coming would come quickly. She wanted to scream Kiera's name.

A door opposite the one by which they had come in opened. The man who entered was powerfully built, a man of about her father's age, dressed in a dark blue velvet gown. He looked over the three of them twice before settling on her. "My Lady Alayna," he said with a bow, his voice indicating surprise and curiosity just beneath the polite manners. "Sir Mordred, so charmed to meet you again. Sir Galen."

"My Lord," the three of them said in unison.

His voice was like a coating of cream on the surface of heated milk. "Castle Burrstone is honored by your presence." That was either empty politeness or for

Mordred's sake, Alayna thought. He couldn't have had any idea who she and Galen were.

Unless, of course, he knew exactly who they were.

But Halbert continued to smile at all of them, and he said, "You, of course, are most welcome to my humble home, and you are welcome to share all I have for as long as you may be in the vicinity. Yet,"—he smiled broader still, showing white, even teeth—"yet, I hope I can say without causing offense that I wonder why three such illustrious young people would choose to leave the glamour and excitement of Camelot for this quiet, modest corner of the land."

Illustrious? Alayna thought. That was a bit excessive.

His eyes kept going back to her—but that may have been because of her outlandish clothing.

"We are on a quest," Galen said with the faintest of smiles, a sign Alayna recognized as tension.

Halbert put on a look of polite interest and absently stroked the pendant he wore around his neck, a crimson jewel. It was probably worth a year's income from the smallest of her father's estates—which was not so very small.

"My sister is searching for her daughter."

Halbert turned to look at her with a concerned frown.

Alayna's hand had found its way to her sword hilt, and she crossed her arms to keep from what had to look a hostile gesture. She saw Mordred's hand clench and unclench, his fingers flexing, a nervous habit shared by many swordsmen. Galen, by the set of his jaw, looked in danger of cracking his teeth.

Halbert said to Alayna, "Then you'd like me to tell you where she is?" That seemed disarmingly direct. For a moment Alayna forgot to breathe, but then the wizard held his arm out to her. "Come," he said, "I have a scrying crystal, which sometimes helps me in such matters."

So he didn't have Kiera. Or—at least—he wasn't admitting to it. But if he didn't have her, what game was he playing at?

Alayna moved to follow him.

Galen whispered hoarsely, "I don't think you need a crystal."

Mordred also had taken a step to follow the wizard. Now he gave Galen an annoyed frown.

Alayna folded her arms again.

"Your faith in me—" Halbert started.

Galen spat on the floor.

Halbert looked as surprised as Alayna felt. "Sir knight—" he started.

Galen said, "Any villain who would steal a five-year-old child away from her family is no better than a dog."

"I?" Halbert said. He rested his heavily beringed hand on his chest, over the ruby on its chain. "You think I would be involved with abducting a child?"

Alayna was left speechless by her brother's suddenly belligerent attitude, not part of their plan at all. Declare and challenge was one thing, open confrontation and rudeness was another—especially given that all along Galen had been the one to urge Mordred to consider that Halbert may, in truth, not be the culprit.

Now it was Mordred who stepped into the awkward silence. "Sir Galen is distraught at the disappearance of his niece." He smiled apologetically at Halbert.

Galen didn't acknowledge either Mordred's warning glare or his attempt to soothe Halbert's indignation. He demanded, "Where is she?"

"I said I was willing to help you look."

Galen said, "I can start with the upper rooms."

"Galen!" Alayna gasped, unsure what to make of this behavior that was neither characteristic nor helpful. If this was part of some plan he and Mordred had worked out between them, she couldn't see the sense of it. And—if it was—they most certainly should have told her.

Halbert had lost his smile. He said, "Sir, if you persist in this insulting manner—"

Galen leaped forward to seize the wizard's throat, but Mordred grabbed Galen and held him back, looking—Alayna was convinced—as surprised and perplexed as she.

"Sir Denis!" the wizard called.

By his quick entrance, the stocky knight must have been on the other side of the door, which really was not proof of anything, but which Alayna noticed nonetheless.

Halbert said, "Our visitors have decided not to stay after all. Please escort them out." Halbert gave them a withering glare. *Was* he as nonplused and outraged as he acted? As bewildered as an innocent man would be? "Good day!" he snapped. With an angry flourish of his dark robes, he left by the same door through which he'd entered.

CHAPTER 7

Alayna felt as though her insides were crumbling.

Sir Denis stood by the room's main door and looked as though he was hoping for the opportunity to let his polite manners drop.

"What," Mordred hissed at Galen, "is the matter with you?"

"That wasn't the plan." Like Mordred, Alayna whispered. She tried to drive the memory of Kiera's face from her mind. *That* wouldn't help now. Stealth. Declare and challenge. It was all meaningless in the face of what had just happened. What Galen had caused to happen.

"You know he has her," Galen protested. "Why play that silly game about"—he mimicked Halbert's self-consciously inscrutable tone—*"looking into his crystal?"*

Sir Denis, still waiting, cleared his throat, the very image of courtly manners. Nevertheless, Alayna doubted that he would really be indisposed to using force.

"Lack-wit." Mordred swept past Galen and out into the corridor.

Alayna followed without looking at her brother. He'd ruined it. He'd ruined everything.

She could still, she thought, cry out, "Kiera!" and see if there was any answer. Was that their last chance, or would she ruin any possibility they might have?

Once they were all in the corridor, Sir Denis went ahead. This might have been politeness, guiding them, though the door was within sight not threescore paces down a straight hallway—or it might have been insult, insinuation that they couldn't be trusted to leave, at least not without theft or causing damage.

Behind her, Alayna heard Galen stop. She was too angry to care, but Mordred stopped also, waiting for him. Alayna stalked past Mordred, but several paces beyond she looked back and saw why Mordred was concerned. Galen was just standing there, a puzzled expression on his face. "Galen?" she called.

He looked from her to Mordred, back to the room they had just left. "Have we already . . . Did . . ." Again his gaze wavered between them and the room. He had the dazed look she'd sometimes seen on knights who'd just had a bad tumble on the jousting field. "What did I say?" he asked.

Alayna saw Mordred, always watchful, glance beyond her. She checked that way also and saw that, for the moment, Sir Denis seemed unaware they were no longer right behind him, and he kept walking.

"Galen?" Alayna repeated.

Her brother ran his hand over his face. "Did I . . ."

Mordred grasped his arm lest Galen prove as unsteady as he sounded.

"I . . . am sorry." Galen's voice was faint and unsure. "I don't know what possessed me. It was as though . . ." He shook his head. " . . . as though . . ."

Alayna felt a familiar tingle up and down her spine. It was the same feeling as when she would find Kiera staring off into space or when, certain times, Toland would say with more assurance than was his wont, about something he should have no control over, "Don't concern yourself about that: I am certain it will work out." Now she took a long look at her brother and said, "Galen, did you feel that that wizard could be—"

At that same instant, Mordred, once more checking back the way they had just come, toward the Great Hall, pulled his sword from its scabbard.

She saw Galen also go for his sword, even before he whirled around to learn what the danger was. She saw all this before finally, over their shoulders, she saw what Mordred had seen: three knights running toward them, having burst from the room where they'd just had their audience with Halbert. Though not armored, they *were* armed.

Mordred spared a glance in her direction, beyond her, before turning back; and by this she knew that Denis was not yet close enough to be a threat.

Belatedly—she *had* said she was competent: what was the matter with her?—she unsheathed Percival's sword that she had accepted without truly expecting to use. She whirled back to check the way Sir Denis had been leading them. Sir Denis, at the entrance to the courtyard, had heard the weapons being drawn and now faced them, his own sword in hand. His eyes flicked from her to her two companions. Obviously he saw her as a minor obstacle and was calculating how quickest to deal with her and get on to the real business at hand.

Alayna went into fighting stance and knew she had an advantage in that Sir Denis no doubt thought she was bluffing.

Behind her, she heard the clash of steel on steel as someone's first sword blow was parried.

Then Sir Denis was upon her.

She saw the look of surprise on his face as she made the first move, a thrust at his exposed neck. He wasn't so surprised, however, that he couldn't block.

Alayna knew that, however skillful, she didn't have a man's arm and shoulder muscles; that was why Percival had given her his broadsword, with a hilt large enough for two-handed fighting while on foot, yet light enough to wield one-handed on horseback. Still, she didn't try to fool herself: The longer this encounter took, the more disadvantaged she would be. So far, Sir Denis wasn't fighting what Mordred had called "all out," apparently at least somewhat reluctant about hacking away at a woman. Alayna felt guilty only until she thought of Kiera. For Kiera's sake, she needed to take every advantage she could.

She played at incompetence, leaving herself open in a way that would have raised

Sir Denis's suspicions had she been a man. But Denis was willing to believe that her first moves had been luck rather than skill, and he came in too close.

Alayna stepped to the side, then thrust forward, closing her eyes only after she felt the blade pierce Sir Denis's rib cage. It was not—at all—like the feel of the practice quintain. Burlap and sawdust didn't bleed. She had never before struck at a real person, but she had never before had to protect herself and her family.

Denis doubled over, then fell to the floor, doing half the work for her of pulling the sword free from his body. He lay still. She knew he could not survive such a blow, that he could not pick himself up off the floor and attack her from behind. He was dead, as surely as Ned, as surely as Toland had been dead, and perhaps he had a wife and child who would mourn him.

Kiera, she reminded herself. *If you must think of children, think of Kiera.*

She steeled herself, then wrenched the sword the rest of the way out, and turned.

Two of the castle's knights were already dead on the floor. Mordred, who had just killed the second, caught her eye for a moment before turning to Galen, who was still fighting.

Her brother had his back to the wall, though the other knight was bleeding from a shoulder wound. Galen dodged to the right just as the knight thrust to the middle, and the blade barely missed him; but Galen's position didn't allow him to take advantage. Alayna saw the knight put his left hand on his hilt and knew before he started that he was about to slash across Galen's belly.

She took a step forward, for all that she knew she wasn't close enough to prevent the blow: Galen was about to die. But then the knight pitched forward, a knife sticking out from his back. She saw the knight fall, saw him twitch, then stop. She saw all this before she saw—by the dropping of his arm—that it was Mordred who had thrown the knife.

It took Galen a moment to catch his breath. He leaned with his back braced against the wall, while Mordred retrieved his knife. "I was capable of finishing him on my own," Galen panted.

Mordred didn't argue; he just nodded back toward the Great Hall from which they had come.

Alayna also kept silent, too relieved that her brother was still alive to be overly concerned about Mordred's method.

Galen looked from her purposefully bland face to Mordred's. "Chivalry is dead," he snapped, "when a knight stabs a man in the back."

"Chivalry is ill-advised," Mordred said. "*You* are the one who was about to be dead." He headed back the way they'd just come, to the door leading to the Great Hall and the main part of the castle.

Alayna started after him, then heard a whoosh and thud, and Galen cried out in pain.

She turned. Behind them, in the doorway to the courtyard, one of the castle guards crouched with his crossbow. The arrow had hit Galen in the stomach, at close enough range to pierce the armor.

Galen dropped.

With no time to reload and rewind, the archer ducked around the corner. But Alayna wasn't concerned with vengeance. She knelt beside Galen. Foolishly the thought came to her that this whole encounter was unlike practice: Just as the burlap and sawdust quintains never bled, neither did they ambush anyone. Galen was still breathing, which of course she had assumed he would be. It couldn't be as bad as it looked, she thought. With care, he'd recover, just as he'd recovered that time he'd fallen from the apple tree. That had looked at least as serious as this.

Almost.

She laid Galen's head on her lap. She concentrated on his pale face rather than the puddle of blood welling out from beneath his breastplate.

Sword in hand and swearing in Cornish, Mordred leaped over the body of Sir Denis. He hesitated at the door through which the archer had fled, and looked to her—*her*—for direction.

"Don't leave us," she said, which may or may not have been good advice. She immediately turned her attention back to Galen and only heard Mordred slam the door and run the bolt to prevent further entry.

Galen squeezed her hand and she tried to smile bravely for him. She was ready to die to save Kiera. But she hadn't known she must balance her daughter against her brother.

She unlaced the breastplate but didn't dare take it off for fear of putting pressure on the arrow.

For a knight, Mordred looked dazed and bewildered. But then, he was a young knight. Perhaps he hadn't had as much experience as she with death and dying. She remembered what it had been like with Toland and wished for anything rather than go through that again.

Mordred knelt beside Alayna. He took a deep breath. He said, to her or to Galen, "Just try to relax. Don't move." He kept glancing from Alayna to the arrow. She noted that he hadn't been able yet to look at Galen's face. "Just," he swallowed hard, "remain calm."

"I," Galen whispered, "am doing fine. I'll be up as soon as I catch my breath. You're the one who is falling to pieces."

Mordred finally looked up.

Alayna gave Galen's hand, sticky with blood, a gentle squeeze and tried to convince her eyes that they would not help matters by misting over.

Galen winced. "Well . . . maybe not . . . exactly fine."

Alayna closed her eyes, but then opened them a second later as her brother tried to swallow back a cry of pain.

She chewed her lip and brushed his fine hair off his forehead. "Don't be afraid," she said, foolish as that was: He had every reason to be afraid. His eyes were losing their panicked look; they were becoming, in fact, unfocused, but he forced a smile in her general direction.

He tried to grip her hand, but she could hardly feel it at all, and then he became totally relaxed. Too relaxed.

Alayna felt Mordred gently touch her hair, and she leaned her head against him, still holding Galen.

She wasn't aware that the door to the Great Hall had opened until she heard Halbert say, "Merciful Heaven!"

Beside her, Mordred tensed, but did not go for his sword.

The wizard came and knelt opposite them.

Not armed, Alayna noticed, *and alone.* Although at that point he could have brought all of Castle Burrstone's fighting force with him and she could not have moved.

Halbert shook his head. "I did not order this," he said, emphasizing every word. "I never ordered this." His voice was shaking. "All I said was to make sure the three of you left. How they could have misconstrued that . . ." He started again. "I have never given"—he looked around helplessly—"*any* kind of order that could make anybody remotely think that I . . ." He drifted off helplessly, looking dismayed. Then he took a deep breath. Much more steadily, he said, "I may be able to help."

"He's dead." Mordred's dark eyes were dry and cold, and the hearing of it was almost as hard as the fact.

Beyond all reason, the wizard repeated, "I may be able to help." He started to move his hand toward the arrow, but Mordred caught his wrist.

"My Lady," Halbert said, bringing Alayna into the question, even though what she wanted was to be anywhere but here, making decisions, having people depend on her. "My Lady," Halbert repeated. "What harm could I do him?"

What indeed? Alayna straightened her back. "Let him."

Halbert removed the breastplate and yanked the arrow out.

She watched woodenly, aware that Mordred's eyes shied away.

The wizard placed his hands over the jagged wound and started chanting. The words were unfamiliar, not English or Latin. Not one of the Celtic dialects, judging by Mordred's vacant expression, nor Greek, whose cadences—at least—she would have recognized. Halbert started rocking back and forth and massaged Galen's chest with his bloodied fingers.

Mordred rose suddenly and walked to the other side of the corridor, his back to them.

The smell of blood was thick, dizzying. When she could look at Galen no longer, Alayna looked into Halbert's face. His eyes were closed, his upper lip damp with perspiration. He had stopped chanting and now repeated one word or short phrase several times. His ruby pendant, reflecting Galen's blood, swung back and forth over the body.

Alayna forced herself to watch. Watch as his hands pushed on her brother's chest, watch as his movement gave Galen's chest the appearance of heaving in and out with breath.

Halbert lifted his hands, and the chest kept moving.

"Mordred," Alayna whispered. She didn't dare take her eyes off Galen, lest she look back and find him deathly still again.

From the corner of her eye, she saw Mordred turn, slowly, and advance.

"Praise God," she whispered. She glanced at Halbert who sat back on his heels and smiled at her, despite his own pallor and the sweat on his face. Then she looked down at Galen, who now seemed to be sleeping peacefully, and finally up at Mordred. Her eyes had finally won out and were letting streams of tears run down her face, but she smiled and reached up to take Mordred's hand.

Slowly, Mordred sank to his knees. "Praise God," he echoed, never taking his eyes off Halbert.

CHAPTER 8

Galen's breathing seemed frighteningly shallow, but Halbert insisted she should not be anxious about it.

Not be anxious. Alayna couldn't get her hands to stop shaking.

Thank God, she thought over and over, that Mordred had been wrong about Halbert. Thank God that Halbert didn't hold a grudge for the awful, accusatory way they had spoken to him before . . . Before.

Halbert summoned servants to ready a room and to carry Galen to it. Several of the wizard's men-at-arms hovered about the area; of course they had come—hearing the sounds of fighting and of servants frantically summoned—but the archer who had struck down Galen was not among them.

All the while, Halbert apologized with every other sentence he uttered, assuring Alayna and Mordred that he had never—ever—given his men orders to attack; that even if they somehow misunderstood something he had said, they should have known enough to seek clarification because he had never—ever (again!)—ordered them to harm anyone; that he would seek out the archer in question to see if anything could be learned from him since—obviously—

something was very much amiss that Halbert's guests should be attacked as soon as he turned his back.

"I would that I could question Sir Denis," Halbert said, wringing his hands as the servants settled Galen into the bed that had been hastily prepared for him, "for now I very much wonder at the manner in which he came to be in my service."

Mordred looked up sharply at that. "He was only recently with you?" he asked.

"Very recently," Halbert stressed. "And now I wonder if there is some connection between that and the matter about which you are here. A strange coincidence, otherwise."

"Yes," Mordred said, drawing out the word as though he thought . . . With Mordred, it was always hard to tell what he thought. "Perhaps," he suggested, "it would be best if the archer were to be questioned in the presence of all of us."

Alayna's breath caught. What was the matter with him? He had seen how Halbert had healed Galen. How, then, could he still mistrust the wizard? Had she been standing closer, she would have been tempted to kick him.

Halbert looked startled. He had to know what Mordred was implying. But, all meekness and ever agreeable, he simply nodded. "If you so wish." He turned, and one of the men-at-arms stepped forward.

"Barth," that one told Halbert. "It was Barth did it. He has already reported to the captain of the guard."

"Bring him here," Halbert ordered. He gestured for all the men-at-arms to leave them, along with the servants who were no longer needed.

That left only one of the serving women, who had just brought in a bowl filled with water and a linen cloth. "Shall I, my Lady?" she asked. "Or will you?"

Alayna indicated she would take over. It was something to do with her hands. She dipped the cloth into the bowl and wrung it out, releasing the tart smell of peony root and yarrow. Gently she wiped the sweat and dirt off Galen's face—Shouldn't the cool water cause him to stir?—then folded the cloth and draped it across his forehead. Should he still be so pale?

While they waited for the summoned archer, Mordred pulled up a stool and began to busy himself with Galen's armor, cleaning off the blood. *Cleaning off the blood.* Now Alayna could think those words, could see the damaged equipment without cringing, could know, as surely Mordred must also, that in truth the breastplate was beyond repair and would need to be melted down and reforged if anyone was to ever wear it again. Now Alayna could acknowledge the blood, and that it had been Galen's, but now he was all right. And Kiera was all right, too—she must be, seeing as how they had made it so far. Soon they would have her back and then every-thing—everything—would be all right. Please God.

Halbert stood looking out the window, having finally run out of apologies, of words.

There was a clatter in the hallway, then a knock on the door. The guard who had been sent to bring the archer entered, and with him the archer himself—who imme-diately dropped to his knees and said, all in one breath, "Pardon, my Lord, I didn't know, I was only following orders, and I thought they were your orders, I didn't know Sir Denis had taken it upon himself, he said that you said, and I didn't know he lied."

Halbert no longer acted the pompous, self-pleased host who had greeted them, nor the shaken, near-to-babbling penitent who had begged them to believe his inno-cence in this matter. His restrained anger showed in the paleness about his mouth and nostrils. "What," he demanded in a voice Alayna would have dreaded to face, "are you talking about?"

The man, Barth, bowed, for all that he was already on his knees and close to grov-eling. "Sir Denis," he repeated, as though that explained all.

"What about Sir Denis?" Halbert asked.

"He said they"—he jerked his head in the direction of Mordred and Alayna and, beyond them, Galen—"would be coming."

Halbert looked in their direction, puzzlement and distress evident on top of his anger. "By name?" he asked incredulously.

"No, your Lordship. He just said 'people.' He said 'enemies of the lord wizard.' He said he would give us a signal. Or you would."

Halbert narrowed his eyes at the man. "*When* did he say all this?" he demanded. "Between the time they arrived and—"

But Barth was shaking his head. His voice was quavering. "A week ago."

A week ago—Alayna thought—was even before Kiera had been taken.

Even Halbert, who didn't know that, was dubious. "*A week ago?*" he repeated. "Denis has only been in my employ for a fortnight."

Barth said, "Then, when I heard the sounds of fighting, when I looked and saw Sir Denis dead and you nowhere to be seen, I feared—"

Halbert made an impatient gesture. "Go. You are dismissed."

The man scrambled to his feet, still bowing even as he backed toward the door. But he hesitated and asked, "By 'dismissed'—"

"From service," Halbert clarified. "I do not want men in my employ who take another's orders and do not question them even if they go contrary to everything you have ever heard from me. Go."

"Yes, your Lordship," the man said, backing out of the room. "I beg your Lordship's pardon."

The guard who had fetched him also exited, closing the door behind him.

"So," Mordred said evenly, as though resuming a conversation started only a moment before, "tell us how Sir Denis came to be seneschal of your estate in two short weeks."

Halbert said, "My former steward died, suddenly. By mischance . . ." He paused, considering, weighing, and then finished, "Which, now, I realize may perhaps not have been chance at all." He paused again, as though in reflection, and Mordred said, "And Sir Denis . . . ?"

"Denis," Halbert said, "was recommended to me by my nephew Sir Bayard."

"Oh, Bayard," Mordred said.

But what it was Mordred knew, or thought he knew, he didn't share, and after waiting a long moment, Halbert opened the door of the room and gestured for one of the servants. To Alayna and Mordred, he continued, "And I find it inconceivable that Bayard would recommend a man such as Denis proved to be." To the servant, Halbert said, "In my room, among my papers, is an opened letter from my nephew that bears a seal of red wax with the impression of three ravens, arranged in a row. This should be near the top of the papers. But look you farther down in the drawer also for any other letter from Bayard. Fetch and bring both letters here." Once more to Alayna and Mordred, he said, "We will see if this is truly in Bayard's clerk's hand, and if it is Bayard's seal."

Mordred turned from Halbert as though to look out the window. As far as Alayna could tell, he was sulking and being stubborn, not wanting to admit he was wrong. For how could Halbert be evil, how could he be against them, if he had . . . She had to admit it: He had raised Galen from the dead.

The servant came back, bearing two letters. Halbert took the papers and, holding one in each hand, set to scrutinizing them.

"Ah!" he cried in a moment. "Look you here." He handed one of the papers to Mordred. He poked at the blob of sealing wax. "Do you see how—"

Alayna was leaning around Mordred for a closer look when he gave a startled cry as the page burst into a thousand red sparkles. He jerked his hand back as though to drop the paper, but it had already disappeared.

Halbert stepped back with a startled oath.

"Are you injured?" Alayna asked, for Mordred was looking at his hand the way someone might after touching a hot kettle—in the moment between realization and pain.

"No," Mordred said, but he rubbed his hand against his leg.

"Are you certain?" she asked, demanding his attention rather than letting her mind settle on what she had just seen.

"I am unharmed," he said testily, but still without conviction.

"There is magic involved here," Halbert said.

"No!" Mordred gasped. "In a wizard's own home?"

His sarcasm and provocation finally needled Halbert into annoyance. "Not *my* magic, you fool. *I* was about to show you." He held up the remaining letter. "The ravens here are exactly straight because that is the way they are embossed on my nephew's seal. What I was about to show you with the other letter was that the ravens did not line up. Someone drew them into the wax separately, by hand. That letter was a forgery. Bayard never did send Denis here."

"So," Mordred said—he was still rubbing his hand as though it tingled or burned—"someone with enough magical power to destroy the forgery, but not enough magical power to create a truly convincing forgery, arranged to have Denis here . . . Why?"

"Probably something to do with you." Halbert nodded to include Alayna.

"Oh, aye, probably," Mordred said.

This time, Alayna did kick him, the side of his foot, anyway. Halbert may not have seen that, but he had to hear her when she told Mordred, "He's trying to help. Somebody has hurt *his* household, too, killed his former steward, misused his trust." She found herself picturing Halbert's former steward as looking like old Ned, whom she had not yet had time to mourn. She said, "It would also explain why Galen acted so strangely in Halbert's Hall. He was bespelled."

But all Mordred said was "Perhaps," and he turned away from both her and Halbert.

"Why," Halbert asked, "did you come here? You said your daughter was missing . . ." He glanced from Mordred to the bed where Galen yet lay, entirely still. Not quite a statement, not quite a question, he finished, "You thought I had her."

"Yes," Alayna admitted.

"Why?"

"Because . . ." She took a deep breath and just said it. "Because she has magical ability."

Halbert's eyebrows shot up.

"We thought a wizard might seek her because of that."

"There are a number of wizards," Halbert pointed out. But he didn't question why they had chosen him. Alayna was going to tell him that other parties had gone out to question other wizards, but before she had a chance to he said, "And one of them, apparently, is my enemy, too." He looked from her to Mordred. "I have a scrying crystal," he said, which he had already told them—it seemed so long ago. "I will get it. I will bring it *here*,"—he emphasized the word, and he looked at Mordred while he said it—"where you can watch me use it. We shall see, together, whether we can find this poor, lost child. And learn who is trying to get to *me* through her."

CHAPTER 9

As soon as Halbert left the room, Alayna turned on Mordred. "What is the matter with you?" she demanded. She bit off what she'd been about to say, that he was acting almost as unreasonably as Galen had in the Great Hall.

Mordred looked at her with that infuriating impenetrable expression.

Galen was alive—despite all reason. And a wizard was going to help them find Kiera. They *would* succeed. They would, she knew it. Yet there was a little voice that intruded on her feeling of well-being, that insisted, *What now?* Desperate to still that voice, she said, "He looks better, don't you think?"

"Yes," Mordred admitted—grudgingly, she thought, reluctant to be in Halbert's debt.

He stepped over to the bed.

"Let him sleep," she started, just as he leaned over to prod Galen. "He needs to gather his strength."

"Galen," Mordred said.

In any case, Galen gave no sign of reacting.

Mordred looked annoyed: She couldn't tell whether at Galen or at her. He said, "You know—"

But just then the door opened, and Halbert came back in. He had what appeared to be a jagged piece of quartz. It had the shape, roughly, of a short, squat, squared-off candle, rising from a jumble of candle parings. The upright portion was clear, the rest milky. This he set down on the chest at the foot of the bed. Then he came to stand by Alayna. "Still asleep?" He touched Galen's shoulder and gave it a gentle shake. She was willing to let him try, because he, better than she or Mordred, knew the limits of the healing spell he had performed. "Sir Galen," Halbert called.

Galen groaned and turned slightly. Alayna was so relieved, she almost missed his words. "The girl . . ." he mumbled, "get the girl . . ."

Alayna leaned closer. "Which girl, Galen?" she asked. "Do you mean Kiera? Yes, we're going to get her, as soon as you regain your strength."

Far from reassuring him, her words seemed to agitate him. *Fool,* she chided herself. She hadn't meant to imply blame, but of course Galen would take it that way, fretting that he was delaying them.

"Galen," Halbert commanded.

Her brother's eyelids fluttered open.

"You're safe. You are among friends. Your sister, Alayna, is here. And Sir Mordred."

Galen glanced at each of them in turn, and Alayna grasped his hand.

"Why don't you sit up?" Halbert eased him up, then said to them, "He'll probably be a bit stiff and confused at first."

And, indeed, Galen looked dazed but unworried.

She gave her brother's cold hand a reassuring squeeze and he smiled vaguely at her. *Is his hand supposed to be that cold?* she asked herself.

"He is doing well," Halbert assured her. "Truly he is."

"Truly," Galen repeated solemnly, and Alayna laughed with relief.

Mordred removed Galen's battered breastplate from the chair where he had set it down, and put it on the floor with more of a clatter than was probably necessary. He placed the chair in front of the clothes chest and straddled it, his arms across the back, watching Halbert.

Halbert's smile was tight. "So," he said. "As Sir Mordred has indicated, it is time we begin."

He pulled the shutters closed over the window, making the room . . . not dark, but darker.

Toland didn't need darkness for his spells, Alayna thought. Then she remonstrated with herself. It was unfair to criticize beforehand. Wait and see what would happen.

Halbert took a candle off the nightstand and placed it on the chest at the foot of the bed, in front of the crystal. He touched his finger to the wick of the candle and it burst into flame.

Toland could do that, Alayna thought.

"Do you have anything of your daughter's?" Halbert asked Alayna. "Preferably a lock of hair, but anything that was hers will do,"—Alayna was shaking her head— "or that she had contact with?"

"Nothing," she told him. "Everything was destroyed in a fire."

Halbert looked disapproving, but he said, "Then put your hands about the crystal, and call her name." He gestured, indicating for her to surround the crystal with her hands.

Alayna knelt before the chest and—reaching around the candle—wrapped her hands around the crystal.

"Call her name," the wizard repeated.

"Kiera," she said. She watched Halbert, expecting him to tell her she was doing it all wrong. Was she supposed to shout the name, as though summoning Kiera from a distance?

But he seemed satisfied with a normal tone of voice. He said, "Picture her in your mind."

Alayna did, fervently.

"Move your hands." Once again Halbert gestured, this time his hands separating and moving down, forming a ring with his fingers.

Alayna did as he indicated, her hands encircling the rough, sparkled base from which the clear crystal jutted.

"Concentrate on the shadow the candle's flame casts on the crystal. See your daughter in that. Picture her."

The picture that her mind formed was from that last morning in the barn: Kiera turning, looking up, her face covered with tears and filled with pain and sorrow.

It was better than no image at all. After only a year, Alayna missed Toland, dreamt of him almost every night, but could only rarely and fleetingly picture him in her waking thoughts.

"Kiera," the wizard said, as though sensing the momentary shifting of her concentration.

Kiera. Alayna pictured her, in the barn. She stared at the facet of the crystal where the candle flame threw its shadow. Kiera was within that shadow, Alayna told herself. She tried to get her eyes to pick out Kiera's features, caught a glimpse of her wild, ginger-colored hair in the flickering movement of the flame, saw a glint that might have been Kiera's eye reflecting the light of the candle, followed a curve that might have been either an angle of the crystal, or a cheek. Like staring into a dark corner. Like forcing sense out of something half seen in the night. Kiera. Alayna drew Kiera's face out of the shadow. Saw the hair, the eye, the cheek.

Someone in the room took in a breath, shifted, but Halbert's voice, steady and calm, said, "Kiera."

"Kiera," Alayna repeated, and the image of her daughter solidified, appeared captured within the crystal, caught constantly in the act of turning, looking up, waiting expectantly for her mother to make things right. Or chastise her. Or disregard her.

"Kiera," Halbert said, louder this time, more commanding, and now he was the one who was moving, who was stepping not quite in front of Alayna—but up to the crystal.

The image of Kiera shifted again. She was no longer in the barn. The wall behind her was stone: Kiera was sitting on a bed, her arms folded defiantly in front of her.

Alayna recognized that stubborn look. A woman—a servant? Alayna assumed she was a servant by the way her hair was tied up in a kerchief, and by the way her sleeves were rolled back and her apron smudged with food stains—a woman sat on the bed next to Kiera, holding a bowl, offering a spoonful of something. Kiera wouldn't look at the woman, the bowl, or the spoon. The woman moved the spoon closer, Kiera turned her head, and the spoon ended up in Kiera's hair. Kiera jumped up, unsettling the bowl so that it spilled. The woman scrambled to clean up, never—apparently— reprimanding.

Halbert made a gesture with his hands, opening and closing his fingers. Slowly the picture of Kiera moved, as though Alayna was backing away.

"No!" Alayna cried, tightening her fingers around the base of the crystal. The rough surface of the base pressed into her hands.

"Shhh," Halbert said, distracted, as though to calm a skittish animal.

Alayna fought to hold the image of Kiera. Someone—it had to be Mordred for Galen was still in bed and Halbert hadn't moved, except for those damn fingers sep- arating them away from Kiera—someone placed hands gently on Alayna's shoulders.

Farther and farther back they seemed to drift from Kiera, so that now they saw more of the room, its tapestries and pillows; now they saw all the room—not a prison, thank God, not a prison. Now they floated out through the window. And still they backed away, though any true observer from this vantage would be a hun- dred feet off the ground, for the window was in a tower and the tower was part of a castle; and then they were traveling, still backwards, over a stream, over sheep fields, over a forest, into a town, past a cathedral . . .

"Montford," Mordred said.

The picture rippled as though water had been poured over it, and dissolved.

"Kiera," Alayna whispered, sure her heart was going to break.

"That's the cathedral at Montford," Mordred said. "The castle must be—"

"Bel Bois," Halbert said.

"Bel Bois," Mordred agreed.

Halbert turned eagerly to Alayna. "Obviously she's being treated well and is unharmed."

"This image we have seen," Alayna said, hardly trusting her voice to work: "is it a true image?" Halbert was nodding, but she needed more reassurance. "Is it what actually is happening—now, not in the past, not in the future?" Halbert was nodding his head or shaking it at all the right times.

Halbert reiterated, "For whatever reason she was taken and is being held, she is unharmed."

Mordred still had his hands on her shoulders. She felt light-headed, loose-kneed—possibly from the disorienting backward flight Halbert's crystal had taken them out the window and across the countryside, or possibly just from relief. Mordred's solid presence may well have been all that was holding her up.

"Who has her?" Alayna asked Halbert.

Behind her, Mordred—who obviously knew, for he had named the place—added, in a silken purr, "Seeing, Lord Halbert, as you do not?"

His continuing plaguing of Halbert, his inability to take the man at his word, filled Alayna with annoyance, ballast that at least made her feet feel more solidly planted to the ground.

Fortunately Halbert was too excited to take offense—pleased with himself, Alayna guessed, that his magic yielded such positive results. "Sir Edgar of Bel Bois," he told Alayna. "I didn't see Sir Osric in my crystal, but they're cousins, and one never strays far without the other."

"Is Bel Bois near here?" Alayna asked.

"We can be there by vespers."

"Can we now?" Mordred purred, just the slightest stress on the "we."

Alayna finally turned, but couldn't read anything from his face.

"I believe I could be of assistance," the wizard said. The model of modesty? Or was Mordred's constant goading as irksome to him as it was to Alayna?

"Yes, please." That was Galen, his voice thick and unnatural. He cleared his throat, and sounded more like himself. "I would feel better for it. Wouldn't you, Alayna? In case any of us needs to be pulled back from the brink of death again?"

"Yes. Certainly." She looked to Mordred for confirmation, but he had gone to open the shutters.

Alayna felt a surge of resentment. "Is Galen fit to come," she asked Halbert, "do you think?"

The wizard nodded. "Don't concern yourself about him. We just have to worry how we can best enter Bel Bois Castle."

"Why should you be willing to help us?" Mordred asked.

Alayna was ready to hit him, but Halbert only said, "Because without me you would never succeed." He moved to the door. "I'll be ready as soon as I change into riding clothes. There is clothing in that chest that should fit you, Galen." He swept up Galen's breastplate. "I will have another of these sent up from stores. This one is useless now." It had belonged to their mother's father, but Alayna bit back her complaint. The wizard was right.

It would take meticulous hammering out to fix the hole, hammering that in all likelihood would dangerously weaken the metal. Galen, to whom the armor belonged, said nothing, and neither did Mordred, who had spent all that time cleaning the blood off it. Who was she to complain? And by the time she had worked all that out, Halbert was already gone from the room anyway.

Galen got out of bed, with uncharacteristic lack of modesty. Alayna quickly turned her back.

"Truly," she heard Mordred ask him: "How do you feel?"

"Stiff," Galen said. "A bit confused. But fit."

After a hesitation, Mordred said, "Good."

She wouldn't have thought that of him: that he could be so petty and vindictive—nipping like a small dog at Halbert's heels, not even willing to allow himself gladness that Galen was recovered and sound—just because he had been proven wrong. She remembered their conversation of the night before, when Galen had warned that Mordred was a person who would hold a grudge. She hadn't been willing, then, to believe it, though Mordred had admitted it, though it had already been hinted at earlier during the King's council.

Still, he had helped her. She didn't want to be angry with him: *She* didn't want to carry a grudge.

With her back still turned, while Galen dressed, she called over her shoulder, "What were you saying?"

"What?" both Mordred and Galen asked.

"Mordred," she said, but apparently that wasn't explanation enough. "Just before Halbert came in. You started, 'You know . . .'"

There was a long enough pause that Alayna wondered if he still couldn't place what she was talking about. Then he said, "Never mind." She wanted to turn around, to try to read his expression. Couldn't he remember? Or was it unimportant, one of those things that made sense at the time, but didn't bear repeating later on?

Or was it something he didn't want to say in front of Galen?

The last, she decided, reluctantly. Probably Mordred was going to say something critical of Halbert, and was ashamed to do so in front of one who—simply by being alive—owed more allegiance to Halbert than he ever would to Mordred.

CHAPTER 10

They arrived in the vicinity of Bel Bois about the time evening was turning into night—which was what Halbert had indicated and Mordred hadn't contradicted. That, Alayna reflected, seemed suddenly the best she could expect of Mordred: that he not contradict everything.

They left their horses within cover of the woods, well beyond range where any noise the animals might make could be heard—for Halbert suggested they approach on foot, under cover of darkness.

As though he and Mordred had never argued about exactly the same thing, Galen silently acquiesced, inclining his head in agreement.

This, Alayna thought, was what Mordred had wanted all along, but he didn't accept winning gracefully. Glowering, he turned his back on all of them without a word, and set about tethering his horse with more concentration than was needed.

They walked in silence. They would have, in any case, but the tension among them let Alayna hear her own breathing, her own heartbeat, as though they echoed in the night. The four of them approached as near as they dared, which was only for so long as they had the cover of trees. They could smell the place before they could see it—or, at least, they could smell the dinner: roasting pig, Alayna guessed. Her stomach grumbled at the unfairness of it; she hoped the others couldn't hear. She had eaten only a cold supper her one night at Camelot, forgoing the communal meal in favor of bed, and she had lived on field rations since. The pig that she could smell, she would have been willing to wager, was likely the most delicious pig anyone had ever roasted. She tried not to picture the skin glistening with fat, the meat practically falling off the bones.

She had seen that Kiera was fed. Or, at least, that her abductors tried to feed her.

Then, finally, Alayna had her first look at Bel Bois to go along with the wonderful smell.

She recognized its general shape from the glimpse she'd had in Halbert's crystal. It was smaller than she had anticipated, smaller even than Burrstone, which was not large, and it didn't have the almost toy-like prettiness of the wizard's castle. But the most daunting thing was its location: in the middle of a wide, fast-moving stream. Alayna had seen the water in the vision in Halbert's crystal, but hadn't realized that the castle was surrounded by it. Whether there was a naturally occurring outcrop of rock rising from the water, or whether men had labored to construct an earthwork mound—the result was still that Bel Bois was an island. The only ready access was the causeway the drawbridge formed to the nearer shore. And that, of course, only when the drawbridge was lowered.

Which it was not.

Halbert stopped, motioning for the others to stop, too—which surely was not necessary: They could all see as well as he that the trees ended here, and that to go farther was to be out in the open.

But neither did Mordred need to look so sour.

Alayna settled down to wait, determined not to look at either of them. She faced Galen instead, to make sure he was fit. Surely a man . . . She pushed the thought away, but it persisted. Surely a man so recently dead shouldn't be riding all afternoon and then lying down in the damp grass.

Anxiously, she watched Galen, wearing his new breastplate emblazoned with the wizard's colors. He was still pale, and uncharacteristically quiet, so fatigued that his hand shook as he covered his eyes, trying to rest until the moon set. Was that normal? Was that to be expected? She wanted to prod Halbert, to demand assurances.

But Halbert sat apart from them. In the almost dark, he had drawn some sort of design in the earth and was doing something with sticks and pebbles. Game to pass the time or wizards' calculations, Alayna couldn't tell. Certainly she had never seen Toland do anything similar.

Beside her, Mordred sat cross-legged on the ground, also watching the castle. Although he appeared totally absorbed in watching the guard who walked the battlements, he would certainly notice if she got up, and would probably take it amiss if she went to speak to the wizard. Alayna was left with her thoughts. No matter what followed, how this turned out, whether they all survived or were dead by morning—now and forever, there would always be this division. There would be the time before Kiera was taken, and time after. *Everything* would be colored by that one event. For the second instance in days, she thought of dyeing wool. There was before the dye, and after. No matter how long the cloth lasted, no matter how it faded or was stained, even if it was dyed again or bleached, it would never be the same as it had been before.

Night deepened. No doubt all that was left of the wonderful roasted pig was its delicious fragrance that still tinged the air. Candlelight shone through shutters in the upper rooms as the castle's occupants readied themselves for sleep. If they knew anything about tending children, Kiera would be abed long since. If they knew. If they cared.

Stop thinking.

Mordred leaned closer to her. Never taking his gaze off the castle, he said, softly, "*Must* you keep doing that?"

"What?"

"That sighing."

"I have not been sighing." Alayna propped her chin up on her hand and stared harder at the castle, willing the people to go to sleep.

Her mind skittered off, once again, in the direction of Kiera. *Sweet dreams,* she used to wish Kiera every night. And if she forgot, Kiera would remind her because she was often tormented by bad dreams. How many of them, Alayna wondered, really came to pass? For Kiera was a smart girl. She knew her mother didn't like to be told what was going to happen. It might well be, Alayna suddenly realized, that most of Kiera's dreams came true, but she only talked about the ones that frightened her.

She sighed, and caught a quick grin from Mordred, which was the way things had been between them before. She was about to protest that it was her first sigh of the evening, but he suddenly put his finger to his lips.

What? she mouthed.

Listen, he answered without sound, tapping his ear lest she couldn't make the word out.

A breeze rustled the leaves overhead, and the night's insects buzzed and whined and chirped. Then Alayna heard the creak of machinery, and in another moment the drawbridge started to lower.

"Galen," she called in a loud whisper.

Galen didn't budge, but the wizard approached at a half crouch and knelt between her and Mordred, forcing Alayna to make room.

"Let him sleep as long as possible," Halbert whispered. "He needs to rebuild his strength."

She nodded her head, first in agreement, then toward the knight who rode out of Bel Bois. "Is that one of them—Edgar or Osric?" she asked, although she knew they were at too great a distance for identification.

Halbert shook his head. "Possibly Osric, but I don't think so. Sir Worthington, maybe, or perhaps Sir Payne." He shook his head again. "Edgar has three or four knights in service, I'm not quite sure how many, and I don't know them well. Edgar wears a full beard to cover scars left by the pox. Osric has much the same face, minus the beard and pocks."

All three of them ducked as the knight rode out, even though he didn't come close to where they hid.

"They left the drawbridge down," she noted.

"Were you planning a frontal attack?" Mordred asked her. "Three of us against we're-not-quite-sure-how-many of them?"

"Four of us," Halbert corrected. "I can hold my own."

Mordred made an apologetic gesture that his half-smile belied. Alayna wondered if Halbert, really, was the one Mordred had been discounting, or whether it had been her, or Galen.

"I only meant," Alayna said, mentally begging Mordred not to start an argument, not now, "that he probably will not be gone long, or they would have closed up after him."

"Probably," Mordred agreed.

"Probably," Halbert echoed.

Still, the open drawbridge was enticing, given that their plan was to wade into the fast-moving and undoubtedly cold stream, then try to scale the sheer wall with grappling hook and nerve, all between rounds of the guard.

But despite their unanimity, the night got cooler and darker, the bridge stayed open, and the knight didn't return.

Galen awoke, and he too agreed that whoever had left must be returning soon. For Bel Bois did not have the look of a place that would be careless about defenses. Alayna would have thought so even without the evidence of seeing—at regular intervals—the guard walking the battlements.

"If I had known we were going to spend the night, I would have brought my blanket," Galen grumbled. He stooped down beside Alayna, and from his borrowed clothes she caught once again the faint aroma of the herbs Halbert had used for storage. "The moon is down. I say we go now."

Mordred looked worried. "Wherever that rider went, we can count on him to return just when it would do us the most ill."

Galen said, "There's danger, too, in being overly cautious."

Mordred obviously didn't like the sound of that.

"I hate to waste the night," Alayna said, though her mind was by no means set. "It would be much easier to steal Kiera away while most of them are asleep, rather than fight our way in and out by light of day."

"I think we should go now," Galen repeated.

Halbert nodded. Which Alayna was sure would set Mordred against going. Still, King Arthur had clearly indicated that Galen was accompanying Mordred, not the other way around. And nobody had ever anticipated Halbert being in charge. She turned to Mordred. She asked, "What do you think?"

"If the three of you are determined to go in, it makes little difference what I think."

"I'm not—" Alayna started.

But Galen interrupted, "So. That leaves you covered no matter what happens."

Mordred looked startled. It was, even in Alayna's estimation, twice now in a matter of moments, that Galen had hinted Mordred was a coward. But Mordred only said, quietly, "Perhaps."

What was the matter with them? They were supposed to be friends. "Whatever is going on in there," she said, mostly to say something to get them to stop glaring at each other, "at least a squire will be waiting up."

Mordred gave her a sidelong glance, as though recognizing her diversionary tactic.

Galen, however, only nodded and said, "Does anybody have an idea how we can get him out here, without making him nervous enough to wake up the whole castle?" He was hugging himself for warmth. "Preferably while the man guarding the battlements is inspecting the far side? And preferably before I freeze to death?"

Alayna rested her hand on his, felt the cold of it. The night was cool, but not cold. She felt a twinge of dread. He never should have come. He should have stayed behind to rest, no matter what Halbert said. She regretted not insisting. Galen obviously wasn't himself.

But she could guess what Galen would say if she recommended he stay here while the three of them went into the castle.

Regrets take too much time and energy, Toland used to say. *We must make the best of a bad situation.*

She and Toland had certainly had bad situations, usually involving the kinds of spells Toland refused to do, or bad luck that townspeople felt he should have been able to avert from them.

What's the good of having a wizard . . . old Croswell had said.

"Halbert?" she began. "My husband used to be able to make a sort of . . . mist, or . . . smoke, or . . ."

"Mist? *Smoke?*" Halbert's tone said his professional pride was stung. He stooped and touched the earth. Softly he began to chant.

Mordred sighed. Loudly.

Halbert glowered at him. "Preliminaries. I must warn the forces of nature that they are about to be manipulated."

Mordred smiled condescendingly.

"Surely your mother knows of such things," Halbert said smugly, reminding Alayna of the rumors that Queen Morgause of Orkney was—depending on one's point of view—a witch or a sorceress. Halbert said, with obvious enjoyment, "Didn't your mother teach you anything?"

"Celtic, of course," Mordred said, a bit too naively to be believed. "A little German."

Alayna saw the flash of annoyance in Halbert's eyes, but he spoke with calm. "A bargain," he offered: "I shall grant that you are young, but not stupid, if you grant that I am old, but not a fool."

Mordred flashed a grin. "Ah! We're talking about magic?"

"We're talking about magic," Halbert agreed.

"My mother is not one to share an advantage." Mordred wore the same sardonic half-smile that the wizard always seemed to bring out from him. "But, then, magic is not always what it seems."

Halbert gave his own cryptic smile. "Nor is life, Mordred."

"Very profound," Mordred jeered.

"Please," Alayna begged in a hiss.

Never taking his eyes off Mordred, Halbert touched the ruby pendant he wore, and simultaneously with his free hand he plucked a dandelion that had gone to seed, and blew.

Some of the seeds flew into Alayna's face, and she impatiently tried to brush them aside, but there were more than she had thought and she closed her eyes and tipped her face away because they were cold. Still they fell. Catching on her hair. Melting.

"Snow!" she whispered gleefully. "Snow in summer!" Already it was sticking to the ground and bushes.

"Impressive trick, wizard," Mordred conceded.

"Look!" Alayna pointed to the castle's portcullis. Halbert had sent a swirl of snow inside, and the amazed squire was coming to investigate. The white flakes formed a dancing halo around his torch.

Mordred silently reached for his bow.

Alayna averted her gaze, unable to watch, even knowing that this may well have been one of the men who had killed old Ned and taken Kiera. Or, at the very least, he owed allegiance to those men.

Mordred released the arrow. The squire made no outcry, but there was a faint splashing sound, and Mordred and Galen simultaneously cursed.

"What?" Alayna demanded in a frantic whisper. The squire was sprawled motionless on the drawbridge. What was wrong now?

"The torch landed in the water," Mordred said.

They waited to see if the sound would attract the guard from the battlements.

Alayna didn't think he'd be able to see the fallen squire, unless he leaned over——but she wasn't sure.

Nothing. He must be watching the unexpected snow accumulate on the trees on the far side of the castle.

Without warning, Galen dashed out from the cover of the surrounding trees and ran toward the drawbridge. Halbert seemed the only one ready for it and followed on his heels. Mordred dropped his bow and was drawing his sword when Alayna passed him.

In a moment she caught up with Galen and the wizard, and a moment after that, Mordred caught up with her. From the trees, the drawbridge had appeared much closer. All the while they ran, Alayna was very aware of what easy targets they made for anyone watching from the walls.

She had planned to look at the face of the fallen man, to see if she recognized him; but he'd landed face down on the drawbridge; and the others moved too quickly. She couldn't take the time to check for fear of being left behind.

They ran with an odd, self-conscious gait, trying for both speed and quiet. They passed the small guardroom by the portcullis, then started down a corridor.

"This will be the Hall," Halbert warned as they came to a doorway from which torchlight shone. The three men slowed.

Determined to be of some worth, Alayna didn't and shot past them. Either someone was there——and if someone was, that person would have heard their approach long since, quiet steps or not——or no one was there. She came to a dead stop only one pace from the entry, and quickly bobbed her head in, then out. She was determined to be of some worth, but she didn't want to make an easy target.

No one was in the Hall. Not exactly.

But she had, she saw, taken an incredible risk.

She turned around and hastily raised her hands, motioning frantically lest the others make any noise. She walked on tiptoe to join them.

Before any of them had a chance to offer complaint of her actions, she said, in a whisper, "There are stairs at the far end, and a second floor balcony. Someone is sitting up there, in front of a closed door. I don't think he saw me."

Halbert closed his eyes and clutched at the red pendant on his chest. "Fifth door?" he asked.

She nodded, then realized his eyes were still shut. "Yes."

"That is where she is. I can see her there. Sleeping."

It made sense. Why else would someone be guarding the room? But still Alayna felt tingly all over, just as she used to when Toland would have one of his sudden insights. She said, "We can't rush at him: He would see us the whole length of the hall, up the stairs, and down the corridor. And have time to wake up the entire household before we got there." The thought of Kiera being so close made her clench her fists in frustration.

Halbert smiled. "The guard is sleeping."

Alayna shook her head. Obviously bored with the night duty of guarding a child's room, he had been trying to balance a knife on his fingertip. "No. I saw him."

Halbert said, "Look again. He *is* asleep now."

Despite the chill this casual use of magic sent up her spine, Alayna tiptoed back to her vantage point and saw that the man's chin was resting deep in his chest.

Directly behind her, Mordred asked, "Will he sleep through anything?" and that was the first she was aware that her companions had followed close on her heels this time.

Halbert said, "Don't concern yourselves with the guard. You and Galen watch this door in case Worthington, or Payne, or whoever that was who left, chooses now to return. Lady Alayna and I will go upstairs."

Mordred's eyes narrowed, then slid to Alayna's for confirmation: He was concerned, she saw, despite all the bickering. But it made sense this way. If Halbert could magically keep the man in front of the door asleep, then best that Galen and Mordred guard their backs from any of the castle inhabitants who weren't asleep.

She nodded reassurance, that she was satisfied with the plan, then she headed for the stairs. *Easy,* she told herself, forcing caution into her steps. *Slow and easy.* She didn't know how strong Halbert's magic was, whether it could keep a man asleep despite any mistakes she might make. She held her breath, as if that could make a difference, until she and the wizard were by the sleeping guard.

Halbert whispered a charm, gently touching the man's throat. Alayna cringed, expecting the man to jump at the touch, but he didn't.

With her hand on the door, Alayna was barely able to control her impatience.

Then the wizard reached into his large sleeve and pulled out a knife, which he plunged into the man's chest.

Alayna's breath escaped in a hiss.

Halbert watched her as he wiped the knife on the man's shirt. "The spell," he whispered, "was so he wouldn't cry out."

Alayna was having trouble breathing quietly, and then she realized that she no longer had to be concerned by that.

Halbert said, "Mordred, I think, underestimates the power of magic. You have a tendency to *over*estimate."

Alayna shook her head. "Wait here so you don't frighten Kiera," she whispered. Silently she opened the door.

CHAPTER 11

Somehow, seeing Kiera every day, she had forgotten how much of Toland was in their daughter's pale and round face. After an absence of four days, she could see it anew, and her heart ached. She brushed the reddish brown hair off Kiera's forehead and bent down close. "Kiera." It was half whisper, half kiss.

Kiera's eyes opened immediately. "Momma." Either she was responding to Alayna's lowered voice, or she had guessed to whisper. She said, "I knew you were coming."

"Of course I came." Alayna ended their hug sooner than she would have wanted. "We must be quick, now. Where are your clothes?"

Kiera kicked off the blanket and Alayna realized she already was dressed, down to her shoes. "I *knew* you were coming," she repeated. "But I fell asleep."

A familiar cold spot started in Alayna's spine, about midway up, and quickly spread. What had been disconcerting in Toland, and now in Halbert, still somehow seemed a perversion in her own little child. Still, "Good," she said, for it would save time. "Come."

Just then there was a tap on the door. "My Lady," Halbert's voice urged.

"That's a friend," Alayna explained as Kiera stiffened. "His name is Halbert, and he's a wizard—the way your papa was—and he helped me find you. Don't be afraid."

Alayna opened the door and Halbert took the time to smile down at Kiera. "Hello, Kiera," he said in a calm and gentle voice.

Kiera clung to Alayna's hand and tried to move behind her leg, choosing—Alayna thought impatiently—the worst time to become timid of strangers.

"Let me carry her," the wizard offered.

"I can walk," Kiera mumbled into Alayna's thigh.

Halbert continued to smile as he reached down for her. "It will be faster," he said.

"Not if I kick and scream."

Halbert froze, obviously weighing how seriously to take the threat of noise.

Annoyed and embarrassed, Alayna said, "I'm sorry. She is not usually like this."

Halbert's smile was gone. "The strain, no doubt," he said in the tone of someone who has never raised children but is confident he would be better at it than most. He gave a mock bow and indicated for Kiera to go ahead with her mother.

"*I'll* carry you," Alayna said, and was relieved when Kiera didn't protest. Alayna picked her up and held her so that she wouldn't see the dead man slumped in his chair by the door.

Kiera let herself be carried down the stairs, but when they got to the bottom, Kiera's fingers tightened in Alayna's hair. In a shaking voice, she whispered, "Who's that?"

Alayna whipped around, her hand going to her sword, recognizing simultaneously both that there was no time to put Kiera down and that, by holding Kiera, she could well be—all unintentionally—using her child as a shield between herself and danger. But it was only Galen and Mordred, Galen standing with his back to them, guarding the corridor to the entrance, Mordred facing them, watching to make sure nobody came out of any of the doors that opened onto the balcony overlooking the Hall.

"That's Sir Mordred," she explained as she put Kiera down. Much, much safer that way. "Another friend." She tugged on Kiera's hand, but Kiera wouldn't budge. She was probably afraid because of the naked sword in Mordred's hand. Across the room, Mordred moved the blade slightly to the side, which could have been to greet or reassure Kiera, or an indication of impatience.

"No," Kiera said, "not that one. Behind."

"That's Galen. Don't you recognize Uncle Galen?"

"No."

Alayna's patience snapped. "Well, come along anyway."

Galen had turned to see what the delay was, but now from behind him came a loud, surprised "Hey!" Quickly followed by, "Sir Edgar! Ho, Osric!"

After being so close to succeeding, the shout left Alayna too stunned to move. The man who had left the castle . . . Mordred's prediction that he was sure to return at the worst possible moment had come true.

Galen disappeared around the corner to deal with the returning knight; Mordred dashed into the Hall to face whoever came to answer the man's shout. He sped by Alayna, Halbert, and Kiera, and took the stairs two at a time.

A man—from Halbert's description of beard and pocks it had to be Sir Edgar—stepped out of a bedroom. He wore only an ankle-length nightshirt, but he was carrying a long unsheathed sword. He looked them over appraisingly, then gave a smile that looked more like an impression of a smile than any real thing.

Alayna finally pulled loose from Kiera's grasp, and belatedly drew her own sword. She pushed Kiera to Halbert to keep her out of harm's way. Surely the greatest danger was from upstairs, where the whole household must be roused by now. It was only a matter of time before they all converged with drawn weapons on the landing.

In fact, Alayna had made it only halfway up the stairs when the door closest to the stairs burst open. This was a house guard, who had taken the time to get not only his sword, but also a shield. He looked from his right, where his lord was fighting Mordred, to his left, to Alayna.

He came toward her: an ugly man, with a big nose, pocked skin, and dark hair. The man who had been with the knights who had attacked her.

Alayna was barely able to make it to the landing before the man thrust to her left with his sword, and simultaneously butted her right shoulder with his shield. The realization that his strategy was to drive her closer to the stair's edge didn't help Alayna, who was forced to take a step back anyway.

Beyond, she was aware of Edgar dropping to the floor with a groan, but now his cousin Osric came at Mordred from the other end of the upstairs hallway.

From behind, Alayna could hear Galen running up the stairs.

The guard she was fighting took a step back and tripped over the body of Edgar.

Alayna hesitated an instant, and in that instant Galen lunged up the final stair and slashed his sword across the man's throat. Alayna watched in fascinated horror as blood spurted. The man dropped his sword, frantically holding both hands to his throat in a vain attempt to stop the bleeding, and looked up at her—*her*—in bewildered pain and surprise before he slumped to the floor.

Beyond the dying man, Sir Osric dropped his sword and fell to his knees. "Mercy!" he cried.

Mordred wavered, undoubtedly wary of a trick, and Osric, still on his knees, sidled up and grabbed his hand. "I don't know what he has told you. But he was behind all this. It was his plan, I swear."

"What?" Mordred demanded, his eyes narrowing. "He?"

Osric looked around the room wildly, finally settling his gaze on Halbert. "Him. He told us to get the child, but Edgar said we could use her, so we said there had been no chance, that we hadn't pulled it off."

Alayna's mind sluggishly refused to sort out this jumble of accusations.

Galen, however, cried, "Liar!" and drove his sword into the man's back.

Still Alayna's mind seemed to lag behind. She stared, unable to react—unable to move, or to think beyond, *Galen killed that man.*

Mordred did not have the same trouble. "He had yielded," he said huskily, thin-lipped and nearly shaking with anger.

"He was a treacherous liar and he would have taken the first opportunity to come at us from behind," Galen countered.

Which was certainly true.

But still it seemed a distorted replaying of the scene in the wizard's castle, when Mordred had scoffed at chivalry and Galen had been angry with him. Nothing was right anymore. Alayna could make no sense of it. *I must go back home,* she thought. She needed to take Kiera away from this, return home and try to put all this behind her. The servants of Bel Bois apparently knew better than to come out, so everything was over. It didn't make any difference whether things made sense or not. She turned to get Kiera.

And saw Halbert, his hand over Kiera's mouth, dragging her to the door.

"Kiera!" Alayna cried.

"Rest easy," the wizard said soothingly. "I am simply taking her to safety, away from these sights unbecoming for a child to see." He was trying to get Kiera under his right arm, to carry her, but his left hand fingered his red pendant, a gesture Alayna remembered and found sudden overwhelming comfort in.

Yes, she thought. *Get Kiera away.* That had been her thought, too. The ruby seemed to glow, even in the erratic candle and torch light, and to show a dizzying depth she hadn't noticed before. Somehow that seemed to be of more importance than anything else in the world.

"Relax," Halbert cooed. "No harm."

"No harm," Alayna repeated.

"Alayna!" Mordred spoke sharply from behind. She heard a scuffle, and knew Galen had prevented him from moving to her side. She wished that they would be quiet, stop their incessant bickering, so that she could concentrate on the beautiful ruby which, even as Halbert stepped away from her, seemed to enlarge and fill more of her vision.

Kiera twisted her mouth away from Halbert's hand, though she couldn't break the wizard's grasp entirely. "Momma!"

Distracted, Alayna assured her, "Hush, all is well."

From behind she heard Mordred cry, "Galen, let go of me. Can't you see—Alayna, don't look at him."

Halbert said, "Gently, Galen."

Alayna could hear and understand his words; she knew that something was terribly wrong—with her, with Galen—but somehow the energy required to be troubled was too far away to summon.

"Try not to harm our young friend," the wizard was saying. "I see an illustrious future possible for our Mordred, one whose purposes run parallel to my own."

"Not likely," Mordred spat.

Halbert shrugged. "Just stay up there. I would rather not kill you, but I might."

"Momma!" Kiera called again.

Halbert whipped her around and shook her. "Your mother wants you to come with me. Now behave."

Alayna knew she should be upset with the wizard for talking to her daughter that way. But she couldn't say so. She knew she should be upset with Galen for preventing Mordred from doing anything to stop the wizard. But all she could say was "Kiera, behave."

"You leave my mother alone!" Kiera shouted at the wizard. She tried to yank herself out of his grip, and he pulled her in closer to his chest. "Let go of me!" She pushed against him with her thin arms, squirming and trying to drop to the floor, her hands tangled in his robes and the chain of his pendant.

Not strong enough, Alayna thought in that deep part of herself she seemed unable to reach. *She's just a five-year-old child.*

"Stop that!" Halbert shook her harder and jerked her out to arm's length to get her flailing hands away from him. But her fingers had gotten caught. The chain snapped, sending the ruby flying. Immediately Halbert shoved Kiera away and scrambled for the stone.

How interesting, Alayna thought vaguely, feeling she was probably witnessing something important, but she couldn't think why it was important and speculated maybe it was important to somebody else, not her.

Kiera also scrambled after the stone. Somebody's foot—Kiera's or Halbert's—sent it skittering across the floor ahead of them. Alayna, from her vantage on the landing, could see where it ended but could only think without excitement or worry, *There it is.*

Halbert looked around wildly. Kiera, younger, shorter, saw where the stone had come to rest; and she reached it first.

Halbert caught up a step later and clutched at her shoulder to yank her away. She stamped her foot down with all her five-year-old strength.

Rubies don't break, Alayna thought. But perhaps it was only ruby-colored. Or perhaps holding magic made it fragile. Up on the landing and half the Hall away, Alayna heard the loud *crack!*

Her vision momentarily shimmered, then focused to an almost unnatural clarity. She saw Halbert's face freeze in a grimace: She could make out each of the indentations made by his fingers in the fabric at Kiera's shoulder.

Then finally—finally—the invisible hand that had seemed to be smothering her lifted.

My God, Kiera! Alayna thought. She ran for the stairs. But before she got to them, she saw that incredible wrinkles were forming on Halbert's face. By the time she was halfway down, the wrinkles had become deep fissures. And as she reached the bottom, Halbert dropped to the floor and fell apart like a log that maintains its form while it burns, only to fall into ashes at the slightest touch.

Alayna fell to her knees and swept Kiera into her arms.

She hated magic. She hated it, hated it, hated it.

Kiera was crying, but Alayna felt only tired, and all cried out. In any case, it was over. It was finally over. "Everything is all right," she assured Kiera. "Everything is fine now."

She looked back to the others. Mordred had stopped partway down the stairs.

Galen, still on the landing, was doubled over. Obviously, he had been more under the wizard's influence than she, and for a longer time. Since Castle Burrstone, she realized now that she thought about it. Halbert had forced his unknightly behavior, which had been the wizard's excuse to send them away, so that he could set his guards on them yet play innocent benefactor when . . . when . . .

Alayna shied away from that thought.

"Galen," she called to him, "are you hurt?"

Mordred went back for him, starting once more up the stairs.

Galen straightened. Then lifted his sword.

Mordred stopped. "Galen?"

"We must get the girl," Galen said, his voice gritty and hollow.

Alayna got up from her knees, but Kiera wouldn't let go, so that Alayna had to either stay where she was, or break away. For a moment she hesitated, and Kiera said, "No, don't go. That's not Uncle Galen."

Which, in her heart, was what Alayna suspected, feared. Knew.

Mordred glanced from Kiera's face to Galen's upraised sword, then took a step back. Hesitantly he raised his own weapon. "Galen . . ." he said in a most reasonable voice.

Galen lunged.

Mordred blocked with his sword, barely in time.

"No!" Alayna took a step closer. It wasn't fair. Halbert was dead. His effect on Galen should have died, too.

Mordred parried another blow, but disbelief, or perhaps it was friendship, prevented him from taking advantage of the opening Galen had left.

"Galen!" Alayna cried, hoping to call him back to reason.

"That's not Uncle Galen!" Kiera shouted. "Uncle Galen is dead!"

Alayna slapped her and Kiera staggered, finally letting go.

Mordred had slammed against Galen, and—still one step lower—backed him into the wall. "Galen," he said from between clenched teeth. *"Galen."*

Galen went limp and closed his eyes. "I don't know what happened," he said, sounding weak and confused. "The stone, the red stone . . ."

Thank God he's come back to his senses, Alayna thought.

Mordred must have thought the same thing. He stepped back, and Galen slashed with his sword, obviously intending a decapitation. Mordred jerked back and down.

Almost in time. But he was bleeding where the sword's tip had grazed his cheekbone.

After all the deaths she'd witnessed since the evening began, the injury was nothing. But this was Mordred. And it was Galen who had done it.

Still only halfway to the stairs, Alayna watched in numb horror as Galen kicked Mordred in the chest. Mordred teetered on the edge of the stair. For a moment he seemed to have regained his balance. For a moment. Then he fell backwards, hitting several steps before he rolled over the open side and dropped about twice a man's height into the Hall below.

Galen started down the stairs.

Mordred staggered back to his feet, but when he tried to pick up his sword, it slipped through his fingers and, in fact, he seemed incapable of lifting his right arm.

Galen was halfway down the stairs.

Mordred held onto his right elbow with his left hand and managed to pick up the sword.

And Galen was three-quarters of the way down the stairs.

Mordred switched the blade to his left hand.

Galen jumped the last step, and Alayna stepped in between, her own sword raised. She said, "I don't know what Halbert did to you, but you have gone far enough." *Galen. Galen! Are you still in there?* she thought. If he didn't recognize Mordred, surely he must recognize her.

"Alayna, get out of the way," Mordred gasped, but he was breathing hard, his sword held clumsily in his left hand.

She said, "Mordred, be quiet. And get Kiera out of here." She was searching deep into Galen's clear blue eyes as she spoke, and she saw nothing there that she recognized. Her voice shook. "If you don't back away, I *will* kill you," she warned her brother. *Back away. Back away.* She could never kill Galen.

The man before her smiled, a smile more reminiscent of Halbert's than her brother's.

His sword came down hard on hers, momentarily numbing her arm to the shoulder.

She slid her sword down and then circled it to the left, but Galen—or what remained of him in this body—could remember old Ned's lessons as well as she, and he was there to block.

"Momma!" Kiera cried.

"Get back!" Out of the corner of her eye she saw Kiera's small form running toward her, her disheveled braids streaming behind. "Get back!"

Mordred was able to intercept her. He grabbed her with his good arm and held her out of the range of the slashing swords. But at the moment Alayna's eyes hovered on them, Galen reached in.

Alayna flinched, her body bending sideways; she felt the pressure of the blow on her ribs, protected only by the leather jerkin. It knocked all the air out of her, but despite the pain, the hit had been a glancing one.

She jabbed, hoping Galen would take it as a feint, but he must have seen her shift balance, and recognized it for the real thing in time to prevent her making contact.

"This is madness, Galen," she gasped, though obviously Galen was beyond rationality. "Halbert is dead."

She was giving ground, using valuable breath to try reason on someone who was no longer there.

They had made a half circle of the room, and now over Galen's shoulder she could again sense, without focusing on them, Kiera and Mordred.

Her feet settled into something vaguely slippery, which scattered. The wizard's remains.

Her arms ached—she had gone into the easier but less agile two-handed stance—and she had a pain in her side, whether from Galen's one hit or from her own ragged panting she couldn't tell. Galen, she realized, was going to kill her. After that, it would take him no time at all to finish Mordred. And then what would he do to Kiera? "Halbert is dead!" she told him in gasps. "*You* don't need Kiera. *He* did."

But with the wizard dead, there was no way to loosen the hold of his spell on Galen.

She tried to move in, but Galen was much stronger, much faster, much better. Any moment she would make a fatal error or he would simply overpower her. There was only one thing she could do.

Pretending to be distracted, she dropped her sword arm. "Kiera!" she screamed, though Kiera hadn't moved. "Get back!"

Galen moved in for the kill, and stepped into her suddenly uplifted sword.

His expression, dying, was neither pain nor anger, but bewilderment. She remembered a time as children, when they'd been walking across a frozen pond, and she had started to slip, and he reached to help her. Just as suddenly, she had regained her balance, but he had fallen before even knowing his feet were no longer under him. That was the expression he wore now in death.

Alayna put her hands on her knees and took great, rattling breaths. The bloody sword dropped from her fingers. But in that position, she could see Galen's face too closely, so she straightened.

Mordred was on his knees, his good arm still around Kiera, his face even paler than hers.

"Momma!" Kiera called, and Mordred let her go.

Alayna took deep breaths of Kiera's fresh clean smell, trying to block out the scents of leather, sweat, and blood. "Oh, Kiera," she murmured.

She had thought there were no tears left in her, but she had been wrong.

PART II

Ninnue

CHAPTER 1

"Sitting around waiting is a waste of time," Merlin had once told Nimue. "Waiting is helped along if one is doing something productive *while* one is waiting."

On the particular occasion when Merlin had told her that, he was referring to waiting for a horse to be shod, and what they did while waiting was to visit various shops in the market district, and what they ended up buying was a dozen tiny silver bells that Nimue had sewn onto a ribbon, which she had given to her niece to attach to her new baby's cradle.

But Merlin's advice was often more than it originally seemed—except, sometimes it was less. For all Nimue knew, he might have been trying to teach her something about horseshoes or markets or babies. Or he might not have been trying to teach her anything at all.

Still, it was by trying to be productive while waiting that—five years now since Merlin was gone—she came to be traveling from village to village, offering her knowledge of herbs and medicines, woven together with a small dollop of magic, to folk too poor to go to the bigger towns to be bled by a doctor.

And that was how, specifically, she came to be in the small town of St. George of the Hills, at Reynard's tavern. Most everyone from the town—eventually during the course of a day—passed through there, and Nimue thought it would be a fine place to learn if there were any who needed the services of midwife, herbalist, or apprentice magician.

"Nothing that I've heard tell of," said Dolph, the young man who last year had married Reynard and Yolande's daughter, Romola.

"Oh," Nimue said with a sigh, for she had walked all morning, her feet hurt, and her stomach was as empty as her purse. This was late enough in the spring that she could find wild strawberries and dandelions which, enhanced by magic, would make a meal. Her magic wasn't strong enough to make it a *good* meal, but she would never starve.

"Why not wait and see," Dolph suggested. "Sit down, have a drink."

Nimue's throat constricted as Dolph poured a tankard of very tempting, sweet-smelling mead. She shook her head.

"I don't think we ever paid you for taking care of that toothache Reynard had last spring," Dolph said.

"Oh, but you did," Nimue told him.

Reynard, who was right there, said nothing.

"No, no," Dolph insisted, "I'm sure we didn't. Did we, Romola?"

"Definitely not," Romola called from the table at which she was serving.

"We'd remember if we did," said Yolande.

Reynard shook his head or nodded it at the appropriate times.

"Thank you," Nimue told them. "That's very kind of all of you."

Dolph winked as he handed her the drink, but she suspected he didn't mean it the way many men would have, for her blond hair and green eyes and fair features. Nimue saw he only had eyes for Romola, and he would have been as kind to any hungry, thirsty stranger.

Romola brought her a platter of meat and bread to choose from, but Nimue had hardly taken a few mouthfuls when the door crashed open with a splintering of wood.

Two knights strode into the room, naked swords in their hands, surveying the scene: fewer than a dozen customers, Dolph just straightening up from the barrel that held the mead, Romola and Yolande waiting on tables. Reynard had just gone downstairs to where the barrels were stored.

Oh no, Nimue thought. She didn't know what this was about, but *Oh no.* On their armor was painted a bold red phoenix, but though she had no idea whose emblem that was, there was obviously something very wrong with the world that knights should be breaking down a door they could have just as easily swung open.

For a moment, no one said anything. Then one of the customers, sounding more surprised than challenging said, "Hey."

And one of the knights swung his sword and took off the man's head.

Nimue heard the two distinctive *thuds* as first head, then body, struck the floor. She had certainly seen people die before, of illness and injuries neither her herbs nor her bit of magic could cure. But she had never before seen anyone killed.

Perhaps the first thing Merlin had taught Nimue, and certainly the point he had repeated most vigorously, was that for every action there is an equal and opposite reaction. This was a law of something he called physics, which Nimue gathered was going to be invented in the seventeenth century by a man called Newton. Merlin said it applied equally well to magic as to apples.

Nimue wasn't very good at history—and particularly at history that hadn't happened yet. But she *did* understand magic. She understood what he meant when he said you couldn't pull a rabbit out of a hat, so to speak, without knowing exactly where that rabbit was going to come from and what were the likely consequences of its disappearance from Point A and subsequent reappearance at Point B. It was damn irresponsible, Merlin used to say, not to take into consideration such things as ethics, spatiotemporal complications, and transmogrificational effects on the sub-etheral plane.

"Not to mention probable damage to the hat," Nimue had pointed out once. But Merlin had gone into one of his foot-stamping, beard-pulling tantrums, and she hadn't brought the subject up again.

Nimue weighed all these problems. She was so busy weighing, she was unable to move even when one of the knights kicked the bench out of his way and shoved Yolande hard enough to cause the innkeeper's big wife to fall.

In the stunned silence that followed, everyone at the inn could make out the sound of Reynard running up the stairs—no doubt he had heard the commotion from the cellar—and the knight moved farther into the room, toward the cellar door, raising his sword.

"No!" Nimue cried, though actions or words sometimes could have as far-reaching and unexpected effects as magic, and though she was well within his striking range.

In this case, the result was the knight grabbed Nimue, digging metal-sheathed fingers into her shoulder.

Time seemed to stop.

Reynard hesitated in the doorway. By chance—or by Nimue's hasty wish for his well-being—he was beyond sword's reach, though probably he had not as yet even seen the sword. He was obviously taking in other matters: his wife sprawled on the floor and the decapitated customer.

Nimue was fervently hoping that her wish for Reynard's well-being couldn't somehow cause something worse to happen; and, simultaneously, she was hoping that her hoping wasn't actually another wish that she'd have to keep track of and worry about later.

The other seven or eight customers stood or sat motionless, most with their eyes downcast and their faces purposely dull lest the knight holding Nimue take offense. The second knight hadn't stopped in the common room but continued toward the back wing, where the overnight rooms were. Now there was a loud crash. Apparently he was searching for something, and apparently his method of search was to kick over the furniture and then throw it against the walls. As everyone waited to see if Reynard was going to get himself killed, there came a ripping noise—a mattress slashed.

Reynard finally saw the knight whose hand gripped Nimue's shoulder. He took a step back, and time seemed to catch up with itself.

The knight obviously dismissed the thought of him—a peasant who had come to his senses, and not worth dirtying one's sword on. But then he did something which, for Nimue at least, was totally unexpected. He flung her away, sending her crashing into one of the unoccupied tables.

Nimue stayed where she landed. Her known affiliation with Merlin, and the strange rumors about his disappearance and her role in that, had resulted in several unpleasant episodes. She'd had trouble with people whom Merlin had helped—who assumed she was a treacherous witch who had murdered him; and she'd had trouble with those who didn't care what had happened to Merlin but thought they had spotted in her an easy opportunity for power. Coupled with her good looks—it would be coyness to pretend she was unaware of the effect her appearance had on men—all of this had made her assume that the destruction at the inn was somehow related to her.

But apparently she had just been another fixture in the way, like the stools and the innkeeper's wife. The knight reached beyond her and grabbed Dolph.

Romola dropped the tray she had been carrying. Tankards of ale splashed over the dirt floor, filling the air with their bitter smell. The knight dragged Dolph outside.

Dolph? Nimue thought.

She had never thought of herself as being quick, but she was still the first to reach the door. She was jostled as the others risked the remaining knight's displeasure by crowding to see what was going on.

Any thought that the sweet-natured, pasty-faced Dolph had somehow crossed these knights dissolved as soon as she looked outdoors. All the way down the street of St. George, doors to shops and homes had been kicked in. She heard cries and moans and knew that more than two knights had swooped down on the town, and that more than the one customer at the inn had been killed.

Nimue started to form a wish that would freeze the knights in their tracks.

But if they were unable to move, then surely the townspeople would set on them in retaliation for the deaths and damage already done. And then either she would have to watch the knights be slaughtered, or she'd have to release them. If she released them, of course they'd fight back and kill more townspeople. On the other hand, if the knights were killed, wouldn't somebody come looking for them? And then wouldn't there be more knights, more destruction?

Nimue hesitated, as—she had to admit to herself—she often did.

Any wish or action she might have started would have been interrupted anyway by the return of the second of the two knights who'd entered the inn. Back in the common room, he pushed through the customers and was suddenly behind her. He gave a shove that caused her to stagger forward, out into the street.

With him, the knight dragged the boy whom Reynard had taken in three summers ago to help clean the rooms and stables and to run errands. She didn't know his name. Perhaps even the innkeeper himself didn't know or could no longer remember, for everyone just called him Boy. The lad, who couldn't have been more than sixteen, was simple-minded and generally fearful of folk, and he was being pulled out of the inn with his head tucked under the knight's arm.

Down the street another knight pulled at the village's young wainwright, who had hold of a large wagon wheel which he had jammed sideways into the doorway of his shop. The knight made to twist the youth and therefore the wheel around, but the youth managed to keep the wheel caught in the door frame.

Angrily the knight gave such a great yank that the wheel wrenched free, and knight and wainwright tumbled into the street. Though the wainwright landed on top, he didn't take advantage of his position, but only bent over his hand and moaned, which probably meant at least some of the fingers were broken.

Boys, Nimue thought, as the image of what she was seeing finally sank in. *They're rounding up very young men and older boys.*

Behind her, Romola pushed through the door of the inn, trailing her parents behind. Yolande and Reynard, recognizing the hopelessness of the situation, were clinging to her, trying to keep her from compounding the family's loss by getting herself killed. But Romola was all flying fists and elbows, and she shouted obscenities into the street where now the only other sounds were the stifled whimpers of grief. One of the knights—Nimue counted quickly, there were twelve—one of the knights glanced in her direction with a scowl. But then one of the inn's regular customers finally came to the innkeeper's aid and helped drag Romola out of view.

Others, too, were retreating, turning their backs on family and neighbors before more harm came of it. A few were distraught or foolhardy enough to lean out of windows, or to peek around doorways. But even a crowd could do little against twelve armored knights.

Nimue found herself alone on the street with the knights and their captives. She took a step—not back into the inn but behind the huge barrel that identified Reynard's establishment.

Crouching, she rubbed the plain gold band of Merlin's ring that she wore on one thumb and tried to concentrate. Who *were* these knights who bore the symbol of the twice-born phoenix, that immortal bird revitalized by its own funeral pyre? And why had they gathered together seven of the youths of St. George?

No, six.

Even as she watched, one of them must have been deemed unacceptable. The knight who seemed to be in charge of this raid had grabbed a strapping peasant boy by his loose shirt and pulled him in for a closer look, then pushed him away hard enough to cause him to bounce off the wall of one of the shops. The youth stayed where he landed—unhurt, Nimue guessed, but fearful enough to be content to leave well enough alone.

In the long days of barbarism between the retreat of the Roman legions and King Arthur's formation of a united Britain, there had been times that groups of mercenaries or knights could settle on abducting a town's maidens as an afternoon's diversion. But since before Nimue's birth, Arthur had declared that the peasants were *not* to be considered fair game, and she couldn't imagine anyone crossing his code lightly.

And not young maidens, her mind kept repeating, young *men*.

The serf who had been rejected was trying to crawl away without attracting notice. He passed by Nimue's barrel and glanced at her. A purple birthmark stood out prominently on his pale face.

Nimue took another look at those who had been chosen. They ranged in age from about fifteen to no more than twenty-three or twenty-four. And they were all nicely featured, even down to Reynard's Boy. Half-wit that he was, it didn't show in his face, as it did in some.

Where? she mouthed at the young man with the birthmark. Where were the knights from? Where were they taking their captives? She didn't have time to ask all that needed asking.

No matter. The young man didn't know or was too intent on escaping before they could change their minds. He shook his head and kept on crawling.

How could she make a reasoned decision on a course of action if she didn't even know what was going on?

She closed her eyes. *Oh, Merlin, help me.* But, of course Merlin wasn't there, as he wouldn't be now for she-wasn't-sure-how-long.

What were they going to do with their captives? She would never find out hidden here behind Reynard's barrel. What should she do? Send to Camelot for help? There were a whole townful of people perfectly able to ride to Camelot—they didn't need her for that. But did they know the phoenix symbol any better than she? Would they be able to tell rescuers *where* to look? And fast upon that she thought: *A little more time spent thinking, and I'll be too late to do anything.*

She squeezed her eyes even tighter and rubbed the ring. Merlin had said she didn't need to rub, but it made her feel more confident.

Casting glamours always made her a bit dizzy, and—before she was quite ready—she took a step out into the open to steady herself.

The leader of the knights looked over. Nimue glanced down at her new body, which looked like that of a seventeen-year-old boy wearing loose homespun.

Too late for second thoughts.

She was grabbed and flung across a horse, like a carcass, like a bag of grain. It had seemed a better plan before it actually started.

Merlin, help me. What should I do? she thought as her ankles were bound. She knew that her indecisiveness had no doubt already cost her opportunities. Yet it was Merlin who had always been after her to keep her wits about her. Merlin *could* think of several things at once.

Perhaps, she thought, if she remained calm and accompanied the knights without fighting, she might be able to help the other captives later on. Wait and see might, after all, be the best immediate course of action. Never one to try to fool herself, Nimue knew it was also the easiest.

CHAPTER 2

imue wished for their well-being so earnestly and so continually that by the time the knights finally halted, she had a headache.

Fortunately, maintaining the glamour that made her look like a boy of St. George required almost no effort. Still, as she was set on her feet along with the others, she swayed dizzily as the blood rushed out of her head and redistributed itself normally. At least she didn't fall.

And at least none of the real young men in the group said anything to draw the knights' attention to her, though they must have wondered who she was, to have suddenly appeared in St. George of the Hills just in time to be captured along with them.

They were in a castle courtyard. She looked around through eyes that wouldn't quite focus. She didn't need sharp focus to see it was a place she immediately disliked. The windows were tiny, high up, and few. The walls were crenelated to provide cover for archers, and the group had passed through three portcullises to get this far. The whole place bristled with guards and armaments. All castles were set up for the possibility of war, but few castellans felt the need to let function dominate form so completely. Either the countryside or the castle inhabitants themselves had to be decidedly unfriendly.

"Ay!" a voice shouted at her. Before she could act on the realization that this was the second time she had been called, one of the knights jerked her toward the doorway.

They went—somehow she had guessed it would be so—down. They had to go single file on the steep stairs, their shoulders brushing rough masonry. The stairs were crudely made—different heights, different lengths—and were badly worn.

Almost at the end of the line, except for a guard, Nimue concentrated on not falling. She didn't dare *wish* not to fall because that could result in too many unforeseen possibilities—such as dying before she had a chance to fall. Dying seemed too close a possibility for her to tempt fate like that. So she watched her feet rather than where the group was headed, and bumped into Dolph when he stopped suddenly.

The lead guard banged the butt of his torch on the armored door before them. "Ay, you awake?" he yelled.

A voice from the other side grumbled an answer that Nimue couldn't make out, then the door opened, releasing a smell of cold, damp earth.

"Well, took your time, didn't you?" the dungeon guard complained to their escort. He lightly tossed and caught a set of dice while, behind him, two more guards waited impatiently for him to complete his throw. "His worship has been fit to gnaw the masonry all afternoon."

The knight in the lead brushed by him. "Move," he told the prisoners. He had to reach over one of the seated guards to get the ring of keys that hung on a nail in the wall. "Simpleton," he growled at the man.

The guard looked neither vexed nor interested.

By the time Nimue passed through the guard room, the three guards had their backs to the procession, only interested in finishing their game. So, she thought, whole groups of prisoners were nothing unusual. That was a worrisome notion.

They made their way down a damp corridor lined with cells, stopping at a door just within the glow of the guard area torches. The lead knight unlocked the door.

"Welcome to Ravens' Rock," he announced, playing at the role of unctuous host. "May your stay be long and profitable."

Ravens' Rock. Ravens' Rock. The name meant nothing to her.

The guard in the back pushed, and the seven prisoners shuffled forward into the unlighted room. One of the knights slammed the door.

Nimue, still at the back of the line, only got one quick impression—that the room was just barely large enough to accommodate them. Then the knights took their torches with them, so that the only light they had was the dim reflection from the torches in the guards' area, about the same illumination as on a cloudy moonless night: just enough light to keep from walking into each other.

The young wainwright sank to his knees, cradling his broken hand. Skittering noises hinted of vermin, but Nimue could also hear bigger noises, albeit still quiet ones, that told of other people present.

Eventually Nimue's eyes grew accustomed to the dark. There were two others in the cell besides the St. George group huddled by the door.

Trying to deepen her voice to sound like a youth, since her glamour affected only her outward appearance, she asked, "Does anybody know why we're here?"

The two unknown men looked at each other but said nothing.

"Can anybody *guess* why we're here?" asked someone from her group. He was a lanky youth, one of Roswald's sons, Evan or Hugh. She knew the family but there were six sons and two young daughters, each with curly red hair and lots of teeth, and she could never keep straight who was who. Whichever this one was, Nimue was glad to know that there was at least one here who wasn't dumbfounded by shock.

A sudden commotion commenced in the hall; someone was banging on the stairway door, and the guards answered that they were on their way.

The two original prisoners dropped to their knees and started in on the *Confiteor*, prayed in fervent, if mostly unintelligible, Latin. It was contagious. Though no one from the St. George group knew what was going on, by the time the door to their cell was thrown open, five had begun prayers for divine intervention. In the bright light of the torches, Nimue looked and saw that it was Roswald's son who remained standing with her.

Four heavily armed knights entered.

And an old man.

The old man needed the support of both an attendant and a wooden staff, and still he seemed barely able to shuffle into the cell. His hand on the staff was badly misshapen. Though she couldn't be sure, Nimue thought that some of the fingers had missing joints, and others were fused together. Then he raised his head. His face was badly wrinkled, like a wadded piece of parchment.

But all that was as nothing.

Neither was her attention drawn to the fact that the right side of his face was almost a handbreadth lower than the left, nor that one eye was only a tremulous slit while the other moved constantly, inspecting the occupants of the room.

The single fact that filled her whole awareness was a sort of alarm that had gone off inside her head, an alarm that clanged and warned she was in dangerous proximity to a strong source of magic.

Now, she thought about Merlin's ring. *If ever, now.* But what, exactly, should she *do* now? Merlin had always urged caution, and one of the guards was already shouting at the kneeling Dolph: "Down! Get your hands down from your face so we can see!"

The old man—he was most certainly a wizard—evaluated Dolph, then his one good eye lingered on Nimue. How could she have been unaware of a wizard of this caliber?

Her heart thudded madly, and she wondered if she had set off some warning bell in his head also, so that he looked beyond her boy's exterior and recognized the presence of magic in her. But, if so, it must have been such a *small* alarm: She was young and inexperienced and most of what little innate ability she had was already occupied with Merlin.

His gaze slid off her and passed on to the youth standing next to her. "You've done well," he told the knights. His voice was a low rumble, spoken through cracked lips that barely moved.

He passed his staff to his attendant, then pulled some sort of red crystal from inside his robes. He held that in one hand and put his other on the shoulder of the youth next to her—Evan, Nimue had finally decided. The farm boy stood firm and met the wizard's gaze with a frightened but defiant steadiness. The old man's half-lowered eyelid fluttered, and his fingers dug into the boy's shoulder hard enough to cause a flicker of pain to show through the youth's resolve.

And the pain and clamor in Nimue's head felt as though it would cause her head to explode. She found herself on her knees with her companions. Let the guards take it for another prayerful gesture. *Too late, too late,* an inner voice taunted. What had her caution cost this time?

And yet *still* she didn't know what to wish. Even to wish for Evan's safety could be disastrous, could result in Evan's death—for what can threaten a man's safety once he is dead?

The wizard was standing straighter and taller, and his victim was writhing but evidently unable to break away. He turned toward Nimue as though he recognized that if anybody could help him, it should have been she.

A red haze filmed her eyes, through which she could make out his face, also transformed with pain. But then she saw it: no, not by pain alone. One of Evan's eyes looked about wildly for help that wasn't there, and the other eye, half closed, seemed to be moving downward on his face, which was crumpling even as she watched. She forced her gaze upward, beyond the strong hand clenched on Evan's shoulder, beyond the other hand still closed around the ruby pendant, to the wizard's face. It was not only young and virile, it was fast taking on the contours and angles that had been the young Evan's.

"No!" she screamed, or thought she did; she couldn't be sure above the clamor in her own head.

Evan, now crumpled and old, slid to the floor.

The wizard, now wearing the face shared by all Roswald's children, finally let go. He stretched his new body, wiggled his fingers, rose on his toes, laughed in exhilarated joy. "Good," he said, either to himself or to the knights. "Very good."

Then he stooped down, hands on knees, and leaned close to Evan, whose old, deformed body was wracked by convulsions. "Thank you," he said, though the boy had not been a willing participant, and was obviously beyond hearing. During the time it took the wizard to tuck the ruby and its chain back into his shirt, Evan's convulsions subsided to twitching and spasms. And then he lay perfectly still.

The wizard straightened and half danced his way to the door.

But he turned back once to look directly at Nimue. "Later," he said.

CHAPTER 3

Two of the knights grabbed hold of Evan's body by the ankles and pulled it out of the cell. The other two knights backed out and closed the door behind, leaving the prisoners once more in the darkness.

Unsteadily, Nimue got back to her feet. *My fault,* she thought. *My fault.* She should have done something. If only she were better at thinking. But she could not let herself be paralyzed by guilt. She found the two young men who had been in the cell before them. Though she looked like a youth herself, she had only her own physical strength. Still, she was angry and frightened enough not to need magic to take hold of the nearer youth by the shirt and haul him up to face her—all without knowing a moment beforehand what she planned.

His teeth were already rattling even before she shook him. "Who was that man? Why do they need all of us here? Answer me." She didn't remember to make her voice deeper, but it was husky from emotion, and the others may not have noticed. She tried to tell herself that if this youth had spoken up earlier, before the wizard had entered, she wouldn't have been so taken by surprise and she might have been able to react quicker. But even as she framed the thought, she knew it was cowardice to blame her hesitation on anyone besides herself.

"We don't know." It was the other who spoke, not the one she held. "We don't know who he be. He ain't never said his name."

Nimue took it for peasant's logic rather than sarcasm. She let go of the shirt. That man still remained tongue-tied, while the other continued, "Whoever he be, whatever be the matter with him"—Nimue could almost feel the young man's shudder—"this . . . this *thing* he does don't last. He'll be back in ten-day looking much the same again. Usually not so bad. He come down once already yesterday and twice today. He looked over me and Griffith here, and he said he'd give 'em till sunset to bring in something better." Obviously the slight was preferable to what they had just witnessed happening to Evan. Any delay was gain.

Neither man was repulsive, though both were too thin, too short, too irregular in their features to be attractive. Could that be a way out? Nimue put her hand on his shoulder. "Look . . . What's your name?"

"Wystan."

"Wystan. Apparently the man is vain about what face he wears. Has anybody tried to work on that?"

"Eh?"

"Has anyone tried to . . ." She tried to think of examples. "Perhaps foul up his hair or . . ." She twisted her jaw and put on a simple look that she wasn't at all sure he could understand, much less see in this light. "Or do something—"

"Bryce banged his face into the wall and knocked out three front teeth."

Nimue winced. "Yes, well, something like that."

"Wizard—he got angry. Bryce ain't here no more."

Right. She sighed. She asked Wystan, "Has anybody ever tried to overcome the guards?"

"William. He ain't here no more neither."

Nimue had no answer to that. Ten days. The wizard would be back in ten days. Could help get to them before that?

She stooped down to feel the earthen floor. In the gloom she tried to pick out details on the far wall of their cell.

Affecting people's minds was the easiest—if the people weren't expecting it. She had done it a few times as a child, for childish reasons, and once shortly after meeting Merlin.

"Never do that again," he had warned, sounding both frightened and angry. "Absolutely, positively never. You go leaping into people's minds, and there's no telling what damage you can accidentally do. Try to get some anonymous peasant to lower the price of his rutabagas for you, and you might end up changing his entire destiny. And suppose he was eventually going to do something important. Or to sire somebody important. Or to encourage somebody to do something important. Why, you might prevent the invention of the wheel. Think of the sociopolitical consequences on the price of rutabagas if the wheel were never invented."

"But, Merlin," she had said, "the wheel has already BEEN invented. And besides, rutabagas don't grow here. You mean turnips. I hate turnips."

"Don't," he had said, "be obtuse."

"You be some lord's son or something?"

"What?" Wystan's question caused the wall to retreat back into the darkness, the image of Merlin overshadowed.

"You talk like gentrys, and the others—they sez they don't know you."

She had thought only a moment had passed while she'd been thinking and that he had been by her side all along. But the others were gathered closer around, and Wystan was now before her instead of beside. "My name is Nevil," she told him—

told all of them. *Some* sort of explanation was definitely called for; but she couldn't trust them with the truth—or certainly not all of it. Nimue of Camelot was too valuable a hostage. To these men with whom she shared the cell, the prospect of ending up like Evan would be strong incentive to try to bargain with the wizard. "I work for Everard the fabric merchant. We had just arrived when the knights came. Now please get out of my way."

"Everard travels alone," said one from the St. George group.

"Thought so," someone behind her agreed. So far they sounded more confused than skeptical. So far they were just trying to work things out.

Nimue said, "Well, he doesn't work alone anymore. Could you stand aside please?"

"But . . ." said Dolph.

"Get out of my way!" she screamed at them.

Everyone backed off.

Still, it wasn't wasted time. From trying to make out their faces as they spoke, her eyes had become better adjusted. She located a spider web in the corner between the ceiling and the wooden beam that braced it. Her eyes picked out an individual strand, then a drop of moisture that hung from that strand. This was supposed to be one of the simple spells, she reminded herself. She let pinpricks of color form, focused on the blue-gold ones, and consciously raised her body temperature. A tiny puff of smoke momentarily obscured the spot she needed, but she continued to see it in her mind. Someone was shaking her shoulder, yelling directly into her ear. She successfully blocked that, along with the other background noise. Finally, the illusion took. Reality merged with thought, and the semblance of fire she had created consumed the spider web. Then the flames dropped to the floor, igniting the wood and straw bedding in the far corner of the cell.

"Nevil, Nevil! Back off! You're too close." It was Dolph who shook her while the others banged on the door and screamed, "Fire!"

For a moment she was confused, couldn't understand why Dolph looked at her and called a man's name, but then he was dragging her to her feet, away from the heat of the flames.

The three dungeon guards were just outside. "Move," the one in command called. "You're blocking the door." If they had been ordinary prisoners of an ordinary castle, the guards probably would just have let the fire burn out—taking bedding and prisoners with it, since it would be unable to burn the stone walls and go beyond this one cell. But they were valuable. The wizard wanted them, and wanted them unmarred.

The door banged open, and the fire heightened from the draft. The guards swore at the prisoners, for whatever it was they'd done, and one of them shoved Nimue and Dolph out into the hallway to have enough room to start beating at the flames with the few old blankets in the cell.

Nimue caught the eye of one of the prisoners, the cooper's nephew, and inclined her head toward the stairs. The others caught on quickly. Only Dolph hesitated with his hand on the cell's door. But whichever guard had unlocked the door had brought the key into the cell with him. And there was no time to look for something with which to block the door, thereby trapping the guards. Any moment now one of them was sure to realize the prisoners were out. Nimue shook her head at Dolph.

We'll probably regret that decision, too, she warned herself as she and Dolph took off down the corridor at a run.

She wanted to call out, *Stay together!* But the others had too big a lead, and she couldn't shout for fear of alerting the guards. So she watched helplessly as the freed prisoners raced ahead.

With his longer legs, Dolph took the stairs two at a time. But then he turned and saw her lagging behind. He grabbed her arm and hustled her up to the outside door. From behind came the sounds of the dungeon guards, who'd finally seen what had happened. They were yelling and running up the stairs.

Outside, too, there was already a commotion. If all eight of them had stayed together and burst through the door en masse, there might have been a better chance for at least some to escape.

Dolph yanked her back inside. "They'll be searching the woods," he whispered, "figuring everybody made a run for it."

Of course they would figure that: It was the only sensible place to go.

Inside, Nimue and Dolph stood at the intersection of three doorways: the one to the outside, the one they had just come through from the dungeon stairs, and one opening on a long corridor that led to the castle proper. If going outside meant walking into the roused castle guards whom they could hear even now starting pursuit of the other prisoners, and downstairs would bring them back to the dungeon guards on their way up, that left only the corridor. But there was no way to make it down that corridor before the dungeon guards reached the head of the stairs, and the only spot that offered even a bit of cover was a small linen-draped table under which there would be room for only one, if that.

Nimue said, "One glance down that hall, and they'll have us. Better to take our chances outside."

Dolph suddenly grinned, though his face was still white with fear. "Nevil, Everard's assistant." He shook his head, put his hand squarely on her back and pushed. "Go!"

Nimue stumbled, knew she wouldn't make it to the table after all, and pressed herself against the wall.

Dolph stepped to the outside door, dropped to one knee, and rubbed the other leg, pretending pain. "Blasted knee," he said. "Hey, lads! Wait for me! Don't leave me!"

From behind, the three pursuing guards burst through the dungeon door and almost fell over him. One of them grabbed his arm, seemingly intent on twisting it out of its socket.

"Easy, easy," he told them. "I'm not going anywhere."

Stupid. Nimue took a shaky breath in through her teeth. *I didn't need that,* she thought. *Why didn't you let me handle it my own way?*

Though, fast on that, her mind asked her, *And what way would that have been?*

They hadn't yet looked in her direction. The guards dragged Dolph to his feet, still with one arm pinned behind and now a sword ready at his back. "Don't try anything," one of them warned.

"I wasn't intending to," Dolph assured him.

Nimue released the glamour that she had cast to disguise her appearance, and instantly replaced it with another. She gave herself dark hair coming loose from under a kerchief, and an apron, damp and food-stained. Her sleeves were rolled up to her elbows, and her hands were red and chapped from work. The spell caused her to stagger dizzily against the wall.

The movement caught the attention of the dungeon commander, but all he saw was a scullery maid. "Hey, wench. You seen anyone?"

"What?" The confused tone came more from the change from one false shape to another than from a calculated intent to appear dim-witted.

"Any of Lord Halbert's boys go down that way?"

"Halbert?"

He looked at her blank face for only a moment, then pushed by her to check the hall himself. He stopped at the table, and jabbed under the hanging linen with his sword.

Dolph stared at her with enormous eyes.

The guard who held him twisted the arm a bit more. "Go on, then," he said. "Back down you go. And any more tricks, and you can roast yourselves." He shoved Dolph toward the stairs.

Behind her, the guard at the table hesitated as if debating whether it was worth his effort to walk all the way down the hall, seeing there was little chance that anyone could have made it that far.

The remaining guard stepped outside to join the search there, and Nimue followed him into the courtyard. Reynard's Boy, the wainwright, and Wystan were huddled into a group guarded by five knights. Griffith was lying face down in the dirt. One of the knights—in fact it was the one who had been in charge of the recent raid on St. George—used his foot to roll the youth over onto his back. He stooped for a closer look, then shook his head, looking annoyed and disgusted.

"Pardon," Nimue murmured, edging past them. The boy's slack mouth and wide-open eyes showed he was beyond magic as surely as he was beyond herbs and simples. Despite the lurch in her stomach, she tried not to seem unduly interested or concerned.

She made it around the corner, where she leaned her forehead against the wall. When she looked up, she saw the cobbler's apprentice being brought back in over the drawbridge. That left only the cooper's nephew unaccounted for. From the surrounding woods, she could hear calls and whistles and barking hounds.

Don't stop now. She knew that was good advice to herself, even if it entailed walking directly by the knights clustered about Griffith's body, arguing over whose responsibility he was.

She resumed walking, keeping her head bent down, which, in any case, was befitting a kitchen servant.

As they passed each other, the knight who had hold of the cobbler's apprentice gave her a pat on the bottom. "Later, girl," he called out, and gave her a wink. She could guess what he had in mind, but his words were disturbingly reminiscent of what the old wizard had said.

She kept walking and didn't look back.

CHAPTER 4

Nimue walked the rest of that afternoon and into the evening. If she had to walk all the way to Camelot, she would, for King Arthur had to be told what was going on at Ravens' Rock. St. George was closer, but what could they do beyond sending for help? And certainly, by now, they would have done that already. But if help came—from Camelot, by way of St. George since Arthur would not know about Ravens' Rock—that would cost an extra day, time that the young men being held prisoner could not easily afford.

On the other hand, north toward Camelot rather than east toward St. George, there were several towns and castles held by lords loyal to Arthur. She would have to decide, later, whether she would do better to stay on the direct road to Camelot, or to veer off in the direction of one of those other castles. A messenger sent by one of those lords could travel much faster than she on foot. But only if, by not going straight, she didn't miss the men Arthur would send in response to St. George's call for help.

She slept the darkest hours of the night, then started again, too tired to think properly, too tired to cry, too tired to avoid worrying that her frantic wishes for the well-being of those held captive would somehow work unsuspected harm— so that her wishes were tinged by self-doubt, which would, of course, diminish the possibility that they would work at all.

Now Merlin, she reflected, could have summoned a horse to carry him, or conjured up one of those infernal riding machines he complained that the people of the future were too fond of. But Nimue's inherent magical ability was slight. And most of it was already occupied, supporting the ongoing spell for Merlin. And most of what was left inclined itself primarily toward small healings.

So she put one foot before the other and tried not to think of where she was going or how long it would take to get there.

The third morning of walking, she heard horses.

They came from the north, the direction in which she was headed. Too early for any response from Camelot. The road was straight and wide at this point, and the riders had to have seen her, just as surely as she saw them. Two knights. Which was good. Unless, of course, they were from Ravens' Rock. But there were only the two, and they weren't dragging helpless village boys behind them. Though that certainly wasn't *proof.*

She considered whether she should leave the road and try to hide in the woods. If these knights were people who could help, hiding would be the wrong decision. On the other hand, they *might* be knights of the Red Phoenix, and if they were, they might or might not decide to pursue her. But—on the other hand—if they were Red Phoenix knights, their main interest was in gathering young men for their wizard, so maybe it would be best to stay on the road and not attract their interest by fleeing. On the other hand . . .

Nimue forced herself to stop. That was altogether too many hands. *Stay on the road,* she decided. She'd never be able to outrun pursuit if that was what these men intended, and—in fact—she probably couldn't walk much farther at all.

She sank to her knees on the road to await them. Although she had long past dropped her disguise as a scullery maid, she knew that—after three days on the road—her true appearance wasn't much better now. Was that good or bad? If these were renegade knights, she didn't want to entice them. On the other hand . . .

Stop with the hands! she ordered herself. Besides, if their sense of chivalry depended on her being attractive, she was lost, for she didn't have the energy to spare.

When she looked up again, the knights were much closer. Both were in black armor, no helmets. Frequently younger sons who had not yet made a name for themselves painted their armor black, being unable to afford a squire to accompany them and polish their armor. She saw that one carried the blank white shield used by novice knights. But, with an incredible sense of relief, she saw the second knight bore the dragon colors of the court of Camelot.

It was the knight with the white shield who dismounted. He knelt beside her, a clumsy maneuver in full armor. He was an older man after all, and already huffing from the exertion. Nimue had hoped it might be Sir Lancelot, who sometimes disguised his identity to raise the odds at a tournament. But this was someone she didn't know. He had a broad and open face—what Dolph's might look like in another twenty years, given the security of knowing from one day to the next where his supper was to come from.

"Lady, what misfortune has befallen thee?" he asked in the formal accents of chivalry.

Acknowledging her as a lady was chivalrous in itself. "Sir knight . . ."

"Sir Dunsten." He smoothed his graying mustache and gave an almost fatherly smile.

She glanced at the second, younger, knight, but he said nothing. "Sir knights," she said, to include him anyway, "there is a terrible thing happening . . . I have been walking three days . . . There is an evil wizard . . ." Traveling, she had tried to work out the best way to tell her story, but now several beginnings got so muddled she couldn't come out with any.

The knight still on horseback looked at her coolly. Impatient or annoyed—she couldn't tell.

The first knight, Sir Dunsten, patted her hand. "There, there," he said in much the same way a falconer might calm a too-spirited bird. "There, there." He eyed his companion. "Would you get down here and help?" he said between clenched teeth, as though that would keep Nimue from hearing or realizing that she was being talked about.

The young man remained motionless for a moment longer, but then slid off, and with surprising grace, stooped down, disarmingly close.

Sir Dunsten, smiled at her encouragingly. "Now. Someone is pursuing you?"

That made her jump, looking over her shoulder. "No," she said, realizing too late that he was just prompting her and that she came out looking a fool, "not anymore. But there were some knights—their symbol was a red phoenix?" Inarticulate and skittish, that was the impression she was giving. Or half-witted and given to spasms.

Dunsten glanced at the second knight, who shook his head. "We regret," Dunsten said, "the device is unfamiliar to us. Where . . ."

She pointed in the general direction. "A place called Ravens' Rock."

"Sir Bayard," the younger man said, finally deigning to speak. "Castle Ridgemont is on a hill called Ravens' Rock." He said the name "Bayard" too evenly, as though she should recognize it. She didn't, but apparently Dunsten did.

"Ah," he said. "*That* one. The phoenix is new, though. Previously it was a raven. What has he done?"

"He has a wizard with him," Nimue said, "Halbert, who is . . ."—she fought down a surge of nausea—"using people, young men, somehow taking their bodies to make himself young." The words sounded so incredible. How could she ever convince them? She should just have asked to be taken to Arthur. Arthur had known Merlin, and was used to the idea of magic, though certainly never in this form. She said, now that she had started, "Apparently he needs to do this every several days. Please help me, there is no time to spare."

"A wizard named Halbert," the younger knight said.

"Yes." She didn't know what to make of his hard, almost brittle tone. Of all the things he might have questioned, why that?

"What, exactly, is going on?"

Nimue shook her head. "I just told you . . ." But he had heard. Certainly he wasn't hard of hearing. He was looking at her as though he suspected—no, as though he were sure—she was a liar. "It's true," she insisted. "There is no time for me to go all the way to Camelot to get somebody else to help." He *didn't* believe her, she could tell. "Please."

Dunsten was looking from her to his companion. Finally he said, "Oh, *really,* Mordred."

Mordred.

Nimue knew she had forgotten much of what Merlin had taught her and mixed up a great deal of the rest, but his warnings about Mordred were something about which she had no doubts. This illegitimate son of King Arthur was destined to bring about the collapse of the Round Table, and possibly Britain itself. She had been caught off guard because he wasn't at all what she had pictured. Suddenly, and for the first time, she realized that Merlin had never actually shown her what he looked like.

Both knights were watching her and it was much too late to pretend she hadn't recognized the name.

Nimue bit her lip. Still, she couldn't believe it was somehow in the best interests of Britain to let all those people who lived around Castle Ridgemont get killed.

She knew she was not talented in lies and subterfuge. It was much easier to keep track of what you'd said if you told the truth. She took a deep breath. "My name is Nimue," she said, and she saw that Mordred looked as startled to hear that as she had been to learn his name. "I was passing through a small town southeast of here, called St. George of the Hills. Some knights came. They killed several of the towns-people, and carried off a half dozen young men. I . . . went with them." Dunsten raised his eyebrows, but didn't interrupt. "And I saw this wizard, this Halbert, do what I have just described to you."

Mordred had gotten over being surprised, but he said nothing, just watched her.

"Perhaps she has the name wrong." Dunsten patted down his mustache again. "Nimue, child," he said in the same kind tone Arthur used, "are you sure it was Halbert?"

"I don't know. One of the knights called him that."

Dunsten smiled benignly. "Well, there you have it. And, Mordred, why do you think it cannot be Halbert?"

"Because he's dead," Mordred said. "Three, no, four years dead."

Nimue asked, "Are you sure?"

"Am I sure?" he repeated. He didn't like being questioned? Well, neither did she. "Yes. I was there."

Nimue took another deep breath. "Let me tell you something about magic. Magic is a sort of force field . . . No, wait." She started again. "All around us . . ." That was no good. "If we could tap into . . ." Both faces looked at her in perplexity. It was so clear when Merlin explained it. "Anyway, I guess I don't need to confuse you by getting into it." That evasion sounded so much more rational and less blatantly evasive when Merlin used it. "What I want to say is that sometimes it is necessary for a wizard to . . . *focus* his or her power. I'm sure you have seen this kind of thing." She widened her eyes and wiggled her fingers in front of her face, then, with a suddenness that jarred her elbow, whipped her arm out, one finger pointing forward.

Mordred and Dunsten both jumped and looked over their shoulders, as if expecting perhaps a burst of flame or at least a visitation by some long-dead saint—which showed that they had missed the point entirely.

"I was referring to the gesture," she said, sensing their disappointment, and held out her forefinger. "That's not dramatics. Well . . . but not entirely. That's focusing.

The more power that is involved, the more necessary it is to focus, and sometimes wizards have to depend on an outside object to help them, like a crystal ball, or some sort of staff, or . . ." She realized she might be putting ideas into their heads, and tucked her thumb into her palm to keep them from noticing her ring.

"Or like a ruby pendant," Mordred finished in a whisper.

That sent a chill up her back. He *did* know Halbert. "The trouble with a . . . focusing instrument"—Merlin had had a special word for it which refused to come to mind—"is that it can be vulnerable. I take it that you did something to this ruby of Halbert's?"

"I saw it done," Mordred said. "It was broken, the pieces scattered all over the floor."

"Where you left them."

She hadn't meant it as an accusation.

"I . . ." For once, he looked momentarily flustered. "Yes."

"Someone, somehow, must have gathered the broken pieces—"

"Bayard," Mordred interrupted. "Bayard is Halbert's nephew. I suspected once before that Bayard was involved in Halbert's plans, but there was no *proof* of wrongdoing, and once Halbert was dead—"

"Halbert is not dead," she told them. "But he is not exactly whole either. When I first saw him he was all bent over and twisted—worse than Richard the Third."

"Richard the third what?" Dunsten asked.

Merlin's references were always getting her into trouble.

Mordred glared at Dunsten's interruption.

Nimue made a vague gesture to indicate it wasn't important. "But then Halbert went through some sort of . . . transformation. He became young, virile . . . whole. But it cost another life. It's as though you left a wounded animal, Sir Mordred." She wanted him feeling at least partly responsible. "Will you help stop him?"

"Of course," Dunsten said, leaping in to agree.

Mordred glanced at him. "Dunsten."

"The problem is," Dunsten continued as though he hadn't been interrupted, "Sir

Bayard is not the type of man to accept a challenge to single combat."

"Dunsten," Mordred repeated.

"Well-fortified place, is this Ravens' Rock?" Dunsten asked her.

Nimue nodded, since he was the one moving the conversation in the direction she wanted.

"Dunsten."

The older knight looked at Mordred in annoyance. "What?"

Mordred nodded over his shoulder, back the way they had come.

"Oh," said Dunsten. "Right."

Nimue looked from one to the other. "What?" she demanded.

Dunsten said, "I am afraid there has been a bit of trouble back at Camelot."

"What kind of trouble?" This couldn't be anything to do with Merlin's predictions about Arthur and Mordred—could it? Surely not yet?

Mordred stood up, another fluid motion despite the bulk of armor. She watched him and was able to tell nothing from his expression.

It was Dunsten who answered. "A matter of . . . an allegation . . . that had to be withdrawn. Sir Mordred was being kind enough to escort me to the border."

She finally managed to look away from Mordred. *Not* that, after all, apparently. Not yet. "You've been exiled?" She found it hard to believe that the plump, cheerful Dunsten had been banished. What could he possibly have done? But he inclined his head toward the white, stripped shield, and Nimue abandoned manners for curiosity's sake. "Why would Arthur do that—"

"Because," interrupted Mordred, his voice quiet as always, "Dunsten pointed out to King Arthur that Queen Guinevere and Sir Lancelot Dulac are lovers, which—by law—makes them traitors to the crown."

She remembered the King's many kindnesses when everyone else accused her of being an enchantress who stole away Merlin's magic and locked him into some old tree, or cave.

Mordred continued, "Sir Lancelot denied it and proved his innocence by besting

Sir Dunsten in trial by combat. Our gracious King Arthur spared Dunsten's life on condition that he leave his family and homeland forever. This has happened before to other knights. Seven, so far." He leaned down close to her. "What do you think of that, royal magician?"

Nimue looked at him helplessly.

"Mordred," Dunsten murmured.

Mordred didn't straighten but continued to wait for her answer.

She tried to keep her voice as even as his own had been. "Arthur has always been like a father to me." She meant only that she could never speak against him. The words came out before she realized what she was saying, to whom she was saying it.

Something almost came through in his smile. "How nice for you," he purred.

He straightened, and meanwhile, Dunsten used his arm to hoist himself back up to his feet. "Yes," said Dunsten, obviously eager to change the subject. "Well. In any case, I have been given just barely enough time to remove myself from Britain. But, come, come, my boy, they have to make an exception for a case like this." He looked from Mordred to Nimue. "Don't you think? Now, one of us has to go to this Castle Ridgemont directly before anybody else gets killed. The other has to take this poor child back to Camelot and bring reinforcements in case . . . well, in case this Halbert is a more competent fighter than I."

Mordred's smile softened to a more genuine one. "No, I think it would be better the other way around. If the King's men discover you here, they may well assume you're trying to raise an army. If you take Nimue and head straight back to Camelot, they at least will give you the chance to explain yourself. And if they do not believe you, they may believe her. I think your chances of survival are better if you go."

"And what about *your* chances of survival?" Dunsten argued. "Surely experience counts for something?"

Mordred just grinned, and swung onto his horse. "Good-bye, Nimue," he said. "I am sure King Arthur will be pleased to see you again." He started to ease the horse past them. "Dunsten."

Nimue got to her feet quickly. "Do you know your way from here to Ravens' Rock?"

"Yes."

"And you think you can take care of everything all by yourself?"

"Yes."

"Wouldn't my knowledge of the place be valuable?"

That wasn't a question he had been expecting. Still, "Not especially," he said.

"What about my magic?"

Mordred looked at Dunsten, who shrugged. The horse moved restively. Nimue smiled her most charming and self-confident smile.

Dunsten said, "I have the longer journey, and I *would* be able to move considerably faster without her." Mordred looked about to say something when Dunsten added, "And we cannot just abandon her here."

She thought Mordred might ask, *Why not?* Instead, sighing, he leaned down to help swing her up behind him onto the horse.

"Shortcut to the left," she said, determined to be of value.

"Just try not to fall off," he answered.

She tightened her grip and told herself that he was Merlin's and Arthur's enemy, and he wasn't to be trusted any more than was absolutely necessary. She also told herself that it didn't help anything to notice how handsome he was.

CHAPTER 5

"Are you aware that you have gone too far west?" Nimue asked.

They had stopped by a stream after Mordred's horse had begun to favor one foot. Mordred was bent over to examine the hoof and didn't spare her a glance. Nimue dipped her scarf into the stream to clean her face.

"Are *you* aware," he said in a voice more quiet than usual, "that we are being watched? Don't look. *I said . . .*" He sighed in exasperation.

Too late. The figure just beyond the fringe of the clearing had seen her sudden turn. For a moment their eyes met. The cold water from Nimue's scarf ran down her arm and onto her skirt. "Romola!" she said, before the innkeeper's daughter turned and disappeared into the trees. Nimue scrambled to her feet, almost fell on the slippery wet pebbles, and raced into the woods after her.

"Romola," she called again. They weren't *that* far from where they should be and she didn't want to attract unnecessary attention. She slowed to a walk, then stopped entirely. In the silence, a squirrel bounded up a tree, its tiny nails clicking on bark. A bird, too far off to identify, shifted from one branch to another and sent a leaf into a slow downward spiral.

Nimue took a hesitant step. "Romola?" It came out a bare whisper. She knew she couldn't be mistaken—it had been Romola. The question was, what was she doing here?

Directly above her, a thrush must have decided that the excitement was over and burst into song. Nimue jumped. She glanced back the way she had come: no sign of the clearing anymore.

Nor of Mordred for that matter.

A mayfly seemed intent on nesting in her hair, and Nimue brushed at it, then took another step. Backwards this time. From her right, a wildly overgrown area, came a muffled scream.

"Mordred!" she yelled back toward the clearing. From the direction of the scream, a crackle of underbrush approached her, but she wouldn't retreat any farther. "Mordred!" The bushes directly beside her stirred, and a mailed arm fought back the branches.

But it was Mordred after all who broke through from that unexpected direction, apparently having stealthily circled around while she blundered through the middle. He had one hand over Romola's mouth and the other held up to caution silence.

Romola kicked him hard behind the knee. The pitch and tone of her muffled voice changed from protest to outrage as her bare foot made contact with armor.

Mordred shifted her from side to front. "Friend of yours?" he asked Nimue.

Nimue nodded.

"Well then, tell her—" Mordred broke off and yelped a startled curse in Cornish. He had removed his gauntlets to examine the horse, and now Romola's teeth had sunk into exposed flesh. He resisted the reflex to let go, instead snapped her head back and slid his mailed wrist into her mouth.

Nimue winced. "Don't hurt her."

"*Don't hurt . . .*" he started to repeat. His voice dropped. "Just tell her," he almost whispered, "if she does *not* stop this noise, I am going to get that nasty little dirk I took from her and start cutting off her fingers, one by one."

"Oh, stop that." Nimue took Romola's arm and gently pulled her away. "Now you've frightened her."

Mordred glowered.

"Sir Mordred would not really harm you," Nimue said with earnest hope that she tried to pass off as certainty. Mordred had been nothing but distantly polite so far, but there were Merlin's warnings . . .

"Traitor," Romola spat at her. Then to Mordred, "Pig."

"The two of you have been friends a long time, have you?" Mordred asked Nimue.

Inexplicably, Romola looked ready to kick and bite Nimue. "So you're one of them," she said venomously. "We wondered where you'd disappeared to. Why'd you do it? What do you want with my Dolph?"

It took several long moments for Nimue to realize what she meant. "Oh, Romola! I never . . . This isn't . . ." She started from the point that could get her furthest. "I didn't 'disappear': I went to get help. Sir Mordred wasn't one of those knights." She considered how best to explain identifying devices and colors to the peasant girl, decided instead that Romola would just have to take her word for it. "Those knights were from Castle Ridgemont over at Ravens' Rock. Sir Mordred is from Camelot."

Romola hugged her arms to herself and kept from looking overly impressed. "The King's court, then? One of Arthur's men?"

Mordred flashed a smile that was a bit too charming.

Romola looked at him skeptically. "So he's it, eh? One knight? And not especially big, is he?"

Mordred kissed her hand. "No, really," he murmured, "the pleasure is all mine."

She snatched her hand away, a heartbeat or so too late for the proper effect.

"Besides," he said, "the next logical question is, what are *you* doing here?"

"They stole Dolph, my man."

"Plan to rescue him, do you?"

If it had been anyone else, Nimue would have given him a good hard pinch for his constant goading.

Romola finally let drop the hand Mordred had kissed. "Well, of course I'm not going to stand at the gate of this Castle Ridgemont and yell for them to give me back their prisoners. I got me a wagonload of beer and ale, and that'll get me inside." She shook her head to get her hair, which was black and very curly, out of her eyes.

"Getting inside is not the problem," Mordred told her.

"Well, I guess I'll just have to wait and see what there is to see before I can plan any farther, won't I?"

Mordred looked as close to laughing as Nimue had seen him. "I guess," he agreed.

"It's not a bad plan," Nimue said.

Mordred glanced at her, then turned and headed back toward the clearing without comment.

"Camelot?" Romola asked.

Nimue nodded, but noticed that Romola looked down at her kissed hand once more before following.

Besides the soft leather undergarments worn under armor, Mordred had a change of clothes in his pack. But, although rather plain for a nobleman, they were too fine to pass as a peasant's. Luckily, Romola found an old shirt of Dolph's in the wagon, and an even older set of breeches.

Mordred, however, chose to be difficult.

"It stinks," he protested, dropping the shirt.

"You'll get used to it," Nimue told him. "You'll need it if you want to pass yourself off as a tradesman."

Romola snorted, just in case anyone wasn't already aware of her opinion.

Mordred poked gingerly at the shirt. "You are a wizard," he said to Nimue. "Why can't you magically change my appearance? That way we could be sure no one would recognize me, *and* I would have the protection of the armor."

Nimue shook her head. "I can only alter my own self."

"Merlin could do it."

"I am not Merlin."

He opened his mouth, but then bit back his answer, which was a wise choice.

It worked out that Mordred was bigger in the shoulders, smaller in the waist and rump than Dolph, and shorter. He looked rumpled, which certainly wouldn't hurt matters, and belligerent, which *would*.

Nimue pulled some of his dark hair onto his forehead, then tied it down with a twisted length of rag. "There, what do you think?" she asked Romola.

"Be still, my heart," Romola answered flatly. "I think I'm in love."

Mordred threw down the cloth and shook the hair out of his eyes. "If you think *that* will stop Halbert from recognizing me—"

"For the moment I'm not worried about Halbert," Nimue put in. "I'm concerned about getting you beyond the castle guards who have orders to take all the comely young men they see."

Unexpectedly, Mordred blushed. His distant manner kept making Nimue forget that he was, in fact, the same age as she—twenty-two. But even as his sudden extra color reminded her of his youth, it showed up for the first time the faintest hint of a thin scar along his cheekbone. And that gave her an idea.

She stooped down and mixed two handfuls of dirt, the black river silt with some red clay.

Mordred watched warily, but offered no objection. She used her muddy finger to paint a dark streak across his cheek. It would be nice, she thought, if when the mixture dried it puckered the surrounding skin to add to the illusion of a badly healed gash. Not that she would *wish* such a thing—she most definitely did *not* wish such a thing, for it might result in a real scar or, worse, a circumstance that would result in a new wound. She smiled encouragingly, but he had retreated into one of his sulks.

With the rag back on to hold his hair, Mordred secured a knife under his breeches' leg and hid his sword in one of the worn brown blankets used to keep the beer kegs from banging into each other. This blanket he rolled up and put on the wagon seat as if it were padding for the rough road. The rest of his things he hid under a gorse bush.

Nobody asked what he thought were the chances that they would ever make it back here at all, never mind whether they could find that particular bush again.

He removed the saddle and harness and gave his horse a *whack* on the rump, for there was no way the fine gray destrier could be disguised as anything but a knight's warhorse. Romola's wagon was pulled by oxen.

Nimue watched the horse sadly, wondering if it would ever make it back to Camelot; but if Mordred had any sentiments, they didn't show.

After covering up the last of his equipment with more branches, he reached to help Romola onto the back of the wagon.

"I can do it myself," Romola snapped at him.

"Of course you can," he said in a friendly tone.

The innkeeper's daughter looked away, then accepted his arm.

Mordred turned to Nimue. If he was surprised to find her suddenly looking like an aging crone, his face didn't show that either.

CHAPTER 6

They arrived at Castle Ridgemont just before gate-closing, which was their intent.

Romola handled the talking, first with the guards, then with the seneschal in charge of supplies. With his new "scar," Mordred didn't seem to attract the guards' interest. No one gave him a second look as he gave the oxen a rubdown. Nimue didn't know if oxen were supposed to be rubbed down the way horses were, but guessed it couldn't hurt. She had made herself look fifty years older than she really was and watching Mordred—who may or may not have been acting foolishly by tending to the oxen—she decided to go further. If being an old woman was a good defense, how much better a mad old woman?

She began to rock back and forth in the wagon and picked at wisps of her white hair, all the while mumbling to herself: "It's a fine night for picking daisies. Why doesn't she hurry up, so we can find daisies before the cats eat them all up? Cats always eat up all the daisies, sneaky creatures that they are. Maybe I should check the wagon to make sure there are no cats hiding. There's one, trying to disguise itself as my foot!" She swatted at her foot. "Damn daisy-eating cat." She continued rocking, and hoped—didn't wish, but *hoped*—Romola would hurry up.

Romola spoke to the seneschal for a long time, made longer by the fact that they were too far away to hear what was being said. But Nimue could see her rest her hand on the man's arm and laugh brightly. When she finally returned to the wagon, she said, "I've struck a bargain."

"I'll bet you have," Mordred said.

"Why, my dear *brother*, I mean for the beer and ale. And for lodging, for ourselves and our granny, since we have been so unexpectedly caught on the road."

Mordred began to lift the barrels off the wagon. "Dangerous game," he warned.

Romola shrugged, then shrugged again at Nimue's look, for Nimue was thinking that Mordred was right: Flirting with the guards *was* dangerous. It could quickly go beyond what Romola intended. Romola said, "Dinner in the lower kitchen whenever we get there, if anything is left. We can sleep there, too, instead of the stables."

Nimue admired her bravery and her ability to speak and act quickly. "Well done," she whispered and gave Romola's hand a squeeze.

"Coming through," Mordred said because Romola stood where he wanted to set down the barrel he held.

"No, no, really," she told him. "Don't mention it. It was nothing." She tossed her black hair over her shoulder and headed for the kitchen.

"Don't," Nimue whispered at Mordred from between clenched teeth, "get her angry at us."

Mordred laid his arms on the barrel, pretending to rest a moment; but Nimue cut him off with a motion for silence: A castle servant was approaching, sent by the seneschal to help unload. Nimue stayed in the back of the wagon, moving from one barrel to another, whichever she guessed the servant planned to pick up next. She cackled, and scratched herself noisily, and made a general nuisance of herself until there was only one small jug of wine left; and for that they had special plans.

"That ain't been sold," Nimue said and slapped at the servant's hand. "We need something to keep us warm on the ride back, my grandchildren 'n me."

"Old witch," the man called her, not knowing how close he came to the truth of it.

By the time they got the oxen bedded and made their way to the kitchen, they found the cook and his helpers setting things out for the next morning. There was no sign of Romola.

Do not be TOO brave and quick, Nimue thought on Romola's behalf. That could easily prove as risky as timid and slow.

Dinner was a round loaf of bread for her and Mordred to share and two pieces of smoked haddock. They found a corner where they would be out of the way and sat on the floor to eat.

"Is she always like that?" one of the scullery boys asked after Nimue bared her teeth and barked at someone who came too close.

Mordred looked at Nimue, then back at the boy. "Like what?" he asked innocently.

After that, they were pretty much left to themselves. But in any case the others soon pulled out blankets and mats and settled down for sleep.

Mordred had brought in the blanket roll in which his sword was hidden, and they used this as a pillow. The wine they kept close by also.

"What about Romola?" Nimue whispered. Where was she? What was she doing? Why hadn't she returned?

Mordred said, "She is not our problem."

Nimue lay with her back to him, furious that he could be so callous. Was Romola in trouble—was that why she didn't come to the kitchen? And if she *was* in trouble, did they help or harm her by not going to look for her? Nimue could argue it to herself both ways. Maybe that was what Mordred meant, why he did nothing.

Wishful thinking, she chided herself. *You could talk yourself into anything.*

But nobody had forced him to help her.

Which proves what? she asked herself. What would Merlin do? Had Merlin ever said that Mordred was totally evil, not to be trusted in *anything?*

Needing to be reassured, needing the proximity—to anyone, even Mordred—she moved closer, not caring that as far as the others knew she was snuggling with her grandson. She rubbed Merlin's ring for reassurance and felt herself dangerously close to tears. She was out of her depth: In a hostile castle, about to face a renegade wizard, here she was bedding down with Merlin's mortal enemy, someone who could blithely say "She is not our problem" about the youngest, least experienced, member of their group.

Merlin was her lover, and he had trained her in sorcery, but they both knew she wasn't an adept. *"Don't lose your head,"* he'd kept warning. *"Don't just jump into things without thinking everything out first."* In this it turned out he had trained her too well. How could anybody ever think out *everything* first? She sent out well-wishes for all of them, and knew that well-wishes would never be enough.

A tear balanced itself on the tip of her nose, and she didn't move to wipe it because she hoped that Mordred thought she was asleep. But he pulled her closer and gently brushed her hair away from her face. For an instant her mind went blank in panic. He wrapped both arms around her before she remembered that she wore a seventy-year-old body. "Go to sleep," he whispered. "I'll watch."

She squeezed his hand, but continued to listen to the noises all around them. The kitchen staff bedded earliest since they would have to be up again before anybody else, but the rest of the castle was becoming quiet also.

Footsteps approached the door, paused as someone apparently looked in. *Romola!* Nimue almost turned her head to look, but then heard the soft clink of metal—a guard on his rounds.

She lay still and tried to match the slow steady rhythms of Mordred's heart and breathing without thinking of the youth himself.

Finally she felt him move his head, then sit up to look around.

No one reacted.

He unwrapped the sword.

She took the wine and crept after him, as silently as possible, to the door.

Still no reaction—which, she hoped, meant everyone in the kitchen was asleep.

Once out in the hallway, Mordred whispered, "Where shall we meet?"

"Meet?" Candles lit the hallway only sporadically, and she was unable to make out his face. Only the dark scar she had painted on his cheek showed clearly. *"Meet?"*

He motioned for her to keep her voice down. He asked, "What is your plan?"

For an awful moment, she thought he was asking for her advice in strategy.

"Why are you here?" he asked.

She didn't like the sound of that "you" as opposed to "we." "What are you talking about? To rescue the prisoners from the dungeon, of course."

"I," he said, "am here to make sure Halbert is dead once and for all. No more resurrections for that phoenix."

She shook her head. Permanently stopping the wizard was important, but the armed men Nimue hoped Sir Dunsten was fetching from Camelot could do that. More pressing, they had to make sure Halbert did no more immediate harm. She told Mordred, "We know where the dungeon is. How will you find Halbert? Ask around which is his bedroom, then slit his throat while he sleeps?"

Mordred gave one of his infuriating committed-to-nothing grins—which may or may not have meant that that was his plan exactly.

"The important thing," she whispered, "is to get those boys out of here."

"The important thing is to kill Halbert. Else we shall never get away from here with those prisoners."

"There would be five extra men to help if we do the rescue first."

"I thought you just said they were boys."

"Mordred!" Her voice was getting too loud, and Mordred again gestured for quiet. "Do what you will," she told him, knowing he would in any case.

Just as he had known she would do what she wanted, she realized, about the time she got to the end of the corridor. That was why he had assumed they would separate. She looked back, but by then he was gone. *Get killed,* she thought at him. *I don't care.* But that was too much like ill-wishing. She sent a hasty wish for his safety after him.

Nimue turned the corner and someone's hand clapped over her mouth.

"Don't drop that jug," a voice breathed into her ear. "I promised it away." The hand lowered.

"Romola!" Nimue was shaking, partly startled, partly relieved. "Where have you been?"

"Where have *I* been? Where have *you* been? And where is your knight, Sir What's-His-Name, the King's friend?"

"Sir Mordred is busy practicing his pigheadedness. And he is not the King's . . ." She decided against complicating things further. "He is not coming to the dungeon with me. He wants to find the wizard first. What about you?"

"Me?" Romola snorted. "I'm not interested in wizards. I got Sir Litton to introduce me to the dungeon guards. They're expecting us—if we can get there before their watch is over."

"Sir Litton? The seneschal you were flirting with?"

"Aye."

Nimue didn't like this plan at all. "Three dungeon guards?" she asked, hoping they hadn't raised the number since her escape—as though three weren't bad enough.

Romola nodded.

"Plus this Litton . . ."

Romola was shaking her head.

"Won't he come looking for you?"

"No."

No. Nimue recalled that the girl had originally gone after Mordred armed with a dirk. Presumably Mordred had given it back. Nimue didn't want to hear anymore details. "Right," she said and headed for the area of the castle from which they could get to the dungeon.

"Ahem . . . Nimue?" Romola said. "The guards are expecting me and my friend, not me and my granny."

"I would have remembered," Nimue told her. Which she might have. Eventually.

She returned herself to her normal age and appearance. She guessed the guards were expecting a good-looking friend.

Romola blinked at her sudden transformation, but said nothing. She took a torch from the entry and led the way down. "It's us," she called. "Romola and Emeline."

The door swung open, and one of the guards had his arm around Nimue's waist before she passed through the portal.

"Spirits!" Romola announced, holding up Nimue's hand that was still clenched around the wine jug. "Don't hold her too tight, Cheston. She's ticklish and she might drop the jug."

The guard named Cheston laughed and pulled Nimue in even closer. The second man, a veteran of some battle or mischance that had left him with one leg shorter than the other, held Romola in similar fashion. The last one in the group was a youth whose face showed the first scraggly signs of a red beard. He put his arm around Nimue from the other side, while relieving her of the wine.

"Ay! Easy!" Romola said when he pulled the cork out with his teeth. "That's the kind of stuff's supposed to be drunk out of a goblet, you lout."

"Yeah, right, a goblet."

"Go on, you heard the lady," Cheston said, though nobody could possibly mistake Romola and Nimue for ladies. "Get out the fancy crockery." He tugged on Nimue's shoulder. "Come on, girl, relax. Don't you ever smile?"

She worked on it, while over his shoulder she watched the other guard kissing Romola's throat. This was going all wrong—and much too fast.

"Well, here, this is the best we can do." The scraggly bearded youth had found a wooden bowl, which he wiped with his sleeve. "A loving cup, just like the Greeks. Or was it the Romans?"

"No matter." Cheston emptied the wine into the bowl and handed it to Nimue. "Here, you need this—make you friendly." As she drank, he twirled a lock of her long blond hair.

What had she gotten herself into?

CHAPTER 7

The bowl went all around once. Then a second time. The young guard with the sparse beard had given up on Nimue and stood behind Romola nibbling her ear while Romola continued to laugh with the other man. Cheston looked as if he was considering a similar move. Nimue wished she could wish she were back in the cave at Avalon, asleep next to Merlin.

"So," said Romola, "are you going to show us what kind of dangerous people you guard down here?"

"Dangerous people," scoffed the man with the short leg, Aric, Romola had called him.

"I mean"—Romola leaned into him—"don't you have any *extra* rooms?"

"Oh, extra rooms." Cheston looked interested again.

The men scrambled to their feet and started marching the women down the hall.

Three men. The two of them against three men: Romola was probably self-confident enough to be satisfied with those odds.

"Excuse me," Nimue said. "We usually have this understanding: one at a time."

The three men looked at one another.

"One *each*, sweets," Romola said. "Not one of you at a time. Don't get all excited."

The two older men turned on the bearded youngster. "You guard the door, boy," Aric told him. "Rank hath its privileges and all that."

"But," the young man said, "but . . ."

Romola patted the young man's cheek and blew a kiss. "Long time till dawn," she said.

He still didn't like it. With a muttered oath, he threw himself onto one of the benches. Then he pulled out a knife.

Nimue's breath caught, but he only flung the knife into the tabletop. Then he pulled it out again. *Thump-thump,* over and over, the sound accompanied them down the hall.

"Here, let me hold that." Nimue took the torch while Cheston unlocked one of the cells. She hoped Romola's plan would start soon. And that it would be a good one.

"This here's a clean one," Cheston told her. "Ain't been used in a while, least not by prisoners. Not for this neither, I'd warrant." He winked at Romola though he still held Nimue's hand, probably hoping to find favor with both of them.

Romola took Aric's hand and led him in.

Nimue motioned, insisting for Cheston to enter first. Then she slammed the butt of the torch down on the back of his head. Whatever Romola's plan—it *wasn't* moving fast enough.

Romola, who had thrown her arms around Aric's neck, suddenly brought her knee up hard enough to leave him too breathless to cry out. From the folds of her skirt she pulled out her dirk and drove it between his ribs.

Nimue's head was beginning to spin. She stooped to pick up the dropped keys, then leaned against the wall. She could smell the warm thick blood even from here.

Romola took a step toward where Cheston was sprawled on the floor, and Nimue said hastily, "A gag will do."

Romola pointed a finger at her. "Don't you give out on me now," she warned. Still, she stepped around Cheston and went to the door of the cell.

"You have blood on you," Nimue warned. "He'll see."

"You get him in here then."

Nimue stepped into the hall. It took two tries before she could call, "Any of that wine left?" Could he hear the quaver in her voice?

The young guard held up the empty jug.

Now what? She swallowed hard and said, "Bring it anyway. We want to show you something." Did she sound saucy and pert, the way Romola did, or did she sound as foolish and scared to his ears as she did to hers?

But he got up; he brought the jug as he started down the corridor.

Nimue saw the glint of the knife still in Romola's hand, and she whispered, "You don't have to kill him."

"Don't start getting soft," Romola hissed.

Start? Nimue thought. This whole business had gotten beyond her even as it began. But Romola was willing to give her at least half a try, for she stepped behind the door, though she still held the knife—just in case.

"Here, give me that." Nimue took the jug from the guard. "Would you like a little surprise?"

He grinned, and probably never saw his friends' bodies before she broke the jug over his head.

She and Romola tied and gagged the two living men, then locked the cell behind them.

Merlin, Nimue thought, would never have believed it.

"Now," Romola said. "Where are they keeping Dolph?"

Nimue led the way to the cell from which she had escaped just four days earlier. But when she held the torch up to the bars, in the sputtering light she could clearly see there was only one person there.

Too late, too late.

But it couldn't be too late.

The wizard needed a new body every ten days. She'd only been gone four.

She had seen one youth killed—Griffith—which left five.

They couldn't, she thought, they couldn't have killed more to punish for the escape attempt. The young men were too valuable.

For a moment the quivering shadows and the surprise confused her, but then she recognized the round baby face of the youth who had been a prisoner before the St. George group got there. "Wystan!" she said. "Where are the others?"

The boy wore a look of befuddled terror. He sat on the floor with his knees huddled to his chest and stared at her for a long moment before he got his mouth to work. "Who . . . ?"

"It's me, Nimue." She saw a flicker of surprise, but she was used to getting a reaction whenever she said her name. "Nevil, I mean. You knew me as Nevil. I brought help." She fumbled with the key and flung the door open.

Wystan scuttled backwards. His hands fluttered anxiously, before settling on his knees, still drawn up close to his chest. "Help?" he asked—with a sidelong glance at Romola.

"We've gotten rid of the guards down here. Someone else is upstairs right now killing that wizard. Wystan, you're safe. Where are the others?"

But he wouldn't be convinced. "Only three of you?" he demanded in a shaking voice. "Three women?"

"Wystan!" she cried, but feared he couldn't be rushed. "The one upstairs is a knight. And, word has been sent to Camelot. *Where are the others?*"

"How has word been sent?" When she only looked at him in befuddled exasperation, he said, "Separate cells. They separated us after you made that fire. *You* made that fire, didn't you? Who is this knight?"

"What difference does that make? His name is Sir Mordred. But do you know which—"

"Because he's in danger. The fire started too quickly and you disappeared too thoroughly. They figured there was magic involved, and they figured you would be back. They've set a trap."

Nimue felt a chill up the back of her neck. "What kind of trap?"

"No time. You get the others." Standing, he indicated himself by resting his hand on his chest. "*I'll* warn this Mordred." He certainly seemed to have found his courage. Perhaps he was used to ordering women around.

Nimue ran her hand through her hair. Why did they have to keep separating? This was all so wrong, she could feel it. *Magic. Magic. Magic.* The warning sounded inside her head. The castle was suffused with this Halbert's evil power.

The boy said, "You'll be safe down here. Find the others, then wait in the guard area, on this side of the dungeon door. I'll bring your friend as soon as I can." His pale eyes lingered on Romola's bloody skirt. "You have a weapon?"

Sulkily, Romola handed him the dirk, which he slipped into his shirt as he stole out of the cell and back toward the guard area.

Nimue shuddered despite herself. "Let's find Dolph," she told Romola.

They went down the hall, knocking and calling at each door until there was only one door left.

"He said they were taken to separate cells," Nimue said. Plotting was hard, and her head ached.

"Maybe this leads to a different wing of cells?" Romola pointed to the latch, which had no lock.

Nimue could imagine. *Deepest dungeon,* she thought. *Torture room.* She stood with her hand on the door. She closed her eyes and tried to concentrate. But her mind felt strange, stuffed with cotton, the mental equivalent of a head cold; and she got vague and conflicting images. She opened the door.

This was a large room: The torch Romola held, which had burned almost to the last, lit only part of it. But that was enough to see she had been right.

The door swung closed behind them, smacking Nimue's bottom. Her attention, however, was on the shackles set high up on the wall, high enough so that a man with his wrists chained would dangle painfully, his feet not touching ground. Whips, of course. And thumbscrews. She recognized the back-breaking wheel and its cousin, the rack. Also an iron maiden. There were other devices with which she was thankfully unfamiliar. There was also a large metal cage where prisoners could be held, presumably to watch others being questioned before their own turn. It was from this dark corner that a voice called out, "Romola?"

"Dolph!" Romola ran forward, bringing the circle of light with her so that Nimue could see Dolph and the five youths with him.

Nimue paused, mid-step.

"The keys, Nimue. Hurry." Romola hugged her husband through the bars.

The *five* youths . . .

Oh, no. Oh, no.

"Nimue." Finally Romola stepped back, looking at Nimue. "What's the matter?"

"Dolph . . ." Nimue counted off. Somehow she managed to keep her voice relatively even. "Then there's the cooper's nephew, Boy, cobbler's apprentice, wainwright—I'm sorry, I don't know all your names." A tremor worked its way into her throat. "So what is Evan—whose body I *saw* Halbert take—what is *Evan* doing in there with you?"

The sixth man, who hadn't approached the front of the cage with the others, remained seated. Finally, slowly, he lifted his face to her: all curly hair and teeth, Evan, just as she remembered. But: "I don't be Evan nor Halbert," he said hoarsely. "I be Wystan."

Nimue didn't dispute it. She knew it for truth as soon as he spoke, and she called herself a fool for having missed all the signs the false Wystan had let pass.

The young men in the prison called out to her:

"Wizard made a second change . . ."

"They kept asking about you . . ."

"He said fight magic with magic . . ."

"It was the same as before . . ."

They all spoke at once, except for Reynard's Boy, who may—for all Nimue knew—have been too simple for speech. "I know, I know," she said, too drained to fight the realization.

"Well, I don't," Romola said. "I don't understand any of it. What is going on?"

Nimue felt cold and numb. Which was good. The pain would set in later. What had she done?

She said, "Halbert transformed himself again—this time before he started to age. Now Halbert looks like Wystan, Wystan has poor dead Evan's body, and I,"— she closed her eyes—"I told Halbert enough to get Sir Mordred killed: The trap was down here all along." She hadn't trusted Mordred, but she was the one who had betrayed him.

Wystan scrambled to his feet. Now he grabbed her hand through the bars. "You be a famous sorceress—Dolph sez. You tell me: What of this body? Will it wear out like all of wizard's other bodies?"

"I don't know," she said as calmly as she could. She wished . . . she wasn't sure how to wish, and so wished, once more, for everyone's well-being. Much good *that* wish had done so far. "I just don't know, Wystan," she admitted.

Romola said, "Well, talking is not going to help anything. Here, give me the keys." She handed Nimue the almost exhausted torch.

But none of the keys fit.

Of course they wouldn't.

"Maybe there's another set of keys out in the guard area?" one of the prisoners suggested hopefully.

Nimue mentally reached out, but this time the barrier was no longer cotton-stuffing soft. "We won't be able to get the door to this room open," she said.

Romola looked up, startled, from trying a key she had already seen wouldn't work. "That door doesn't have a lock."

It didn't. Wizards didn't need locks.

Nimue said nothing.

Romola looked at her quizzically. "It doesn't have a lock," she insisted. She started to back up slowly, then turned and ran to the door. She pulled, she pushed, she beat her hands on it. "It doesn't have a lock!"

The torch sputtered one more time, then went out entirely, leaving the darkened room with an oily, singed smell.

Nimue blindly eased down with her back to the torture chamber's cage. She could hear Romola still raging against the door and someone behind her, presumably Wystan or maybe it was the wainwright with his broken fingers, whimpering softly.

Calm down. Think rationally. Think like Halbert. She closed her eyes, mere habit for there was nothing in this total darkness that could interfere with concentration. What would the wizard's next move be? Her mind fluttered off in several directions at once.

And suddenly settled on: Sir Dunsten.

She bit her lip and clenched her hands to keep from crying out loud. That was something else she had told Halbert—blithely handing out lethal information—that they'd sent to Camelot for help. She went over the conversation trying to remember the exact words. Had she actually volunteered the portly knight's name?

No, she decided. She had not spoken his name. And the wizard hadn't pressed, perhaps afraid to arouse suspicion.

Now, if she were Halbert, how would she stop an unknown knight from alerting the King? Men sent after him tonight would never catch up. Magic? Difficult, very difficult on a nameless, faceless man. He'd need more details first.

A shiver coincided with the memory of what room she was in. A room made to wring details out of the reluctant.

Oh, Merlin, she moaned to herself. *What have I done?* And, more importantly, *What should I do now?*

CHAPTER 8

A long time passed in the darkness.

Then, finally, from the other side of the unlocked door that wouldn't open, a voice warned, "Do not try anything. Sir Bayard has a knife to Sir Mordred's throat."

Bayard. According to Dunsten and Mordred, Bayard was the lord who held Castle Ridgemont. A lord who, apparently, had no complaint against aiding a wizard-uncle who stole young men from the countryside and used them to prolong his own life. A lord who either took his orders from a renegade wizard, or had similar goals.

If Romola, still by the door, had a plan, and if someone having a knife to Mordred's throat disrupted it, she made no sound to indicate so.

The heavy door banged open and the room was flooded by the light of torches, which flickered and crackled and stank of pitch. A dozen armed men crowded in, the first of whom did, indeed, have a knife to Mordred's throat.

Nimue scrambled to her feet. "Don't let him into your minds," she warned the prisoners, remembering how Evan, Roswald's son—the real Evan—had died not even struggling. "Make him fight for every advantage."

The man she now knew as the wizard Halbert, dressed in Wystan's body, swept into the room. "Ah! So nice to have everybody back together again. I *do* enjoy a good reunion, don't you? Get up off the floor, my dear, there is no telling who has died on that spot." This last was addressed to Romola, who was on her knees by the door. Apparently the sheer number of armed knights and guards was enough to persuade her not to try to take them on. Then Halbert grinned at Nimue, which twisted the baby fat of Wystan's face into a leer. "At last we meet properly, my Lady Nimue. I have looked forward to this occasion for the past several years."

Ignoring him, Nimue asked, "Sir Mordred, are you unharmed?"

"He is quite undamaged," Halbert answered before Mordred had a chance to say anything—assurance that he was unharmed, or complaint that her foolishness had brought them all to this. "For the moment," the wizard added. "Unfortunately, the same cannot be said for several of Sir Bayard's guards." He gave his leering smile again. "Sir Bayard is quite distressed."

Nimue did not think Sir Bayard looked at all overcome by grief.

"You will be next," Mordred promised Halbert in his quiet, dispassionate voice.

Though Bayard twisted Mordred's arm a bit higher, his uncle never reacted. He only said, "Bring the girl."

Nimue braced herself, but it was Romola they went after. One of the men grabbed the innkeeper's daughter by the arm and hauled her to her feet. The wizard smiled at each of them in turn: Nimue and Romola. "'Word has been sent to Camelot,'" he said, Nimue's own words come back to haunt her. "By whom?"

"Don't answer," Nimue said. "His power is less not knowing."

Romola had joined them after they'd parted with Sir Dunsten and had no way of knowing his name, and she simply continued to glare at her captors.

Mordred's face showed not a flicker, but Halbert had caught to whom Nimue meant her warning. He said, "We have time. There is no way any messenger could have reached Camelot yet. Except for Merlin. And Merlin is no longer with us." He smiled a bit too benignly. "Is he, Nimue?"

By his patronizing tone, he believed the stories that Merlin was her prisoner: As though a powerful magician who could tell the future would suddenly go mad for a silly young thing—unable or unwilling to stop her from implanting him in an oak tree. She said nothing to correct the misperception.

His left hand clutched at his chest, at the ruby pendant she now knew was hidden beneath his shirt. But he reached out with his other hand and touched her hair. "Pretty," he mused. "I like pretty things." The back of his hand rubbed her cheek.

She flinched, which he seemed to like. His finger traced her jaw, caressed her neck.

There was a momentary disturbance: Mordred twisted to break the hold of the knights who held him. Halbert's nephew, Bayard, kicked Mordred's leg out from under him, which caused the arm already twisted behind his back to go higher yet. One of the other knights reached in and yanked the back of his hair, bringing his chin up so that Bayard could get his knife in closer. Halbert's men all moved quickly and efficiently.

In the interval between two heartbeats, Nimue tried to impose her own will on the wizard while he was distracted. But she knew she was outmatched, and she doubted her decision even as she made it.

Which lessened her power still more.

The cell was totally silent as the knights waited for their orders, and the prisoners waited to learn what would become of them.

None of them was aware of the struggle that had decided everything.

In the silence, the wizard's voice sounded inside her head: *Shall I give them the word, my Lady?*

She answered, also without words: *Please spare him.*

Give me the ring.

Nimue closed in around herself.

Halbert raised his eyebrows at his nephew. The knife, already touching Mordred's throat, started to indent the skin. Bayard grinned, not averse to follow his uncle's orders.

Nimue saw that he *was* going to do it. She pulled the ring off and threw it at

Halbert's face. "Use it and die," she said, halfway between warning and threat, with a bit of wish thrown in.

The wizard caught the ring in midair. He slipped it on his little finger, then slapped her with the same hand. "Stupid girl," he hissed. "I do not like children, and I do not like children's games. Did you think your silly disguises could fool me long? Hmmm? Young *boy*? And this." He indicated the mud-daubed scar on Mordred's cheek. "Wash that off," he ordered.

"Tell me," Mordred demanded of Bayard, "do you enjoy being this second-rate wizard's lickspittle?"

Unperturbed, one of the castle knights knocked the lid off a large barrel in the corner, and Bayard finally put his knife away to free both hands so that he could be the one to force Mordred's face into the water.

Mordred came up sputtering and spitting. But before he could catch his breath, Bayard pushed him back under.

Mordred's free hand tried to grab hold of him, but one of the other knights twisted that arm too. Bayard let him up for one gasp, dunked him again, kept him in this time.

"Word has been sent to Camelot by whom?" Halbert asked.

Nimue kept her mind blank.

"Word has been sent to Camelot by whom?"

She fought away a mental picture of Sir Dunsten.

"Word has been sent to Camelot by whom?" Halbert was losing his temper, and that affected his concentration, making him less difficult to withstand.

Bayard jerked Mordred back, which allowed him to slump to the floor, coughing almost to the point of retching.

"Wrong tactic, wizard," Mordred finally managed to gasp. "She doesn't like me enough to care what you do."

Though Nimue would have wished for this to be true, somehow it already wasn't.

The wizard smiled. "We shall see."

But Bayard jerked his head toward the door and said to his uncle, "We need to talk."

Between great hacking coughs, Mordred said, "What makes you think he cares what you have to say?"

Nimue hoped the moment of satisfaction he got from saying this was worthwhile, for Bayard gave him a vicious kick before leading his uncle away from the group.

Nimue strained to hear their conversation in the far corner, but couldn't make out anything. Once she realized this, she knelt beside Mordred, who was pale and still bent double, with his hair hanging limp and dripping. The guards did nothing to stop her as she anxiously laid her hands on Mordred's shoulders—a swordsman's powerful muscles there, she couldn't help but notice, despite his professed disdain for knighthood and the chivalric code.

One of the other knights stepped forward and pushed her away with—not exactly a kick—but a foot placed squarely on her shoulder.

"No talking," Bayard snarled, coming up behind them.

"Got you all straightened out now, has he, Bayard?" Mordred asked.

Halbert scowled, but Bayard, the one belittled, smiled. Actually he had a pleasant face which, along with his too-round body, hinted at good humor and an enjoyment of the easy life. But his eyes had nothing of laughter in them. "Lord Halbert has special plans for your body, boy, or I would cut out that foul tongue of yours and shove it down your throat."

But Mordred only said, "You could try."

Nimue cringed inwardly at this reckless bravado, which at best could get Mordred killed.

Bayard's hands curled into fists, but he kept them at his belt. "Oh, believe me, I will. If there is anything left after my uncle is through with you."

Once more Nimue pictured Evan—his body being dragged out of the cell, crumpled and maimed. And still alive? She had assumed they were removing his corpse.

But he may have been simply dying, not yet dead. With Evan, surely it didn't make that much difference: He must have died within a very short time. And the guards had no grudge with him. Still, she reflected, whether the wizard's victims died as part of the magical process, or soon afterward, Mordred wouldn't want to spend his last moments with a vengeful Bayard. All she had to do was look around this room to know he had the skills and equipment to make someone's last moments interminable.

"Well-trained lap dog," Mordred goaded Bayard. "You're incredibly fearless—virile even—with a wizard behind you."

Bayard's breathing was suddenly audible.

"Enough," the wizard snapped at Mordred. He put a hand on his nephew's arm. "He is all talk because he knows he is helpless—a snapping little dog."

"His prattling bothers me not one whit," Bayard said, trying for the supercilious smile again. But then he dropped it. "He just seems to have such delicate sensibilities for what he is: bastard. Bastard born of *incest.*"

Mordred's expression was set. No doubt he'd had this thrown in his face often enough before.

"I don't know how he can stand to think what he is," Bayard continued. "An abomination before God and man. If I were you, Uncle, I would be revolted at the idea of inhabiting his vile body, no matter what the gains."

Gains? Nimue thought.

Mordred said, "Which shows why he's the master and you the lackey."

"Just put him in the cell," the wizard commanded before Bayard could answer. "He would say anything to delay." Then, as one of the guards yanked Mordred to his feet, Halbert cautioned, "Gently. Gently. I don't want any bruises on what will soon be my body."

The guard who shoved Mordred into the cell, then jerked his head toward Nimue and Romola, in a questioning motion.

Halbert said, "The women stay out."

Which surely did not bode well.

As the door clanged shut, the wizard continued in a conversational tone, "Sir Mordred, you may be interested to know it was Sir Bayard who pointed out that we should not kill you. I wasn't thinking properly, what with memories of old times and all. You have cost me dear. But if that gives you any joy, think what you have cost the peasants around Castle Ridgemont. Consider—if you had minded your own business four years ago—all the young men who would still be alive, contentedly working the fields hereabouts today."

Nimue could see a spasm in Mordred's hand as he held on to one of the bars of the prisoners' cage.

Halbert continued. "All I needed was the right opportunity. To get back at you. To get back at that wretched woman and miserable child who ruined everything last time. Their turn will come later, when I go to Camelot and everybody thinks I am you. And, oh Nimue, think of the possibilities there."

It made sense. Oh, damn, it made sense. She had had a hard time reconciling Merlin's dire predictions with the young knight she had come to know over the past day: Stern. Arrogant. Ruthless perhaps, but not cruel. And in fact probably not nearly so ruthless as he would like to be thought. But Halbert . . . Halbert in Mordred's body . . . That thought left a cold, empty spot in her chest.

"Now, the two women." Halbert circled Nimue and Romola, stroked his chin and pursed his lips. "And, once again, the question of who was sent to the King. How best to discover that? Your thoughts, Bayard?"

"The witch," Bayard recommended. "She's the one who knows."

The wizard smiled. "That is why I would say the dark-haired beauty. She doesn't know the name of the messenger, so if she dies . . . no loss."

Bayard shrugged, indifferent.

Dolph, in the large cage, stretched his hand out to his wife, but couldn't quite reach. "Romola."

"Oh, no maudlin displays, please," the wizard said. "Not from you, anyway. Only from someone who knows something. Sir Bayard, what do you recommend? Metal-tipped whips, hot brands, the knives?"

"Hmmm," Bayard said. "Still, there is no need to mark up her body right away, is there? Some of us may go in for that sort of thing but others get their pleasure"—he smiled—"different ways. Eh, Sylvanus?" He nudged one of the guards. This got a favorable reaction from all of them. "I see no reason not to please everyone."

"No!" Romola cried. But the man named Sylvanus was already behind her, and he pinned her arms back. She tried to kick and wriggle her way free, but the man was so much stronger.

"Now, now, my dear," the wizard said. "It will all be over soon. Well, eventually."

The ominous effect he wanted to create was disturbed by the clatter of feet on the stairs and the sound of panting. Distracted and annoyed, Halbert thundered, "What in the name of all the powers of Hell is it now?"

Bayard held his sword at the ready, but when the door opened, it was one of the other knights from the castle. "What?" Bayard snapped at him.

"Sir, someone is at the castle gate."

"It's the middle of the night."

"Yes, sir, it is."

Bayard paused to take a calming breath before answering, "So tell whoever it is to go away."

"It is Sir Lancelot Dulac, sir, and he will not go away."

Nimue was already facing Mordred, so she saw the flicker of surprise. An instant later, when Bayard and Halbert turned, it was gone.

Still facing the prisoners, Bayard told his man, "Tell him to come back in the morning."

"Wait," said Halbert. "When has Lancelot ever stopped by here for a friendly visit?" He looked from Mordred in the cage to Nimue, and Nimue hoped her face told as little as Mordred's. Slowly, as if to convince himself also, Halbert said, "Word could not have reached Camelot yet. *Could not.* It has to be a coincidence."

"Coincidence or not," Bayard said, "we do not want the man here."

Halbert continued to scrutinize the prisoners.

Mordred smiled enigmatically.

The wizard's hand was at his chest, stroking the ruby pendant under his shirt.

Nimue, who didn't dare wish that Lancelot would demand entrance because that might endanger his life, held her breath.

"I think," Halbert said to his nephew, but hesitantly, "I think you had better talk to Sir Lancelot yourself and try to find out how much he knows."

As soon as Bayard was gone, Halbert said to the remaining knights and guards, "I believe we were about to try an experiment of sorts with the girl."

"Sir Dunsten," Nimue said.

Mordred, for once taken totally by surprise, swore.

Halbert's eyes shifted from one to the other, weighing, evaluating. "Thank you," he said, but cautiously. "That was unexpectedly reasonable of you."

"Little good it will do you," Nimue said. She was making this up as she went along, and dared a wish that her gamble wouldn't cost Dunsten his life. Everything hinged on the fact that the first thing Halbert had demanded from his position of power had been—not the name of the messenger—but Merlin's ring. She said, "Mordred overrated you when he called you a second-rate wizard. Merlin would not have rated you so high."

Halbert grinned. "But Merlin is dead."

"No, he is *not*."

Halbert shrugged. "Entombed or entrapped someplace safe, out of the way for both of us."

Nimue couldn't help but smile. "Safer than you think," she told him.

Halbert held up his hand. The ring caught a reflection of the torches and sparkled. "But his power, how safe is that?"

"Safer," Nimue repeated, "than you think." It was as close as she would come to warning him.

The wizard grinned at what must seem to him desperate bluster. It was a grin such as the real Wystan would never have worn; there was condescension there, and cruelty—and it looked ludicrous, though deadly, on his chubby, childish face. Halbert lifted his other hand too, and now held both above his head. "By all the powers of darkness," he intoned, "in the name of Lucifer, whom God himself could not contain—"

There was a sudden flash of light that engirdled the wizard: no thunder, but a crackling that Nimue recognized as some distant relation to what Merlin called static electricity. One of the prisoners cried out, perhaps misunderstanding, perhaps only frightened by the sudden brightness that overcame every shadow in that torch-lit room. Nimue squinted, and saw Halbert's smile frozen. She had to blink several times, but the next image she caught was of the wizard clawing at his hand that bore Merlin's ring. "Get it off!" he screamed. "Get it off!"

One of the guards stepped forward warily.

"Get the ring off!" The wizard dropped to his knees, then fell writhing to the floor.

The guard cringed, but put his own hand through the dazzling outline that surrounded the wizard. And jumped back with a howl of pain.

Nimue turned her face, but could still smell the singed flesh.

"Somebody help me!" Halbert cried. "Damn you! I can heal any injuries! I can reward you beyond your dreams!"

But most of those who were not looking at him in fascinated horror were eyeing the guard who knelt bent over what was left of his hand; and the rest were gazing at the door, looking ready to bolt.

Nimue found that she could see the far wall through Halbert even as he continued to threaten and beg. And he was quickly fading.

"Somebody *do* something!" But by then the wizard's voice was just about all that was left. "Do something," it repeated, or echoed, "do something, do something . . ."

And then the light was gone.

As was the crackling energy in the air.

And the wizard.

There was a dull *clunk!* as Merlin's ring hit the dirt floor. Nimue thought she might have heard a tiny squeak of pleading that lifted and carried itself away on little bat wings, but it was lost before she could be sure it had ever been there.

One of the guards swore, and pushed her aside on his way out the door. Most of the others followed, though three remained, not counting the injured man. One of these looked too stupefied by the events to be of any concern. Of the others, Nimue chose the one closer to her and ran at him full speed. The collision sent him staggering backwards.

Ever-quick Romola put her foot out and he toppled, falling against the prisoners' cage.

"Witches!" the man snarled. His balance recovered, he took a step toward Romola, who was closer.

But Mordred grabbed him through the bars and slammed him back against the cold metal.

"Don't move," Nimue warned, though that hardly seemed necessary, as Mordred had already whipped away the man's dagger from his belt and was holding it to his throat. "Twitch, and I'll roast your innards." That was pure fiction: She'd had nothing to do with what had happened to the wizard. It had been the ring, defending itself. But the expressions on the surrounding faces showed little doubt of her ability. "Now . . ."—she pointed at the one guard who remained, beyond the one incapacitated by injury and the other by fear—"who has the key?"

The man looked around, desperate to believe she could be addressing someone—anyone—else. "Sylvanus," he finally whispered, "my Lady. One of the ones who ran away."

"There must be more than one."

"In the guard area, my Lady."

"*In the guard area?*" she repeated, letting all her anger, her exasperation, show.

"My Lady, I swear it's true."

"I want you to get it."

Several of the prisoners started to talk at once, offering advice, though it was Romola's voice that cut through. "It would be safer if I—"

Nimue held up a warning hand, and the silence was instant and total. There was too much danger of someone passing by the top of the stairs, of glancing down and seeing Romola. Very quietly, very calmly, she asked the guard, "Do you think my magic cannot go around corners?"

He shook his head vigorously.

"If you go and get the key—quickly—and bring it back, you will not be harmed," she assured him. "Do not let me *suspect* your sincerity. Do you understand?"

"My Lady," he whispered.

"Do you understand what I'm saying?" she repeated, for it was urgent that he believe.

Wordlessly he nodded.

And, indeed, he was back before Nimue would have thought humanly possible. But then it took him twice as long as it should have to unlock the door, because his hand kept shaking.

"In!" Romola commanded the third guard, the one who—since this whole thing began—had not moved except to shiver. The cooper's nephew yanked up the man with the burnt hand and fairly threw him in also.

"Come," Nimue said to Reynard's half-wit boy who had worked himself back into a corner and showed no sign of moving. The others had practically knocked each other down in their haste to get out. "The worst is over now." She sincerely hoped she was right. "You are safe."

The youth finally came out, and Nimue turned to find Mordred had swept up one of the dropped swords, and now he had it pointed at the chest of the man who had gone for the key.

"Wait! I promised if he cooperated we wouldn't kill him." Even as she said it, she knew why, of all the guards, Mordred would have cause to kill this man: He was the guard who had helped Bayard hold Mordred under water.

"Never," Mordred told her, "do that again." When he was angry, he didn't get loud, but instead would lower his voice and speak from the back of his throat. "Don't *you* ever make promises *I* am supposed to keep."

Nimue nodded.

Mordred slowly lowered the sword, and the knight hurried into the cage unbidden, to be locked safely away.

"Let's go," the wainwright said, "before anybody of 'em others comes back."

"Wait." Nimue frantically searched the floor.

"I have it." Mordred held out Merlin's ring in his palm. "It rolled after it fell."

She breathed a sigh of relief. How could she have let it out of her sight, out of her thoughts, even for a moment? She reached, and Mordred subtly changed position: He didn't exactly close the hand, but suddenly his long fingers were curved more protectively, more possessively, around the ring.

"Is that how you did it?" he asked. "With this?"

Nimue spoke very evenly. "The ring has defenses of its own."

"But it doesn't harm you," he pointed out.

Nimue sighed. She had repeatedly misinterpreted and misjudged Mordred, but it hurt to see that he didn't understand her, either. "People persist in seeing me as a rival to Merlin, a competitor." She shook her head. "Merlin was sick. He was worn out and dying. He had me put him under a spell until such time as Arthur and Britain would need him. He gave me the ring—not for the ring to protect me, but for me to protect the ring. Not," she added, "that it needs much protecting."

"So you're the only one who can use it?"

"Yes." She said it for Merlin's sake, who was defenseless and couldn't be revived without it.

Mordred didn't believe her. She could see that. Nobody would who considered the matter: Why would the ring need to be protected if she was the only one who could use it? She had realized he might not believe, and might be angry at her deception. What she hadn't counted on was that he didn't believe—and he was hurt by her lack of trust.

"I see," he said. His eyes, that unlikely shade of gray, looked away. For once—rumpled, damp, and bedraggled—he was the one who looked in need of protecting. He seemed to suddenly notice his hand, half closed around the ring, and he held it out to her, flat-palmed.

Nimue quickly snatched the ring away without looking at him, lest he change his mind.

"I would have given it to you anyway," he said as she slipped the band back on her thumb.

Because she had hurt him, after time and again he had proved true, she admitted, "Halbert died because of the way he obtained the ring—by force." She sent a wish flying that her betrayal wouldn't cause harm later on. "If the ring had been freely given, or found, that would have made all the difference."

As you found it, she might have said.

Mordred stepped back, and gave her a formal salute with his sword. He addressed the men who had been the wizard's prisoners. "I would suggest that you stay together. I doubt anyone is going to be willing to take you on after what they have witnessed happening to the wizard. If Lancelot is still at the gates, you might want to get the drawbridge down to let him in." He looked them over.

As did Nimue.

Untrained, badly armed peasants. Besides the sword Mordred had taken, there were two more from the other two guards, plus the one dagger, and a club one of the guards who had fled the room had dropped. It took years of training to master a sword. Nimue guessed anybody from this group who tried to use one would likely be more hazard to himself and his friends than to any enemy.

"Or stay here," Mordred advised earnestly. "But whatever you do, stay together." He turned, then suddenly turned back, pausing only long enough to sweep up Romola's hand and give it a kiss, and then he was running up the stairs.

"Be careful," Nimue called, but she couldn't tell if he'd heard.

Dolph came and stood by his wife and gave a snort of disapproval. "Where's he off to, then?" He took her hand that Mordred had kissed and held it, an uncharacteristically possessive gesture. "And why's he wearing my clothes?"

Nimue only bothered with the first part. "To kill Bayard, I imagine. Come, let us go."

Sluggishly, the group began to move toward the door.

Young Wystan, looking like Evan, grabbed her arm. "Look at my face," he said. "Tell me. Do there be any change?"

"What?" she asked, distracted, her mind arguing with itself: that the safest place for these people might, in fact, be here.

"He sez"—Wystan indicated the wainwright who pretended to be preoccupied with the abandoned dagger—"that I be growing old. Like wizard."

"Oh Wystan!" Nimue took a closer look, saw nothing more than fatigue and worry. "Even if you were, he couldn't tell that in this light." That, obviously, was poor reassurance. Wystan surely needed to hear better than that. She added, "We're all a bit haggard. We have been up all night, and we have all been very afraid. Truly, I don't see anything else." She nodded toward the wainwright, happy for the excuse to look away from Wystan. "He's been in a great deal of pain—his hand was broken almost a week ago, and he's taking his pain and frustration out on you. I *have* to go now. The drawbridge needs lowering if Sir Lancelot is to get in. You'll be fine."

He let go of her arm but didn't answer.

The cobbler's apprentice, who had chosen the abandoned club as a weapon, tossed Wystan a long, sharpened stick that had been propped against one of the walls. Dolph and the cooper's nephew had picked up the swords that had belonged to the guards. The wainwright, with at least a couple broken fingers on either hand, wasn't going to be of much use, but he chose the dagger. Romola took the poker that was by the fireplace, and Nimue wouldn't take any weapon. The only other unarmed person was Reynard's Boy. He clung to Nimue and in any case nobody trusted him with anything sharp.

In fact, seeing the improper way most of the weapons were held, and the way the men were swinging them about, Nimue felt a cold dread that they would probably be of more help to Bayard than to Mordred.

If the former prisoners were counting on a fight, the men of Castle Ridgemont didn't seem willing to oblige them. Nimue and her companions made it outside without seeing anyone, which was odd even for this hour somewhere between night and morning. It wasn't until they rounded a corner on the way to the drawbridge that they surprised two fully armed knights headed the same way but coming from a different direction.

Dolph lifted his sword, brandishing it much as a housewife might wave a flail to beat a rug.

The two knights took one look at Nimue, then turned and ran.

"Behind every successful man, there stands a strong woman," Dolph observed, with a wink for Nimue, to show he had no delusions why they had run.

Despite the seriousness of the situation, she couldn't help but smile. In another moment, the sound of nearby fighting turned the smile to a grimace.

"Hush," one of them said to Boy, who was humming loudly. Then, "What is it?"

Unsure of her voice, she pointed to the left, and up one level. "Sword fight," she managed to squeak. She could hear the distinctive clash of metal on metal.

Mordred, she thought, *don't get yourself killed now*. Lancelot was the most competent knight of Camelot. Why didn't Mordred leave the fighting to him? "Look." She pointed. "The bridge is down that way. If anyone is guarding it . . ." She looked at Dolph's sword and hesitated.

Dolph grinned. "Don't worry. If worst comes to worst, I'll call out, 'Nimue, get this guard!' and they won't even stop to check if you're really there."

She wanted to hug him, but there wasn't time. She ran in the direction from which she could still hear the metallic clangs. She was dimly aware of shadows that scurried out of her way, but she didn't stop for them.

Mordred and Bayard were fighting on the bastion that overlooked the drawbridge—moving much too fast for her to dare try to intervene with magic. She could hear Sir Lancelot from below, yelling at whoever manned the bridge, demanding entrance.

Nimue stifled a cry for Mordred to look out: He knew what he was doing, and she could prove a fatal distraction.

He ducked the blow, missed an opening that could have ended the fight, but forced Bayard to take a backwards step.

"My Lord, look out!" one of the Ridgemont guards called as Bayard came dangerously close to an open embrasure—a fall to certain death.

That was Mordred's bad luck, but when Nimue heard the sound of running behind her, she whirled around. "Don't move," she warned the knights who were rushing to Bayard's aid.

Their eyes glinted in the starlight as they looked, each to check the others' reactions. One by one their swords lowered.

"Get back. *I said back!*" She used what Merlin had called his best John Barrymore voice. Whoever John Barrymore was, it worked.

There was a loud *screech* and *thud*: the drawbridge. Somehow the inexperienced youths of St. George had accomplished their task. Lancelot wouldn't join the fight, now that Bayard and Mordred had engaged in single combat, but she hoped Lancelot could keep the fight fair. Once he actually got up here.

Mordred seemed to be holding his own: Bayard was more experienced and had the advantage of strength, but Mordred was quicker and in better physical condition, so he would have more stamina. Their swords locked for a moment; Nimue could see that Bayard said something, although the dawn breeze carried away the words. Mordred didn't answer the gibe; he slid his sword down and around while he jumped to the side.

Bayard got his leg behind Mordred's, and the younger knight staggered, parried a blow, fell, rolled in time to avoid another thrust that skewered a corner of Dolph's shirt. But Bayard's sword snagged on the uneven stone banquette, then skittered uncontrollably, and put him, momentarily, off balance.

Mordred's own foot lashed out. Bayard threw his weight backwards, and he fell out of Mordred's reach. Mordred was back on his feet first, but Bayard had landed by the parapet and found a loose stone that he heaved at Mordred's head. Mordred ducked, and then Bayard was back up also.

Lancelot's head suddenly appeared over the edge of the battlement, which meant that—once through the gate—he had climbed the sheer face of the rampart rather than follow the boulevard that wound its way about the inside of the walls.

"Lance!" Nimue yelled warning as Bayard swung wide, level with Lancelot's neck.

Mordred jumped in to protect Lancelot. But, although Lancelot had earned his reputation as Arthur's best knight almost a quarter century ago, it was not merely memory of past glories that kept him first. His head bobbed down behind the wall, then he seemed to ricochet back up and over the edge to land on his feet.

Mordred, however, had overreached in his attempt to keep Lancelot from decapitation. Bayard swung hard, and Mordred's sword went flying. Mordred spun, retrieved the sword, and turned back at a ready crouch.

But Bayard was not there. Instead of going after Mordred, he had faced about and engaged Lancelot. It made no sense at all, for—as long as the fight had proceeded fairly—Lancelot was restrained by the rules of chivalry from interfering. And if anyone could be counted on to abide by the rules of chivalry, it would be Lancelot.

Bayard had been hard-pressed against Mordred. Against Lancelot, he had no chance at all. In another instant his sword clattered to the ground.

It was then that his logic suddenly became clear.

"Mercy, sir knight," he said, dropping to his knees. Then, to his men, "Everyone." They all offered their swords, hilts first.

Lancelot sheathed his sword, and indicated for Bayard's men to do likewise.

"No!" Mordred cried. "Kill him!"

Lancelot looked up, startled. He grabbed the younger knight by the wrist, as though afraid Mordred would go after Bayard himself. "I have granted him mercy."

"No, listen." Mordred's voice shook, but in another instant he had it back under control. "This man is responsible for abducting countless young village boys who—"

"It wasn't me!" Bayard objected. "It's my uncle, the wizard Halbert! I have done nothing wrong. Find him."

Lancelot looked to Mordred for a response.

"He's dead," Mordred said.

Nimue, watching Bayard, saw no reaction.

"It was the two of them," Mordred conceded. "Halbert needed the boys to perform his loathsome rejuvenation spells, and Bayard provided them from the surrounding area."

"It was not *just* rejuvenation," Bayard said. "He needed them to live. And the effects on the youths were temporary; they were returned unharmed."

"Unharmed?" Nimue cried, unable to keep silent, to leave this to the men. "They were dead."

"No!" Bayard protested. "You must be mistaken. Weak, yes. Perhaps temporarily confused—"

Nimue shook from anger. "I saw Evan, Roswald's son, of the town of St. George, *dead*. Not weak. Not confused. Dead."

Bayard looked from Nimue to Lancelot, avoided Mordred, came back to Nimue. "Merciful saints in Heaven," he said, his voice a reedy whisper, "he tricked me.

Uncle Halbert assured me . . . If I had ever thought . . ." He shook his head. "This is terrible."

"It seems," said Lancelot, "you have all been ill-used. But the man responsible is now under God's jurisdiction."

"No," Mordred protested. "No, we are not that gullible." To Bayard, he said, "You almost killed me in there, and you were about to—Lancelot, he was about to rape and torture a young peasant woman who was in our company, and he stood by while Halbert maltreated Nimue. He knew. *He knew.*"

"Was anybody killed?" Bayard asked, having found his voice again. "Was anybody tortured? My dear boy, my only intention was to frighten you. You must admit: You *were* frightened?"

Mordred's fingers tightened on his sword.

Nimue saw Lancelot was watching warily, as if expecting Mordred to try something rash and sneaky. As if he were suspicious of *him.*

"My Lady Nimue," Bayard pleaded. "I was not there when you saw the terrible things you saw. Was I? Tell him I was not there when Halbert did his evil magic. Tell him whether you saw me actually harm anyone."

Nimue had to admit, "He wasn't there. He harmed no one in my sight."

"This man is guilty of heinous crimes," Mordred protested to Lancelot, "against me, and against my companions. Once before he was involved in his uncle's crimes, and slipped away from just retribution by claiming ignorance. I demand that you withdraw from a situation in which you are not involved, and let me finish what you have interrupted."

"When he raised his sword at me," Lancelot said evenly, though Nimue knew him well enough to suspect he was becoming heated, "I became involved. It seems to me that misunderstandings and harsh words have compounded—"

"Oh, really!" Mordred said in exasperation.

"Yes, well,"—Lancelot's tone remained stoically polite despite Mordred's bitter sarcasm—"in any case, now it is for the King to say."

"Dammit! He's mine!"

Lancelot raised his eyebrows and stopped trying to convince Mordred.

"You fool!" Mordred's voice was a throaty whisper. "You interfering stooge! You have no idea what has been going on here. How dare you come in here, with your archaic sense of fair play, feeding your sense of self-worth with empty magnanimous gestures that endanger all? This is not a game."

Lancelot's had always been an open face, no subtlety or guile hid his emotions. He took a moment to calm himself before answering. "I have never taken chivalry as a game. But I have overcome this knight in fair combat, and I have granted him mercy. He and his men will present themselves before King Arthur and the Lady Guinevere, and *they* will decide his fate. Whatever your grievances are, and I am sure they must be great to make you so forget yourself, you can address them to the King."

Nimue put her hand on Mordred's arm. He was breathing harder now than he had when he'd been fighting Bayard. He was right. She knew he was right. But so was Lance.

Behind them, she could hear running footsteps: the group from Sir Bayard's dungeon finally catching up. Neither Mordred nor Lancelot paid any attention.

"And what will the King decree, do you think?" Mordred asked. "Confiscation of one or two feudal properties, perhaps? A novena offered for the souls of the dead? Then again, he seems to favor banishment lately."

"Mordred, Lancelot," Nimue pleaded. The older knight was perhaps the most decent man she knew. She hated the pain she saw in his clear blue eyes, and she hated the thought of what he could do to Mordred if he so chose.

But she had never seen Lancelot lose his temper, and she didn't see it now. He bent to kiss her hand. He indicated for Bayard to rise to his feet. Then he turned back to Mordred. "Will you be accompanying us to Camelot?" he asked. Very formal, very cool.

Mordred's eyes narrowed. "You were *following* me," he suddenly said. "*That* is how you came to be here in so timely a fashion—you met Dunsten on his way back to Camelot. But why?"

"You left court in company with someone who had just lost in trial by combat—a proven criminal who had been banished."

"I was accompanying a friend whom I may never see again, thanks to you, to the border."

"You seem to have a number of friends among those who have been banished," Lancelot said with a tight smile. "But, there too, I am not the judge."

Mordred stood with his teeth clenched and bared. Then he gave a half smile, and an apologetic flourish with his hand, and he walked away.

Nimue recognized that there was nothing she could do, nothing she could say, and so it was Romola who ran after him.

Romola asked, "Where are you going?"

"Home, it seems. To Camelot. But to get there, I need to borrow a horse from Bayard's stable."

Romola stopped following him and faced the former prisoners. She announced, "My father's cart is here. There is room for everyone. We're all going home."

The ragged group cheered.

Dolph came up behind Romola and gave her a hug. "And I want you to know I'll always love you," he said, "no matter what."

Romola looked at him quizzically. "And I'll always love you," she answered. "What do you mean 'no matter what'?"

Dolph made a vague gesture.

"I just meant,"—he saw that everyone was listening, but continued, perhaps thinking they must know what he was about to say anyway—"you know, after what happened. *Whatever* happened. Not that I want to know," he added hastily. He gave a solid glare that included everyone. "And it's nobody else's business."

"Dolph."

"Yes?"

"I have no idea *what* you are saying."

It was what Nimue would have told him, too.

Dolph lowered his voice, which only served to make everyone listen harder. "With the guards." He nodded toward her skirt, which was stained with the blood of the man Romola had slain. "I mean you're still my woman, and I'll never have you put aside or anything because you certainly couldn't help what they did to you, and it's best if we just forget the whole thing happened and pick up our lives from here."

Nimue's heart sank.

Romola considered this speech, a long one for Dolph, for a moment. "I'm . . . What . . . They . . . Dolph, this isn't my blood."

Now it was her husband's turn to look at her quizzically.

"Dolph, I killed a guard. I . . . stabbed him. This is his blood."

"You . . ." Dolph lowered his voice even more. But by this point he couldn't have lowered it enough to exclude the others. "You killed a guard?"

Romola nodded.

"You just walked right up to a guard—an armed guard, I'm guessing—and stabbed him?"

"Dolph," Nimue said, remembering how he had let himself be recaptured so that she would have a better chance at escape. "Dolph."

"No, I didn't just walk right up to him," Romola said. "I . . ."

"You what?" Dolph snapped.

"Pretended to like him."

"We both did," Nimue said, but Dolph wasn't interested in what she had done. "Romola was very brave," she said. "She came here to rescue you."

But Dolph's gaze was centered unshakably on the skirt.

Lancelot took a step closer to Nimue. "Who *are* these people?" he asked.

Romola tossed her hair off her shoulders. She took hold of Lancelot's arm in an overly familiar gesture, which the knight accepted graciously, while she started to tell him all about the town of St. George and her parents' inn.

Arm in arm they headed down toward the gate, with Dolph behind, close enough to keep stepping on Lancelot's heels. The wainwright, the cobbler's apprentice, and the cooper's nephew crowded about and interjected their own bits of information as Romola spoke. Boy skipped along in front of them, moving backwards. Bayard, and the rest of the knights who were to present themselves to Arthur, trailed behind.

Nimue counted, came up short, and glanced around.

Wystan was sitting on the parapet, holding the sword Dolph had abandoned.

With a start, she realized he was trying to catch the first of the dawn light, to see his reflection on the burnished steel of the blade.

"Wystan." She touched his shoulder. "Wystan, I'm certain you will be all right. You look fine. If you were going to start aging, I'm sure you would have already—and you haven't."

He laid the sword down. "I haven't." He said it tonelessly, neither question nor affirmation.

She shook her head. She forced a smile, though there was little enough to smile about. "So. Where do you come from? Sir Lancelot, Sir Mordred, and I can escort you back to your village. How would you like that? That would shock the socks off your friends and neighbors."

"Socks?"

"Never mind. It's just an expression a friend of mine used to use."

Wystan said, "Who would know me? This don't be the face I left with."

Nimue bit her lip.

"And I can't be going back with your friends and pretending to be the man whose face this was."

"Oh, Wystan," she said, seeing he was right.

He avoided her eyes, but picked up the sword. He stood straight. With determination he said, "But, then, maybe this be a new chance for me—to start new someplace different. Somewhere. It may be." His voice got less and less sure. Still, he forced a smile. "We better hurry, or they'll be leaving without us," he said. "Those friends of yours seem set on bickering and snarling all the way, and they may well overlook you."

When Nimue and Wystan got to the stables, Dolph and Romola were sitting in the cart with the rest of the St. George group, but they were quarreling bitterly, and Mordred and Lancelot had started a debate on chivalry. Bayard wore a self-satisfied smirk.

"Without strict rules of conduct," Lancelot was saying, "civilization itself would disintegrate. How can you call Arthur's ideas old-fashioned? The old way was to look out only for yourself, and if your neighbor had something you wanted and if he wasn't strong enough to keep it from you—well, rotten luck, neighbor. You want to go back to anarchy?"

"I am not against people being decent to each other," Mordred protested. "Or against table manners or social etiquette, either. But you have made a mockery of—"

"By honoring ladies? By declaring the house of God a place of sanctuary? By establishing that once a man yields, he should not be cut down anyway?"

Mordred jerked his head to look away from Lancelot.

"You have no idea of the brutality of life before King Arthur. Why, the first time I heard of Arthur . . ." Lancelot had started to smile at the memory, but the smile faded, as did his words, when he saw that Mordred wasn't paying attention. Mordred sat on his borrowed horse looking far away at nothing in particular. "Yes, well . . ." Lancelot cleared his throat.

In the silence that surrounded them, Romola's voice carried. "What am I supposed to do: Be grateful that you'd still have me? So what? I'm not impressed."

"Outgrown us village folk, have you?" Dolph sneered.

Mordred whirled on him and snapped, "Has anybody ever pointed out what a horse's ass you are?"

Romola grinned, but Mordred had already stopped paying attention and missed it.

"Here, let me help you up," Wystan said to Nimue.

She swung up on the pony that had been readied for her. She started to thank Wystan, then saw that he had frozen. She looked at his stricken face, moved her gaze down to his hands. He had laced his fingers together to give her a lift, but the fingers wouldn't work properly. They couldn't—for they were bent and misshapen and several joints were missing.

Boy shook the reins to the oxen, and the cart started with a jerk.

The men's horses followed. "Listen," Lancelot was saying, "and I will tell you a story about chivalry . . ."

Bayard rode in the middle, wearing an expression that said *I am eager to listen to every story you are willing to share.*

Mordred was in one of his silent sulks.

Bayard's men, looking chastised and ready to be forgiven, followed.

From the cart, the cooper's nephew looked back and saw Nimue. "Come on," he called after her. "You don't want to be left behind."

Wystan slapped her horse on the rump.

The last she saw him, he was sitting on the step just inside the gate, elbow on knee, chin on disfigured fist, the first pink of dawn behind him.

PART III

Kiera

CHAPTER 1

"alking to animals isn't even a big kind of magic," Kiera protested to her mother just as they reached the shady area Agravaine had pointed out as a good place to stretch their legs and rest the horses.

Her mother, as usual, refused to be reasonable. "Honestly," Alayna said in exasperation, "you'll be the death of me yet."

"No," Kiera said. "It won't be anything to do with me."

She recognized her words for a mistake as soon as they were out. A death prophecy wasn't the kind of information most people wanted to hear—least of all her mother. The unsolicited prediction hung between them, just as so many things did lately.

It shouldn't take magical sight, Kiera told herself, for someone who had reached the age of fourteen years old—and been invited, after this one last trip with her mother, to begin training as one of the Queen's ladies-in-waiting—to have the sense not to blurt out such stupid things.

Still, her mother was the one who had started it.

Alayna dismounted without waiting for one of the

men to help her: Agravaine, who had come with them as escort, or his younger brother Mordred whom they'd chanced to meet on the road home as he traveled with Nimue.

"Thank you for the ride," Kiera whispered to her pony, who wiggled an ear at her.

Agravaine rushed over, too late to help mother or daughter dismount. His quick green eyes darted from one to the other, and must have caught the tension, for he spoke a bit too brightly: "Nimue says we had better make this a short stopover if we are to arrive at Camelot before the rain."

"Yes," Alayna snapped. "So Kiera's horse was just telling us."

Agravaine raised his eyebrows, but Alayna was already looking beyond him, her attention on his brother, who reached up to help Nimue dismount. The beautiful young enchantress leaned forward, laughing, her golden hair hanging close to Mordred's dark brown. Abruptly, Alayna turned and walked away.

But Mordred must have heard at least part of what had been said, or he could read the situation by the set of Alayna's shoulders, for as soon as he reached Kiera he whispered, "Have you been arguing with your mother again?"

Kiera shrugged. When Mordred didn't move away but waited for an answer, she said, "I just told her that my horse said it felt like rain." The rest of it, she thought, was best not repeated, and nobody's business anyway.

"Oh, Kiera," Nimue said, "you know your mother gets upset when you use magic."

Upset? Kiera thought. No. Her mother was *terrified* of magic. She was fearful of almost everything.

Kiera knew that, years ago and to the scandal of her great-aunts, her mother had learned to use a sword. She had accompanied Mordred on a quest once, and had fought as a man would, a dim memory from Kiera's earliest childhood. *That* was a mother Kiera could have gotten along with. It was hard to reconcile that image with the plump, pretty woman who spent most of her time treating the imagined ailments of the wealthy old ladies of court. In fact, that was where they were coming back from now: the country estate of a baron whose wife had too much time on her hands and worried excessively about herself.

Kiera wondered, not for the first time, how different things would be now if Nimue had not come to Camelot five years ago.

"It isn't even a big kind of magic, talking to animals," she told them. But—as obvious as that sentiment was—they didn't seem any more willing to accept it than her mother had been. And who was Nimue—an enchantress renowned throughout the realm—to lecture *her* on not using magic? She had thought Nimue would be on her side. "And, anyway, what am I supposed to do when a horse or a dog talks to me—not answer? Pretend I don't hear? My father was a wizard, and it is only natural that I have some of his ability."

The adults exchanged a look she couldn't interpret, then Mordred, without a word, started after Alayna.

"Nicely done," said the usually agreeable Agravaine. "I especially liked that part about natural ability." He strode off to check the horses. Upset with *her*, Kiera realized. As though her mother's bad mood was *her* fault.

Adults always took one another's side.

Kiera went to fold her arms over her chest; but that was awkward ever since this past January when—all of a sudden, it seemed—she had developed a bosom. *You're not a child anymore*, her mother had lectured her. *I was wed when I was not that much older than you*. But in many ways—all the wrong ways—she continued to treat Kiera as a child.

Now, Nimue patted her hand and gave a gentle smile. "It used to be," Nimue broke the silence, "there was all manner of magic in the world. The art was stronger then, and those who practiced it were respected. But it's dimming. All the while dimming. Some people seek to control the weaker magicians, which is one thing for a mother to worry about. And some say the reason there is less magic is because it's a gift from Satan and it's being slowly destroyed by Christianity. Your mother loves you, Kiera. That's why she's afraid."

She doesn't ACT like she loves me, Kiera thought, *always criticizing, always expecting the worst of me.*

Did Nimue have a mother who worried about her? Kiera suspected the question was childish, and though she wanted to know more about the mysterious and usually elusive enchantress, she also wanted to be sophisticated and self-assured, the way Nimue was. So she didn't ask.

But she *did* say, "I've never called on Satan."

Nimue laughed, softly. "Nor have I." But then she looked at Kiera thoughtfully and asked, "What is it? What's wrong?"

"Nothing," Kiera said. Generally, this was the safe answer for her mother.

"*Nothing* wrong," Nimue repeated. "My goodness. Not too many people can say that."

Kiera shrugged. When the silence dragged on longer than she could bear, she said, "It's just . . ." Nimue looked at her attentively. It might be good to talk to someone for whom magic wasn't a *plight,* like her nearsightedness, or a stomach complaint. "It's just, the last few days . . . without looking for it . . . I'll be doing something, and all of a sudden I'll see . . ."

"Yes?" Nimue urged.

"A sort of mist . . ."

This time Nimue waited, not pressing.

All in a rush—the same way the visions came—Kiera said, "I'm surrounded by gray, and by a silence I can almost feel. I know that I have to get someplace or do something, but I don't know what. And I'm afraid. And I don't know why." She regretted having started any of this—and here she'd been concerned that asking about Nimue's mother would sound childish.

But Nimue didn't rebuke or belittle her. She sighed, and answered seriously. "I've never had the Sight. Or very little anyway. My magic has primarily been small healings." She shook her head. "You really should be trained, your power given a channel, so that you can control your magic rather than the other way around."

This was not like anything her mother would have ever said.

"A channel?" Kiera repeated. A sudden realization blossomed. Though the ring Nimue wore on her thumb was so plain it would be easy to overlook, Kiera asked, "Such as that ring of yours?"

Nimue opened her mouth, then closed it. She jerked her hand behind her back, then tried, twice again, before she got words to come out. "Where did you hear that?"

She'd said something wrong. It took no Sight to see that. "No place," Kiera said. But that obviously wouldn't do. She added, "I can just . . . kind of . . . feel it."

"You *do* need to be trained."

Kiera couldn't be sure if she meant in magic or in manners. She had overstepped her bounds. *Oh please don't be angry,* she thought. She wanted so much for Nimue to like her.

For a long while Nimue said nothing and Kiera didn't dare speak. They stood side by side, facing down the hill, with Agravaine behind them tending the horses, and Mordred and her mother too far down the slope to see clearly. *Nimue* could probably see them, as Agravaine probably could, too, if he were facing the other way. But Kiera's eyesight was weak.

Except when she saw those things that weren't there.

But then Nimue spoke again, very gently. She held her hand out, displaying the gold ring. "This ring belonged to Merlin. He was perhaps the greatest magician of all time. He was my teacher, and I loved him, and he was dying. I know what people say," she added in a rush before Kiera could interrupt, "but people are wrong. I did not entrap Merlin and steal his magic: Together we wove a spell and he sleeps safe in Avalon."

Kiera worked on that thought for a moment. "Then *you* must be the greatest magician of all time." Nimue's face went blank at that, and Kiera explained her reasoning: "Since you have the ring, and the ring has both Merlin's magic and your own."

Nimue checked to make sure where each of the others was standing, to make sure no one was within hearing before she answered. "Most of the ring's power is used just to sustain Merlin. Otherwise, it could be a most dangerous instrument." Nimue sighed. "And this conversation is dangerous, too. Only Vivien and the other Ladies of the Lake know. It is *not* to be repeated."

Why was she being so secretive when there was nobody around besides Agravaine and—farther away—her mother and Mordred? "What about Mordred?" Kiera asked.

"What about him?"

Kiera started at the brusque tone. That happened, sometimes, from asking an adult too many questions. Though never before with Nimue. And she didn't truly believe that was what had happened now. "Doesn't Mordred know all about the ring?"

Nimue gazed down the hill. "He knows some of it. With Mordred, it often is difficult to tell how much he has guessed."

But surely you trust him? Kiera was about to ask.

But she didn't.

She had assumed that Nimue loved Mordred, that she was his lady. And it turned out Nimue didn't even trust him. *My mother would trust him,* Kiera thought. If she had any secrets. Which Kiera doubted. She wondered if Mordred trusted Nimue.

"Go and apologize to your mother for vexing her about magic," Nimue said. Before Kiera could protest that she was always the one who had to do the apologizing, Nimue added, "When we get back to Camelot, I will urge her to let you study with me, if that is something you would like."

"You would teach me?" It was more than Kiera would have dared hope for.

"Enough to keep you out of trouble." Nimue glanced at the sky. "And warn them to hurry or we'll never get home before the rain."

Kiera started down the hill, wanting to run for joy, but remembering that was not lady-like. She could see the two figures and, beyond, she could just barely make out a sparkling band, a stream. But despite the increasing darkness of the sky, the sun shone so bright it dazzled her eyes, and the closer Kiera got, the more the water glistened, until her eyes teared. And the more her eyes teared, the brighter the sun glared.

She momentarily closed her eyes against the brightness . . .

. . . and opened them to find herself surrounded by mist. She blinked again, but the gray remained, too thick to penetrate.

She reached her hands out in front, to the sides, but touched only damp air. Gone were the chirp of birds, the rustle of meadow grass in the breeze, the jingle of the horses' trappings from the nearby road. There was only a low drone. And she smelled something, nearby, burning.

Never before had she been caught outside by the vision. "Mother?" Her voice shook. "Mother, I can't see. Where are you?"

She stepped forward, tripped over something large and hard, and fell. The mist shifted. Several paces away, human shapes hovered, but when she called to them, nobody answered. Gingerly she put her hand to the ground. No grass, where there had been grass moments before; just packed dirt. She moved her hand and found what she had fallen over: metal, she thought, but sticky. She snatched back her hand, and found it smeared with blood. The mist shifted again, and she looked into the glazed eyes of a dead knight, a stranger. Then, the gray swallowed him up again.

For a moment she couldn't find her voice. Then, "Mordred!" she screamed.

There! She glimpsed him just off to the right. Inexplicably, he was wearing armor, and he didn't answer. He disappeared back into the mist. "Mordred!" she called again. "Agravaine! Help me!"

She hugged herself to keep from trembling, then saw blood on her sleeve from her hand that had touched the corpse. She shut her eyes, welcoming the friendly blackness, and screamed.

Hands grabbed her shoulders and she inhaled deeply, ready to scream again, but then she recognized Mordred's voice: "Kiera! Kiera! What's wrong?"

She blinked in the sunlight and saw him kneeling on the grass before her. He pulled her close, hugged her, murmured that everything was all right. She pressed her face against him and he smelled clean like leather and horses, and there was no smoke, nor blood, and he wasn't wearing armor after all, but only his own shirt of soft blue linen.

Alayna caught up. She threw her arms around Kiera, almost toppling all three of them. "What happened?" she demanded. "Are you hurt?"

"I . . ." Kiera held out her hand to show them the dead man's blood, but there were only grass stains on the whiteness of her skin.

"Did you hurt yourself?" Alayna took the hand, examining it for broken bones.

As if she'd be such a baby, to tumble and bawl. Resentfully, Kiera pulled her hand away. "There was a man here," she tried to explain.

"Where?" Mordred's eyes swept the line of trees beyond the stream.

"Here. Right . . . here. A dead knight." She realized how outrageous her words sounded—how she herself would react if someone else were to speak the same way.

Whatever they would have answered was interrupted by Agravaine's arrival. "She's not hurt, is she?" Though a young man, he was starting to lose his hair, and he always took meticulous care arranging it to hide that fact. His run down the hill had exposed his high forehead and the thinness on top, but he was too worried to notice. "Is she all right?" he asked, looking down at Kiera anxiously.

"She . . ." Alayna started to say, but then she gave up.

"Did you recognize the man?" Mordred asked, taking her seriously after all. "Was it anybody you know?"

Kiera shook her head.

"What did he—"

"Stop it!" Alayna commanded. "Leave her alone!"

So . . . they both believed.

Mordred gave Alayna one of his cool stares, his gray eyes hard and cutting. Kiera had seen the King back down—once—at just such a look, but her mother, still kneeling, did not.

Nimue finally caught up. "What happened? Is the child injured?"

"Kiera had some sort of vision," Mordred explained tightly. "Alayna does not want to discuss it." He had turned it around, so that Alayna sounded like the foolish one. Kiera was both relieved and disturbed.

"Ah!" Nimue said as though Mordred's summation had explained all. "Well, Alayna is her mother."

"But she saw—"

"Mordred." Nimue used the same tone on him that Alayna was wont to use on Kiera.

Now they were going to argue, Kiera thought, and it was all her fault. Sometimes she wanted them to argue. Sometimes she thought that if only Nimue weren't there, Mordred would spend more time with her mother. But sometimes she thought this was unfair of her, considering how kind and concerned with her Nimue always was. And now Nimue had promised to teach her. These visions wouldn't be able to waylay her then. "Please, can we go?" she said.

"Are you sure you are well enough?" Alayna asked. "Well enough to ride?" She still clutched Kiera's hand, as though she'd never let go.

Embarrassed by all the attention, Kiera nodded, eager to leave, eager to put this behind her.

CHAPTER 2

Not until they had been riding their horses for two or three miles did Kiera suddenly touch her hair and realize something was wrong. "Oh no," she cried.

"What?" her mother demanded, all wide-eyed and pale.

"The ribbon Nimue bought for me at last year's fair. I must have dropped it."

Alayna closed her eyes. *Silly*, Kiera could imagine her thinking. But she only asked, "Do you have any idea where?"

"Probably back where we stopped," Kiera admitted.

"Oh, no," Alayna said. "We are not going back there."

"I didn't drop it on the hill," Kiera said. "I felt it in my hair while we were walking up. It must have come loose after we got back to the horses. I'm sure of it." Kiera herself wouldn't go back if it meant going down that hill again.

Alayna sighed, eyeing the dark clouds.

Nimue, who had overheard, told her, "I'll get you another this year."

It wouldn't be the same. It had been the most lovely thing Kiera owned, and it had made her look so grown up, so elegant. "Please," she begged. "I can go back by myself. It won't take any time at all. You won't have to wait."

"You would never find it," Agravaine said, patting his own hair, as he had done at least a dozen times already.

"I'll go back with her," Mordred offered, which was the best possible solution. "We can catch up."

Just her and him. It would be worth the lecture he was bound to give about getting along better with her mother. There had been a time all three of them had gotten along better. Her mother hadn't seemed so skittish about everything, Mordred had spent more time with them, and she had played a secret game where Mordred was her father and he was only pretending to be just a friend because . . . because . . . Kiera couldn't remember what reason she had made up. But it had all changed with Nimue. Mordred visited less often, Kiera learned enough of life to realize he was too young to make a likely father to her, and her mother . . . Her mother seemed to find fault with everything.

The ride was pleasant but when they got back to where the horses had been tethered, there was no ribbon.

Mordred looked down the hill. "Wait here," he said. "*I* will check by the stream."

He had already started when she spotted a patch of pink and lavender in the nearby grass by the road. With a sigh of relief, she picked up the ribbon and then waved it over her head calling out: "Mordred!"

The shout echoed inside her head: "Mordred!" she heard her own voice cry. Impossibly close, he looked up. Turned. Mist swirled about her knees, mist composed of earthly fog and magic and the smoke of battlefields. She heard herself scream his name again, and saw him turn again. Echoes and re-echoes, sluggish repetitions—one moment she saw him head-on, the next, a side view—all in unnaturally sharp clarity. The mist thinned. Mordred stood in armor. He staggered, his eyes in a daze of fear and pain. She was

aware both of standing next to her pony Ebony on the road, and of being
surrounded by shadows in a land where the gray mist grew and thickened,
and she couldn't tell which self was real.

But then his arms were about her again, steadying her—his voice soothing her
back to reality. Again the mist thinned, and she could see his face once more, no fear
or pain, just concern in the green eyes that watched her steadily.

She shook her head to clear it.

Gray. She knew Mordred's eyes were a dark shade of gray: It was Agravaine who
had green eyes.

A tendril of mist reached between them, and she saw Agravaine lying on the stone
floor, his eyes wide and empty. Or was it Gareth? None of the brothers of the
Orkney clan—Mordred, Agravaine, Gareth, Gaheris, Gawain—none looked especially alike, yet suddenly she realized she couldn't tell whose death she was foresee-
ing. "Mordred," she whispered, clutching at the solid reality of his hand.

He came back into focus, his eyes the right color this time. "I'm here."

She thought to tell him of the danger meant for him—him or one of his brothers. But when she opened her mouth, the name her voice formed was: "Nimue." She
didn't know where it had come from, but she knew it was real. She said, "Nimue is
in danger."

He lifted her onto his chestnut-colored horse, then swung up behind. He had
them at a full gallop before her poor Ebony knew what was going on. Kiera was
aware, without turning, that the faithful pony followed, but the powerful strides of
Mordred's mount seemed just short of flying.

The road was narrow here, crowded by the forest, winding and hilly. They
rounded a curve, and there was a long, long level stretch, with the rest of their party
in sight, traveling leisurely. Mordred never slowed. Kiera saw Agravaine look back,
no doubt wondering at their breakneck speed.

In the same moment, seven armed knights broke out from the trees and bushes that had carelessly been allowed to grow too close to the road.

Agravaine saw their raised swords and lances, and whipped out his own sword.

He must have called out a warning, still too far away for Kiera to hear, but her mother and Nimue faced about.

"Down!" Mordred pushed her forward, down onto the horse's neck. Kiera turned her face, and saw that two more knights had broken from cover near them. Mordred had his own sword out. He slashed at one of them without slowing down, then wheeled about and went after the second.

Kiera saw the body of the first knight, caught by the heel of his solleret on the stirrup. The horse made close circles, trampling the bloody ground. She closed her eyes.

Mordred rode too low, vulnerable, and a bad position for fighting, but he was bent over in the saddle to give her what protection his unarmored body could.

Who would attack them practically on King Arthur's doorstep?

She was getting dizzy and almost opened her eyes, but at that moment Mordred shifted balance. Her own body felt the shock that jarred his right arm as he parried a sword blow. His left hand was on the reins, but the arm was holding her in; he was mostly guiding his mount with his legs. "Gently," she whispered in the horse's ear, "our lives rest with you."

The destrier gave no indication whether it heard.

She waited for the blow she was sure would kill them both.

But then she realized the pained, ragged panting so close to her ear was not that of Mordred but his opponent. She heard a sharp intake of air, and Mordred didn't wait to see the man fall. He jerked the horse around, lifted Kiera off and onto the ground, and was halfway toward the others before she fully caught her balance.

There were two more of the attacking knights down, and one horse. Her mother must have picked up a sword from one of them, and she circled one of the knights. Kiera had a sudden clear memory of Alayna in a strange castle Hall, holding a sword, circling, circling a tall blond man who looked something like her mother, but whose eyes were soulless. Kiera shivered at the fragment of memory.

The other four knights were closing in on Agravaine when one of the attackers' horses screamed in panic, a disconcertingly human sound. The animal reared and twisted and frothed at the mouth as the rider pulled up tight in an attempt to regain control.

Kiera covered her ears, but could still hear, could still understand. The horse's cries were frenzied, maddened, speaking of conflicting, fantastic, horrific images. The other horses backed away, struggling against their riders. She watched in horror of her own as the afflicted horse threw itself on the ground. Its rider managed to untangle himself from reins and saddle just in time to avoid ending up under the horse.

Nimue, Kiera thought. *Nimue can't stop the knights, but she's affecting the horse's mind.*

In the confusion, Mordred whipped through the crowd from behind, slashed at two knights, killing one and gravely injuring the other. Then, without breaking stride, he came against the knight who fought Kiera's mother. Now Agravaine had only one knight to overcome. Meanwhile Nimue, a look of dismay on her face, watched the dying horse thrash.

"Nimue!" Kiera shouted, seeing the knight whose horse it had been struggle to his feet. "Nimue!" But her small voice didn't carry above the sounds of battle. *"Nimue!"*

Finally—finally—the young enchantress looked up.

Too late. The knight dragged her off her horse.

The last of the mounted knights had been killed. "Nimue!" Kiera screamed yet again, and finally Alayna, Mordred, and Agravaine turned to find Nimue with a sword to her throat.

"Don't," that knight warned from between clenched teeth.

"Pinel," Mordred said, and that was when Kiera recognized him. Pinel was a lanky young knight whose lack of skill made him a liability on tournament teams, though he was personable enough to always get invited anyway. Then, a fortnight ago, he'd attempted to poison the head of the Orkney clan, Sir Gawain. Kiera assumed there must have been a reason, of the kind that the adults were unwilling to talk about in front of the young people. All she knew was that the plot had been discovered and Pinel had disappeared from court.

And now he tightened his grip on Nimue and touched the sword point to her throat. "Not exactly as I planned it," he said, "but here we are anyway, Mordred. *Keep back.*"

Mordred had dismounted. He sheathed his sword, then stepped back, his hands before him, palms out as a token of peace. "Since when do you fight ladies, Sir Pinel?"

"Just your lady."

Mordred's voice was quiet and even. "Your quarrel is with me."

"Back-stabbing bastard," Pinel growled. Then, "Keep your hands where I can see them." That was directed behind Mordred to Agravaine or Alayna—Kiera hadn't seen. "And I told you to keep back."

Mordred, who had not moved, took a backwards step.

Pinel was shivering, like a man fevered. *Dangerous,* Kiera thought, *very dangerous.*

"Mordred—" Nimue began.

Pinel shoved her to her knees. "Back!" he screamed at Mordred and the others.

Kiera bit her hand to keep from crying out.

Pinel dug the fingers of his left hand into Nimue's shoulder and aimed the sword at her back.

"Don't!" Mordred cried. Kiera had known him most of her life, and it was the first time she had ever heard him raise his voice. Then, more calmly, he said: "Don't hurt her."

"That's the way you killed my cousin," Pinel said, "in the back."

"No," Mordred said. "I killed Lamorak in fair contest—"

"Murdered him!" Pinel shouted.

Mordred swallowed hard. ". . . in fair contest with—"

"Liar!"

". . . witnesses," Mordred finished.

"Gawain and Agravaine," Pinel spat. "Your brothers. Who held him down while you butchered him."

"Nobody held any—"

"Shut up!"

Mordred closed his eyes and didn't dispute.

"There was another witness that you did *not* know about: Sir Bayard of Castle Ridgemont of Ravens' Rock."

The name meant nothing to Kiera, but Mordred swore. Then he said, practically spitting the name, "Bayard. Bayard was nowhere near—"

"You and your brothers have been trying to annihilate my family for years," Pinel said. "Your mother . . ." He took a deep breath, got his voice to sound less strangled, more under control. "I'd always heard Queen Morgause was a witch. She must have been a powerful one to seduce my cousin when he was young enough to be her grandson. And you killed him—you killed both of them—for that. Bayard saw you gang up on Lamorak, while Gaheris stayed inside, and Bayard never guessed . . ." He shook his head. "A foolish seventeen-year-old boy and *your own mother.*"

"Bayard and I have an old score between us. He lied about being there, and he lied about what happened. I killed Lamorak in a fair fight, and Gaheris killed our mother by accident."

Pinel's fingers dug deeper into Nimue's shoulder. She flinched. Head bowed, one long blond curl hung beyond the edge of the cloak's hood—Mordred's cloak, because Nimue hadn't brought hers and they had all been worried, not an hour gone by, about getting rained upon.

"Don't hurt her," Mordred said. "She is not involved. Your fight is with me. Not Agravaine, not the women. Me."

"I said keep back!" The sword above Nimue shook.

Mordred's hand clenched and unclenched, but he kept it away from his sword.

"Did Lamorak beg for his life?" Pinel asked. "Did he?" And when Mordred didn't answer, he asked, "Agravaine?"

Agravaine shook his head.

"I didn't think he would. My kinsman was young, but he was a good knight. He probably would have begged for your wretched mother's life, if it had ever occurred to him that she was in danger from her own sons. A cold-hearted, degenerate brood of devils, you."

"Pinel," Mordred started, "you are—"

"Can you stand there and watch your woman bleed?"

"What do you want from me?" Mordred asked.

"I want to hear you beg."

"What do you think I've been doing?" Mordred screamed at him.

But even this wasn't enough for Pinel. *"I want to hear you beg,"* he repeated. "I want you on your knees. And I want you to say, 'Please, Pinel, spare Nimue.'"

Kiera, where she stood, mouthed the words.

Mordred dropped to the ground, never taking his gaze off Nimue. His voice was quiet, but barely controlled. "Please, Pinel, spare Nimue."

"No." Pinel raised his sword.

His arm had just started to plunge, when Agravaine flung his sword. The blade went in at the base of Pinel's throat and out through the back, no doubt killing him instantly.

But it could not stop the momentum of his swing.

Pinel's sword sliced through the huddled form at his feet, hard enough that the sword passed completely through Nimue and lodged itself into the ground. Only then did his own dead body pitch forward to land on top.

"Lord in Heaven," Agravaine whispered.

For a moment no one moved. Then Kiera darted closer, unwilling to believe what she knew to be so. Her mother leaped off her horse. "Don't," she said. "There is nothing we can do."

There had to be something. There was always *something*. Kiera bit her lower lip to stop her teeth from chattering.

Agravaine had dismounted too. He stood with his hand on his brother's shoulder. Mordred still knelt. He hadn't moved at all.

Eventually Agravaine moved away. Kiera closed her eyes, knowing where he was going. She felt her mother's fingers tighten in her hair.

Then Agravaine stifled a surprised oath.

Kiera forced herself to look, ready to avert her eyes quickly. Agravaine had used his foot to roll away Pinel's body, for it had fallen on top of his victim. Now they could see the cloak, flat to the ground, pinned there by the sword.

It was Mordred who moved first, and it was Mordred who yanked the sword out. He stooped and gathered up the cloak.

No body.

How could there be no body?

There was blood, quite a lot, but no way to tell whether Pinel's or Nimue's.

"Could she do that?" Mordred asked nobody in particular. "I don't . . . think . . . I ever saw . . ." Very gently he gathered up the cloak, and something dropped: Merlin's ring. Mordred picked it up, held it tightly, looked as though he might be praying. When he spoke, it was in a hoarse whisper. "She would never have left this behind."

No, Kiera thought.

"Perhaps . . ." Agravaine started.

"What?" Mordred jumped at the promise of the vague word.

Agravaine made a helpless gesture.

"Perhaps," Mordred finished the thought the way he wanted, "she . . . somehow . . . traveled to safety. And she will come back."

Yes, Kiera prayed.

"Oh, Mordred," Alayna said.

"It could be," Mordred insisted.

Alayna looked away. "It could," she murmured.

Kiera could tell she didn't believe it.

In her heart, Kiera didn't believe it, either.

Mordred looked away also. He bit the knuckle of the fist that held the ring. "So we shall wait here until she comes back."

Agravaine and Alayna exchanged a look. Then Agravaine checked the sky, which was darker than ever. The air smelled of imminent rain. He said, "We must bring these"—he indicated the bodies of the knights—"back with us lest we get accused of ganging up on someone again." Their wounds would be proof—Kiera knew he was saying—against the accusation of treachery and stabbing in the back.

Mordred said nothing.

"Kiera, stay . . ." her mother started, but then apparently realized that there was no good place for her to stay.

Kiera looked back the way they had come, and saw that Ebony had caught up but stopped far back on the road. The little pony wouldn't pass the first dead body but just stood there, all lather and heaving sides.

She went—her own eyes rigidly forward—to fetch the frightened pony and scratch his nose. For the first time she realized she still clutched the hair ribbon. She opened her hand and stared at it, all crumpled and damp. "Oh, Ebony," she said. *Poor, poor Nimue.*

The pony butted her gently with his head.

She looked back once, saw her mother, Mordred, and Agravaine arguing. Agravaine had strung the surviving horses together, with the dead attackers tied across their backs like so many practice quintains with the stuffing knocked out. It was harder to hate them now that they were dead. Kiera buried her face in Ebony's neck.

After a while, Alayna came from behind and caressed Kiera's hair back from her cheek.

"Ebony says it feels like a bad storm coming up," Kiera mumbled into Ebony's mane.

Her mother let it pass. "Mordred will wait a little longer. Agravaine will stay with him."

Kiera looked to where Mordred still knelt in the middle of the road. Agravaine was crouched beside him, the picture of controlled impatience.

Her mother walked between Kiera and the horses with their grisly loads. Ebony snorted, but allowed himself to be led to the head of the line.

Kiera couldn't think of anything to say. She had always felt a nagging resentment of Nimue: Who could compete against that beautiful face and perfect hair and easy self-assurance? The young enchantress had come between Mordred and Alayna, between Kiera and her expectations for the two people she loved most. Nothing had been the same since her coming. Nothing. From her childhood Kiera remembered the almost imperceptible scar Mordred had had along his left cheekbone, a reminder of the adventure he and her mother had shared, the time they had rescued Kiera from the evil wizard. Mordred had been injured and her mother, with her knowledge of herbs, had cured him so that the scar was so thin and faint you couldn't even notice it unless you knew it was there. Then Nimue came, and took it away with her magic. And then she had taken Mordred away. But now she was gone, and neither herbs nor magic would bring her back, no matter what Mordred chose to hope.

But Kiera couldn't just leave. She went to Mordred and kissed his cheek, and he squeezed her hand. Still, he didn't look at her and she didn't think he really knew she was there.

Agravaine had moved onto the grass, where he sat hunched up in his cloak.

Her mother pulled her away, and the raindrops started before they reached the first curve in the road.

CHAPTER 3

Alayna and Kiera reached Camelot in one afternoon.

Agravaine took five days, Mordred seven. In the end, Gawain, the eldest of the Orkney brothers, went out after him and brought him back.

It had rained and been unseasonably cold much of the sennight of Mordred's absence. He was pale and thin and hollow-eyed, and many expected he would sicken and take to bed before the end of the council the King convened to determine exactly what had happened. Kiera was aware that there were several wagers riding on the outcome.

Normally, councils were held in a special room. But so many people were related to the participants, or involved one way or another with the outcome, or simply curious, that this hearing took place in the Great Hall. Rows of benches had been arranged, but still there were more people than seats. There were, in fact, more people than even the Hall could accommodate, and the large doors were left open for the overflow of spectators. Kiera was one who got to sit, but the people were so tightly packed together in the rows ahead of her that she had to constantly shift to see around heads.

King Arthur had asked Alayna to stand before the assembly and tell what had happened. Kiera knew that her mother was probably dying inside at having to speak before so many. Several times, people in the back called for her to speak louder.

Alayna told of how they had been ambushed, and of how she and Mordred and Agravaine had fought off the knights. She didn't mention the spell Nimue had cast to cause Pinel's horse to panic.

"What, exactly," King Arthur asked, "did Sir Pinel say while he held the sword to Lady Nimue's throat?"

Alayna took a deep breath. "He said—"

"Louder!" someone called out.

"He said," Alayna repeated, marginally louder, "that Sir Mordred and his brothers had killed his cousin Lamorak and that he was going to make them pay. Mordred said that he alone had fought Lamorak, and that it had been a fair fight. But Pinel would not believe him. He said Sir Bayard of Ridgemont had witnessed it all, and that Mordred and the others had murdered Lamorak."

"That is not true," a loud voice cried out, overpowering Alayna's faint one.

One of the knights leaped to his feet, a tall, broad man whom Kiera didn't know. Sir Bayard, it had to be. Kiera felt dizzy and could hardly breathe.

"I never told Pinel that," Bayard protested. "I never claimed to be anywhere near Lothian when Lamorak was killed."

Kiera slumped in her seat willing herself not to be sick, not to have to leave.

Bayard continued. "I was at a dinner with Pinel and several others," he admitted. "We discussed rumors about how young Lamorak and Queen Morgause were killed. Several rumors: many ridiculous, many contradictory." Bayard repeated all of them for the benefit of the assemblage. Several times he mentioned what was already well known: that Morgause had been Arthur's sister as well as the mother of his son, and that Lamorak had been a godson.

Kiera could see that the court loved it.

Her mother hesitantly sat down, her part apparently done.

Arthur called on the men who had eaten with Bayard and Pinel: Sir Lancelot, Sir Bors, Sir Ector de Maris, Sir Lambert—knights of unimpeachable character, and, in the case of Lambert, a stickling adherence to detail that was almost enough to cause the assembly to lose interest. The knights all verified that Pinel had seemed distraught at the death of his cousin but that he had given no indication he planned any action. And they all agreed that Bayard had only reported the rumors circulating around Lothian, without crediting any, without stressing any, without claiming to have been there.

Mordred was called on to give his testimony. He stood somewhat unsteadily, which brought a murmur of sympathy from some of the spectators. He looked levelly at Bayard and said, "You tried to kill me once before."

The crowd burst into excited chatter.

"Enough," Arthur said. He was a king who had not often needed to raise his voice, and he didn't do so now. Kiera couldn't see much of him beyond the bulk of the woman who sat in front of her, just his silver hair. Eventually the crowd stilled, somewhat, and only then did Arthur continue. "We are discussing what happened seven days ago, not five years since."

Kiera saw Gawain put a hand on Mordred's arm. They stood near enough that Kiera could clearly see the whitened scar on Gawain's right hand. The little finger was missing, cut off during a sword fight, a sword fight Gawain had subsequently won.

If Arthur saw how angry Mordred was, he gave no indication.

If Mordred saw how desperate Arthur was, he gave no indication either.

Mordred turned to Lancelot. "And you," he said, "have been Bayard's unwitting dupe before. What makes you think that Bayard didn't talk to Pinel after your dinner?"

"I didn't!" Bayard protested.

Arthur said, "These endless old feuds, this refusal to give in no matter the cost—will destroy us all."

In the end, Arthur sent Bayard away from Camelot. Not banishment, the King stressed, but for his own safety till tempers cooled.

It was a solution that pleased no one.

The people around Kiera got up, stretching, talking, comparing opinions. Between them Kiera caught occasional glimpses of Mordred at the front of the Hall, still glowering despite his brothers and his friends gathered around him. Kiera followed his gaze and settled once again on Bayard. She forced herself to look at Bayard as he spoke quietly and earnestly to his friends. She had never met him before—everyone acknowledged it was the first time in years he had come to court.

And yet she *had* seen his face once before.

She had seen it that day on the hillside, white and drained of blood, with lifeless eyes staring up into the swirling gray mist.

CHAPTER 4

*K*iera was in the field of gray mist again.

At first, all she heard was a loud, hollow sound: THUMP. THUMP. THUMP.

My heart, *she thought.* Something was wrong with her heart.

But the sound also came from outside her, a steady wooden drumming.

Eventually she realized that what she heard was the clash of swords—laboriously slow, as though the fighters were hurt or weary. And it came from all around her: many, many fighters.

After that she could make out stifled moans and frantic cries. A riderless horse broke through the mist. It came within an arm's length of trampling her, close enough that the breeze of its passing rippled her hair. She gasped, and choked on the bitter taste of smoke.

She turned her head to rub her burning eyes and saw the body of a knight on the ground, his eyes open and glazed.

Bayard, *she thought.*

Now he had a name and she shouldn't be afraid.

But it wasn't Bayard. It was King Arthur.

Oh no, *she thought.* Oh no, oh no, oh no.

Not the King, who had always been so kind and gentle and good.

In horror she leaned closer to the corpse, and one of its eyes slowly winked at her. She slumped back, her heart racing to the same beat of the insistent pounding that was somehow louder than the other, closer sounds.

Hesitantly, afraid, she called, "Mordred!"

He turned, always there, but his hand was to his side and he staggered,
so slowly, blood running over his fingers and down his arm.

"Mordred!" she screamed. She wanted to run to him but something
tripped her, something held her down. She twisted herself and saw the dead
knight's gauntleted hand clasped around her ankle. Except that this time, it
wore Agravaine's face. "Agravaine," she whimpered.

She couldn't get loose, and something was approaching: The banging noise
got louder, faster, more urgent, and she had never been afraid of Agravaine
before. "Agravaine, no!" Her muscles were all tensed, but her limbs wouldn't
move. A high-pitched moan made its way out from the back of her throat.

"Kiera, Kiera, hush, dear. You have been dreaming."

Kiera sat up. She had to stop to think before she recognized it was sweet, plain-faced Hildy who leaned over her in the bed, her hair hanging down in disarray. It took another few moments for Kiera to remember where she was: in the bedroom shared by Queen Guinevere's ladies-in-waiting. Somehow she'd forgotten the most important thing that had happened in her life—being chosen to train as one of the Queen's ladies.

In a soothing voice Hildy said, "Go back to sleep. It was just a dream."

But it wasn't.

"Agravaine," Kiera said—whimpered—her voice shaking.

"The King's nephew?" Hildy smiled. "Home and safe, and in his own bed." She considered. "Or somebody else's."

Was that all people around here cared about?

Always the smirking. Always men and women and beds. She didn't like thinking about it—Guinevere and Lancelot, they whispered. Mordred and Nimue.

Mordred and Alayna, they had probably said, when she'd been too young to understand it.

Agravaine and somebody.

Surely there was more to growing up than that.

Hildy said: "Quiet now, before you wake the others." Though she was probably more worried about the Queen in the adjoining chamber, she nodded toward the rest of the room where the other ladies-in-waiting slept—two or three to a bed, for that was the best way to keep warm.

"But what was that noise?" Kiera insisted. "That banging noise?"

"Shhh. There's nothing, dear. Listen."

Kiera did listen, and heard only her own heavy breathing and one of the other ladies who murmured in her sleep.

"See," Hildy said gently, not mocking the way some of the others had a tendency to do, "just a dream. Sometimes it is hard, the first few nights away from your mother."

My mother has nothing to do with this, Kiera came close to telling her. But her mother had begged her to please, please try to make friends. She bit back her answer, realizing even as she did so that Hildy would mistake it for a homesick gulp.

Hildy patted her hand, pulled the blanket up to her neck, and started to lie back.

Then stopped at the loud noise that came from the Queen's room, someone pounding on the heavy oaken outer door.

"Open up in the name of the King!" someone—*Mordred?*—shouted.

No, Kiera begged. *Go away.*

There was a slight scurrying noise from next door, but no answer. And Arthur was away. Arthur was on a hunting trip.

Guinevere and Lancelot, they said. Guinevere and Lancelot.

Was it true, the Queen and Camelot's best knight?

The banging resumed—not the honest sound of knocking, but with a metallic ring to it: Someone, in the middle of the night, within the very heart of the King's castle at Camelot, was using a gauntleted fist or the hilt of a sword.

Another voice spoke up, this time with the stiff formality of chivalry. "Sir Lancelot Dulac, wit we well ye are in the Queen's chamber and we are fourteen of us, on allowance of the King. Open the door for thou canst not escape."

Perhaps Hildy recognized Agravaine's voice. Maybe the banging was enough. She rolled out of the bed, took a step backwards from Kiera, and made the sign of the Cross. The others were beginning to stir at the noise, groggily asking what was happening. Somebody started to cry.

Wasn't anybody going to do something?

Kiera swung out of bed and went to the door that connected their room with the Queen's. "My Lady," she called softly, not to alert the men in the hallway.

"Do not be alarmed," Guinevere answered. "There is no danger." Kiera could hear her say something else, in a quiet voice, to someone in the room with her. Guinevere and Lancelot.

The pounding started again, and the cries for Sir Lancelot to show himself. Nobody was smirking now.

One of the Queen's women stifled a startled squeak, then pointed at the other door in their own room, the one that opened onto the hallway. The latch shook as someone surreptitiously tried the lock.

"My Lady," Kiera whispered, even though the door was locked. "Someone is trying to get in here."

The door connecting to the Queen's room flew open. Lancelot stood there, dressed in rumpled shirt and breeches, while Guinevere, in the background, pulled on a dressing gown.

Oh no, Kiera thought. She had assumed the Queen's innocence would protect her.

The room had gone perfectly quiet. Even the outside door was still now. Lancelot went to the window, where he leaned out to check the distance to the ground and to examine the surrounding walls. No armor, Kiera saw, no weapons.

He turned to Guinevere, who stood in the doorway, and shook his head. She was pulling her long, graying auburn hair out from underneath her dressing gown.

"Nobody will get hurt," the Queen told her women. "Simply stay calm and out of the way."

"Traitor knight!" someone from outside shouted. "Traitor Queen!"

On the other side of their door there was a *clank* of metal, perhaps a shield brushed against a stone wall, or an armored toe stubbed.

"They're going to kill you," one of the women whispered. "They're going to kill all of us."

"Nonsense," Guinevere said.

But she didn't look as though she thought it was nonsense.

Lancelot ran his fingers through his hair, which was also graying. Mordred despised Lancelot, Kiera knew that. In her loyalty to Mordred she had always felt obliged to hate Lancelot, too. But she had never been able to muster more than a vague resentment, for Mordred's sake. And now she felt a grudging respect for the old man. *Go away, Mordred and Agravaine,* she thought. *You have gone too far.*

Lancelot, by the window, turned to Guinevere, by the door. "I can do nothing without a sword," he whispered.

"I know," Guinevere answered.

"If I just give myself up, once Arthur gets back to court—"

"They would never let you live that long, and you know it."

"I can do nothing without a sword," he repeated, an edge to his quiet voice.

And, once again, with that stillness: "I know," Guinevere said.

"My Lady," Kiera said, "Sir Lancelot. That's Sir Mordred and Sir Agravaine out there. They would not—"

Hildy interrupted with a hiss: *"She* knew! *She* spoke in her sleep, and she knew! This is some sort of trap."

"No," Kiera said, shocked that Hildy could think that of her. She didn't know what to make of the look Guinevere gave her. "I didn't know. I only—"

Somebody shoved her from behind, pulling on her hair.

"Stop that!" Guinevere commanded.

Kiera looked from her to Lancelot, then around the room. They were all stand-ing huddled together. Some of the ladies actually clung to each other, but even the rest stood close; the Queen and Lancelot, with the length of the room between them, still—for the moment—had each other. Only *she* suddenly stood alone, and the physical distance that separated her from them was the least of it. "I did *not* know. It was just a dream."

Lancelot accepted it, she could tell from his eyes. Perhaps it came from having known Merlin: a habit of seeing the impossible and believing without explanation. For a moment he rested his hand on her head. But he didn't muss her hair, the way Agravaine was accustomed to; instead he put finger to lips for silence and motioned Guinevere to go to the hallway door.

The Queen waited with her hand on the latch, while Lancelot yanked a blanket off one of the beds and wrapped it around his arm.

Protection, Kiera realized. He was expecting them to come at him with weapons. She still wanted to say that they all were wrong—that Mordred and Agravaine wouldn't do anything like that—but he gave a quick nod.

Guinevere yanked the door open.

The knight on the other side tumbled in. Kiera, from where she stood, could see that he was alone: The other men were still gathered at the Queen's door. The knight was, after all, not in full armor though he did have a chain-mail shirt. In the instant before Lancelot hit him in the mouth with the heel of his palm, Kiera saw that it was Agravaine. She stifled a cry of sympathetic pain.

Agravaine would have staggered backwards, out into the hallway, but Lancelot was anticipating that. He had hold of Agravaine's sword arm, and he jerked him back into the room. Immediately he let go, then drove his elbow into Agravaine's face.

Guinevere slammed the door shut behind them and secured the bolt.

Kiera backed into a wall, too shocked for tears.

Lancelot brought his knee up in Agravaine's groin. Then, before Agravaine could straighten, Lancelot jerked his knee up again, this time slamming him under the chin, snapping Agravaine's head back. Then Lancelot kicked him in the chest so that he fell. Agravaine must have been stunned, his grip on the sword loosened, for Lancelot was able to wrest the weapon away. He brought the hilt down hard at the base of Agravaine's skull, and Agravaine dropped flat onto the floor.

Unsure of her legs, Kiera slid down the length of the wall until she was sitting on her heels.

The Queen leaned against the door, her face pale. She was breathing almost as hard as Lancelot. "Is he dead?" she asked. This time her whisper seemed more shock than desire for secrecy.

"No," said Lancelot.

He should know. Surely he had enough experience and should know. Kiera prayed he was right. He knelt and began to strip off Agravaine's protective mail.

Kiera brought her knees up to her chest. She rested her forehead against them, gulping down a wave of nausea. Then she pushed her damp hair away from her face and got to her feet. If Agravaine was to get help from anybody in this room, it would have to be her.

Before she could move, the door behind Guinevere rattled with a sudden jolt. "Agravaine!" It was Mordred's voice. Kiera's teeth started to chatter.

Lancelot recognized Mordred's voice, too—Keira could tell. He finished unfastening the mail shirt and started to put it on. Guinevere went to help him.

"Agravaine!" Mordred called again, unaccustomed urgency in his voice.

Kiera used her hand to push herself away from the wall. Agravaine was breathing, but he bled from nose and mouth and—more dangerously, she knew—from the ears. She folded the blanket Lancelot had discarded and put it under Agravaine's head. Although he was sweating profusely, his skin seemed unnaturally cold.

And Mordred practically screamed: *"Lancelot, what have you done to Agravaine?"*

Kiera bit her lip. Lancelot looked across at her, then down at Agravaine. He sighed, then knelt beside her. He forced the fallen knight's eyes open. The pupil of his right eye was larger than that of his left. Lancelot swore and sat back on his heels. He looked about the room, shook his head, swore again.

Other voices joined Mordred's: "Sir Lancelot, open this door."

Lancelot looked at Guinevere, who had her own eyes closed. Agravaine was, after all, her nephew. "If there had not been so many of them . . ." Lancelot said. "If I had brought my own sword in with me . . ." Kiera saw him swallow hard. Then he wiped his hand, sweaty and bloody, on his leg and picked up Agravaine's sword.

"Keep out of the way," he told the ladies-in-waiting. "You are not in danger."

He started back toward the Queen's room, but stopped when he realized Guinevere had followed him. He took her hand and kissed it. "Your ladies need you," he said.

"Yes," Guinevere said. She pressed his hand to her cheek.

After a moment he released her hand.

This tenderness wasn't what Kiera had expected, not from the whispered titters, the smirks people gave each other.

Guinevere returned, shooing the women into the corner of the room that was farthest from both doors. All except for Kiera, who stayed by Agravaine's side.

Lancelot strode into the farther room, away from the Queen, away from the women, away—Kiera realized—from Mordred, who pounded at this door, frantic to find out what had happened to his brother. Lancelot yanked open the Queen's door. Very quietly—very quietly—he said: "If you have a quarrel with me, here I am."

They must have recognized the shirt and sword. "He's murdered Agravaine!" several voices shouted.

Kiera averted her gaze. She turned her attention back to Agravaine. That was bad enough. She didn't look up at the sound of clashing swords. With every breath, blood bubbled and foamed around Agravaine's nose and at the corners of his mouth. She used her hand to wipe it away.

Someone knelt beside her: Lisette, who, until Kiera's arrival, had been the youngest of the Queen's ladies. She held out a pale yellow kerchief, but kept her face tilted away so as not to see.

There was a yell from the other room. Kiera jumped and involuntarily glanced over. Through the doorway, she saw at least three men already down, but Lancelot was being forced back by the sheer number of opponents.

A loud, rattling breath seemed to catch in Agravaine's throat. It wasn't followed by another. She turned back reluctantly, knowing what to expect before she saw it: His chest no longer heaved and the blood at his nose and mouth no longer stirred with breath. Only one drop still worked its way across his cheek.

"Oh, Agravaine," she said. The ballads were always full of heroic last words, of destiny fulfilled. This was just a body that no longer moved. She stared at the crumpled bloody cloth in her hand because she couldn't look at his face any longer.

Someone must have crashed into the table where Guinevere kept her perfumes and cosmetics: Glass shattered and wood splintered. Lancelot was being forced to give way, although more of the intruders were down. Now he had been backed practically into the room of the ladies-in-waiting; he fought two knights at once.

Lisette tugged on Kiera's arm. She was suddenly joined by Guinevere, and the two of them dragged Kiera out of the fighting men's way, for she had no feeling in her body and couldn't move on her own.

The pair that fought Lancelot got in each other's way in the narrow confines of the doorway. That, and their reluctance to get in as close to him as they needed, caused Lancelot to start regaining lost ground. But suddenly both his opponents fell back entirely, making way for someone else.

Guinevere's fingers dug into her shoulder, and Kiera went cold all over.

Lancelot was fighting Mordred.

Framed by the doorway, Lancelot didn't have enough room to maneuver; he had to shorten his swings and couldn't dodge to the side. But he was the best swordsman in Camelot. And Mordred . . . Despite her love for him, even Kiera knew that Mordred was no better than average.

Lancelot parried a jab, feinted to the left, then thrust right. Mordred blocked, trying to force Lancelot into a tighter angle against the wall.

Kiera didn't know much about fighting—she didn't like tournaments and had only attended a few—but it didn't take an expert to realize that Lancelot was passing up opportunities. The first time, Mordred had swung too wide, misjudging the width of the doorway. His sword grazed the stone arch, leaving him exposed a moment too long. But Lancelot didn't take advantage of the opening. Then it happened again: a clear chance to sever Mordred's hand at the wrist, but instead Lancelot pressed forward, and Mordred was able to block.

Lancelot was only trying to disarm him, Kiera realized suddenly. He was trying very hard not to kill him. The relief was almost enough to start her crying again.

Mordred made a quick move that Lancelot mistook for a feint. Almost too late, he stepped back; but now Mordred was confined by the doorway and Lancelot had the freedom of movement.

Lancelot worked to his own left, cramping Mordred's sword arm, then suddenly he aimed for the head. Mordred started to shift balance, but it was a feint after all, and Lancelot swung back, pinning Mordred's weapon against the wall.

There was no time for him to slip down through the bottom: Lancelot grabbed his hand and slammed it against the stones that formed the arch of the doorway. Mordred winced, trying to pull down, but Lancelot jerked the hand back and hit the wall with it again. Then again, and again. Mordred tried to twist around, to get at Lancelot with his left hand, but the older, bigger knight had thrown his weight against him. The back of Mordred's fist hit the wall yet again. This time he was unable to suppress a cry of pain, but Lancelot relentlessly repeated the motion. The next time, Mordred's sword dropped from his fingers.

Lancelot's grip shifted lower on his arm. He yanked Mordred into the room and threw him on the floor. Already two of the other knights had made it through the door, and Lancelot defended himself against them without a glance to see where Mordred landed.

Kiera only just kept from crying out. Mordred had instinctively put out his right hand, the injured one, to break his fall and now was on his knees bent over in pain, with his eyes closed, unaware that what he had tripped over was his dead brother.

Mordred began to get up.

And then, *then* he opened his eyes.

Guinevere suddenly jerked Kiera away. The motion snapped her head back, and she saw that while Lancelot fought two knights, two others had circled behind and were running toward the corner where the women were.

Guinevere put herself between the ladies-in-waiting and the men, before anyone had a chance to think that she was the one who most needed protecting.

Kiera knew these people. She knew the men who were fighting and dying. She wanted to scream, *Stop it, stop it!* What was the matter with them? There: That was Sir Mador de la Porte, a kindly man who had given her piggyback rides when she'd been younger. Now he grabbed Guinevere by the arm and spun her around, holding his sword near her throat. The other knight was freckle-faced Sir Lionel, and he faced the ladies as though to ensure that they wouldn't try to sneak up from behind.

"My Lady!" Hildy screamed.

Lancelot whirled around.

"Hold!" Sir Mador said.

For a moment, everyone was motionless. The Queen didn't struggle against Mador who held her. Kiera and the ladies faced Lionel silently. The two who had been fighting Lancelot had frozen midstroke, their swords still up. Mordred remained on his knees next to Agravaine.

Then Lancelot grabbed the knight nearest him and heaved him against his companion.

Sir Mador's sword came closer to the Queen's throat.

Lancelot raised his sword, but took a backwards step. He was looking not at Mador but at Guinevere. "I will come back," he promised. Again he moved backwards. Then he did look at Mador, and told him, too, "I *will* come back."

"Get him!" Mador yelled to the other two, who were still trying to disentangle themselves from each other.

Lancelot turned and fled.

The two knights followed him, and Kiera heard their footsteps running down the hall. But then that was gone also, and all that was left was the sound of Mordred, his face against Agravaine's chest, crying softly.

ight knights were dead, and two seriously injured, besides Mordred. People who for years had been willing to laugh and shrug about Guinevere and Lancelot, people who had said, "Ah, well—passion!" with a wink and a nod, now spoke of bitter betrayal. Adultery was treason for a Queen, and she and Lancelot had been caught together. The trial on which Arthur insisted was simply postponing the inevitable, people complained.

Many put the blame squarely on Lancelot rather than Guinevere, as a man and a knight, he should have known better, they said. Others put the blame on the Orkney brothers—not only Mordred and Agravaine, but also Gawain, Gaheris, and Gareth, who had not even been there—for forcing the King to publicly acknowledge what he had surely known, or at the least suspected, for years.

But whomever else people blamed, the person they most found fault with was Kiera—the witch girl who had known what was coming and refused to warn any-one.

Hildy and Enid and some of the others took to intentionally bumping into Kiera. Or they would tip over her embroidery stand, causing it to crash to the floor: threads and needles skittering under rugs and furniture, never to be seen again. Or they would jar her elbow as she ate so that her dinner ended up in her lap. Queen Guinevere caught them at it once—she walked into the room and found them pouring stagnant water from a flower vase into Kiera's clothes chest. She made them launder the clothes, and even checked to see that they had done a good job. But that didn't serve to make the girls nicer—just more careful.

Kiera's perceived guilt overflowed onto her mother. For years Alayna's healing skills had been recognized and sought out by the ladies of Camelot. But now she was the traitor witch's mother, and instead they went to the tinsmith's mother, a midwife, or they waited for Padraic, the old former sergeant and one-time friar who tended injured knights. If Alayna spent a good deal of time taking care of the injured Mordred, she had a good deal of time to spare.

On the day of Queen Guinevere's trial, Alayna sat on a chair by Mordred's bed, working on some lap embroidery. Even with her weak eyes, Kiera could see the large knotted loop her mother was trying to pick out of the thread; sewing had never been a talent of hers.

Kiera couldn't quite look at Mordred. With his pale face and closed eyes, he gave the impression of being dead.

Like the knight in her vision.

His right hand, the one Lancelot had broken, was wrapped with wet gauze. Padraic had treated the hand with hot oil, and it had become badly swollen, with a throbbing redness that extended almost to the elbow. Alayna had finally convinced Mordred that hot oil festered more wounds than it healed and that she could do better. Since Padraic had begun hinting that the hand might have to be cut off, Mordred was willing to be persuaded.

So far, her hot compresses seemed to have stopped the advance of the bad blood, though he remained alarmingly weak.

If Nimue hadn't died, she could have healed him.

If Nimue hadn't died, she might have taught Kiera how to heal.

If Nimue hadn't died, might none of this have happened?

Gawain entered the room, and Alayna put down the piece of linen she was embroidering. "He needs to sleep," she warned.

Gawain countered, "I need to speak with him."

Alayna shook her head, but it was too late. Mordred's eyes opened.

Feverish, Kiera saw, even as she returned his weak smile. His eyes had that same too-bright quality she had noted in Pinel. She sat hunched over her own embroidery.

Gawain sat down on the edge of the bed. Kiera knew what he was going to say before he said it—not from any magical vision, but from his stormy expression. "The trial is over," Gawain said. "Arthur has just declared the Queen guilty of treason."

Somehow, someway, Kiera had expected that it wouldn't have come to this. That there had been some proper and valid reason for Lancelot being there. A reason Guinevere had to keep to herself till the last possible moment, such as . . .

Such as . . .

"So," said Mordred, struggling to sit up, "that was expected."

"Yes." Gawain offered his brother no assistance. He got up and walked to the window. "Good view," he said. "You should be able to see the execution from here."

"*Execution*," Mordred scoffed.

But even if Mordred took the word lightly, Kiera couldn't.

Gawain turned on him sharply. "Yes, execution. You know the penalty for treason: Trial by combat, or this new civil thing—it's still death. You forced the issue. You backed Arthur into a corner. For God's sake, man, what good will it do you to have the Queen burned at the stake?"

Mordred said, "Arthur has no intention of burning his wife at the stake."

"Then why has he spent all this time listening to the most hateful, despicable—"

"He's waiting." The strain of even this short a conversation was already showing. They all had to lean forward to hear his words. They all looked at him blankly. Mordred added, "For Lancelot."

What in the world was he talking about?

There was a long moment of silence. It was Alayna who spoke. "Arthur isn't that devious. He wouldn't use Guinevere as bait to lure Lance."

"No," Mordred said. "Arthur is honestly counting on Lancelot to come and rescue her. *I* am using her as bait."

Oh, Kiera thought.

Gawain pointed a finger at him. His face was flushed and his voice an angry rumble. "Lancelot again! When will you leave off Lancelot? The man never did harm to any of us—"

"He killed Agravaine."

Kiera fought away the memory.

"Because you came at him. But Lancelot is the one who knighted Gareth. He rescued the whole lot of us from Sir Tarquin—"

"He killed Agravaine," Mordred repeated. His voice was just as even, but the fevered gray eyes sparkled.

"You came at him armed." Gawain practically shook with rage. If Kiera could have fled the room, she would have, rather than listen to them argue. "So he was the Queen's lover," Gawain said. "How did that harm you? Or Agravaine? But the two of you just kept at him and kept at him. *They hurt nothing.* If the King was willing to live with it, *why* . . ." He made a helpless gesture and regained control of his voice. "Why? If I had known what you two planned that night . . ." Again he had to stop. "What a stupid thing to die over."

"Yes." Mordred sank back into his pillow and closed his eyes.

Gawain looked up sharply, perhaps suspecting sarcasm.

"What do you want me to say?" Mordred whispered. "That I weighed Agravaine's life against Lancelot's and thought the risk worth taking? *I never suspected it would end that way.*"

Gawain shook his head. He walked to the window and back. "Peace, Mordred," he said. "Peace."

For the time being, Kiera thought.

With that, the church bell started to ring, a slow, solemn *Bong! Bong! Bong!* The death knell: letting the countryside know the King's decision.

"Damnation," Gawain whispered.

The bell seemed to go on forever. Like the pounding in Kiera's dream, which had turned out to be Agravaine banging on the Queen's door. Demanding entrance. Demanding to be killed.

Mordred waited for it to stop. Then: "When?" he asked.

"Two days hence," Gawain said. "Sunset."

So soon? Kiera thought.

Mordred said nothing.

Kiera looked from him, to Gawain, to Alayna. Her mother, biting her lip, picked up her embroidery again and once more tried to get the thread unknotted. But she worked in impatient, jerky movements and finally tugged, snapping the thread. She pulled the end through to the wrong side, then pulled on the right side, again on the wrong, violently removing that length, starting all over.

"I like Guinevere," Kiera said. "She's very kind."

"Nothing bad is going to happen to her," Mordred said, barely more than a whisper.

Perhaps he believed it.

Gawain stared out the window, and her mother kept undoing the thread.

CHAPTER 6

Guinevere was restricted to her rooms, but she was allowed to keep her ladies-in-waiting.

Once, she suggested that Kiera might return to her mother.

"Are you sending me away?" Kiera asked, thinking of the rumors told about her and her mother and the Orkneys.

"No," Guinevere assured her. "I am only giving you leave to choose for yourself whether to go or stay."

Kiera stayed.

Then it was the last day, and Kiera thought, *The next time she offers, I will go.* But as the time drew near, she watched the ladies one by one excuse themselves and never come back.

Arthur had been there already, sitting with Guinevere for a long time, holding her hands, the two of them talking so quietly that those of the ladies who remained could not hear. And before he left, they embraced, and several more of the ladies departed.

The royal apartments faced north. Usually candles were lit there before they were necessary elsewhere. But this afternoon the ladies did their stitchery by feel, unwilling to acknowledge the coming of dusk.

Father Jerome had come as the shadows grew longer, and now he, too, was gone.

And they were suddenly aware that Guinevere was ready. They had fussed with her long hair, braiding it over and over, never satisfied, until she had called enough, and now the braids were circled around her head, and neither Kiera nor any of the other three remaining ladies could pick out a flaw with which to keep her hands busy. The Queen sat in her plain yellow shift, with her own hands folded on her lap, and they could barely see her face in the gloom.

Someone knocked on the door, softly, hesitantly. Hildy began to cry.

Guinevere waited a moment. Then, when it was obvious not one of her ladies was going to move, she got up and opened the door herself. "Gareth," she said softly. "Gaheris." She looked at her two nephews, and at Father Jerome, who stood behind the two younger men, his head bowed. "Are you to be the ones . . . Are you my guards?" She stood even straighter.

The brothers had neither swords nor armor. Gaheris bowed first, taking her hand and kissing it, and then Gareth did the same. "Lady Queen, we are not your guards, but your honor escort," Gareth said. He bent to kiss her hand again, to hide the tears in his already-red eyes.

Guinevere laid her hand on his cheek. "Gentle Gareth," she whispered. She ran a finger along Gaheris's jaw line. "Sweet Gaheris."

"My Lady," Gaheris said, because it was obvious Gareth couldn't say anything, "it is time."

Guinevere turned to Hildy. "Stop that," she commanded, more sharply than was her wont.

But Hildy only cried louder.

Guinevere tried to reason with her: "Hildy, I cannot be accompanied by someone . . . Please stop. I cannot go out there if . . ." Her voice had begun to tremble.

Kiera saw the Queen's gaze pass over her. Just a child: She knew Guinevere thought it of her, though fourteen was a woman. Only Enid and Selma were left. "Enid," Guinevere begged, because Selma—though quieter than Hildy—was crying just as hard.

Enid shook her head. "I can't," she mouthed, though no words came out.

Guinevere took a deep breath and turned to the door. "I am ready," she told the men.

"I will go with you," Kiera said.

Guinevere shook her head.

Kiera ran after her, tugging on her sleeve. "I'll go."

"It would not be seemly for you to be alone," Gaheris said to the Queen.

Guinevere rested her hand on Kiera's head. "Only," she said, "only if you promise me, give me your word that you'll leave . . . before . . . Before."

Kiera nodded. Did they see she'd agree to anything rather than abandon her Lady?

"Then I thank you. I would be pleased to have you accompany me," Guinevere said. Her face pale, she said: "Now we are ready."

Still unable to look at her, Gareth extended his arm for her. Gaheris took Kiera by the elbow.

Father Jerome stepped to the front. Slowly swinging a censer, he intoned, "By the Cross and Resurrection of Jesus Christ, our Lord and Savior, our faith affirms that we die so that we may live forever."

They started down the hall to the courtyard. The open door at the end of the hall blew the bitter smoke of incense back into Kiera's nostrils, creating a gray fog about her face. She closed her eyes for a moment, letting Gaheris guide her. *Something has to happen*, she thought. *The Queen cannot really die. Arthur can't let that happen. Mordred can't.*

And then the bell started to ring.

The bell tower overlooked the courtyard, almost directly overhead. The noise shot all the way through her: *Bong! Bong! Bong!*—the same solemn tones as when Guinevere had been sentenced.

Kiera stiffened and stopped. Gaheris was brought up short for an instant, then he pulled her along with him. *Don't let yourself get dragged out there,* she tried to convince herself. What was the matter with her? What of the Queen's dignity? She took a few hesitant steps, but Father Jerome and Gareth and the Queen were a good distance ahead of them now, were already outside.

"Yea, though I walk in the Valley of Darkness . . ." Father Jerome began.

Several voices cheered, perhaps to show love and support for Guinevere, like Gareth and Gaheris, or maybe because the interesting part was beginning. The sound was drowned out by another clamor from the bell. Whoever was in charge let each peal fade away before ringing the next. Birds—wrens and sparrows—that normally roosted in the tower alternately wheeled and fluttered uncertainly.

She and Gaheris were in the courtyard now. Kiera looked at the grim faces surrounding her. Who were all these people, like waiting vultures? Could their lives be so drab that they welcomed the diversion of a public burning no matter who the victim was, or were they specifically interested in seeing the Queen die? A man, a local peasant by his garb, had brought in a wagon and was loudly trying to sell sausages.

Ahead of them, Guinevere had mounted the platform that held the stake. She was stepping over the bundles of kindling. *Bong! Bong!* the bell continued. The courtyard spun and Kiera put her hand out to keep from falling onto the grass.

Grass?

But that made no sense: The courtyard was flagstone, not grass. Blue gray flagstone, with blood between the cracks, and there was Agravaine, bleeding from a massive chest wound.

Agravaine?

But he was already dead.

And of an injury to his head, not his chest.

She blinked, stiffened again, and heard herself whimper, but Gaheris chose not to notice. His job was to escort her to the stake, and they had already fallen too far behind the others.

Bong! Bong! Bong!

Kiera screamed and fell to her knees. Gaheris whipped around, looking for the source of danger.

And the bell stopped. There was a *thud!* instead of a *bong!* As though the bell ringer had—what? Stopped in midtug? Just as Gaheris had finally stopped and was now

suspended midway down in crouching beside her . . . As the black-hooded executioner had stopped tying Guinevere to the stake . . . As the crowd stopped murmuring
and shuffling.

Then the bell rang again. But fast this time, frantic, a call to arms, a ringing such
as the people of peaceful Camelot hadn't heard since Arthur had become High King.

"Lord, have mercy on our souls," Gaheris whispered.

The man beside whom they had stopped threw back his rough peasant's cloak,
revealing a long sword. Armed knights jumped out of their hiding places in the
sausage wagon. "Lancelot!" someone called, a cheer. "Lancelot! Lancelot!"

And then another voice yelled: "Burn her!"

CHAPTER 7

Instantly everyone was on the move. Friends and family members got separated. Already the crowd had divided into three contingents: those who wanted the Queen rescued, those who wanted her executed, and those who wanted to get out of the way as quickly as possible while the first two groups fought it out.

On the raised platform, the executioner wavered. He was looking toward the castle, to see if King Arthur watched from one of the windows, obviously hoping the king would give him a sign.

"Go!" Gaheris hauled Kiera to her feet and pushed her back toward the doorway from which they had just come.

The force of his push caused her to stagger forward several paces, but then she stopped to look over her shoulder, to watch what he was going to do. A dog, scrambling out of the way of all the suddenly running feet, got entangled in her legs. She put her arms out to regain her balance, and hit somebody in the face. As she turned to apologize, someone else ran into her, and she flipped over the dog, smacking her palms and scrapping her knees even through her dress. A woman heavy with child, already fallen, screamed into her ear.

The dog gave one warning growl, then began snapping at the surrounding knees and calves. Someone tried to kick the animal, hitting Kiera's elbow instead. But the menacing snarls kept the crowd back long enough for her to get to her feet.

In another instant she was almost trampled down again, but this time she clutched at the nearest person and managed to stay standing. Her hands were swatted away, and she was swept along with the crowd, facing backwards.

"Gaheris!" she called, unable to see over the mass of stampeding bodies—for, though she was too tall for a girl, at least half the crowd were men.

Nobody warned her, and the next moment she backed into rough masonry, the castle wall. The flow of people angled sharply off to the right, toward the nearest door. But it was already impossibly crammed with those trying to get through, away from the courtyard.

Her back scraping against the wall, Kiera forced her way instead to the left. She suddenly broke through the surge of humanity and had an unobstructed view of the courtyard.

There were knights killing each other—Arthur's men, recognizable by the winged dragon that had given the Pendragon family its name, and Lancelot's supporters, who wore no emblem.

But it was not only knights. Townspeople fought each other, using knives or stones or bare hands. Others ganged up on individual knights, often ones who were already wounded. The blacksmith had leaped to the front of the platform where Guinevere was tied, and picked up a bundle of the kindling. Now he waved it before him, jabbing its bristling ends at anybody from either faction who tried to approach. Half-trained squires retrieved weapons of knights who had already fallen, and they were, in turn, cut down.

Kiera squinted, unable from this distance and with her poor eyesight to recognize individual faces. There was one cluster where several of the palace guard fought, and she guessed that to be where Lancelot was. But something was wrong—there weren't as many of the King's men as there should have been. Even given that some would risk the accusation of treason by refusing to fight their former captain, they should have vastly outnumbered Lancelot's group, which couldn't have been more than fifty or sixty.

The sweat on her back and arms chilled and began to prickle as she thought of Gareth and Gaheris unarmored. Once more she entered the crowd, pushing her way closer to the fighting.

A holiday-garbed merchant lurched into her, even though that portion of the crowd which was doing the most frantic pushing had already clustered at the various doorways. "Excuse," the man muttered, his breath stale with wine.

She edged sideways.

He took hold of her shoulders, tried to straighten her dress that was all twisted from sliding against the wall. "Excuse," he repeated, tipping forward.

"Get away from me!" she cried, loudly, to be heard over the clamor of the bell.

He backed away, bowing. "Looking for the door," he said. "Excuse." He sat down suddenly, looking surprised.

Kiera circled around him. "Gaheris!" she called. "Gareth!" Her voice didn't carry. She herself could barely hear it over the ringing of the bell and the clashing of swords and the shouts of men, both battle cries and death cries. *Let the others do this on their own!* she wanted to warn them. Oh, let the others do it.

A hand grabbed her shoulder from behind. She whipped around, suspecting the drunken merchant again, but it was Gaheris. She was ready to hug him, but he held her out at arm's length and shook her. "I thought you were safe inside. Dammit, I can't be nursemaid to you."

She opened her mouth to try to tell him the awful danger he was in: how she had seen him and Gareth, as well as Agravaine, dead.

"Burn her!" shouted the man standing next to them, his voice drowning out hers.

Gaheris flashed him a look of loathing.

"Gaheris," she tried again. Already his attention had moved off her, was focused instead on the center of the courtyard, where Guinevere was still tied to the stake, where Gareth stood, arguing with the black-hooded executioner who held his lighted torch. The blacksmith, whichever side he'd been on, was sprawled face down among the kindling. "Gaheris," Kiera insisted.

"Burn her!" the townsman next to them yelled again, and threw a rock that hit Gareth on the back, between the shoulder blades. Gareth whirled to scan the melee.

But Gaheris was closer, was there already. He took handfuls of the man's shirt and flung him against the sausage wagon. The man staggered and Gaheris kept him from falling by bouncing him off the side of the wagon again, and then again.

"Gaheris!" she begged, but he wouldn't be diverted. She looked toward the stake again. She couldn't hear, but she could tell that Gareth was angry by the way he waved his arms at the executioner, who, in return, shook his torch practically under Gareth's nose. Gareth grabbed his wrist and the man tried to pull away.

Another rock flew from a different direction to fall harmlessly among the kindling.

And then a third stone was hurled, and this one struck the executioner's hand. He jerked back.

And dropped the burning torch.

Into the kindling.

The dried wood burst into flame, and the crowd erupted into noise—cheers as well as cries of dismay.

Kiera caught a glimpse of Lancelot, wading through the concentration of Arthur's men who had positioned themselves around the platform. Not enough, she realized: They'd never stop him. He swung his broadsword before him, and his own followers were having a difficult time keeping up. She saw Sir Aglovale go down, and Sir Belliance, then lost sight of Lancelot.

She turned to Gaheris and found that he was gone, too. She finally made him out already halfway to the stake. There Gareth stamped on the flames. Guinevere shrank back against the stake, away from the fire. Then Kiera noticed the executioner. Apparently he had decided that in absence of a decision by the King, he'd take the fallen torch as a sign from God. He was running full-tilt at Gareth from behind.

"Look out!" she yelled. Not in time, even if she had been loud enough. Gareth went sprawling.

Just beyond the platform, Lancelot crouched as a peasant swung a thick, rough-hewn stave at his head. He sprang erect, his sword angled, and impaled the man. At the same moment Lancelot was yanking his sword free, Gareth was trying to get back to his feet. He must have heard the commotion behind him, for he whirled around, still at a half crouch, just as Lancelot leaped onto the platform.

And Lancelot ran him through.

"Gareth!" Kiera screamed.

Yet even if she had been close enough, he was already beyond hearing.

But there was still time to try to save his brother. "Gaheris!" Kiera screamed with all her might.

Gaheris swung onto the platform just as Lancelot sliced the ropes that bound Guinevere. Gaheris froze when he saw Gareth's body.

"Gaheris!" Kiera pushed through the crowd. "Lancelot, it's Gaheris!"

Lancelot must have caught Gaheris's movement out of the corner of his eye. His movement, but not his face. Lancelot gave a backhanded swing of his sword without noticing that the figure did not threaten, did not—in fact—move. The blade sliced Gaheris's throat, and Lancelot didn't check to make sure he was dead, nor even to see whom, among all the many, he was.

Kiera dropped to her knees, covering her eyes, unwilling to witness any more.

Sir Bors's voice rose above the confusion. "Lance! The rest of the guards!"

Reluctantly, Kiera pulled her hands down from her eyes. From somewhere, Lancelot's people had brought out readied horses. But now, two or three dozen of the palace guard were streaming into the courtyard, all on foot, all from the direction of the gate.

Numbly, Kiera realized that she was between the two groups of armed men. Arthur's men had been waiting, she saw, expecting a frontal assault, not infiltration. And now they were straggling in, a few dozen at a time, out of breath from the run in full field armor, and found themselves in the unaccustomed position of foot soldiers facing the lowered lances of mounted chevaliers.

From behind she heard Mordred's voice, yelling to the King's men to fall back, not to stand up against the horses.

Lancelot, mounted behind Guinevere and surrounded by his men, dug his heels into his destrier's sides. The group formed a wedge, and aimed themselves at Arthur's men, who scattered.

Move! Kiera told herself, but there wasn't time. She threw her arms up to protect her head—much good *that* would do, but it was all there was time for.

An arm circled her waist, dragged her backwards, so that she and the person who had pulled her back tumbled to the ground. She felt a tug on her dress, felt and heard the tear of fabric, and knew that a horse's hoof had landed on the trailing hem.

She recognized the feel of her mother's arms, then the voice, shouting in her ear, cursing Lancelot's men as savages who endangered the lives of innocent children.

Kiera twisted around to gape at Alayna, this soft-spoken, soft-bodied woman who shunned situations of crowding and noise, who had somehow been close enough to see her danger.

Now that Lancelot and Guinevere had escaped, those of the townspeople who remained in the courtyard were joined by many who had initially retreated indoors. Dead bodies were identified. The widow Clive's son. Sir Priamus. Young Sumner who had just been accepted into the Woodcrafters' Guild. Friends and relatives with caved-in skulls or gaping wounds. The summer evening was pierced by voices raised in mourning, sending chills up the backs of all who had not yet located their loved ones.

Once again, people were running.

A second pair of arms plucked Kiera off the ground, away from her mother. Mordred held her while he called directions for the setting up of an infirmary for the wounded, then impatiently, as if he had asked before, demanded where the horses were. There was still no sign of Arthur, and the people seemed to instinctively acknowledge Mordred as being in charge.

"I'm not hurt," Kiera said as soon as she could speak without interrupting him. "I can stand."

Mordred set her down. He had been supporting her weight mostly with his left, uninjured arm and didn't look as if he could have done so for much longer. But still, he looked at her closely before turning away. "Gawain, go see if you can find out what the delay is at the stable. They will be half the way to France before we ever get started." He raised his voice to carry into the crowd. "Has anybody seen Gareth or Gaheris? And would somebody please get that fool to stop ringing the bell? Sir Lucan . . ."

Kiera felt her mother's arms around her again, and realized she had swayed, almost fallen. "Mordred," Kiera said, unable to get much louder than a whisper.

He had hold of her other elbow. "Can somebody—"

Several people were yelling all at once. "The horses. They've gone and killed the horses."

Two squires tried to force their way through the crowd to Mordred's side.

"Move!" Gawain, behind them, pushed one insistent man out of the way, intimidated the rest with his voice and sheer bulk. He grabbed Mordred's arm, which made his younger brother wince. "Lancelot's men," Gawain panted. "They've killed the stable master and his assistants. A good quarter of the horses are dead or cut up. Much of the equipment is slashed and unusable. They tried to get a fire going, but thank God our people caught it before it spread too far."

Mordred swore. "Get together what you can . . ." Mercifully, the clamor from the bell cut off abruptly. "See what you can salvage—"

"Done, it's done. They'll be out as soon as they can, but good Lord, Mordred, the horses! There was no need for that."

"Did you see Gareth or Gaheris?"

Gawain shook his head. "I had trouble convincing Arthur to stay inside. Maybe they're with him."

"Mordred," Kiera said, still not much more than a whisper. "Gawain." She noted the quick looks behind their backs and knew she wasn't the only one who had seen. Why were they leaving this to her? Why didn't one of the adults tell them? Somebody had hold of Mordred's arm, was asking about the Channel crossing should Lancelot's men get that far.

Kiera tugged on his shirt, despite Alayna's continued fretting. "Mordred."

He gestured for her to wait, and she repeated his name much more loudly. He turned, even though the squires had started to bring out the surviving horses, accoutered in what remained of saddles and bridles. Gawain, asking something of one of the squires, realized he was suddenly the only one in the vicinity talking, and stopped midsentence.

Mordred's dark gray eyes surveyed the crowd. Perhaps he recognized the hunger, the way their eyes expectantly flicked from him to Kiera.

Vultures, she thought again. *They're waiting to feed on him.*

She searched for the right words, but there were none.

"He didn't see them," she blurted out, not any reasonable way to start, but the silence could go on no longer. "Mordred, he didn't mean it."

Mordred's eyes narrowed.

"Lancelot," Kiera said, and in that moment, he knew. She could see he knew. She said, "There were so many people, armed knights and townsfolk throwing stones."

Mordred turned to face the platform, the stake.

How had she come to this, that she was defending Lancelot, who was destroying the people she loved most? She insisted, "He didn't recognize them!"

People moved out of his way faster than they had done earlier for Gawain. Gawain was fighting comprehension, obviously trying to fit a different meaning to Kiera's words, but his face was pale above his beard. "Not Gareth," he said, laying his large hand on her shoulder. "He would never have hurt young Gareth."

But a path had opened from them to the platform, and his keen eyes would have been able to sort out the sprawled forms at the foot of the stake. His hand fell from her shoulder and he walked woodenly after Mordred.

Kiera ran after them.

Mordred had knelt next to Gareth, but looked up at the clatter they made mounting the platform. "They weren't armed," he said—though everyone could already see that.

"Apparently that don't matter to Sir Lancelot," somebody yelled up. "My neighbor's boy, Kent, warn't armed neither."

The crowd murmured, sympathy or impatience. Several of the knights hesitantly mounted the readied horses.

Gawain sat down heavily between his two dead brothers and looked from one to the other.

"They weren't armed," Mordred repeated.

"No," Gawain agreed numbly. He ran both hands over his face, covered his mouth.

Kiera felt icy fingers brush against her heart. For as long as she had known him, Gawain had always had a beard—the only one of the five brothers who did. Now, with it momentarily hidden, Kiera saw that his resemblance to Agravaine was greater than she had ever realized. An image of Agravaine, dead in the Queen's chambers, forced itself into her mind.

Gawain let his hands drop, and he was suddenly just Gawain again. "It could *not* have been Lancelot," he said. "He was always a friend to the boys, especially Gareth. For God's sake, he *knighted* Gareth."

"It was Lancelot," someone called out. "I seen it."

"Me too," another voice said.

"Aye, he never saw who it was," a third added, grudging concession, "but it was him."

"I told them it was madness." Mordred seemed oblivious to the crowd that closed in. "Honor guard. I told them to keep out of it."

"I never thought . . ." Gawain started. "Lancelot has never . . . Oh, God, *they weren't armed.*"

Mordred sat back on his heels. He pulled something from his shirt. For some rea-son, the gesture gave Kiera a rush of unexpected panic, an echo of a recurrent though never quite recalled nightmare. But it was only Nimue's ring, held around Mordred's neck by a thin strip of leather. He held the gold band in his fist, his eyes closed, his face tipped back toward the evening sky. Gawain, on the other hand, bent over Gaheris so that his hair—dark shot through with gray, much the same as Lancelot's—fell forward and hid his face. Yet his shoulders shook. Everyone could tell that he was crying.

And they approved, Kiera could sense it. Tears for a dead brother were something they could understand. Mordred's control, however tenuous, was *not*.

Alayna took Gawain by the shoulders. "Gawain," she told him, "he couldn't have meant to do it . . ."

He pulled away. Stood up.

Kiera reached for his hand, but he didn't see, or chose to ignore. He jumped down from the platform, then stooped to pick up one of the swords that had been dropped during the fighting. "Mordred," Alayna said sharply, urgently.

Mordred turned, and saw that Gawain had taken the reins of one of the horses. "What are you doing?" he asked.

"Going to Joyous Gard, if need be," Gawain answered, which was Lancelot's cas-tle in Brittany. The crowd of knights and half-armed townspeople began to show signs of life at this. Blood feud was something else they could understand. Somebody started a cheer, which was caught up by others. They suddenly had a leader.

"Hurry with the rest of those horses," one of the knights shouted toward the sta-ble, for all the first group was suddenly taken.

Mordred got to his feet—didn't anybody else see how much that cost him?—and strode to Gawain.

Alayna and Kiera followed before the crowd closed in again. They were right behind when Mordred rested his arm across the saddle so that Gawain couldn't mount. His voice was quiet, but it had always had a tendency to carry. "Gawain, this isn't the time—"

"Isn't the time?" Gawain could barely get the words out. "Mordred, Gareth loved him. All Lancelot had to do was ask, and he would have gone against anybody for him. He would have chosen him above King Arthur . . . Mordred, he would have chosen him above us. *You* wanted this; you pushed for it. You and Agravaine against Gareth and Gaheris, with me in the middle. Well, now I am on your side. I admit you were right about Lancelot all along." He swung onto the horse, and Mordred had to move his hand lest his brother sit on it.

"This . . . this is not what I wanted." Mordred raised his voice, playing to the courtyard. "We are *not* riding out tonight with only a few score of horses. That would just get more men killed. We are going to pull in horses and equipment from the countryside, and when we ride out we will be organized and under King Arthur's direction."

Gawain made a move as though to hit him across the face, and only refrained at the last instant. He spoke in a shaky whisper. "You have always been good at calculations: This is three-fifths of the family gone, you . . ." He bit off the rest of what he'd planned to say. He dug his heels into the horse's sides, but Mordred grabbed the reins. That, and the closeness of the crowd, confused the steed enough that it stopped, pacing restively.

Mordred winced at the jarring on his hand. "Whatever King Arthur's feelings are," he said, still loud enough for everybody to hear, "Lancelot has treacherously attacked people under the protection of Camelot and wrongfully killed knights bound by oaths of fealty to the King and performing their duty under his law."

This was an appeal to reason that the people could understand. They murmured and muttered, knowing that Mordred was right, yet perhaps distrusting him still for being level-headed at a time like this.

"Gawain . . ." Mordred's voice dropped so that only those standing nearest could discern his words. "Gawain, please. I can make out the mathematics of it, too." His eyes were bright, whether from tears, or the last vestiges of fever, or reflected starlight—Kiera couldn't tell. He was pale and shivering.

Gawain rested his hand on Mordred's head. "All right," he whispered. "All right." He turned to the crowd. "We wait for King Arthur to lead us." He was crying, and the words were just about indistinguishable, but it was all they needed.

They gave a subdued cheer.

Very tasteful for the circumstances, Kiera thought.

Stop it, she told herself. Amiable Gareth and the stormy but kind-hearted Gaheris were dead, as was Agravaine, who had always been able to make her laugh; and all she could do was fall back into distant mocking. But with that thought, the distance was gone, and she began to cry. For she suddenly realized what she had seen on that hillside with her mother and Nimue and Mordred and Agravaine. She had seen all the brothers from Orkney dead: Agravaine, Gareth, Gaheris—and Gawain, too. Mordred mortally wounded. King Arthur dying. Nothing left of Camelot: a puff of smoke, a pile of ash, sated buzzards. The knights and ladies and all their dreams forgotten. The towers dismantled, their stones used to shore up a peasant's wall. The Round Table burned piece by piece in a shepherd's cook fire. *Oh, Mordred, don't do it*, she thought.

But she didn't know what it was he shouldn't do.

CHAPTER 8

Kiera missed much of the turmoil of the days that followed. Servants and nobles alike scurried to prepare and pack wagonloads of food, clothing, medical supplies, and extra military equipment. Craftsmen worked late into the night making swords, saddles, harnesses, barrels, anything that might be needed for the siege on Lancelot in his castle at Joyous Gard. Horses throughout the countryside were requisitioned.

Arthur, gaunt and silent, seemed everywhere at once, and Mordred was always at his side. Somewhere during that time, the last of those who had persisted in calling Mordred Arthur's nephew began to acknowledge him as Arthur's son.

Even before the army left, peasants from the surrounding land started to drift in, to throw together hasty shelters or find dry corners within the outer walls. Those who lived in the outlying regions knew that without the protection of Camelot's knights they would make easy targets for the kind of men who were always there to take advantage of unsettled, unvigilant times; and they drew in, a closing spiral, each wave taking over the cottages and holdings abandoned by those who had moved on before them.

Kiera caught glimpses of the preparations, but she spent most of her time help-ing Alayna in the rooms that had been set aside as an infirmary. There had been enough people wounded in what was already being called the Courtyard Massacre that at first they weren't particular about who tended them.

But the day the army moved out, with Arthur at its head, and Mordred left behind as regent, Kiera and her mother were thanked for their help in tending the wounded and were asked to keep away from the sick room.

"Stupid, ungrateful, superstitious . . ." Alayna crammed her things—powders and ointments and tinctures—into a bag, muttering loudly so that Padraic, standing close to make sure she took nothing of his, could hear.

Padraic didn't care.

Nor did Kiera, who had become anxious about some of the looks she and her mother had been getting the last day or so. As if they had spent all those hours changing fetid bandages and ministering to the weak and delirious only to poison them at the first signs of health. Many of the men who had never before bothered much about religion had suddenly taken to wearing rosary beads around their necks. Kiera would walk into the infirmary and be greeted by a flurry of bowed heads and mumbled prayers. She and her mother were lucky to be out of it, she thought, if only Alayna didn't provoke anybody.

Alayna pulled her bag off the table. "It has been delightful working with you," she told Padraic. "Delightful and inspiring."

Padraic shrugged.

Tight-lipped, Alayna looked around the room, at the knights in their various stages of recovery, as though she still hoped for some word or acknowledgment from somebody whom they had helped.

Nothing. Not one sign of reluctance to see them go.

"God be with you," she said. "May you all prosper under Padraic's skilled and gentle care."

Still nothing.

Alayna turned and stalked out of the room so abruptly that Kiera had to run to catch up.

For Kiera, and the other women and children of the castle, things quickly settled into a routine, a routine involving refugee peasants who had taken over the public halls and rooms and who were always underfoot with their bundles of clothes, their children, and their squealing, squawking, or bleating livestock.

As for the men, there were constant skirmishes as adventurers harried the ill-fortified border lands. To support the thinly deployed knights, Mordred announced he would begin to train a troop in the use of longbows. Anybody—anybody—could join.

Over the years, Kiera had often enough overheard her mother and Mordred debate the morality of arming peasants. It had been a familiar argument between Mordred and Arthur, too, during their last days together.

No doubt those of like mind to the King sent word to him.

No doubt Arthur sent word back that Mordred's special troop was to be disbanded.

But if so, Mordred ignored the order. And though the knights complained about fighting side by side with commoners, it wasn't long before everyone saw that even this small, raw group of archers had a devastating effect in battle.

By autumn, the serfs felt safe enough to return to their fields for the harvest. Only a small number of holdings had been burned, and Mordred saw to it that those affected were provided for, which pleased both the peasants and the inhabitants of Camelot—who could finally walk down a hall without tripping over somebody.

With each peaceful day that passed, Mordred became more popular. And as his popularity grew, the antipathy toward Kiera and her mother finally lessened.

They are just waiting, Kiera thought. It wouldn't take much to change their mood again.

Dispatches came from Brittany. Lancelot and his men were entrenched in Joyous Gard and would not come out to fight Arthur's men. Arthur had settled down to wait for Lancelot to run out of supplies, which probably wouldn't happen until spring or early summer.

Knights who had been banished for denouncing Lancelot during the early years returned to court to reaffirm their loyalty, to offer Mordred their service. Others came whose exile had had nothing to do with the out-of-favor Lancelot, but who hoped to be welcomed back because of the general atmosphere of harmony and forgiveness that Mordred was promoting.

One of these was Sir Bayard of Castle Ridgemont at Ravens' Rock.

CHAPTER 9

Kiera was sitting at the edge of the pond talking with the ducks. They had been complaining about a pair of boys who had found some of the nests and were stealing eggs. That should have been warning enough, when the birds went into a sudden panic of squawks and beating wings and left without a good-bye. But Kiera put it down to ducks' flighty temperament, and she remained where she was. She leaned back, savoring the spring sun on her eyelids, the tickle of the new grass on her bare legs, the breeze that lifted wisps of her hair.

Behind her, a pebble rattled down the hill. Kiera sat up, rearranged her gown to cover her legs, and called out, "Hello?"

A twig snapped, but no one answered.

The air suddenly seemed too chill for her to be out here alone sitting on the damp ground. Standing, she tightened the ribbon that kept her hair back from her face and stood. On one of the bushes at the top of the slope that lead down to the pond, a branch moved. She didn't call again, but only picked up the basket in which she had been gathering flowers.

Someone laughed softly.

Then there was a war whoop, and the clatter of

someone half-running and half-sliding down the hill. Two of them, town boys: She knew them well enough to recognize them. They were three or four years older than she and had the rough, swaggering look of bullies. So, she thought, they were hunting for duck eggs after all. But then they reached the bottom of the hill, and they didn't go straight, to the pond, but swept along in a wide curve to the right, toward her.

She hesitated, and already it was too late. The boys separated, one on either side. As they passed, one snatched her flower basket away, the other yanked on her hair ribbon, undoing the knot, tugging her hair. "Stop!" she yelped. "That hurt!"

They stopped running and now tossed her basket to each other, spilling butter-cups, violets, and alyssum.

"Stop that," she said. She stepped forward, but they danced away, always just beyond her reach. She pulled the trailing ribbon out of her hair before they could seize that, too, and held it tightly in her fist. "Give me back that basket."

"Oh, she wants her basket back," one of the boys taunted. He held it out toward her, balanced by its handle on the tip of his finger. "Come and get it, then."

She took a step toward him and he swung his arm in closer to himself.

"Come on," he taunted. "Come and get it." He shook his pale blond hair out of his eyes and met her anger steadily.

Kiera put her hands on her hips, refusing to play this game.

"Don't you want it? Let your animal friends fetch it for you, then. Witch." He heaved the basket into the pond. It disappeared into the water, leaving behind a rain-bow swirl of daisies and bluebells that bobbed and floated on the surface. The boys laughed and whistled.

Bullying was one thing.

Calling her a witch was much, much more dangerous. Kiera turned and ran, head-ing for the woods. But she'd taken only a few steps before one of the youths hit her from behind, making her fall. He forced her to sit up, her arms pinned behind her. It had to be the blond, short one who held her, for the dark, gangly youth stood before her, poking her with a stick.

She aimed a kick at his knee, but couldn't reach.

"Witch," the blond boy said. "Hold still! Hold still, or I'll twist it off." He forced one arm up higher. Then, to his companion, he warned: "Don't let her look in your eyes, Lowell, and she won't be able to put a spell on you."

The second boy averted his eyes from her face but continued to poke at her.

Kiera jerked her head back, smacking it into the face of her captor.

He grunted but held her all the tighter. "Look what she's done!" His voice was a mumble around his pain. "My mouth's all bleeding!"

He shoved her away then, and the dark youth, Lowell, grabbed a fistful of her hair and twisted. She didn't cry out, though her eyes swam with tears of pain. She saw the blond one put his hand to his mouth, then take it away again. "Miserable witch!" He slapped her, hard.

Lowell demonstrated he was as stupid as his friend by using *his* name, which any fool should have known was a more dangerous thing to give a witch than even a direct look in the eyes. He said, "Know what they do with witches, Eldred?"

Eldred's cut and bruised lips twisted into a slow smile. "Same as we did to her flowers."

They wouldn't, Kiera told herself. They wouldn't risk that she couldn't swim and might drown. Still she tried to squirm away, but they both had her by the hair, and now the blond Eldred had once more forced her arm behind her back.

They dragged her to the edge of the pond. There, they picked her up—one taking her arms, the other her legs. "One," they chanted. "Two. Three."

She still thought it was only a threat until the moment they flung her loose.

The water closed over her head, instantly soaking the layers of her clothing, weighing her down. Kiera didn't know how to swim and she had no idea how deep the pond was and already the breath she'd instinctively taken right before she'd hit the water was burning in her lungs.

At first she couldn't tell which way was up. But then she felt the bottom, sucking mud and clinging water weeds. She got her legs beneath her, was on her knees.

Her head cleared the surface, the water coming barely to her chin.

They'd probably known that; they'd probably just wanted to frighten her.

Or so she thought, until—sputtering and spitting, and fighting both her own hair and her clothing—she felt one of the boys grab the back of her neck and force her face once again under the water. She tried to hit and kick at the encircling arms and legs, but the water pressed against her movements, slowing them, weakening them, making them ineffectual.

They *were*, she realized. They *were* trying to kill her.

And then suddenly, just as she knew her lungs would surely burst, there was an extra pair of legs in the water. One of the boys let her go, and then the other, and she bobbed to the surface long enough to suck in the breath she needed. She found the bottom again and got her feet beneath her and stood.

An armored knight had Lowell by the front of his shirt. She didn't recognize the man's insignia—a crow?—and he had his back to her; but he was big—big enough to hold the lanky youth off the ground and to shake him hard enough to cause his dark head to snap back and forth.

On the shore, Eldred struggled to get out of the bush into which the stranger had thrown him. Besides the bruises she had made with the back of her head on his face, he had deeper gashes from the sharp branches, and he held one elbow in close as if the arm might be broken. He struggled to his feet, but made no effort to help his friend. Instead he tried to get out of the clearing, staggering and weaving.

The knight saw him, and dropped the limp body of Lowell into the water. The youth was face up, and he floated, but Kiera knew he was dead by the angle at which his head was tipped. His neck had to be broken.

Good, she thought. But she didn't feel good.

"No!" Eldred screamed when he saw the knight coming after him. Despite the man's heavy armor and the water streaming out of it, his longer stride and the youth's battered condition made it a one-sided race.

The knight grabbed the back of Eldred's collar. He whipped him around and struck him with his heavy mailed fist. Then he picked him up and flung him against a tree.

From where she stood, Kiera could hear the *thud* as Eldred's head struck the tree trunk. She had spent too much time these past weeks ministering to broken bodies, listening to the crying of families, and could find no satisfaction in what was happening. She had seen how fragile life could be. Watching this violence, she felt in her heart that they deserved it, but she could take no satisfaction from it.

The knight stepped back. He turned from one motionless body to the other, then faced Kiera. "Are you all right, little maid?" He waded into the pond, then went down on one knee. His dark eyes inspected her anxiously.

She stood there, cold and dripping and wondered if she would ever feel warm again. She nodded.

"Yon young ruffians will harm you no more."

"No," she agreed, unable to get her voice more substantial than a whisper.

He stood, extending his hand to her. "Let me help you out of there."

Kiera just hugged her arms to herself.

"Do not be afraid," he said. "I have seen you at Camelot. I am from there, too, though just recently, so you don't know me. My name is Sir Bayard of Ridgemont." He smiled. Fatherly. Brotherly.

"I know who you are," she told him.

"So. Well." Before she could resist, he had put an arm under her knees and the other around the upper part of her body, and he picked her up.

Her heart pounded so hard she thought she would die from it. *Mordred's enemy*, she thought. *Mordred's enemy.*

But his horse was there, tied to a tree just a few yards from the clearing. He set her down on the saddle gently, then took the bridle and walked the horse down to the path that led to the castle, asking over and over to make sure she was unharmed.

Kiera kept her gaze on the back of the horse's neck, holding tightly to the saddle, which was too big to give her enough support, and slippery with the wetness of her clothes.

In the courtyard, people started to gather. Bayard snapped at them, ordering them out of the way, declaring that the young lass needed to be tended to.

"I'm fine," Kiera said. "I am *not* hurt."

But he paid her no heed.

More people came to see what all his fuss was about. At the castle gate, he tossed the reins to a nearby squire and lifted Kiera off the horse.

"I can walk by myself," Kiera assured him, but he didn't set her down, so she pressed her face against his chest, unwilling to look at the people, to let them look at her.

She felt him climb the stairs. There was a back way to the room she shared once again with her mother, now that the Queen was in Brittany with Lancelot. But Bayard was new to Camelot, so perhaps he didn't know where the women's rooms were. He headed for the Great Hall.

Kiera tried to make herself smaller.

Then she heard her mother. "Out of my way!" Alayna demanded, her voice shrill with anxiety.

Finally, finally Bayard set her on her feet.

The next moment, Alayna almost knocked her over. She threw her arms around her. "Are you all right? What happened? Are you hurt? Oh, Kiera."

"She is uninjured, madam," Bayard said, more loudly than necessary—for the crowd's benefit. "Just shaken and frightened. She was set upon by two local ruffians, but I intervened in time. She has not been hurt."

Her mother took her chin in her hand and looked into her face, then hugged her again. "Oh, my poor, poor dear."

Voices called out from the crowd, demanding details.

"Who was it?"

"Where?"

"What happened?"

Why didn't they stop shouting? Why didn't they leave her alone? All she wanted was to get away from them, all of them.

Bayard explained. He said: "By the duck pond. Beyond the north pasture. I was exercising my horse when I heard her scream. I don't know the youths' names, but I've seen them before. I . . . I think somebody better go back there and see to them. They were trying to drown her. I was so enraged that I . . . did not take into account that they were little more than boys, and unarmored."

Kiera remembered the way the one boy's head had snapped back on his neck, and how the other had been thrown against the tree. She stole a glance at Bayard, then looked back down at the floor.

Still holding onto Kiera, Alayna dropped into a deep curtsy. She took Bayard's hand and pressed it to her cheek. "We are forever in your debt, kind sir."

"My Lady," Bayard murmured, and kissed her hand.

There was a sudden movement in the crowd. The people in front of Kiera were parting, not reluctantly as they had for Bayard and Alayna, and without being shouted at this time. They moved aside soundlessly, and Mordred strode into the sudden clearing that had formed.

He looked first at Kiera, then quickly to Bayard, and back to Kiera. "Are you all right?"

"She has had a bad fright," Bayard said. "But I came in time to see they did her no lasting harm."

Mordred didn't even look at him. He put one hand on Kiera's shoulder and the other, in a gesture mirroring Alayna's, under her chin. "Are you all right?" he repeated.

Kiera nodded.

"What happened?" he asked in what Kiera always thought of as his dangerous voice—soft and slightly husky.

"Nothing," she whispered. "Nothing happened." How could she tell them that the youths had tried to drown her as a witch? In the stillness she thought she could hear the breeze in the trees again, the far-off quacking of the ducks, the raspy breath of the two youths.

Then, "Sir Bayard rescued the maid," called a voice from the crowd.

"Did he?" Mordred's cool gray eyes shifted to Bayard, who inclined his head in acknowledgment.

"Yes," someone said, and then another.

"She was attacked by a pair of ruffians, and Sir Bayard came along just in time to save her honor."

She didn't correct them. She didn't tell them that they had called her witch.

Someone said, "Justin has gone to see who they were."

"About to rape her, they probably were."

For a moment, everyone was talking, then they were all still again.

Kiera closed her eyes, reliving it:

> *The spilled bluebells . . .*
>> *Eldred's swollen lips . . .*
>> *"She's uninjured, madam," Bayard said. "I intervened in time . . ."*
>> *She felt their solid grips on her wrists and ankles, tasted the water again . . .*
>> *"By the duck pond," Bayard said. "I heard her scream . . ."*
>> *She saw Lowell's body, like a boneless thing in the water, and heard the* thud *of Eldred against the tree . . .*
>> *"I did not take into account that they were unarmored . . ."*

She shook her head to clear it.

"Bayard," Mordred said, acknowledging the man with an all but imperceptible bow.

With a tight smile Bayard again inclined his head.

The crowd began to make way again, for them to pass, but then there was a commotion near the door. Would she never get away from all these people?

"What is it?" asked Bayard, who had started to follow Mordred, Kiera, and Alayna.

"Make way, make way," a huffing voice called. After some shoving and complaining, finally one of the older knights pushed his way through—Sir Justin, who had not gone with King Arthur's group because his joints were so stiff that in rainy weather he was barely able to walk. He waded through the crowd with his peculiar rolling gait, all the while dragging by the shoulder a boy of no more than ten, who looked and smelled to be a goatherd.

"My Lord," the stocky knight managed to puff out when he saw Mordred. He steered his reluctant charge toward them. "I was riding out to that duck pond yon fellow was talking about, when I saw this young laddie break from the woods, heading for the castle like the devil's own hounds were after him." He pushed the boy closer. "Tell 'im what you told me, boy."

The goatherd pulled his gaze away from the ornate woodcarvings and wall hangings, beyond the sumptuously dressed lords and ladies in their everyday clothes. He looked at Mordred, probably the nearest thing to a king he would ever see, and gulped.

"Tell 'im what you saw, boy." Justin gave him a little shake.

The boy's voice was a whisper, which they leaned forward to hear. "Well, sir, one of the goats, Teaser, he goes off from the rest of them, sir—"

"Not that part, you young fool." Justin cuffed him.

Again the boy gulped. "Eldred and Lowell, sir," he whispered, "an you please, sir."

There was a sigh from the crowd, the release of a communally held breath.

"And," Justin urged him. "And . . ."

Kiera felt fingers digging into her hair, hurting. She felt her lungs empty and aching, with the water pressing to get in.

The boy took another breath—his one moment of importance—and looked, for at least two heartbeats, directly at Mordred. "They was dead, sir."

Mordred's eyebrows lifted.

"An you please, sir. Eldred, his skull wor bashed in against a tree, sir, and Lowell, his neck wor broke. Sir."

Bayard sighed. "I never . . . In the heat of the moment . . . My only thought was to get them away from the girl."

Mordred said nothing, only looked at Bayard appraisingly.

Bayard said, "I never meant to kill them."

"You never mean to kill anybody," Mordred said. "I remember that."

"Mordred!" Alayna gasped. "Bayard has—"

"Bayard was a nephew of the wizard Halbert. You do remember Halbert?"

The vision of her mother, and the sword, and the tall blond man with her mother's features and the empty eyes came back to Kiera. And Halbert . . . But that memory slipped away.

"Didn't you hear what they tried to do to Kiera?" Alayna said. One hand still encircled Kiera's shoulders. Now she rested the other on Bayard's arm. "Sir Bayard rescued her."

"She's uninjured, madam," Bayard said. "I heard her scream." She saw him shake Lowell until his neck snapped. "I intervened in time."

"Certainly Sir Mordred, also, would have helped," Bayard said silkily, "had he been there."

Mordred's chin raised slightly, but he said nothing.

The rattle of a pebble. Her basket sinking in the pond. The roughness on her palms as she slid on the ground. She felt their fingers trying to pull out her hair. She couldn't breathe, couldn't breathe.

Bayard's gaze surveyed the crowd. "Please, somebody, find out the families of the youths. Despite Sir Mordred's doubts, I had no wish for their deaths, no matter what crime they intended against this child. I would make restitution to the parents." He laid a hand on Kiera's head.

She ducked, edging away, and Bayard was left with one hand in the air. He took Alayna by the elbow, and smiled. "Shall we get the lass out of the crowd?" he murmured and started to force his way through, still holding onto her mother.

At the doorway, Kiera turned back. Old Justin was ushering out the young goatherd who was still trying to take in all he could of the Great Hall. Mordred stood in the center of the diminishing crowd, his gaze hard and intent on the backs of Bayard and Alayna. And the rest of the people were beginning to drift away, many of them no doubt headed for the duck pond.

I heard her scream, Bayard had said.

But try as she might, Kiera couldn't remember screaming.

CHAPTER 10

The next day Bayard called on them, to see how Kiera fared.

And the day after he came again, bringing as a gift an intricately woven basket, much finer than the one Eldred and Lowell had thrown into the pond, and he said he would be pleased to escort Kiera and Alayna on a flower-gathering picnic if they'd so honor him.

No, Kiera told him, she didn't quite feel up to it.

But he came back the following day, with a different basket and the same offer. And then again, and again, until her mother agreed they would go.

He came even more often after that, one time bringing a pretty lace handkerchief, and another some sweets in a painted tin box, and—on Kiera's fifteenth birthday—a pink hair ribbon edged with silver thread.

"Thank you," Kiera said for each of the gifts, and handed them directly to Alayna without really looking at them or Bayard. Except for the time he gave her the ribbon. That reminded her too much of the one she had lost on the sunny hillside draped in magic gray. The images would give her no rest: she and Mordred returning . . . a curl of Nimue's golden hair hanging below her hood . . . the *thud* of Pinel's sword into the ground . . . Agravaine—his face as pale as death—Agravaine . . .

Kiera dropped Bayard's ribbon into the midden.

"Oh, Kiera!" her mother said in exasperation when she asked after the ribbon and Kiera told her what she'd done. Alayna paused in her weaving and gave Kiera a long hard stare.

Kiera pretended to concentrate on the cloth she was making. It was aqua, a shade she knew would make her look sallow and unwholesome, but she had chosen the dye because it reminded her of Gareth's eyes.

"You should be more careful of things that people have given you."

"Yes, Mother."

"Sir Bayard has been so kind . . . so generous . . ."

"So constantly *present*." Kiera pictured the man, his fine, large teeth flashing as he laughed, his hand resting on Alayna's arm. He was good at getting Alayna to laugh. So had Agravaine been, though Mordred never was. "We hardly have any time to ourselves anymore," Kiera said. "Why, he has only been here once this morning, so I imagine he'll be back any moment now."

"Kiera," Alayna said in a warning tone.

Kiera pretended not to notice. "Why do we never see any of our old friends anymore?"

"We don't have any old friends."

"Well, what about Mordred?"

"What about him?" There was some of the old tension back in her mother's voice that hadn't been there since her mother had been so concerned about her. "Don't blame me if Mordred feels he has outgrown us."

Kiera let her shuttle drop from her hands. "What has Bayard been saying about Mordred?"

"Oh *Bayard!*" Alayna flung her shuttle angrily across the room, causing the loom to tip precariously, bunching the threads. She got up and walked to the window. Quietly she started again. "Mordred has been very busy with the governing of the country. Very busy." She picked absently at some imperfection in the stone that formed the sill.

Kiera looked away, confused by the sudden bitterness in her mother's voice. She said, "Well, but now Arthur is coming back." And Lancelot was bringing Guinevere. It had taken the Pope's threat of excommunication to bring such a measure of accord.

"Yes, and then everything will be happy and agreeable. Is that what you suppose? After all that has happened—the adultery, the killing, the fighting at Joyous Gard, the changes Mordred has made back here despite Arthur's express commands—now the Church says, 'Give her back,' and everyone will say, 'Oh, what a fine idea! Why did we not think of that?'"

Her mother's vehemence was uncharacteristic and unsettling. Kiera picked up her shuttle and studied it. Very softly she asked, "Why does Mordred hate Bayard?" Out of the corner of her eye, she saw Alayna make a vague gesture of dismissal.

"It's too complicated," Alayna said.

"Does it have anything to do with Halbert?" Still Kiera didn't look directly at her mother. She had the feeling she was approaching something she would never again be able to back away from, no matter what she learned. "Mordred mentioned Halbert that day . . . that day Bayard rescued me. It seems I should know the name . . . Shouldn't I?"

Alayna came and knelt beside her. She sighed twice and swallowed repeatedly before saying, "Halbert was a wizard, an evil man who had great power . . . and wanted more."

"Mine?" Kiera asked. Of course hers. Why else would her mother have such trouble saying it?

Alayna hesitated, then nodded.

"And Bayard worked with him?" Kiera guessed.

"No! I mean yes, but . . ." Alayna got up, and started to pace. "Bayard did not *ask* to be Halbert's nephew. And Halbert used people. He had enough power that he could force people, or trick them." She turned to face Kiera. "Halbert was the cause of how your Uncle Galen came to die."

That was part of the quest Alayna had been on, so many years ago, that nobody—not Alayna, not the great-aunts—ever wanted to talk about. Kiera pictured herself very, very young—probably no more than two or three years old—and her uncle, holding her by the hands and twirling, twirling, twirling her, while she kept saying, "Do it again!" And she realized—for the first time—that he was also the vacant-eyed man she had occasionally glimpsed in her visions.

Alayna was saying, "He used me, too, for a while."

Kiera shuddered, yet couldn't think why.

"But Mordred remembers what he wants to remember. And Mordred's perception of things does not allow for Bayard to be as much a victim as I was." Alayna forced a cheery smile. "Surely we can talk about this some other time."

Kiera forced herself not to give in, not to make peace. She asked, "How many years have you been telling me that?"

Alayna straightened her loom. She picked up the shuttle and began to undo the part she had ruined. "Bayard is a good man," she said. "You can see it in his eyes. Besides, would the evil accomplice of an evil wizard have helped you?" For one moment, she looked directly into Kiera's eyes. "Sometimes Halbert worked with corrupt people, but he forced good men to his will, too, and that didn't make them any less good."

Kiera could see that. "Yes, but—"

"I do not want to talk about this anymore," Alayna said so firmly that Kiera knew she would not learn any more today.

She sighed. "No, Mother," she agreed.

CHAPTER 11

Kiera saw little of the sweeping changes Alayna had been afraid Arthur's return would bring, but neither did things go back to normal.

Then again, Arthur only stayed for one day.

Lancelot formally committed Queen Guinevere to Arthur's care, then immediately returned to France, to Joyous Gard.

Kiera glimpsed Guinevere, accompanied by the ladies who had waited on her at Lancelot's castle, but she was not invited to join them. They made immediate preparations to leave for London, away from court for an indefinite stay.

Meanwhile Arthur, looking dull-eyed and stooped, announced that he, too, was leaving again at dawn. Now the men were confident of an easy victory—for at last Lancelot could no longer hide behind concern for the Queen. People gleefully reminded each other that Merlin had prophesied Arthur would never lose a battle throughout his life. Camelot's mood was one of exhilaration.

Kiera stood at a parapet and watched the army leave once again. Below, sunlight shone on burnished metal and brightly colored caparisons; but all around her, Camelot began to settle down to the routine of the working day. A servant girl leaned out of a nearby window, not watching the army, but shaking out linens, while the voice of the new stable master called to his assistants.

Long after the army had become indistinct in the distance, Kiera remained where she was, letting the early morning breeze blow her hair away from her face.

Finally she pushed away from the balustrade, but then she leaned forward again. A sudden fog had formed in the hollow the men were just entering. It was too quick to be earthly fog, for in a moment it had engulfed not just army and hillside but was sweeping up toward her.

"No," she whispered, but had no power beyond that to resist.

> *The gray swirled up and she could no longer see the balustrade, just a hand-breadth away from her fingers. The air hissed about her and stung her eyes and she saw the shadows of knights fighting near her, although that would mean they were suspended high above the countryside.*
>
> *"Arthur," she called, though she couldn't get her voice above a whisper for she saw the King bent double, on his knees, his silver armor bloodied.*
>
> *"Mordred," she heard Arthur gasp. "Mordred."*

Kiera stepped back, unmindful that her senses had become confounded and she might be heading for the edge. "No," she said, afraid of what her vision could possibly mean. "Please, Mordred, no."

> *She glimpsed him in his black armor, his sword raised, turning to face her.*

"No!"

> *The scream was echoed by the buzzards that wheeled above.*

She covered her face, staggered, felt the rough stone of the parapet against her knees. The air smelled of dew on grass, not burning bodies, and the sun was warm on the back of her hair. She lowered her hands. Far away, King Arthur's army continued to march under the cloudless sky, and—not quite so far—a herd of sheep grazed unperturbed on a green hillside.

She passed her hands over her face and turned to go back indoors.

And met the appraising gaze of Hildy, watching her steadily. Hildy, who had been so friendly that first day in Queen Guinevere's service.

Hildy said, *"Please, Mordred, no—what?"*

Kiera moved to walk by her, but Hildy put her arm out to block the way.

"You said, 'Please, Mordred, no.' And you also said, 'Arthur.' Why?"

She was not answerable to Hildy, but she said, "I . . . I must have just been thinking out loud. Daydreaming."

Hildy glared at her with loathing. "Another dream?" she said. "Such as the one you had that night in the ladies' chamber?"

"Please," Kiera said, "it's *not* that *I* caused anything bad to happen. I had a nightmare."

Hildy folded her arms and asked, "Oh, yes?"

Her sneering tone made Kiera add, "And you can't seem to make up your mind if that makes me a traitor or a witch. But I am neither. It was just I . . ." How could she possibly explain this, her confusion, her constantly shifting vision of what she now realized was a battlefield? ". . . I dreamt I saw Sir Gawain's dead face, only it didn't even happen exactly as in my dream—"

"Sir Gawain?" Hildy asked in an outrush of breath.

Kiera clapped her hands over her mouth. What had she said? "Agravaine," she whispered. "I meant to say Agravaine." She fought back a wave of nausea. "Of course Gawain is still alive. I just misspoke. I dreamed Agravaine was dead the night he was killed. But it didn't happen the way it did in my dream, so it wasn't any kind of prophecy—please don't hate me: I had that dream, and Agravaine is dead, but Gawain is fine, and I didn't mean to say Gawain, truly I didn't."

Hildy was watching her with a smile that was eager and hungry.

"I have to go now," Kiera said.

"Witch," Hildy called her.

It was no use arguing. Kiera turned to go.

"Witch," Hildy repeated, much louder.

Kiera fled indoors, but Hildy followed.

"Witch!" Hildy shouted.

People looked up. People stopped what they were doing.

"She's a witch!" Hildy's face was all red and puffy. "She just put a curse on King Arthur."

Kiera whirled around. "I did not!"

"She's a witch! She just put a curse on King Arthur! She's a witch!"

Hildy just wasn't going to stop. Kiera ran down the corridor and still Hildy followed, shouting, demanding attention. Kiera gathered up her skirts and ran down the flight of stairs leading to the level where she and her mother had their room.

"She's a witch!" Hildy screamed yet again.

As she reached the bottom of the stairs, Kiera looked back just in time to see Hildy start down after her. Except that Hildy was too busy pointing to hold up her skirts.

"She's a witch! She just put a curse—" Hildy's foot came down on the hem of her dress. She grabbed for the walls, but tumbled all the way down.

Mercifully, she didn't hit her head. Kiera ran to her side, and for a few moments, Hildy was too shaken to utter a sound. Then she began to wail. And finally, when it seemed everyone in the castle was gathered there around her, Hildy sobbed, "She's a witch! Did you see her make me fall? I heard her put a curse on King Arthur, so she tried to kill me."

"That's not true," Kiera said to the horrified faces around her.

"She looked at me," Hildy insisted. "She has the Evil Eye and she willed me to fall."

"I didn't do anything!"

"No," Hildy said, fighting back a sob, "and she didn't know anything about Agravaine's plans the night he broke into the Queen's chambers, either."

It didn't matter that Kiera couldn't find an answer. They wouldn't believe her anyway; they chose to believe the injured Hildy instead.

Somebody was pushing his way through the crowd—Padraic from the infirmary. But he hardly made note of Hildy. He took hold of Kiera's arm, hard enough to hurt. He told her, "You are an abomination against the natural order of God and his most Christian church."

"But," Kiera said, "but—"

"Throw her in the river and see if she floats," someone suggested.

Kiera whirled around but couldn't tell who had spoken.

Padraic smiled. "We shall bring her to Prince Mordred," he said. "We shall present our testimony. The result will be the same: trial by ordeal, trial by combat, or trial by jury—the truth shall be known, regardless of who may try to hide it. Then, Mordred himself will have to condemn her."

CHAPTER 12

*K*iera didn't know what they called Mordred away from, but he was obviously displeased. Sitting on his father's throne in the Great Hall, with a crowd of loud people all demanding immediate action, he looked at her coldly. She had hoped she would be brought to him in the smaller council room, where only a dozen people could fit—if that many—beyond whichever twelve men were seated at the Round Table. But this, apparently, was a matter for the entire court.

Alayna came rushing in, before the hearing started, but the guards that kept the crowd at bay would not let her approach where Kiera stood, along with those who would testify against her.

Mordred didn't even look at her. Kiera rested her fingertips against her throat and could feel the pounding of her heart there. It was only Mordred, she told herself, and she had never been afraid of Mordred before.

And so it began . . .

"She looked at my sister," Enid addressed the assembly. "From across the courtyard—glared at her, and my poor sister miscarried."

"Across the courtyard?" Kiera said. "I would not

have even been able to recognize her from that far. I can't see that well."

Enid sucked in her breath. As did several others.

"Even if I had wanted to," Kiera added belatedly. Mother Mary, she'd made things worse.

"You heard her!" Enid cried. "She admitted it! She was after my sister!"

"No!"

"Four fine babies she has had," Enid persisted. "Four healthy, perfect babies in four years, and never a problem until you look at her. Explain that."

Mordred said nothing, and Alayna finally managed to push her way forward. Kiera fought the inclination to cling to her, as a toddling child might. *Can she see?* she wondered. *Can she see how grateful I am to have her here?*

Not that she believed there was anything her mother could do to save her.

Alayna stepped between Kiera and Enid. "Come, come. These things happen, ask any midwife. You can't—"

"Well, what of my cakes then?" asked an older woman Kiera didn't even recognize. "I'm making sweet cakes for my niece's first-born's Christening, and *that one* comes by my window, and none of the cakes turn out. They're all hard and heavy and no good to eat, and sweet cakes has always been my specialty."

Some people were nodding their heads, others shaking theirs. Kiera hoped that meant not all took this foolishness seriously; she thought some of them were smiling indulgently.

"What about Eldred?" shouted the butcher's wife. *That* wiped away all smiles. "He wor always a wild boy, but never meanlike."

Some in the crowd shuffled their feet, for many had known Eldred. "Oh, well, now," someone started.

"Yes!" the butcher's wife insisted. "And I can tell you something else. Did you hear about them gashes on Eldred's face? I *seen* them. I went to see the body, first thing, there in the woods, and there they was: marks like she'd clawed him."

No, Kiera wanted to say. *It was when Bayard threw him in the bush.* But her throat was too dry to get the words out.

"By the time they got him back home," the butcher's wife continued, "I was the one who first said it: 'Look,' I says, 'the marks have got bigger,' I says, 'deeper. Looks like a wild beast laid into him,' I says, cause I know about witches, and what they can do. And that night them wounds begun to fester, even with him dead and all. I set there with him, me and his ma, and his two sisters and their men, and his three brothers and their kin, and we used three months' worth of candles, and we all seen it, spreading till they was deep gashes, covering half his face. And I says, 'Better call Father Jerome,' I says. But soon as the light of Father's candle falls on Eldred's face . . . Nothing. Just scratches again."

This was the first Kiera had heard this story, but from the knowing looks people were exchanging, it wasn't new. She searched for a friendly face. *Somebody* had to see the truth of it.

Mordred . . . Mordred was scaring her, sitting there, listening to this, his expression impassive. Mordred did what suited Mordred, her mother had always said. Would he abandon her now?

"I was out one day," a young man said, "and I saw her walking in the meadow, and I called out to warn her because there's a fairy ring there, clear as anything. At night sometimes you can see the tiny lights flickering in the grass, and we lost three pigs last summer that must of wandered too close and the fairies took them for their feasts. Even during the day you can see what it is, with the grass all flat where they dance, but she's heading right for it. So I'm jumping up and down, yelling and waving my hat." He paused to look around the Hall, at everybody except Kiera. "And she walks right through it. Unharmed."

She could feel the release of tension, as though everyone exhaled at once. The constant background of muttering grew louder. People began shouting to have their say.

"Mordred." Her mother tried to make herself heard above them.

He looked at her coolly and she must have wilted inside, just as Kiera did.

Behind her, another voice was saying: "Well, her father practiced the black arts, too . . ."

Loudly, to the left: "What about my cakes?"

From the butcher's wife: "Don't forget Eldred . . ."

Kiera pressed her hands to her ears.

"And what about Agravaine?" she heard Hildy insist.

The doors burst open, and a flicker of annoyance crossed Mordred's face.

Kiera squinted to see across the room, even though her mother always warned that squinting made her face fierce and unlovely. Bayard, she saw. And—for no reason she could name—her heart sank.

"My Lord!" Bayard had Father Jerome in tow. "In defense of the maid, we have a character witness here. A man of God whom we all know and who has known this girl most of her life and whom I have persuaded to testify despite his great personal trepidation at offending his superi—"

"Shut up, Bayard," Mordred said.

Kiera felt as though someone had doused her with a pail of water. As from a great distance, she saw the shock in Alayna's eyes, the pleased surprise in Padraic's.

Bayard's mouth remained open for a moment or two before he remembered to close it.

What are you doing? Kiera thought at Mordred. *What are you doing?*

Padraic gave a frigid glance at the pale Father Jerome. Then—indicating Hildy—he said, "This fine woman—"

"No," said Mordred. He pointed at Hildy. "You. You are bringing the complaint. What have you to say?"

Smirking, Hildy said, "She talks to the devil."

"And have you heard him answer her back?"

The question flustered Hildy. "Of course not, I'm a good Christian. But I've heard *her* talk to *him*. And she plots against you and your family, my Lord—including the King." She pointed at Kiera. "She groveled on the floor, speaking to her invisible master, her eyes glazed, her face with a light not of this world, and,"—her finger swung around to Mordred—"*and she asked for your death. Lord Mordred, and that of your father, our beloved King Arthur!*"

The room burst into excited murmurs. Mordred sat back, calm but indecipherable.

Merciful Savior, Kiera thought, *what is he thinking? He can't believe all this.* She had a fleeting recurrence of the vision that she had had on the parapet—Arthur dying, Mordred dying, Camelot in ruin—and what had this to do with her? Until now she had been able to force it from her mind. That Mordred could try to kill Arthur . . . it was too distant from the Mordred she knew. But now she watched his cold eyes and realized she couldn't guess what he would do from one moment to the next.

"My Lord," Hildy said, "she cursed your brother Agravaine, moments before he was cut down by the traitor Lancelot. And Gawain, too. Before she had fully gained her senses and realized who I was, she asked her demon lord for Gawain's death."

Mordred started at that news, then folded his arms across his chest.

Oh, Mordred, Kiera thought. *You know I wouldn't.*

Padraic stepped forward, pulling out a letter. "You have already read the dispatches which came at dawn?" he asked, but continued before Mordred gave any indication of yes or no. "But most of these good people have not. Friar Guillaume, whom you all know went to France to see after the spiritual well-being of King Arthur's army, has written to me. He says in this letter that has arrived only today that our good Sir Gawain has been sorely wounded while in mortal combat with Lancelot and may, even now, be with our Lord and all the saints in Heaven."

Gawain! Kiera heard someone gasp—it may have been her mother, it may have been herself. It was not news to Mordred—that she could tell. He was watching Padraic.

And Padraic was watching her. "Yes, little one, what a terrible shock! Oh, so surprised! But you knew it. You knew it before I said so."

"No," Kiera said, "I—"

"You knew it!"

"I—"

"You cursed him!"

The crowd started rumbling, louder and louder as each person tried to tell his or her opinion. No one was smiling indulgently now.

"Mordred," Alayna called, but he watched impassively until they were all talked out, until his continued silence could no longer be ignored, and the last murmurs faded.

That had to be a good sign, didn't it?

When every pair of eyes was on him, Mordred said, softly, "How much foolishness do you expect me to bear?" He looked from person to person in the room, and if they all felt as Kiera did, they felt personally responsible for all the foolishness of the world.

He stood, and those nearest him took a step back. "Yes, Padraic, I am aware that Gawain has been injured. Your concern is a solace to me. But is anybody aware of how many others have been injured—how many have been killed—while Arthur abides steadfastly by Lancelot's rules? Is there anyone in this room who has lost no one, who remains untouched by this ill-conceived and badly managed war?"

People shuffled their feet, looked at each other, but nobody spoke.

And what had this to do with her?

"Lancelot DuLac," Mordred said. "Undefeated in tournament or combat. Acknowledged as the strongest and most skilled knight of Camelot. A strategist of renown. Does Arthur take any precautions? Does he deviate from the battle plans he and Lancelot himself worked out when they overcame second-rate barons and Pict outlaws in their good old days together? No. Heaven forbid we should try anything new. He has with him no brothers or fathers or sons to lose."

Kiera felt Padraic, beside her, fidget. "My Lord Regent, this may be true, but—"

"This court," Mordred said evenly, "is dissolved."

Kiera looked at her mother, unsure whether this was good news or bad.

"I decree an end to Arthur's ridiculous civil code," Mordred continued. "Terminated. Abolished. Dissolved."

There were scattered cheers.

"And I find this girl innocent of all your silly charges,"—Kiera gasped, Hildy opened her mouth to protest—"on the grounds that I declare her so."

So it was good news. For her. She felt her mother grab hold of her arm.

"You cannot do that," Padraic said.

There was instant silence in anticipation of Mordred's reaction. But he only smiled. "My second decree," he said, "is this: Since Arthur seems unable to overcome Lancelot at Lancelot's own game, I resolve it is time we change the rules of that game."

While Kiera was still trying to sort that out, her mother's fingers tightened on her arm.

"It's about time!" someone near them yelled.

"Send in the longbows!" called a rough peasant voice.

"He won't be able to argue with success."

"Once he sees us in action—"

"Mordred will show them how it's done!"

Though the majority was cheering, some shook their heads.

Surely, Kiera reasoned, Arthur—who had not been convinced by argument—would not change his mind by having his decrees ignored.

Mordred started for the door, but Alayna grabbed his arm. "Mordred," she said, echoing Padraic's words, "you cannot do this."

Kiera saw his dark eyes take them all in. She was painfully aware how much—with the way Bayard stood behind them, one hand on her arm and one on Alayna's—they seemed to present a united, almost a family, group. She squirmed away from both of them, but knew it was too late.

"You cannot do this," Alayna repeated yet again.

"Which?" Mordred asked ingenuously. "Absolving Kiera?"

"Stop it. Mordred, please, Arthur trusted you . . . You know what he'll say when you turn up with that longbow corps that he has already disbanded once. There can only be trouble. Think what you're doing."

Mordred looked at Bayard before returning his attention to Alayna. "My Lady," he said, matching her tone, "think what *you* are doing."

Alayna flushed. "You have no right," she whispered hoarsely.

Mordred turned again to Bayard and gave a tight smile. "As for you, Sir Bayard, I think I would feel safest were you where I could watch you at all times. So you will accompany us."

"How dare you!" Alayna clutched and twisted Bayard's hand as though it were a glove or kerchief. "Besides saving Kiera's very life, Bayard has been good and kind to both of us while you were too busy to notice us. And now you want to prevent that, too. You'll never be the king Arthur is. And you'll never be the man Bayard is!"

Mordred's expression never changed—it just froze where it was. He gave a slight bow and turned his back on them. He was enveloped immediately in the crowd, which chattered about details of the departure.

Kiera stared into the crowd, knowing that she teetered on the precipice of the land of swirling gray mist.

It was Bayard's unwelcome voice that called her back from the edge. "Well," he said, sounding relieved, "what we wanted but not quite the way we expected it—eh, my dears? Just so long as Kiera is safe." He enveloped the two of them in a hug, and Alayna started to cry.

Kiera looked up, surprised.

"There, there," Bayard said. He pulled Alayna close to his chest and patted her head, which only made her cry more. She threw her arms around his neck and he rocked her gently.

Let her go, Kiera wished at him. She couldn't remember ever having seen her mother cry. And why, oh why, did Alayna turn to Bayard for comfort? Kiera stared at her hands until her own eyes began to fill with tears. Annoyed, she tossed her head, brushing at the hair sticking to her face. For one instant she glimpsed Bayard's face while he was unaware of being seen.

Although he still held Alayna with all the tenderness of a parent, and although he murmured comforting endearments, and although his voice was warm and distressed, he smiled.

Like a cat crouched in the fish market, he smiled.

CHAPTER 13

The dispatches came addressed to Sir Kaye because, as seneschal in charge of managing the household, the King's aging foster brother was the closest thing to a man of authority they had left. Sir Kaye had them read out loud in the courtyard because—as he said—he had long outgrown any interest in power and empire. What Kiera suspected was that he wanted to share his responsibility with as many others as possible, should any decisions be called for—should anything go wrong.

The news that she heard in these courtyard sessions went from good to bad to worse.

First, before Mordred's group would have made it beyond Britain's borders, they received word that Gawain was doing well and, with rest, would recover completely.

But the next rider from the front reported that Mordred and Arthur had argued bitterly and that Arthur had commanded Mordred to return to Camelot immediately.

On the heels of that came the devastating news that Mordred had only pretended to leave, but had instead circled behind Joyous Gard in the dark of night—and had mistakenly slaughtered one of Arthur's patrols.

The messenger, still astride his horse to be better seen, told off the names of those killed: twenty-three of Arthur's men, two of Mordred's. Despite the obvious superiority of Mordred's peasant-soldiers, the King had ordered their longbows confiscated and burned. "He assembled the entire army," the messenger said, "and burned those bows for all to see, even Lancelot and his pack sitting in their damned castle, no doubt laughing their faithless heads off. And the King, he talks more and more of making peace with Sir Lancelot."

"That's all we have had with Arthur lately," someone in the crowd called out: "concessions and endless war and in-fighting. Mordred did better the little chance he had."

Others grumbled agreement.

Kiera, who'd heard enough to make her head ache, decided that she needed less of people and more of horses. She stopped at the stables to get an armful of apples to offer as gifts. The warm, friendly scent of the animals and their leather accouterments, the sweet hay, the tart crispness of the apples—all these blended for a feeling of familiarity and well-being. She straightened from picking the apples out of their bin, and heard a voice, from the other side of the wall, from outside.

"So now they have lost Willis, too." It was the name that had been given as one of Mordred's archers who had been killed.

She didn't recognize the voice of the man who spoke, and there was no reason for her to listen or be interested, but she stood motionless and held her breath for quiet's sake. Nobody had bothered her since Mordred had declared her innocent of witchcraft, but she knew safety lay in not attracting attention.

A second man asked, "Willis—which one was that, the youngest?"

"No, second eldest, the one after young Eldred, who came to such a bad end."

"Sir Bayard's friend?"

One of the apples slipped out of the crook of her elbow as her arm twitched. She had to scramble to keep it from hitting the ground.

The first speaker must have been taken by surprise, too, for there was a long pause before he said, "If Eldred was Bayard's friend, God protect me from friends."

"Bayard and Willis, you dolt," the other corrected. "Willis was always running errands for him, doing this and that for a bit of copper. Though I imagine Bayard knew Eldred well enough, too. Double the tragedy of him killing him like that. Paid 'em off good though, I'm told—the family."

"Still, bad fortune to lose the two boys." The voices faded as the men moved away.

Kiera finally remembered to breathe.

Then jumped when Bayard's voice whispered, "I heard her scream."

Kiera whirled around, scattering the rest of her apples.

But Bayard was a week's journey away, with Mordred's army.

By then it was too late to stop the vision.

> The ducks scattered. The two young toughs came running down the hill. They ripped the flower basket from her hand. They chased her, pulled her hair, knocked her down.
>
> "I don't know the youths' names," Bayard said. "I was exercising my horse. I heard her scream."
>
> Eldred's hands closed around her wrists, Lowell's around her ankles. She couldn't breathe.
>
> "I heard her scream," Bayard said.
>
> She came up sputtering and choking.
>
> "No!" Eldred screamed—Eldred, not her, and Bayard was there already, snapping Lowell's neck—"No!" And what was that expression on the doomed Eldred's face? Pain? Certainly. Fear? Recognition? Betrayal?
>
> "Always . . . doing this and that for a bit of copper," a disembodied voice proclaimed. "Paid 'em off good . . ."
>
> She heard the thud of Eldred's skull against the tree.
>
> "Yon young ruffians will harm you no more."

She found herself on her knees, rocking back and forth, her hands covering her face.

He'd paid them. He'd paid them to do that to her. Then killed them. She wanted to rip her skin off where they'd touched her. She wanted to use her fingernails on their faces the way she'd been accused of doing. She wanted to hurt Bayard, and hurt him, and hurt him, and hurt him.

Her thoughts frightened her. She put her hand out to steady herself. She needed to stop this. She needed to stand up and walk to her mother's room and tell her how things really stood with Bayard. That was what she needed to do.

But she put her hand out while her eyes were still closed and felt a dead man's face.

That was how she had first seen Bayard, bloodied and glaze-eyed on the misty gray field she'd seen on the hillside the day she and her mother and Agravaine had crossed paths with Mordred and Nimue, the day that first introduced misfortune into her life.

But now she wanted it. She wanted to see him dead. She opened her eyes . . .

. . . and it was Gawain she saw, his face white beyond reason and the eyes fixed upward.

No, she thought. *He recovered.* The messages had said so. This couldn't be.

"No!" She whispered the word, as though there might be more strength in the denial if she spoke it out loud. "No!"

And she saw Mordred turn. And Arthur's voice echoed hers: "No!"

The mist caught in a draft from the stable door and dissipated, leaving her entirely alone.

She forced herself to stand. And she put one foot in front of the other until she reached the north pasture even though what she wanted was her mother, the comfort of her arms, the calmness of her voice.

But she had let events control her long enough, and the time for action, if not past due, was now.

"Tempest," she called, for her own pony, Ebony, was too small for such a journey. "Tempest!" She climbed over the stone wall and was immediately assaulted by the colts and breeding mares who nudged her and got in her way, jostling for the apples whose scent they caught from her clothes. "Tempest!"

She squinted at the hill in the back section, and her heart sank at the thought of having to walk that far. She was bumped from behind. "Oh, go," she said, still trying to pick out movement in the distance. "I don't have anything with me." Not trying to hide their disappointment, most of the horses wandered away, but the persistent one from behind snuffled in her ear.

"Stop," she said firmly, and turned around, but it was Tempest after all. She threw her arms around the old destrier's neck. "Oh, Tempest, please help me."

He nuzzled her—comfort, yes, because he was sweet-natured despite the battle training—but also she knew she still swelled of those apples she had dropped in the stable.

"I'm sorry, I lost them," she said, rubbing his large head between the eyes. He was palest gray, even closer to white than in those days when he had been Mordred's destrier, the young knight's first.

To show there were no hard feelings, Tempest moved closer to rub his head against her, placing his immense feet carefully so as not to step on her.

"Mordred is in trouble," Kiera said, "and so is his friend Gawain." Horses had trouble with the concept of family, but friendship was something they could understand even better than many humans. "I want to help them, to warn them."

Tempest moved closer still, no longer playful, but for her to mount.

Destriers were bred big, tall and broad to support the weight of a knight in full armor. It took her two tries before she managed to scramble on. No dainty sidesaddle seating, of course. She settled herself, straddled, putting her arms around his neck. "We have to get to the sea as soon as possible," she said, leaving the worry about how to cross till they got there. "Do you know—"

Tempest didn't take the time to answer, but took off at a full gallop straight for the stone wall that fenced in the pasture.

Afraid to watch, Kiera buried her face in his neck. *Trust*, she told herself. She felt his muscles tense, then there was the sensation of hurtling through the air, followed by a jolt where her heart and her body caught up to each other.

By the time she felt confident enough to look up and back, all she could see of Camelot were the tips of the highest towers.

It took four days.

They had to stop when Kiera became too tired to hold on, and other times to ask for food from cottagers who gaped dumbly at her on her aging but splendid war horse. Nobody questioned her. They just disappeared inside for a few moments, then came back with dark bread and cheese, or smoked fish. Sometimes they brought hay or a bit of oats for Tempest, though mostly he foraged by the roadside. They looked afraid not to comply, these dark-eyed peasants and their too-silent children. Was it the strangeness of her appearance that upset them, or had her reputation spread this far, or had they just seen too much? Best not to ask. She gratefully accepted what they gave and left as quickly as she could, knowing that every delay might cost Gawain's life.

Finally she was sure she could smell the sea. It was almost dusk—and how was she ever going to find a boat for hire?—when they crested a hill and she saw camp-fires below.

Tempest stopped to let her look. "Mordred," she said, for her eyesight was good enough to make out the black and white of his flag. But the camp was too big for him alone. Arthur must have returned with him after all, though she couldn't tell if there were any of the red and gold dragon flags.

She urged Tempest to the edge of the hill, then let him pick his own way amongst the rocks and bushes. She was debating whether the probable safety she'd gain by getting off and walking alongside was worth the effort of having to get back on, when a figure stepped out of the shadows.

Tempest stopped, his nostrils flaring.

A knight, Kiera saw, an outpost guard.

The man held his hands out, to show them weaponless, which meant he had seen her long before she saw him—and recognized her. She didn't know him. She patted Tempest's neck. "Easy," she murmured.

Tempest snorted.

The man looked from her to the horse, no doubt trying to estimate how much control she actually wielded.

"I am looking for Sir Mordred," she told him. "Or Sir Gawain." *Please let Gawain be still alive,* she prayed.

"Right," the man said. Did Mordred intentionally pick men whose faces gave away as little as his own? Carefully, he eased ahead of them, helping to clear a path.

People from the camp must have been watching their progress. They had hardly reached the bottom, when the curious left their campfires, heading toward them.

Her escort made a move as though to help Kiera dismount, and Tempest reared back on his hind legs.

Somehow she held on.

The knight jumped out of the way of the flailing hooves. No telling if he realized that—had Tempest's intent been serious—the man couldn't have moved fast enough. "Right," he said again. "Just come this way then." He led her toward the officers' tents, but checked over his shoulder several times, nervous with Tempest at his back.

CHAPTER 14

The flap of the center tent was pulled open, but it took Tempest to whinny softly, and the knight to bow his head with a murmured, "my Lord," before Kiera saw it was Mordred who had stepped out.

Silently, he helped her dismount. She leaned close to Tempest's ear. "Thank you," she whispered. "You can go with this man now." He probably would have anyway—satisfied, once Mordred scratched him in the spot between his eyes, that all was well.

Mordred held the tent flap for her, and she stepped inside.

Two knights looked up from a field table spread with maps and papers. She recognized one vaguely, though she didn't know his name: one of Mordred's friends who had returned from banishment after Lancelot's treason. The other knight's face was unfamiliar.

Mordred motioned them out, but then stopped them at the entry, for one final quiet word.

Kiera paced impatiently. Where was Gawain? She made a wide circle of the interior to avoid the suit of black armor that was set out. She forced herself to see no more than what was actually there. No mist. No blood. She touched a wall of the pavilion, taut reality.

There was a pallet in one corner, its blanket unfolded. Next to that was another table, smaller than the one in the middle of the tent, but just as cluttered. This one held weaponry—broadsword, crossbow and bolts, an anlace whose intricately worked handle indicated very old craftsmanship—also a leather shirt, several rings and armbands, an extra helmet. The whole assortment looked to have been simply dropped there. She shook her head. Meticulous as Mordred might be in matters of tactics and strategy, he had always been careless about personal possessions.

She picked up the shirt, and had started to fold it before she realized it was much too big to be Mordred's. Her eyes reluctantly went back to the helmet she had moved to get at the shirt. Silver-colored, not black like Mordred's armor. And one side was caved in. She felt light-headed. Surely if the metal was so badly damaged, the skull it was supposed to have protected would have been . . . She went to cover her mouth, thinking she might be sick, but she still had Gawain's shirt in her hand.

She felt someone loosen her fingers, take the shirt, and finally she focused on Mordred, who had stepped between her and the table strewn with Gawain's possessions. She saw him try to gauge how much she guessed, how much she needed to be told.

"I saw Gawain dead," she said.

His eyes widened slightly. He let go of her, putting his hand to his chest, clasping Nimue's ring, still on its strip of leather around his neck.

And she felt the cold gray mist swirl about her ankles. "I came to warn him," she said, her voice close to a whisper. Obviously she was too late. "I came to warn you."

He turned back, looked at her levelly.

Say something, do something, she wanted to cry. *Let me know you feel something.* "You're in danger, Mordred, mortal danger." She was afraid that if she cried, it would weaken her argument, make her seem childish, but he did not look worried. He just gazed at her blandly.

"Yes," he finally said. "Nimue says so, too."

"Nimue?" This time her voice *was* a whisper.

Mordred's hand tightened on the enchantress's ring and his eyes seemed to look beyond her. "Yes. But she's so distant . . . so unclear . . . I can see her, but I cannot make out . . ." He looked directly at Kiera again. "Has she contacted you? Is that what you're saying?"

"No." Kiera wasn't sure she had spoken loud enough for him to hear. "No, it's these visions I've been having since before . . . since . . . all along. I . . . Mordred, *don't* fight with Arthur."

Mordred raised his eyebrows. He started to say something, then cut himself off. He took another breath; but instead of speaking, he began to pace. "Nimue," he finally begun again, "Nimue . . ."

Kiera watched him, anxious because she had no idea what to expect. He was full of energy, but vague, flickering energy, like a flame; and something was wrong with his eyes, which wouldn't meet hers directly and reminded her of swirling mist.

He stopped in front of her. "Nimue has always been, first and foremost, Merlin's friend," he said.

Lover, Kiera mentally corrected him. Everybody knew that.

And perhaps Mordred did, too, for he continued, "Nobody—nothing else—was as important." The intensity with which he had begun vanished. "She always took care to make that clear."

What? she thought. *What are you trying to tell me?* "Yes?"

"Did you know that Merlin tried to have me killed? When I was a child? Gawain . . . Gawain told me."

She had heard the stories. She couldn't get her voice to work, and simply nodded.

"Merlin said I was a danger to my father, that I would destroy him and the Round Table. Of course, that was before there was a Round Table, so it didn't make sense, but Arthur took him at his word. He always . . . took him . . . at his word." Once again, Mordred seemed to have been distracted by a thought midsentence.

What's wrong? she wanted to ask him. Besides the obvious, of course. But she was a nobody, despite all his previous kindnesses, a hanger-on—and he was the King's son.

"Merlin," he continued, "Merlin was his teacher, his friend. He was a father to him, and he made him High King against the opposition of everyone—everyone— and helped him stay there. Can you imagine the power that gave him, the influence? And then he says, 'Mordred will destroy all this. Kill him.' I don't blame Arthur for believing him. But I *cannot* understand why Merlin said it. I could never have competed with *him*. Why did he say it?"

What? What answer did he want? She would give it to him if she only knew. All she could do was shake her head.

"Afterwards," Mordred said, "he kept trying to make it up to me. He said, 'Even the world's greatest wizard is entitled to be wrong once.' But it wasn't true. He didn't believe Merlin was wrong. He never trusted me. I'm not quite sure Nimue did either."

Don't ask, Kiera mentally begged, remembering how shocked she had been. *With Mordred, it often is difficult to tell how much he has guessed,* Nimue had said. Could Mordred read that thought on her face?

He said, "She told me exactly what you just did: 'Don't fight with Arthur.' But whose interests does she hold: mine, or Arthur's, or Merlin's? But you're on my side, Kiera. I can trust you, can't I?"

She took his hand, tried to sound gentle and reasonable like her mother, despite his odd ramblings. *I'm not an adult,* she thought, though she had been protesting for the better part of a year that she was. "Of course I'm on your side, Mordred. But are you sure it is Nimue you have seen?"

She could see the question startled him. He dropped her hand. After all this time of his believing in her visions, here she was doubting his. It had to hurt. Still, she remembered the day she and Nimue had talked, and Nimue deprecated her own talent, insisting that she wasn't a powerful wizard. *Small healings,* she had said. That was a far cry from reaching out from the dead.

How long had Mordred been talking this way? That was probably why Arthur had abandoned the siege on Lancelot's castle. He had to have become worried enough about this odd fancy of Mordred's that he wanted to get him back to the safe, friendly confines of Camelot.

But then things seen and things unseen came back to her. The banners she had viewed from the hill—had any borne the winged dragon that was the emblem of the High King of England? And this pavilion, placed in the center of the encampment, the leader's position, should belong to Arthur. So why was it filled with Mordred's things? And why was Mordred engaged with two knights—neither of them from Camelot—in a war conference the King did not attend?

The gray mist, which these past four days had never seemed farther away than swirling about her ankles, reached cold tendrils to her knees. "Mordred," she said very gently, "where is Arthur?"

"About a day's march inland."

"Then who,"—she tried to steady her voice—"who are all these people, if not Arthur's army?"

"Mine. My army."

She closed her eyes.

"Knights from the North Country, Scotland, Cornwall. People who were deposed, whose lands were confiscated for opposing Lancelot before it became fashionable to do so. The disenchanted." Mordred smiled wryly, as though still capable of seeing the irony of it. "They can't be trusted, of course; but for the moment they follow me."

"Oh, Mordred," she said. "What have you done?"

He looked at her coldly, and when he spoke it was with distant civility. "Kiera. It was very good of you to come to warn me. I thank you on behalf of Gawain and Nimue." He said it in a perfectly normal tone of voice, as though it were a perfectly normal thing to say. He took her arm, guiding her to the exit. "But this is not a safe place for you. I am afraid you must leave immediately, tonight. We can give you some provisions for your return trip, but I cannot spare any men to accompany you. Alayna will be frantic. You must ride Tempest as quickly as—"

"Bayard—" Kiera spoke loudly to get his attention, and was about to repeat the name, but Mordred had stopped instantly.

He spun her around, and put his finger to her lips. *"Shhh."* He dropped to a crouch, pulling her with him, and held her in close. Again he motioned her to silence, though she had made no sound. "There is always somebody listening." Furtively, he peered outside as though to make sure no one was close enough to hear. "What about Bayard?" he finally whispered.

She spoke quietly. "Bayard knew those boys who attacked me. He *paid* them to attack me so that he could rescue me. And then he killed them." Had Mordred always gotten that vague and faraway look when he was thinking? She averted her own eyes. "What better way to get to my mother than through me?"

Mordred's attention snapped back to her and he turned her question on its head. "What better way to get to you than through your mother?"

For a moment she dismissed it as a play on words, as more of Mordred's disconcerting mood.

For a moment.

She tried to back away. "No." She thought of Bayard, always hugging, always laughing, his large hand resting easily on Alayna's arm as they walked together. Would he really have gotten rid of her, as readily as he had gotten rid of Eldred and Lowell? Would he have killed her, if she hadn't trusted him, because he had no real interest in *her* but only in her daughter?

But already Mordred was focused beyond her, no longer seeing her. "I will tend to Bayard," he said, hugging himself as though for warmth.

"Mordred . . ."

Again he put his finger to her lips. Then he helped her to her feet. "But you must leave. Arthur's men are moving. We have caught some of their advance spies already. The main force will be here to attack by dawn."

"Mordred! Arthur would never attack your people. He would never really fight you." The thought of how much ill Mordred's misguided suspicions could cause nearly took her breath away.

Mordred just looked at her.

"If it ever came to that—"

"It has already come to that." Now that Mordred had committed himself to her, he insisted on telling her all. "There has already been a battle," he said. "Not a foray or a skirmish, a battle. Do you understand? The fighting has begun. I had to give the order—make the first move—or he would have forced us into a corner. It has gone beyond anything that could be patched over and forgiven. I'm sorry that there is no time for you to rest, but you have to go now."

She threw her arms around his neck. What could she say: *Good luck against Arthur? I hope you win?* "Take care," she told him instead. She pulled away before he could answer, if he would have answered, and she stepped outside.

One of the knights who had been talking with Mordred, the one who had at least looked familiar, got up from the watchfire by which he had been sitting. He smoothed his mustache and said, as if it were the most natural thing in the world, "My Lady, may I accompany you to your mount?"

Kiera followed without a backwards glance to check if Mordred watched. Although the sunset still reddened the western sky, most in the camp were already bedded down for the night, and few bestirred themselves to see who passed.

Somebody had found a saddle for her, and Tempest was fidgety over it. This still wasn't a lady's saddle, but it would make staying on easier. "Tempest," she murmured, stroking his muzzle. "We're to go home."

Tempest shook himself, jingling the metal of his bridle.

"Mordred said for us to go home."

Tempest snorted, tossing his head.

"You are certain you can handle such a steed by yourself?" The knight's chubby, good-natured face peered at her skeptically.

She nodded and he gave her a boost onto Tempest's back.

"I will see that you find your way."

Whistling tunelessly, he took the reins and led Tempest up the slope of the hill. They saw no one, though there was an occasional rattle of pebbles off to the side. Perimeter guards, she realized. Her escort, dressed in heavy armor, had begun to puff loudly at the exertion of the climb; but all the while he continued to whistle. Proof, she decided, that he was more for the benefit of the sentries than for any difficulty the path itself posed.

"Thank you," she said once the man stopped, well beyond the crest of the hill.

He had made the climb at Tempest's pace and was still panting. He nodded. "Now, there is no need to rush in the dark. Just keep a steady pace for as long as you have light and you will be beyond any danger."

"Yes." She was reluctant to break this final contact, but saw that he took her hesitation as fear. "Thank you," she said, putting her heels to Tempest's sides. "Farewell."

The first time she looked back, she saw him silhouetted against what was left of the sunset; but the next time she turned he was gone. She lifted her face to the quickly blackening sky. The moon would be in its first quarter, rising late and setting early. There would be several hours of total darkness before dawn, and she planned to stop before then, rather than risk Tempest's breaking a leg in a rabbit hole or some such unseen hazard.

But they hadn't gone far when Kiera noticed that Tempest's gait had stiffened, becoming self-consciously chary.

Despite his assurances that nothing was wrong, and despite her knowing that dismounting was easier than getting back on, she slipped off his back. "Did you step on something?" She lifted his right front leg without giving him a chance to answer. Nothing wrong with his hoof. She ran her hand down from forearm to fetlock. "You might have pulled a muscle." She glanced back the way they had come to gauge the distance, which—in truth—was not all that great. "Do you think you could go a bit farther if I walked, or should we stop here?"

Tempest also looked back. Kiera had explained that there was to be a battle, men fighting, and that was the thing for which Tempest had trained all his life. And Mordred was there, who had been Tempest's responsibility. He looked at her, his large dark eyes confused.

"We can't go back," she told him. "We can stay, or we can go on. But we cannot go back."

He nickered softly, pushing against her hair. Then he turned and faced the way home.

She twined her fingers into his mane and walked beside him until the moon disappeared under the horizon.

hen Kiera awoke, it was early morning. Her clothes were still damp from the dew, though the grass around her had dried. She got up stiffly, barely able to move.

"Tempest," she called too loudly when she didn't see the horse immediately. Panic set in at the thought of being alone.

But he had only wandered as far as the edge of the hillock where they had stopped for the night. They were in the middle of a small woods, but when she got to Tempest's side, she realized that they were high enough to be able to see over a good many of the trees. When she squinted and concentrated hard enough, she thought she could see back to the edge of the woods. Beyond that would be the gently rolling plain they had crossed, and beyond that, Mordred's camp. If he had anticipated correctly—if Arthur had attacked at dawn—both men could be dead by now.

Arthur would *not* have, she tried to convince herself. Arthur was too kind. Arthur was . . .

Arthur was King. And if Mordred posed a threat to his kingdom, Arthur would do whatever he had to do.

Was that smoke on the horizon? No. Only morning fog. She listened. Birds. Insects. The barest whisper of a breeze. She chided herself for finding comfort in the near silence. The sounds of battle wouldn't carry this far in any case.

Neither she nor Tempest had appetite for the food she had discovered in the saddle pack last night, gift from Mordred's men.

Tempest's leg had stiffened so that walking was even more painful for him than it had been the day before. With a mixture of reluctance and relief she led him away from the hill with its almost-view of what she had left behind. Little by little they walked, until nightfall, which was just one more rest period of many.

Late the following afternoon they were in a stretch of woods when they rounded a curve and came upon Alayna.

Would her mother be angry or relieved?—Kiera had no idea. She decided to remain aloof, just to be safe.

Alayna jumped off her horse almost before it stopped, and ran toward her.

Kiera abandoned her plan and threw herself into her mother's arms. "How did you find me?" she asked. "How did you know I was here?"

Alayna, oblivious to her own tears, wiped away Kiera's. "A dispatch came from Mordred shortly after you disappeared. As soon as I heard his name, I just knew you—"

"Oh, Mother, they're fighting: Arthur and Mordred—"

"I know."

"I mean really fighting. Yesterday. About a day in from the coast, they—"

"I know. I met a royal messenger yesterday. They're both still alive. Sir Deems was killed, and Galton. Bevis. Scores of men on both sides, but neither Mordred nor Arthur was hurt."

Deems had had a talent for making up silly songs that always made her laugh. Galton could tame wild birds to take seed from his hand. Bevis had struggled with the decision to become a knight or a priest. Kiera couldn't think of them as dead, or allow herself happiness that Arthur and Mordred were not.

Instead, seeing that her mother was wearing page's breeches and a leather jerkin—and had a sword by her side—she said, "You came to rescue me."

Her mother looked away self-consciously. "You're a terrible daughter," she said, but Kiera knew she didn't mean it.

"What else?" Kiera asked. "What else did the messenger say?"

"That Arthur won the battle . . ."

She felt drained, that was all. How could she feel happy or sad?

". . . but that it wasn't decisive."

There had to be a clear victor. There had to be or . . . "They're going to fight again? That's . . . that's . . ."

"Madness. Yes." Her mother took a deep breath. Then another. "Oh, Kiera, let's go home."

Kiera glanced at Tempest and wondered how much of this he understood. Not much, she guessed, or else he trusted her completely, because he waited patiently. She faced Alayna again. "Mordred has been talking with Nimue."

The flush left Alayna's face. She asked, very reasonably, "Can he do that?"

Was Nimue dead? It had always seemed more believable that Nimue's dead body had somehow dissolved, rather than that she had escaped into thin air. Else, why hadn't she returned once the danger was gone?

"I . . . I don't see how."

And there was also the question of why Nimue would come back now, and why she spoke only—apparently—to Mordred.

Alayna said, "Kiera, there is nothing we can do."

She had no answer for that.

"There is nothing we can do," her mother repeated.

"I know," Kiera admitted.

Her mother twisted her palfrey's reins around her hand until her fingers turned red. "What do you expect of me?" she cried. "Even if we got there in time, since when does he listen to me?"

Kiera knew that, too. "I didn't say anything."

Alayna shook the reins loose. "All right," she said. "All right, all right, all right."

Another day and a half later they caught up to the two armies. They were camped within easy march of each other on a huge plain that seemed particularly well suited for large groups of men killing each other.

"What do you think is going on?" Kiera whispered, though they were far enough away that even her mother, who had keener eyes, had trouble picking out details.

"Can't tell." Alayna also whispered.

In the failing light of evening, they lay on their stomachs at the lip of one of the hills that rimmed the field. The incline was a long slope with much rubble, impossible for fighting; but the plain was large enough to accommodate both armies, each spread out in its own corner, and an empty expanse between. It reminded Kiera of the old Roman arenas, which were no more than ruins now, where men had fought to the death for the entertainment of the crowds. But *this* battle would be fought by the crowds.

Her mother said, "A truce perhaps. A parley."

That, Kiera thought, was wishful thinking.

Alayna pointed to the right. "Arthur's personal standard is there."

Kiera had seen it all her life: a red-winged dragon—but even knowing what she was looking for didn't help; from this distance, the very colors of the banners shifted.

"And there"—Alayna pointed left—"is Mordred's." That would be the stark Latin cross, black on a field of white, that had become identified with Mordred during last summer's border wars: a symbol of hope, in tones of mourning. Alayna sighed.

Then gasped.

Kiera turned slowly. A knight stood next to her mother, his sword extended so that it rested easily against her shoulder.

"Sir Dodinas," Alayna said to the knight who held it, one of Mordred's men. "We mean no harm."

"Unfasten your scabbard and—very slowly—hand it to me. Now get up, quiet and easy, one at a time. You first." He tipped the point of the sword toward Kiera. "Away from the edge so that nobody down below can see you."

"Dodinas," Alayna said. "Don't you know us? Alayna De La Croix, and Kiera."

"Keep your voice down. I see who you are. Now move, very slowly. And don't try anything. Should you escape from me, the hill is covered with patrols—Arthur's and our own. You would not get as far as your horses. And they are no longer where you left them anyway."

Alayna held her hands palms up in a gesture of peace.

Kiera stood, afraid that every innocent move she made screamed of guilty intentions.

Dodinas inclined his head for her to step to the left. "Now you," he told Alayna. "Keep down till you're away from the edge." His voice, though a whisper, rasped harshly.

"Sorry," her mother said, in truth sounding more put out than sorry. "But nobody could see—"

"Move." He pushed Alayna, not roughly, not gently, into the lead. "The girl stays by me. This way. And remember: You are being watched."

Kiera followed her mother, and Dodinas followed her. And he had yet to put his sword away. As they moved downhill, the trees blocked the remaining light from the sky and the underbrush became denser and harder to make their way through.

Off to one side, there was a crackle of brittle branches, then a muffled cry, quickly followed by a low-pitched whistle something like, but not quite, a warbler. Then, once again, silence. Thinking about that, wondering who—someone she stood a good chance of knowing—had just gotten killed, Kiera slipped on a patch of leaves.

Dodinas caught her by the elbow. "Keep moving," he whispered into her ear.

They stopped at an outpost, to wait while somebody was sent for. The sentry was someone's squire, no older than Kiera, and his eyes shifted nervously from mother to daughter, until Kiera wondered what would make the strain unbearable for him, what little inadvertent thing might make him lose control. She looked away, lest staring be it, and tried not to breathe too hard. Then again, he might consider calmness suspect. She and her mother could die here tonight, and no one who cared would ever know it.

Two knights approached, and Dodinas stepped aside with them.

The longer the three knights argued, the more audible their whispers became. Nobody, it seemed, wanted to be responsible for deciding what to do with them.

"Listen—" her mother said, stepping forward.

Four swords whipped out and pointed at her.

Alayna took a step back, her hands raised before her. "Peace," she said. "All I wanted was to suggest you ask Sir Mordred what to do with us."

"Easy for you to say," one of the men muttered.

Since when were Mordred's men afraid to talk to him?

They continued their discussion in muted tones, watching Kiera and her mother warily. Whichever side won, Dodinas left abruptly—Dodinas, the only one they knew.

Kiera watched as he went back up the hill without a backwards glance for them.

"Come," one of the others said impatiently, but at least they kept their swords sheathed.

They stopped in front of Mordred's pavilion, presenting arms to the guards who stood before it. And that too was something new, that Mordred felt he needed guards. *There's always somebody listening,* he had told her. What, exactly, was he afraid of? Spies from Arthur, or something less tangible?

Once again the whispered arguments, though this time they didn't last long. One of the men who had accompanied them unceremoniously tugged Kiera and her mother, then pulled back the tent flap and pushed them forward. Kiera felt Alayna put her hand on her shoulder at the same time she heard the man say, "My Lord."

Mordred turned.

But it wasn't as in her vision: He, of all the knights in the camp, was unarmored, and his expression was only mild surprise—quickly turning to annoyance.

"My Lord," the knight repeated, stepping into the torch light, "these women . . ." He saw the scowl on Mordred's face and grabbed a handful of fabric by Kiera's shoulder and another by Alayna's waist, and started to pull them back. "I beg your pardon, my Lord. No doubt it can wait till—"

"They stay," Mordred said, waving the man out. He followed him to the tent flap, then stayed a moment to make sure he had truly left before turning to Kiera. "Bloody hell, I told you—"

"Mordred," a woman's voice interrupted, "that is no way to talk to a young lady."

CHAPTER 16

Kiera jerked, startled. Her attention had been centered on Mordred, and she had not noticed the tall, dark-haired woman.

The woman arose from the edge of the field cot where she'd been sitting, and smiled. "You must introduce us." Her diaphanous black gown sparkled with each graceful move. She took a step forward, and Kiera found herself taking one back. "Mordred," the woman repeated, "who are these charming people?"

Kiera felt the tent's guide rope rub against her shoulder; she couldn't get any farther back without making a big step over the rope or walking around her mother.

Mordred was watching her, too. "The Lady Alayna De La Croix," he finally said, "and her daughter, Kiera. I don't believe either of you has ever met my aunt, Morgana?"

That explained it. The smile was familiar because it was Gareth's—at least, the mouth was. Kiera didn't think anything could touch those eyes. She curtsied, taking the opportunity to look away. Morgan le Fay, people called her, Morgan of the Fairies. But then, people also called Kiera a witch, and *that* wasn't true. Still, she couldn't meet those disconcerting eyes.

Morgana stepped forward; and for the first time Kiera realized that what she had thought was a loose collar around Morgan's neck was actually a black and brown snake—an adder. It stuck its long forked tongue out to taste the air between them.

"Let them breathe, Morgana," Mordred said.

Mordred's aunt stepped back, her smile wry. *This is to humor Mordred,* her expression said. She never shifted her gaze from Kiera.

Mordred was looking from Alayna to Kiera. He asked one, the other, or both of them, "Did Arthur send you here?"

Her mother finally stopped graping at Morgana. "No. Mordred, of course not. I needed to talk to you."

Mordred watched her warily.

"Mordred, this is madness." Kiera guessed this was probably not the best way to begin, but her mother continued, "You cannot win this fight. If you kill Arthur, you will have started a blood feud the like of which this vengeance-hungry country has never seen. Even should you survive tomorrow, you will be poisoned or pushed down a set of stairs or stabbed in the back within the year. What can you do, kill *all* of Arthur's supporters, *and* their entire families, *everyone* you're not sure of? Who will you have left to rule? Assuming you don't get run through tomorrow."

Kiera suspected her mother's words were pushing Mordred in exactly the opposite direction she intended.

Mordred gave a smile disturbingly similar to his aunt's. "You always have a way of putting things in perspective, Alayna. But—it so happens Arthur and I are not fighting tomorrow. We *have* been negotiating. Arthur has agreed to give up Cornwall and Kent. All that is left for tomorrow are the formalities."

"You're dividing the country?" Alayna's voice was breathless. "Arthur spent his whole life uniting Britain, and you're dividing it?"

"Until his death," Mordred said with a shrug. "Then it will all be mine."

"I love happy endings," Morgana purred. "Don't you, Buttercup?" She stroked the adder's head with one finger.

Buttercup hissed and once more tasted the air.

Very quietly Alayna said to her, "Please stay out of this."

"Oh, now you sound like Vivien," Morgana told her. "You haven't been talking with Vivien, have you?" She looked Alayna up and down and said, smirking just a bit, "No, you would not have been. Vivien is the Lady of the Lake, Nimue's grandmother. Nice old granny—you would like her. She doesn't wear interesting trousers the way you do, but she does like to go around telling everybody they're always wrong about everything." She smiled sweetly. "She was here just a short while ago, trying to persuade Mordred to give up the only keepsake he has of poor, dear, dead Nimue."

Kiera saw that Mordred still wore the ring on its leather thong. She looked back at the beautiful Morgana, who was watching her. As was her snake.

"In fact, kind Vivien has offered to take Mordred away from all this," Morgana said. "To misty Avalon. What do you think, Kiera—should he go?"

"That's enough," Mordred warned.

Morgana cooed, "I'm only looking out after your interests, my dear boy. Of course, Vivien has magic of her own, but she wants that ring. Naturally, she would use it to help Arthur. But if you would let me show you how to use it, you would not have to settle for Cornwall and Kent. We would be done with Arthur so quickly, his friends wouldn't know what happened to him; they wouldn't know what happened to *them*. You would hold the destiny of Britain in your hand *now*. We want the same thing, my boy. We should work together."

Mordred lifted his eyebrows. "Should we?"

Morgana held her hands out, palms up. "What have we come to, that you don't trust your own Auntie Morgan?" She smiled, all teeth. "You know you're my favorite nephew."

"At this point, I'm your only nephew," Mordred pointed out.

She laughed quietly. "Yes."

Kiera looked to Alayna. Her mother, who had always been timid around talk of magic, said, "Mordred, please—"

"Alayna," Mordred said, sounding reasonable, "I am not going to do anything rash. Arthur and I are meeting tomorrow with the already agreed upon terms. Unless there is treachery from Arthur's side, this is where this matter ends."

There would be no treachery from Arthur, Kiera was sure.

Her mother hesitated, then threw her arms around Mordred.

"How sweet," Morgana said exuberantly. Then she added, "Such a relief—don't you think, Kiera?—that she got over Sir Bayard so quickly."

Kiera's heart sank. She had said nothing to her mother about what she had learned of Bayard. She prayed that her mother would misunderstand, would assume that Morgana was simply referring to the fact that Bayard had come here with Mordred while Alayna had remained at Camelot.

But Alayna was giving Mordred and his aunt a quizzical look. "Where *is* Sir Bayard?" she asked quietly.

Morgana put her hand to her mouth and said, "Oh dear. My mistake. Never mind." She turned her back on them and picked up a small wooden cage that held a brown and white field mouse. "Time for Buttercup's feeding."

Kiera focused her eyes on the ground at her feet.

"Mordred," Alayna said, "where is Bayard?"

Mordred must have known, from Alayna's tone, from Kiera's face, that Kiera had not told her mother what she'd told him. But he made no attempt to soften the news. "Dead. I had him executed three days ago."

Alayna shook her head. "Why?"

"Because he was the one behind the attempted drowning of Kiera. He hired those youths to menace her so that he could make the heroic rescue, and then he killed them to make sure they would never talk."

Alayna looked around helplessly. "Bayard said this? He confessed to you?"

Mordred's eyes shifted. "Yes," he said, and even Kiera knew Bayard had never willingly confessed.

"I wanted . . ." she started to tell her mother. "I didn't know how . . ."

Alayna turned on her. "You knew this?"

"No," Mordred said. "She told me her suspicion, but she didn't know——"

"You accused him?" Alayna looked at Kiera in horror.

"Alayna, he admitted it." Mordred tried to take her by the shoulders, but she shrank away.

Her voice was a hoarse whisper. "You had him tortured, didn't you? He admitted under inquisition." She looked from him to Kiera. "You always hated him, both of you." She took a step back as if to make sure neither of them tried to touch her again. "You murdered him. You took the word of a confused girl, without trial, without——"

"You did not mind when I overrode the trial system for Kiera's sake."

"He wouldn't have done it!" Alayna screamed at him. "For what possible reason?"

"For Kiera," Mordred said. "She was the prize: Kiera. As always." He grabbed Kiera's arm and her mother's, standing them face-to-face. "Listen to me," he hissed. She would have bruises from where he held her, but for the moment it was his eyes that hurt, that cut into her and reflected empty gray mist. Could her mother see it, too? "It's time for both of you to grow up. You cannot pretend Kiera is just a little girl anymore. Don't you understand? There isn't enough magic to go around these days, and nobody will leave you alone. Either they will fear you and try to destroy you, or they will try to use you. And if you get in the way, Alayna, you will only get yourself killed. Those are the only two possibilities."

It was true. Kiera knew it was true. Her mother opened her mouth, and Kiera thought she was going to deny it; but when finally she got the words to come, what she said was, "Unless somebody stronger comes along."

Mordred blinked.

"Like Nimue."

He still seemed to be trying to work out her meaning.

Alayna pulled away from him. "Halbert wanted to use Kiera, and perhaps Bayard did, too. But what about you? Why did you befriend us, why did you make us think you loved us, how are *you* different from Bayard except that you met Nimue and decided her magic was stronger than Kiera's?"

Mordred shook his head and let go of Kiera to hold Alayna, but she flailed at him with her fists, and he stepped back in surprise.

"You have done what you set out to do," Alayna said. "You've killed Bayard, ruined Lancelot, destroyed Arthur. And all it cost was *everything*. I hope vengeance feels good, Mordred. I hope it is warm and comfortable. So now you can just leave me and my daughter alone." She grabbed Kiera's wrist and dragged her out of the pavilion.

Kiera expected him to deny it, to try to stop them, to follow.

But he did none of those things.

Mordred, tell her it's not true.

Is it?

"Mother," she said, "where are we going?"

"Arthur's camp."

"It's the middle of the night. The archers will shoot us halfway through the neutral zone."

"Arthur isn't like Mordred."

That wasn't fair, but Kiera didn't say so. She said: "But they're expecting treachery."

Her mother sat down abruptly and started to cry. "Why didn't you tell me about Bayard?"

I was afraid, because I thought you loved him, she wanted to say. *I thought you loved both of them.* She bit her lip and shuffled her feet.

Eventually Alayna stood up, pulling her after again. Did she hear the footsteps behind, someone following but not closing the gap? She didn't look back, and neither did Kiera.

As they passed through Mordred's camp, faces peered out of the darkness at them, but nobody tried to stop them. When they passed the last campfire, there were guards, but they looked beyond mother and daughter to whoever followed—

Mordred or one of his people. And whoever it was must have signaled for them to be permitted to pass. Someone gave a low trilling whistle, a signal to those beyond the glow of the fire. And still her mother refused to soften her heart. She called out in a loud voice, "This is Lady Alayna De La Croix and Kiera, coming to King Arthur's camp. We mean no harm. Please let us pass. This is Alayna De La Croix." She held her hands up in front of her, palms forward, and Kiera did the same.

The area was level, with short grass and a few bushes. Something small darted in front of them, breaking cover at the last moment, but there was no sign of any soldiers.

Her mother must not have believed that meant no one was there. "We come in peace," she continued to announce. "We seek shelter."

Kiera narrowed her eyes. They were still a good way from the closest watchfires of Arthur's encampment, but they had to be approaching the first outposts by now. Cold sweat trickled down her spine to the small of her back. Her mother was insuring that nobody could mistake them for spies, but at the same time her noise made them into targets the bowmen could track even in the absence of light. Still, they must have come within range of crossbows long since, and if they were to be killed out of hand, surely they would have been already.

"This is Lady Alayna De La Croix. My daughter and I come unaccompanied—"

Kiera's foot caught on a stone and she started to pitch forward. A pair of hands, gauntleted, steadied her.

"Keep walking," a man's voice said. "There is no need to shout anymore—King Arthur has given you leave to approach."

They were led through the silent camp. Most of the men were already asleep, an early night in case the next day proved a need for battle after all. Those who were still awake watched them with suspicion and curiosity.

King Arthur stood just outside his tent, waiting for them in his nightshirt. "My poor, dear child!" he exclaimed.

It gave Kiera a start to realize he addressed not her, but her mother. In the candlelight from the open doorway, she could see the streaks that Alayna's tears had made on her grimy face.

He embraced Alayna, laid his hand on Kiera's head, and urged them inside. "Thank you, Bedivere," he said to their escort, whom she knew but had been too frightened to recognize.

Bedivere nodded and disappeared back into the night.

Arthur sat her mother down on his cot, then sat beside her. "What has happened, my dear?"

Alayna shook her head, crying again.

"It's Bayard," Kiera said. "He's dead."

Alayna shook her head more violently. "That's not it," she finally managed to say. "That was just a surprise. It's Mordred."

Arthur's hand tightened on Alayna's. "Mordred?" he repeated, perhaps thinking she meant he was dead.

"I don't know what is the matter with him," her mother said. "He is doing things I don't understand. Your Highness, he has become erratic and strange."

Arthur seemed to suddenly realize how tightly he squeezed Alayna's hand. He let go and stood. "Ah! Just the usual then." His face belied the lightness of his tone, and he turned away as though to work a kink out of his knee.

"And your sister is with him, the Princess Morgana. I . . ."

Arthur raised an eyebrow.

Alayna finished, "I am uncertain of her intentions."

Arthur made a choking sound, but Kiera saw that he was laughing. "Knowing Morgana, she is probably encouraging Mordred to chop my head off when I'm not looking: 'Look, Arthur! What's that behind you?' Then *slash!*" He made a crosswise motion with his hand.

Her mother sat very straight and said what Kiera was thinking: "That is not funny."

"Well. But you don't know Morgana." He took Alayna's hand, helping her to her feet. "She tried to have me killed once—in a particularly nasty way—when we were both young."

Alayna shifted her weight, and even Kiera was uncomfortable at the reminder that Morgana, who looked younger than Mordred, was actually Arthur's older sister.

Arthur patted Alayna's hand. "She and I go back a long time, more years than *she* will admit to. And I know not to turn my back on her. If Mordred has any sense at all, he knows so, too. Now, the hour is late, and tomorrow is a big day . . ."

Alayna was letting herself be led to the door. Kiera threw herself to her knees at Arthur's feet and grabbed his hand. "You aren't planning to fight him, are you?" she asked. "I'm sorry, I know that's no proper way to talk to a king, but—"

"Kiera, Kiera," he said. "Mordred's representatives have agreed to the terms I laid out." His look hardened. "Unless you know something I do not."

Don't let something ill come because of me, she prayed. She shook her head. "He said that, barring treachery on your part, he wouldn't raise his sword to you."

Arthur helped her to her feet. "Then we are safe. For, barring treachery on *his* part, surely I would not be the first to raise a sword against my son. Satisfied?"

Slowly, she nodded.

Still, the gray mist that had been swirling at her knees crept up to her waist.

CHAPTER 17

Kiera and her mother waited for daybreak, neither able to sleep, in the tent from which three of Arthur's officers had been evicted for their sake.

Shortly after daybreak, Bedivere came to ask them to accompany the King's party to the meeting place, halfway between the two camps.

"But why?" Alayna asked.

"King Arthur thought it might be a nice peaceful gesture," Bedivere said, "since you have maintained friendly ties with both sides." His expression said he didn't approve.

Kiera saw Mordred turn, his hand pressed to his side; blood ran between his fingers, down his arm. Beside him, Arthur dropped to his knees with a clatter of his silver armor, and coughed, spitting up blood.

"Kiera!" Her mother was shaking her.

Kiera tried to speak, but no words would come. She saw Bedivere was watching her with a combination of disgust and trepidation.

He pulled the tent flap back to walk out, but readjusted his features quickly. "My Lord," he said, bowing.

The vision dissipated entirely as, through the tent opening, she glimpsed Arthur passing by on his way to the horses.

"I do not think it would be appropriate—" Alayna

started to say to Bedivere's invitation, but then she interrupted herself. "Is he going like that?" she asked in horror. "Without armor?"

Bedivere snorted. "Show of faith for the peace conference." He shook his head. "Lord have mercy on us all."

"No." Kiera exhaled slowly, finally daring to hope. In the visions, Arthur and Mordred were both in armor. She wanted to laugh out loud with relief. "No, this is a good sign."

Bedivere's expression was blank, somewhere between desperation to believe that everything would work out and fear that she was demented.

"I saw him," Kiera explained, wanting to share her relief, "*with* armor."

Bedivere's look became more skeptical. "When?"

That would not ease his mind "What about Mordred?" she asked, "Will he be wearing armor?"

Bedivere tapped his head. "I doubt even Mordred knows what Mordred is going to do from one moment to the next."

Kiera wouldn't allow Bedivere to ruin her belief that everything might, after all, work out differently from her vision. "It doesn't matter," she told him, told her mother, told herself. "Arthur is not—so that changes everything."

She swept ahead of him, hearing her mother curse under her breath as she hurriedly gathered up her things.

The knights, all armed and armored except for the King, were waiting. Horses had been saddled for them and somebody Kiera didn't know lifted her to straddle the smallest, an easygoing sorrel. Kiera wondered how Tempest fared, over in Mordred's camp.

Alayna caught up, puffing and muttering, one boot and her sword under her arm as she laced her leather jerkin. She glared at Kiera, but said nothing. She had to sit on the ground to get the boot on, then fastened the sword at her waist. One of the squires, biting his cheeks to keep from laughing, helped her up. Now she would be angry about that, too.

Arthur faced the waiting army. "By the grace of God, we ride forward to peace.

I expect no treachery, or I would not lead you here. But be alert, and if—God forbid—the unexpected should happen"—Arthur's gaze took in the entire group—"I expect you to follow your captains as you would me."

The men raised their swords, and their rhythmic chant filled the air: "Arthur! Arthur! Arthur!"

The King nodded to Bedivere, who carried the flag of truce.

Bedivere gave a soft grunt of disapproval, but moved his horse to the fore.

Arthur's group, twelve men plus the two women, came next; and the rest of the army followed several furlongs behind. Kiera knew that on the other side of the plain Mordred's people would have set out, probably in much the same formation, the moment they saw the blank white standard move forward.

Once she could make them out, she squinted until Mordred came into focus. He was dressed in black—but it was cloth, not armor. She exhaled in relief, and her mother, riding beside, gave her an uneasy look. Kiera smiled, to say that everything was going to be all right, but Alayna had already looked away.

Bedivere and the standard bearer from Mordred's army met. The two white flags fluttered listlessly.

Arthur raised his hand for the army behind him to stop where they were, and Mordred gave a similar signal to his men. The two advance groups edged closer.

With further relief, Kiera noted that Mordred was not wearing a sword, only Gawain's anlace tucked into his belt. Every difference in detail reaffirmed that her vision would not come to pass. Whether the future had been changed or only deferred, today—at least—was safe. Her gaze continued over the rest of Mordred's group.

And stopped at Morgana, who winked at her.

Kiera looked away quickly, but the gray mist had already closed in, tightening around her chest.

They were beginning to dismount. Kiera half fell, half jumped from her saddle and joined the semicircle around Arthur, who had taken two steps and then stopped, waiting for Mordred to come to him.

Mordred paused, with a smile that bordered on a smirk. *I know what you're doing,* that smile said, but he approached anyway, arms extended to show his hands were empty. "Father," he said smooth and cold as ice.

"Son," Arthur replied in a tone that matched. But then he clasped Mordred's wrists and pulled him into an embrace.

Mordred pulled away, too fast for Kiera to read whatever it was that flickered across his face. He stepped back into the security of his own group, which had formed their own crescent around him. Only Morgana stood apart, still by her horse, tugging on the saddle straps, adjusting the cinches.

"So," Mordred said, still in that infuriating, distant voice. "What *is* the proper protocol for treaties? You have made so many over the long years, and this is my first." He folded his arms over his chest.

Arthur set his jaw.

Kiera averted her gaze, and the mist closed about her throat: Mordred was wearing Nimue's—Merlin's—ring. It was no longer about his neck, but on his finger.

As long as she was looking for signs, surely that was not a good one.

"Kiera," Alayna whispered frantically in her ear, dragging her back from wherever she had been.

Time had continued to pass, while she hadn't been paying attention. Kiera clutched at her mother's hand.

"Well," Morgana was saying about something, "I certainly do not think you should let him get away with that."

Mordred didn't react, but Arthur—who must have been interrupted several times already—pointed his finger at her. "See here, Morgan, I—"

"The devil take you!" one of Mordred's men exclaimed, whipping out his sword.

Mordred whirled around, but Morgana was holding onto his arm, and this slowed him.

"*Jesu* protect us!" Bedivere cried at the naked blade. "Treachery!" He pushed Arthur back, out of harm's way, and pulled his own weapon from its sheath.

Kiera heard the scrape of metal all around her. What had happened? She had seen nothing amiss.

"No, wait!" Mordred lunged away from Morgana, grabbed at Bedivere's arm. "Reeve," he shouted over his shoulder to his own man, "put that away."

"Stop this!" Arthur commanded, trying to make his way through the cordon of men who were determined to protect him.

Bedivere swung his sword at Mordred's face. Mordred jerked back, and another of the King's men grabbed him from behind, his arm around Mordred's neck.

Morgana added her shrill screams to the confusion.

But Kiera saw her face: She wasn't afraid.

She wasn't afraid.

And that made Kiera look back at the man who had started it all—Reeve was his name—who was fighting with one of Arthur's men.

Alayna was trying to push her back, but Kiera ducked under her mother's arm, all the while searching the ground near Reeve's feet. He moved hesitantly, gingerly, despite his danger from the other swordsman, clearly distracted.

She finally spotted the slither of black and brown.

"Snake!" Kiera screamed. "He was only startled by Morgana's snake!" At her cry of "Snake," Reeve dropped his guard entirely, and the other man jabbed his sword through his lifted visor.

Mordred swore in Cornish. "Didn't you hear?" he yelled when he made it back to English. "He was just after the snake."

"Snake? What snake?" the other scoffed, but the last word was choked and he pitched forward, an arrow in his back. It had come from the main body of Mordred's troops, no doubt under orders similar to Arthur's regarding treachery.

"No!" Mordred cried, trying to break away from the King's man who still held him. "Let me stop them!"

Kiera could feel the trembling of the ground, could hear the hundreds of horses.

"Merciful Lord," someone muttered, looking from Mordred's side to Arthur's. "And we're right in the middle."

"Move!" somebody shouted.

The man who held Mordred shoved him toward Bedivere and scrambled for the horses.

Mordred stumbled and Bedivere grabbed him by the shoulder with his left hand, meanwhile drawing back his right arm, his sword arm.

"Stay!" Arthur commanded. Kiera saw he wasn't looking at Bedivere, but meant the others, those intent on getting out of the way of the two converging armies.

Still, Bedivere didn't know. He checked himself midswing.

Arthur pulled one knight off his horse. "Stand fast. They will not run us down if both leaders are in the way."

Kiera prayed he was right.

The man eyed the fast-approaching fronts skeptically.

Bedivere still hesitated, still held fast to Mordred.

"My Lord," one of Mordred's men said—Kiera recognized the good-natured knight who had escorted her up the hill—"there are archers on both sides. They will pick us off as soon as they are within range—any moment now. The flanks are too wide to stop."

Mordred's eyes moved, but that was all.

Bedivere remained totally motionless.

"Your Highness, he's right," Alayna said. "We cannot stop this from here."

Several of the men moved toward their horses again. This time Arthur didn't stop them.

Kiera fought every instinct that screamed at her to run.

"If you let go of me," Mordred told Bedivere, "Arthur and I can rejoin our armies. Once we get back in control, we can countermand the attack orders. Unless that is not what you want."

Arthur seemed to finally notice them. He nodded. "Bedivere, put your sword down before it's too late."

Bedivere watched Mordred's face.

Mordred said nothing.

Kiera looked longingly at her horse, and tried to ignore the other horses—seemingly just beyond—bearing down on them.

"Bedivere," Arthur said. "Put down your sword."

Bedivere released Mordred's shoulder, sheathed his sword, turned toward Arthur.

Mordred spun him back around, the small but deadly anlace to his throat.

Arthur, who had already moved for his horse, was helped up by two knights who had hurriedly dismounted. By the time he looked back, Bedivere and Mordred were still again. Bedivere wore an expression that said he had expected this all along; Mordred's face was unreadable.

"My Lord," urged the knight from Mordred's group who had spoken earlier. He held the reins of Mordred's horse in readiness.

Alayna shoved Kiera toward her horse. "Move."

Kiera half fell against the horse's flank. Instinctively she reached up for the pommel, but her attention was on Mordred and Bedivere. Alayna continued pushing her, and she clambered into the saddle.

Mordred moved the point of the knife in even closer. Bedivere braced himself, which seemed what Mordred wanted, for he smiled—one of his more unpleasant smiles.

"My Lord," the other knight begged, "there is no time."

Mordred hesitated another moment, then the knife was back in his belt and he had stepped out of Bedivere's range. He leaped onto his horse, then turned back to Arthur. "See if you can control your men," he said, "and I will hold back mine."

It probably wasn't all boast, for only two of his surviving thirteen had mounted before him; while of Arthur's group, only Bedivere and Alayna were as yet unhorsed.

Arthur tugged on his reins, heading back to his own lines.

"Go!" Alayna yelled at Kiera. Her own horse, perhaps sensing battle from all the shouting, had suddenly become high-spirited, and pulled to one side so that she had a hard time mounting.

Kiera pulled in closer, trying to help. Bedivere, already mounted, hesitated between following his king and helping Alayna, who had been his responsibility previously.

On the other side, Morgana had finally located and picked up her snake, but her horse had bolted. "Mordred!" she called. "I need help."

Mordred turned back, regarding her coldly.

Kiera remembered that he hadn't seen Morgana's face. As far as he knew, her bringing the pet snake to the peace negotiations was no more than thoughtlessness. Kiera opened her mouth, prepared to tell him, but then closed it again. He would leave her if he knew.

As awful as Morgana was, did she deserve to be abandoned between two advancing armies?

"Mordred." Morgana stepped forward, and an arrow hissed just behind her. "Mordred!" She searched the faces of Mordred's men, seeing no expression more friendly than her nephew's.

"Put down the snake," Mordred said.

"But Buttercup will get . . ."

Mordred yanked on his reins, and Morgana threw the snake to the ground. "He's down, he's down."

Mordred pulled back around, and swung Morgana onto the saddle with him. She would have complained against the ungainliness of it, Kiera suspected, just as several more arrows whizzed through the air, from both directions.

"Kiera!" her mother shouted. She had gotten a good hold and had finally swung up.

Bedivere now took off after the King.

Kiera put her heels to her horse and followed after Bedivere.

"Head back and to the right," her mother shouted. Kiera could only make out every other word or so, but put it together as best she could. "They're curving in, and we cannot outrun them, but they will be spread thinner at the edges. If we get separated, head for the camp."

Kiera signaled that she understood—

And then they were engulfed by the first wave of Arthur's men.

It was similar to the day of Guinevere's rescue in the courtyard—trying to fight the current of a mass of humanity. But this time Kiera had a horse to do the work for her. On the other hand, the people she faced now held weapons at the ready for the enemy they were about to face.

Her horse shied to the left as a knight, seeing her break through from the direction of Mordred's camp, aimed himself at her. He moved his arm in a circular swing, and she heard the *whizzz* of the spiked ball on the end of its chain before she saw the mace. He must have realized his mistake as he spun the deadly morningstar over his head, for he didn't lash out at her, though its momentum precluded his putting his arm back down. He charged by her, and she twisted around to make sure he didn't use his readied weapon on her mother. There was no sign of Alayna, although in such a press of people that was not proof she wasn't there.

Kiera faced forward again and was clipped on the side of the head by the edge of somebody's shield. Dizzily, she slumped to the right. She felt her horse compensate for her shifting weight just as he should be moving to avoid another horseman.

At the last instant he was forced into a close turn, and she felt herself slide farther to the right even as she tried to pull herself back up. Again she was grazed by a knight passing too close, his armored sleeve scraping against her bare arm. He yelled back, but too many others were shouting for anybody to hear: those behind whipping their courage up to a frenzy for the coming battle, while others at the fore were already dying.

Her left foot had slipped out of the stirrup and was halfway up her mount's back. She pressed tight with her legs, thinking, hoping, there could not be that many more ranks of soldiers left.

Her horse was jostled, and she closed her eyes rather than watch the ground slip ever closer to her face.

They swerved once again, then she felt his muscles tense even more. They were hit almost head-on this time. He pitched forward, his legs tangled with the other horse's. Both animals cried in pain. Kiera's arms and legs gave out—it felt as though someone tore her away—and she fell face forward on the ground.

She was aware of the horses screaming, their hooves flailing as they thrashed on the ground, and she wondered if she would be killed by her own crippled mount or by someone else running over her. But then the sky began to rotate on an axis located just between her eyes, spinning faster than the spiked morningstar ball.

Silly, she told herself, *the sky can't be moving—it has to be the earth.*

And, sure enough, the ground kept on spinning, faster and faster, until she fell off the edge of the world.

I can't be dead, Kiera thought, *it's too dusty to be Heaven, and too bright to be Hell.*

She was aware of herself lying on the ground, the body of her dying horse close enough to protect her from the hooves of Arthur's onrushing army.

But at the same time she seemed to be hovering several feet above the confusion. When she turned her head—even though she knew her face was still pressed unmoving against the ground—she could see the red dragon banner of King Arthur. Before she was even aware of wanting to go there, she was drifting above it.

Arthur was flat on his back on the ground, just as she had left herself, except that he was surrounded by a cordon of men to make sure he didn't get trampled. She wondered if he also floated above himself and if their spirits could collide into each other up here.

Farther away, her mother rode back and forth, getting in people's way, calling, "Kiera! Kiera!" But when Kiera tried to answer, no sound came from where she felt her mouth to be.

Bedivere was farther still, at the front, arguing with one of the captains, trying to convince him that he spoke for the injured Arthur.

"You show me some token of the King's authority," the captain said. "Otherwise, I take my orders from Arthur himself. Good Lord, man, they don't know how to fight! We're getting hardly any resistance at all. They're falling back almost as fast as we can move forward. I am not stopping that advance for anyone less than the King."

"Don't those ears of yours work?" Bedivere shouted, partly to be heard above the din of swords and shouts and horses, and partly out of frustration. "The King had his horse shot out from under him. He was on his way to tell the men to fall back because he has an agreement with Mordred. *That* is why you are finding it so easy: Mordred is holding them back. But any time now he is going to give up on us, and once he starts fighting, that will be the end of you."

Even Kiera knew that was the wrong thing to say; it was not the wording to convince anyone.

The captain's mouth twitched. "Maybe so and maybe not. You just send Arthur to tell me what he wants." He tugged on his horse's reins, and disappeared into the press of fighting men.

Bedivere sat for a moment longer, as if considering whether he should follow that captain, seek out another, or return to Arthur. With a cry of disgust, he wheeled his horse about, farther down the line, to the next company.

Kiera planned to follow him, but found herself, without having moved there, in someone's tent.

Here was an old woman, with yellowing hair and small eyes lost in a mass of wrinkles. She sat, cross-legged, in the middle of a pentacle drawn in black powder on the floor, her long fingers working, working, working at something. At Kiera's entrance, she jerked her head up as though she sensed something but didn't know what. With the woman's hands momentarily stilled, Kiera saw it was a lock of hair over which the fingers had fluttered, a lock of white hair—short, a man's. And even though she was still in the tent, Kiera saw Arthur, on the field, being helped to his feet—and then suddenly stagger forward, his hand to his chest.

No! she cried. No sound came out, but the old woman's head whipped around to look directly at her.

It was the eyes Kiera recognized: Morgana's.

The King's sister hissed. She dropped the lock of Arthur's hair, reaching out her gnarled and spotted hand to snatch at Kiera.

Kiera stepped back.

The grasping motion turned into a finger pointed in warning. Then Morgana swept her arm in front of her face, a flurry of black cloth.

She felt the rush of air. There was a moment, or perhaps it was an eternity, of nothingness—falling, falling in total blackness—but then the arm moved back and it wasn't diaphanous silk, but black armor. The aged Morgana was gone, and it was Mordred she watched now.

He sat on his horse, in the midst of the fighting, his hands gripped tightly on the reins. Even with his visor down, she knew his eyes were closed.

She felt the pulsating glow of Nimue's ring. The air crackled with summer thunder and lightning, and two of Arthur's men fell from their horses.

Mordred! she called, but he gave no sign that he heard. The hairs on the back of her neck and upper arms stood up.

There was another flash, an actual flame this time. The knight it was aimed at rolled off his horse, and the flames that danced over the surface of his armor were smothered as he thrashed on the ground. But the panoply of his mount—leather and brocade—flared and erupted into fire. The animal bolted, heading for Mordred's ranks. The horses of Mordred's knights shied away, close to panic.

Kiera mentally closed her eyes, covered her ears, held her breath, but couldn't be rid of the images and sounds and smells of the horror. She wished herself away . . .

. . . And found herself sitting on a small boat in the middle of a lake.

A woman, older than Morgana, but with a gentler look, sat at the other end of the boat. She looked directly at Kiera. "Etheral transference is a risky bit of business at any stage of development," she said. "But if you are determined to try it, you really should practice with shorter distances first."

Vivien, Kiera thought at her. The Lady of the Lake.

Vivien inclined her head, and her white, waist-length hair fell forward. When she spoke, it was with a voice, like normal people. "And you, of course, must be Kiera. Patience, Kiera. Practice. One level at a time."

They're using magic, Kiera thought at her: *Morgana and Mordred.*

Vivien raised her eyebrows.

In her mind, Kiera said, *I don't think Mordred exactly knows what he is doing.*

"No, I think we can safely assume that he does not." Vivien shook her head. "But you must go back to where your body is. I will do what I can." She leaned forward, and Kiera could have sworn she felt the long fingers gently brush her face. But that was impossible, she realized; she had left her face behind, pressed against the ground, next to a dying horse.

She opened her eyes. She was sore all over and had a mouthful of dirt. Gray fingers of fog curled among the stones and sparse grass on the ground. She sat up before she thought about the advancing army, but they had bypassed her already, long since.

The horse she had been riding was dead. She rested her head on her knees, knowing there was no time for mourning, that people were dying—and that people were more important than horses—but it was hard. She forced herself to stand.

What could she do? A young woman—a girl—just barely fifteen years old, involved in the affairs of kings, trying to prevent a war the entire countryside seemed determined to have. The air crackled with magic, and here she was with her puny visions and her ability to talk to animals and her pathetic desire to save the people she loved. For a year and a half she had first suspected, then known, what was coming and had been unable to do a thing about it. The most reasonable course of action now was to find a horse and get out of here, try to build whatever life she could away from those who knew her, who would always fear her—her, with her ridiculous, ineffective magic. Why was she cursed with being different if that difference was unable to help her? Visions of a future that could not be changed—pure vexation. Conversations with animals—so what? She must find a horse . . .

Something tugged at her mind. She must find a horse . . .

She must find . . .

She sucked in her breath. She must find a horse and explain to it that the knights could not fight without their steeds. That this battle was a misunderstanding which could be worked out in the time that would be gained if the horses refused to partake in this folly. The knights' field armor was too bulky, too ungainly for sustained hand-to-hand combat—all she had to do was convince the horses, get them to pass the word.

She glanced around, trying to gain her bearings, and saw a man approaching. He was tall, about the King's age—a lord, she could tell by the way he walked. But she stepped back warily, wondering who would stroll through a battlefield without armor, dressed in a velvet gown.

He smiled, holding out his right hand to her. His left hand rested gently against his chest, holding something that hung from a chain around his neck—a disturbing gesture, which was reminiscent of Mordred, which in turn was reminiscent of . . .

"Halbert," she whispered. The past, which she had thought beyond her recall, seemed to slap her across the face. *She felt his fingers digging into her shoulders, and heard her mother, strange-eyed and distant say, "Behave."*

His smile broadened. "Kiera," he said. "Little Kiera, come to be with me at last." His hand moved down, showing the red stone that sparkled too brightly for this gray day.

She took a step back.

"Look at me. Surely, you don't think I would hurt you?" He beckoned with his right hand.

She turned and ran.

She couldn't hear, over the sounds of the nearby battle and the pounding of her blood in her ears, if he followed. Only when her sides began to hurt did she slow down. Then, prepared to run again, she spared a look over her shoulder.

Bodies—men and horses. Dropped shields and lances. And the fog, thickening, getting higher from moment to moment. A raven, perched on a saddle—no horse, just a saddle—flapped its black wings and cawed, but didn't take flight.

She came to a full stop, turned entirely around. Within her field of vision nothing moved. But the fog made the distance she could see not much at all. Who was behind that? she wondered. The wizard Halbert? Morgana? Mordred? Vivien was the only one she could think of who would have a reason to cut down visibility: If the knights couldn't find each other, they couldn't fight.

If Vivien truly didn't want a battle.

The raven pecked at a bridle bell, the only sound nearby.

Kiera wiped her sweaty palms on her grimy dress.

A shape solidified from the fog, moved relentlessly toward her, the hand extended, the long-nailed fingers beckoning.

She ran.

She headed for Arthur's camp, thinking there might be spare horses that hadn't been used in the first charge, but still the dead wizard followed. She veered off to the right, to the left, a zigzag he couldn't keep up with, but did.

She made it past the edge of the camp, beyond to the dense underbrush that bordered the field. Branches snapped, leaves crackled. She was smaller; she should have been able to get through places the pursuing wizard would have to go around. But still she could hear him close behind her. She dove into a pile of leaves near a giant oak. Her breath came in retching sobs.

If Halbert wanted her that badly, he could have her.

In another moment she calmed down enough to cram the back of her hand into her mouth to muffle the sounds she was unable to stop making.

She heard his footsteps—how could such an old man not get winded?

He slowed. He walked beyond the tree, then returned. "You cannot get away from me," he said softly, and his fingernails clicked against the red stone on his chest. "Come."

Come and get me, she thought. But he must not have known for sure that she was here, for he did not approach. She tried not to squirm under the gaze that she was sure must be directed at her, and closed her own eyes as though that would help. She resisted the temptation to check whether the leaves covered her entirely.

She heard his footsteps, not a handbreadth from her face. Then he kept on walking.

Kiera kept her eyes closed. Her shoulders shook. If he returned, he would see the pile of leaves trembling, but she couldn't stop.

A long time passed, and she caught her breath.

A longer time passed, and she thought about climbing out. Eventually, she brushed away the leaves from in front of her face.

From where she lay, the angle of her body, the tilt of her head—she could see nothing but more leaves, ground, bushes, the roots of the oak. If Halbert had circled back, if he was—for example—behind her, he had already seen her move and she needed to be ready. She jumped up, and out of the corner of her eye caught a movement. She whirled, with an involuntary gasp, and the jay she had startled gave an uncharacteristic *squawk* and almost toppled from the branch it had just landed on.

It beat its wings, started to fly off, then returned, on a higher branch, to chatter down insults at her.

Kiera sat heavily on the ground, half laughing, half crying, knowing she was making enough noise for even the most inept of wizards to find her.

The jay swooped down as though to make sure Kiera understood its opinion of her.

"I'm sorry," Kiera said. "I thought you were this bad man who is chasing me. I know how ridiculous that sounds, but that's the truth." She put her hand out. "Come, don't be angry with me. I have few enough friends as it is."

The jay landed on her finger—birds were the least likely of any creatures Kiera knew to keep a grudge—and immediately it started preening itself.

She smiled, looked up, and saw Halbert watching. "No," she whispered.

The jay fluttered about her head, screeching at her to flee.

Halbert smiled and crooked his finger at her.

She stood up. She took a deep breath.

The jay launched itself at Halbert's face.

"Don't!" she cried, for the wizard could blast it into a cinder.

And the bird flew through Halbert's head.

She blinked, disbelieving what she knew she had seen.

Halbert continued to smile, continued to beckon.

The determined jay made another diving swoop into his face, again coming out on the other side.

Kiera picked up a stone, threw it at the smiling wizard, and heard it hit the tree behind him. And still he only menaced, never approached, never touched. Unable to find a bigger rock, she scooped up dirt and leaves and pebbles. He was nothing but an illusion, a trick. She flung the handful of debris at him, saw it spatter on the ground behind. Somebody had set him on her all this while . . .

She felt her insides turn cold.

Morgana.

A second handful of pebbles dropped from her numb fingers.

Morgana.

"Come to me, little Kiera," the illusion of Halbert purred. "I will not hurt you."

She walked through him, and felt nothing. She began walking faster, toward the field.

"Come," Halbert continued, for that was what he was created to do. "You will come." He followed after, running but never catching up, his footfalls making sound, but not disturbing the leaves he passed over.

The field was an ocean of fog. She ran along the edge. There was a clear bound-ary: no trailing tendrils or patches of half-visibility. When she felt she was close to the middle, she stepped into the mist.

The nature of it changed as she advanced. It tasted of dust here, and smelled of burnt wood and meat, which didn't bear thinking of. She could hear others now, horses and men. Some were dying, and some were shouting to get their bearings, but many were still fighting: Swords clashed, maces thudded, a lance clunked against a shield.

"Arthur!" she screamed. "Mordred!"

Shapes moved close by, but none approached or tried to interfere with her or with the still-trailing figure of Halbert.

CHAPTER 19

Behind her, Kiera could hear hooves tear up the ground as two of the still-mounted knights came at each other. Metal crashed. Someone cursed. The momentum of the horses carried both men forward beyond the point where they could find each other again in the mist.

She rubbed her hand on the skirt of her dress to ease the sudden burning sensation. The more she walked, the stronger it got: Nimue's ring was nearby.

She came upon two men: One was a knight sprawled on the ground, half under a horse that still twitched; the other was a peasant, sitting on the ground, using his back to push against the dying horse. For a moment she wondered if he couldn't see, or wouldn't admit, that the knight was obviously beyond help.

But at the noise of her approach, the peasant pulled a sword out of the burlap bag by his feet and held it, two handed, pointed in her general direction. A looter.

She made a show of holding her hands away from the folds of her dress lest he think she had a weapon of her own.

The looter's eyes, blank in an empty face, shifted to the wizard, a half-dozen paces behind her.

"He's with me," she explained.

Halbert stopped when she stopped, for he had been created to threaten, not to actually touch, which would have given him away. "Come with me," he urged her.

The peasant said nothing.

Kiera eased to the right, a wide circle around knight and peasant and burlap bag.

The tingling of her hand lessened, and she saw she needed to edge back to her original path. But a hand came out of the particularly dense mist, and clasped hold of her wrist. She jumped. "Morgana," she gasped.

But there were two women, and though one was a once-again-young-and-beautiful Morgana, the one who actually held her was Alayna.

"Kiera!" her mother said. "Thank the Lord! I was so worried—" She stopped, gazing beyond Kiera's shoulder, her eyes wide with fear and surprise. She took a step backwards, pulling Kiera with her.

"He's not real," she assured her mother. "He's an illusion. Morgana made him to keep me from helping Mordred and Arthur."

Mordred's aunt shook her head. "No," she said, all hurt innocence. "Who is this man? I've never seen him before. Your mother and I have been looking everywhere for you. We have been together all afternoon." She raised her hands, palms outward, toward the figure of the wizard, who waited patiently just beyond reach, his arms folded on his chest. "But you are right," Morgana continued, "he is insubstantial; he cannot harm us. Maybe he is some trick of Vivien's. She must have been afraid you would help Mordred. She has ever been interested only in Arthur."

Kiera hesitated, weighing all this. But she remembered the snake.

"We were so worried," Morgana was saying. "I'm so relieved we found you." She sniffed and buried her face in her hands. "We became lost in the fog . . . We looked everywhere. We couldn't find you, we couldn't find Mordred . . . I was so frightened."

Alayna was finally able to take her eyes off Halbert, and now she watched without comment as Morgana's shoulders shook with loud sobs.

"This isn't yours?" Kiera asked, nodding toward the wizard, her confidence shaken but not broken.

Morgana shook her head, her face still behind her hands.

Kiera considered. Perhaps. It was hard to insist the woman was a liar in the face of her tears. The fact that she cast spells to make herself appear young and beautiful proved nothing. "You may come with my mother and me, then, if you wish."

Morgana grabbed her arm. "Oh, no, please! Just give me a moment. You don't know the things I've seen: Dead men. Pillagers slitting the throats of the wounded. Scavenger animals . . ." She covered her face again and shook her head. "Please be patient with me. I'm sorry."

Alayna glanced at Kiera. She had always had to work at being patient with helplessness. "Really . . ." she told Morgana.

From the direction in which Kiera had been headed came the clash of swords.

"I'm sorry," Morgana wailed. "I'm sorry, I'm sorry."

But Alayna also had heard the fighting. Eyes flashing, she turned toward Morgana. Kiera stepped backwards.

Once again Morgana's hand whipped out to hold onto her, but this time Kiera noticed that the hands, as well as the face, were perfectly dry—no tears at all. "There's a looter there," Morgana said in a frightened voice, "with a knife."

Kiera hit her hand. "Let go of me."

Morgana's fingers tightened. Her left hand scrabbled for a hold on Kiera's dress at the waist. "If you'll only just stay—" she pleaded.

"Mordred!" Kiera screamed. She pulled Morgana's wrist in front of her mouth and bit.

Morgana slapped her, but had to release her hand to do so. Kiera twirled around. She felt the fingers of Morgana's left hand dig into her side, trying for a more secure hold.

"Let go of her!" Alayna shouted, prying at the fingers.

Suddenly freed, Kiera staggered several steps backwards.

Alayna grappled with Morgana, and both fell to the ground.

Kiera turned and ran.

Before her, shadow shapes fought; behind, she could hear footsteps—her mother's, Morgana's, or Halbert's, she didn't turn to check. Suddenly she broke through the mist.

Mordred and Arthur fought in a clearing as totally devoid of mist as the woods had been. Neither seemed aware of her. Both had their visors up—a calculated risk that weighed exposure against the ability to breathe—indicating they had been at it for a while already. For the moment their swords were locked.

Mordred forced in closer, twisting upwards. Metal scraped against metal. Mordred pushed Arthur backwards. Arthur put one foot back to steady himself, then swung his sword, Excalibur, in and up. But Mordred had already begun his own swing, a wide one that left him open, but gave him deadly momentum.

"Mordred!" Kiera screamed. "Don't!"

The sound rebounded off the walls of surrounding mist.

Slowly, in dream-time, Mordred looked up—distracted from Arthur—and turned toward her, his gray eyes wide and startled, perhaps searching for some secondary threat. And settled on the illusion of Halbert that had broken through the mist beside her.

Slowly, in dream-time, the point of Arthur's sword continued its swing. Kiera saw Arthur set his teeth, start to shift his point of balance, try to hold back the force of the blow. Her scream continued to reverberate off the inside surfaces of her skull.

And then the moment ended.

Arthur's sword pierced Mordred's armor, angled up under his rib cage. The follow-through from Mordred's aborted swing caught Arthur, flat-edged but powerfully, against the side of his helmet.

Both men staggered. Arthur dropped to his knees. Mordred had his hand to his side, and blood ran through the fingers, down the sword he still clutched.

Kiera looked on helplessly.

Behind her, Alayna broke through the mist. Seeing Mordred standing, Arthur on the ground, she gasped, "Arthur!" and she ran to help the King, to pull off his helmet.

That left Mordred. Kiera stepped toward him, but before she reached him, his sword dropped, and he followed, landing hard on his knees. The arm of his black armor was slick with blood.

She tried to pry his fingers from his side, but he was bent over. "I can't breathe." He gasped for breath, sounding close to panic.

The mist quivered, almost closed in on them, then she felt Morgana's hands steadying her own. For a moment, she almost went for the other woman's throat; but together they got the helmet off and Mordred gulped at the air.

"Mordred," Morgana said, "give me the ring." She had twigs and pieces of leaves in her disheveled hair, and the sleeve of her gown was split at the shoulder from her struggle with Alayna.

"No," Kiera warned.

Breathing hard, Mordred took all this in, and said nothing.

"I can't hold the mist back from us much longer—Vivien's magic is stronger than mine. You know she is on Arthur's side. She doesn't care if we lose you in the mist and you bleed to death. Mordred, trust me. I just want the ring to get rid of this fog so we can get help for you."

"Mordred," Kiera said. "That was just an image of Halbert you saw." The wizard was finally gone. "Morgana created him. And she released that snake of hers on purpose—she *wanted* the battle. Don't trust her."

Morgana's eyes flashed. But she said very calmly, "Silly child. You have misinterpreted everything."

Mordred shifted his gaze from one to the other. He took his hand away from his side, wincing, and pulled off his gauntlets. His right hand was sticky with blood, and Kiera averted her eyes. Morgana bit her lip, saying nothing. Mordred closed his eyes, curling his fingers into a fist around Nimue's ring.

Kiera felt the tingle in her hand again, all the way to her elbow. There was an audible *ffffttt!* and the mist was gone.

Mordred sucked in his breath. The effort had obviously hurt. He coughed, bringing up blood, and her own chest ached.

"See," Morgana said. "I told you to give it to me."

He looked up sharply, then turned to see how Arthur fared.

Alayna had him sitting, with his knees drawn up, and his head resting on them. The bandage that had been wrapped around his head after his earlier fall had fresh blood on it. He lifted his incredibly pale face and looked around them, at the carnage the mist had hidden. He held his hands up, palms out. "Enough, Mordred," he said, between puffing for air. "Enough." He held his sword out, hilt first; but Mordred, unable to stand or reach, made a dismissive gesture. Arthur let his arm drop.

"Let me take that off," Kiera said, reaching to unfasten the breastplate.

"No," Mordred said. Then, more steadily, "No."

Arthur took Alayna's fluttering hands into his own to still them. "Just one too many knocks on the head," he told her, and hushed her when she started to protest as he got to his feet.

Careful, Kiera wished him. *Oh, be careful.*

Unable to prevent him, Alayna helped support the King as he staggered to where his son knelt. "I am sorry," Arthur said, easing heavily to his knees. "I saw you look away, but I couldn't stop the swing."

"Chivalry." Mordred said the word with amused disdain.

Arthur gave an apologetic shrug. "Still. I didn't mean it. A stray blow, a lucky shot." He had to lean closer to hear Mordred's whisper.

"Bad block."

Arthur gingerly moved himself into a sitting position. "Well, yes," he said. "That too."

Mordred had his hand to his chest. Even without the helmet, he still seemed to be having trouble catching his breath.

Behind them, there was a scrape of metal.

"Put it down, Bedivere," Arthur said wearily. "I have already surrendered."

Bedivere stepped forward, staring at the five of them incredulously.

Morgana flashed a dazzling smile at him.

Bedivere backed away with a hurried sign of the Cross and an expression that was all too familiar to Kiera. He sheathed his sword, then threw himself to his knees at Arthur's feet.

Arthur put his hand out. "Gently, Bedivere," he said. "We tried. We did try."

Bedivere shook his head. "Sire—"

"No," Arthur said. "Bedivere." He put his hands on Bedivere's shoulders. "It is over." He shook his head, and echoed more slowly, "It is over." Then he looked up and said, "If Mordred agrees, though I offered him my sword, I have a debt to pay."

Bedivere's eyes slid to the doubled-over Mordred.

Arthur tugged on Bedivere's shoulder, forcing his attention. "Years ago, when I was first made King, Merlin brought me here." Arthur looked around. "There." He nodded. "Just beyond those trees. There is a lake below, and within that lake, though none can find it lest the Ladies that dwell there wish it so, is the island of Avalon. When I was a young man, Merlin brought me here. And a hand . . . draped in white silk . . . rose from the water, holding Excalibur."

Arthur closed his eyes, almost smiling at the memory. On reopening them, he seemed to have trouble focusing and blinked repeatedly. "Excalibur was mine on loan," he said, "as was Britain. And it must be returned."

"My Lord," Bedivere said, and shook his head helplessly.

"Take the sword," Arthur told him. "Throw it in the water."

Bedivere bit his lip. "My Lord," he said again. But this time he picked up the sword and headed in the direction Arthur had indicated.

"How touching," Morgana said. "I just love sentimental endings, don't you, Kiera? If we're lucky, they'll live long enough for everybody to hug and kiss and be friends again."

A familiar voice spoke from behind. "Be still, Morgan," it said gently, "or I shall see to it that you look your true age."

Kiera turned to see the aged Lady of the Lake walking toward them.

"Vivien," Kiera whispered.

Morgana shrugged to show her indifference to Vivien's threat—but did not speak.

The Lady of the Lake, Nimue's grandmother, glanced at Kiera, gave a polite nod, then turned her attention to Arthur.

Alayna's look of near panic quickly turned to a defiant tilt of the head, but through it all she remained where she was, at Arthur's side.

Vivien spared her half a glance, then ran her wrinkled hands over the King's face, over his shoulders and chest. Then she took his face in her hands, giving the impression of mother and child, and she told him, "It is time. You must come to Avalon now."

Alayna looked at Kiera, who was remembering what Nimue had said about the ancient and dying Merlin: *He was dying. Together we wove a spell and he sleeps safe in Avalon.*

"No," Morgana said.

Vivien turned toward her.

"You promised Mordred," Morgana said.

Vivien's eyes narrowed.

"I have you," Morgana gloated. "And you know it. Last night, when you were trying to persuade him not to fight with Arthur. Remember? Remember?" Her bright eyes momentarily lit on Mordred. She said to Vivien, "You tried to tempt him with Avalon. 'If you change your mind,' you said. 'Whenever you choose,' you said. Same promise you made to me twenty years ago. You just wanted to get us out of the way, but we take you up on your offer. Now."

Kiera looked at Vivien expectantly. But, "No," the Lady said. "You can't all fit in the boat at once. Two at the most."

"Ooooh," Morgana purred. "Rotten luck, Arthur."

"He needs the healing powers of Avalon," Vivien protested.

"You have always told me I did, too." Morgana smiled sweetly. "You told me I had a dried and shriveled old heart."

"You do," Vivien acknowledged. "But you can wait."

"But I do not choose to," Morgana said. "And you gave me that option. As you gave it to Mordred. *Whenever you choose*," she repeated.

"No," said Mordred between teeth clenched in pain. "No, I have not asked to go."

Kiera tightened her grip on his arm. Alayna looked at him in surprise.

"You'll die." Morgana said it coldly.

"This is not as bad as it looks," Mordred said.

"Oh, but it is," Morgana assured him brightly.

"Mordred," Arthur said, also surprised.

No, Kiera tried to say, but nothing came out. Why was it always a choice between Arthur and Mordred?

"What would I do in Avalon?" Mordred shook his head. "Enough," he whispered, an echo of his father. "Enough."

Arthur shook his head weakly, looking as though he would pitch forward onto his face without Alayna's support.

"Arthur." Vivien forced his chin up, to look into his eyes. "Come with me to the boat."

"Wait," Arthur said.

Wait? Kiera thought. Was Morgana the only one who wanted to go? Kiera turned to follow Arthur's gaze and saw Bedivere was returning.

"You did as I told you?" Arthur asked him.

Bedivere nodded morosely.

"And what did you see?"

"What did I see?" The knight's eyes shifted.

Arthur ran his hand over his brow. "Bedivere, throw the sword into the lake."

"Waves," Bedivere said hurriedly. "Wind." He shrugged, still not meeting Arthur's eyes.

Arthur stared at him without a word.

Bedivere finally looked up. "My Lord, Excalibur in the hands of your successor could hold this country together—"

"What successor?" Arthur demanded. "What survivors, Bedivere? *Throw the sword into the lake.*"

Bedivere backed off in the direction in which Arthur pointed. "My Lord," he whispered once again, then turned and ran.

Arthur leaned back, breathing hard.

"It is time," Vivien urged him yet again. "It is past time. Morgan . . ."

Morgana folded her arms, refusing to give up her place in the boat, perhaps yet hoping that Mordred would change his mind.

Vivien set her jaw. "All right then, Morgan, at least you can help me. Alayna,"— Alayna looked startled, that the Lady of the Lake would know who she was—"try to make Sir Mordred as comfortable as possible until I return."

Morgana looked at each of them angrily, but there was nothing she could do to make the situation any worse.

"Mordred," Arthur said, but when Vivien and Alayna and Morgana lifted him to his feet, he swayed dizzily, and his head hung limply.

"I will come back for you as soon as I can," Vivien promised Mordred.

"Spare yourself the effort," Morgana said. "He'll be dead by then."

"Enjoy your stay in Avalon," Mordred said to his aunt, but his eyes were closed, and there was blood at the corner of his mouth.

Morgana flung her black hair over her shoulder and turned her back on them.

Vivien studied Mordred for a moment, then Kiera. "I *will* be back as soon as I can," she repeated.

But Kiera feared that Morgana was right in this: It would be too late.

The old woman put her arm around Arthur and—with her on one side and Morgana on the other—they started walking.

Alayna said to Mordred, "Let me take a look at that wound."

Mordred shook his head.

She reached to unfasten his armor, but he flinched. "Just . . . leave it," he whispered.

Kiera looked helplessly in the direction Vivien had gone. *Hurry*, she thought. *Please hurry.*

"Come," Mordred said, "let us find Bedivere."

"No," Kiera and her mother said, in horror at the thought of his moving.

Alayna tightened her grip on his arm. "Mordred . . ."

"In the end," he said, "it will make no difference." He got to his feet, breathing hard, and that looked as though it would be the finish of it. But then he started walking, not down and toward the shore where Vivien had landed her boat, which—were he determined to walk—was the sensible direction, but up toward the bluff that overlooked the lake.

Kiera followed, despite the hopelessness of it all.

Alayna gave a cry of exasperation, then hurried to catch up.

When they got to the top of the hill, Mordred sat down heavily.

Bedivere was still there, looking out over the water.

It was windy up here, and Kiera had to hold her hair back from her face. She could make out the boat, and the other side of the water, but there was no sign of an island.

Bedivere, still not looking at them, said, "I saw a hand."

Alayna glanced at Mordred, trying to gauge whether he believed such a thing could be true.

Tonelessly, Bedivere said, "It caught the sword. Waved it three times. And then disappeared." He finally looked at them, for a long moment. "Where is the King?"

Mordred nodded toward the lake. "They took him in the boat."

Bedivere asked, "What boat?"

Kiera looked again at the lake, as did Mordred and Alayna, and then they looked at each other.

Nothing.

The only sounds were the waves and the cries of gulls.

The wind continued to whip their hair.

Bedivere sighed. He turned to the lake again. "Now what am I supposed to do?" he asked softly. Again he sighed, then slowly, without waiting for an answer, he started down the hill.

Mordred leaned back against a large rock. He seemed to be having trouble staying awake, and that was something Kiera had seen before in mortally wounded men.

She knelt beside him and took his hand, sticky as it was with blood. "Don't die, Mordred," she whispered.

He squeezed her hand, but kept his eyes closed.

At her words, Alayna had turned from the still lake and now knelt at his other side and looked at Kiera helplessly.

"Mordred." Kiera put her hand on his shoulder and shook him until he opened his eyes. "Please. We need you. My mother and I need you."

He was looking at her. He may even have forgotten that Alayna was there, too. "Since when," he asked, "has your mother ever needed anybody?"

"That's not fair," Kiera said, looking beyond him to the hurt on her mother's face.

Alayna's hand, resting on his leg, twitched; but he wouldn't have felt it through the armor. She said, "I have always loved you."

Mordred looked up sharply, but the sudden move must have hurt—Kiera saw it on his face before he put his head down to his knees. Bent over, he shook his head, but reached for Alayna's hand. "You . . ." he started, but then choked off a cry of pain and pulled away from both of them, keeping his face averted.

When he'd regained control, he pulled Nimue's ring from his finger and held it in his palm. "Vivien says she's in Avalon with Merlin," he told them. "Vivien says they are both asleep, that there is no way for her to communicate with anyone . . . It's"—he was obviously using Vivien's words—"'beyond her realm of power.'" He sighed. "Especially with me wearing the ring, draining their vitality. That's what Vivien says. She says my hearing her . . . is my imagination."

"Stop," Alayna commanded. "Save your strength."

But he struggled to his feet, standing closer to where the hill overlooked the lake.

"The boat is on its way back," he said, slurring the words a bit. "Despite Morgana's opinion."

Kiera saw that the boat was again plainly visible.

Her mother said, "Mordred . . ."

He wasn't steady on his feet, and Kiera felt a sudden lurch in her stomach at the thought that he might intend to hurl himself off the edge. Alayna must have had the same idea, for they moved simultaneously, one on either side of him.

"Morgana, on the other hand, says it is all a matter of practice." Mordred turned to Kiera, and Alayna grabbed his arm to keep him from falling. He didn't seem to notice. "*She* says I could draw on our combined energy—mine, Nimue's, and Merlin's. Do you think so, Kiera?" He held the ring in the flat of his hand. "Could I still be the ruler of all of Britain?"

She avoided his eyes. "Perhaps."

"Perhaps," he repeated. His hand tightened into a fist. Then he drew his arm back, and flung the ring with all his might.

She saw the flash of gold, high over the lake. Then she lost it, but her eyes followed the path it must take.

The water rippled, bubbled, flew up in a great spray—too much to be a splash from such a small object. Then a lady's arm broke through the surface. The hand clasped shut, and then it disappeared back into the lake.

Mordred whispered, "Bedivere *wasn't* making it up," but the last word was lost in a gasp of pain. He dropped to his knees, bent over double, his breathing loud and ragged.

"Mordred!" Kiera cried. Her fingers and her mother's began to fumble with the fastenings of his armor.

"No," he said, though he still couldn't catch his breath.

They ignored him, got the breastplate off, then pushed the bulky armor out of the way.

He had stopped resisting. In fact, his eyes were clear and unafraid and filled, Kiera thought, with the wonder of someone surprised to be alive. His soft leather undergarment had a large gash and much of it was saturated with blood, but he didn't flinch at her touch.

Carefully, tenderly, Alayna pulled the shirt up.

The skin was smeared and crusted with blood, but there was none of the damage to flesh and internal organs that had to have occurred from the sword stroke Kiera had witnessed.

Mordred had his eyes closed, his head tipped back.

"Small healings," Kiera whispered.

Slowly, her mother nodded. "She always said her specialty was small healings." Alayna gave a short laugh, shook her head, then laughed again. She took Mordred's head between her hands and laughed and cried at the same time.

Mordred threw his arms around her, buried his face in her neck, between her shoulder and her hair, then drew Kiera into the circle with them.

Finally he held both of them back, at arm's length. He started to say something, but his attention was diverted below, to the shore.

Kiera followed his gaze and saw Vivien, just now climbing out of her boat.

The Lady shaded her eyes with her hand, searching the nearby hills.

Kiera waved her arm.

Vivien waved back, and started for the path that led up.

"You aren't going?" Alayna asked Mordred, her voice shaking. "Are you? Now that you don't need to? Or . . ." She didn't dare ask the question Kiera knew she wanted to: *Will you go there in the hope that Nimue, when she revives, will choose you over Merlin?*

"No," Mordred said. He shook his head for emphasis. "No, there's nothing in Avalon for me."

Alayna looked light-headed from relief. "Shall we meet Vivien halfway?" she asked. "Let her know she made the trip back for nothing?"

Softly, hating to dispel the happiness so quickly, Kiera said, "No."

"Kiera." There was fear in her mother's voice once again.

"Mother." Kiera found it difficult to meet Alayna's eyes. "Mordred asked what there was in Avalon for him. What is there here for me? People afraid of me? People hating me? People wanting to use me?"

"No! It doesn't have to be like that. We'll find a place where nobody knows any of us, and we'll be happy together. We'll protect you. Won't we, Mordred?"

"Yes," he agreed, too quietly. "As best we could. As long as we could."

Kiera knew it was the truest answer he could give. It was the truest answer anybody could give.

Alayna turned back to Kiera. "I love you, Kiera," she said—in the end, the only argument she had.

And it was almost enough.

"And I love you," Kiera said. She reached for her mother's hair, caressed it away from her face as Alayna had so often done with hers. "Be happy," she wished them.

She turned back only once, just before the path curved away to the beach. But by then she was too far away to see them. And if they could see her, she never met them again to ask.

The Legend of King Arthur, According to Sir Thomas Malory

Britain was less a country than a gathering of battlefronts, fought over by innumerable petty kings and barons. Still, with the help of the enchanter Merlin, and a magical sword given him by the mysterious Lady of the Lake, Arthur Pendragon became King of Britain.

Queen Morgause of Orkney, the widow of one of the leaders of those opposing Arthur, was also Arthur's half-sister. Whether Morgause was aware of this relationship, *Le Morte D'Arthur* never says, though Malory takes care to mention several times that Arthur was not. In any case, Morgause came to court with her four sons, Gawain, Gaheris, Agravaine, and Gareth, and—in Malory's words—"She was a passing fair lady, wherefore the king cast great love unto her, and so was Mordred born."

Upon learning that he was guilty—however unwittingly—of incest, and haunted by Merlin's prophecy that Morgause's child would destroy him and all the knights of his realm, the young King tried to have his infant son killed. By the time he learned that Mordred had escaped, Arthur had come to regret his cruel plan, and he accepted Mordred at Camelot.

By then Merlin was gone.

Malory tells us that Merlin, the clever magician who could see into the future and knew that Nimue would betray him—and how, and when—was nevertheless "assotted upon" the damsel of the lake, and so he let her lock him in an underground cave, never to be heard from again.

What Malory doesn't explain is why, despite Arthur's love for Merlin, the King bore no grudge against Nimue. In fact, Nimue was welcomed at Camelot on several occasions. One of these times she warned Arthur about a gift sent by another of Arthur's half-sisters, Morgan le Fay—a cloak, which, it turned out, caused the wearer to burst into flame and be reduced to ashes.

Over the years, the knights of Arthur's Round Table had many adventures, and gained a reputation for helping women and the poor and weak. But a darker side to chivalry was beginning to show itself: an underlying disregard for human life, a perverse pleasure taken in anger and the seeking of revenge, an unwillingness to forgo any challenge—no matter the cost.

Throughout *Le Morte D'Arthur*, whenever Malory mentions Mordred, it's to say he was knocked off his horse at a tournament ("and there he smote Sir Mordred from his horse, and brised him sore"), or to show him in some cowardly act. Yet when—in Arthur's absence—Mordred declared himself King of Britain, he was able to rally enough support that Arthur was unable to win a decisive battle.

Unfortunately, when they met on the field to discuss terms, one of the other knights present drew his sword to kill a snake that had appeared out of nowhere, and the waiting armies converged.

Eventually, with hardly anyone left alive on either side, Arthur killed Mordred, just as Mordred gravely wounded Arthur. Then, says Malory, "pillers and robbers were come into the field . . . And who that were not dead all out, there they slew them for their harness and their riches."

Morgan le Fay (Arthur's oft-times enemy) and the Lady of the Lake (his oft-times benefactor) came in a barge and, weeping, took the injured King and disappeared.

Queen Guenevere became a nun at Amesbury; and Lancelot, who had hastened back to Britain to help Arthur against Mordred—only to arrive too late—took the vows of priesthood. The remaining knights scattered, and the last of them were killed in the Holy Land.

As for Arthur, Malory says he died. He says the women on the boat had planned to take him to Avalon to be healed, but didn't get there in time. And he says a hermit buried him in a little chapel in the woods.

Then he says: But then again, maybe not.